Annie Mundy

ANNIE MUNDY

Robert H. Fowler

STEALTH PRESS

ANNIE MUNDY Copyright © 2000 by Robert H. Fowler. All rights reserved. Printed in the United States of America. No part of this book may be reproduced or transmitted in any form or by any means, electronic or mechanical, including photocopying, recording, or by any information storage and retrieval system, without written permission from the publisher, except in the case of a brief quotation embodied in critical articles or reviews. For information address Stealth Press, 336 College Avenue, Lancaster, PA 17603 (www.stealthpress.com).

PUBLISHER'S NOTE
This is a work of fiction. Names, characters, places, and incidents either are a product of the author's imagination or are used fictitiously, and any resemblance to actual persons, living or dead, events, or locales is entirely coincidental.

ISBN 1-58881-013-5

FIRST STEALTH EDITION FEBRUARY 2001

Stealth Press books are published by Stealth Media Corporation. Its trademark, consisting of the words "Stealth Press" and/or bomber logo is registered in the U.S. Patent & Trademark Office and in other countries. Marca Registrata.

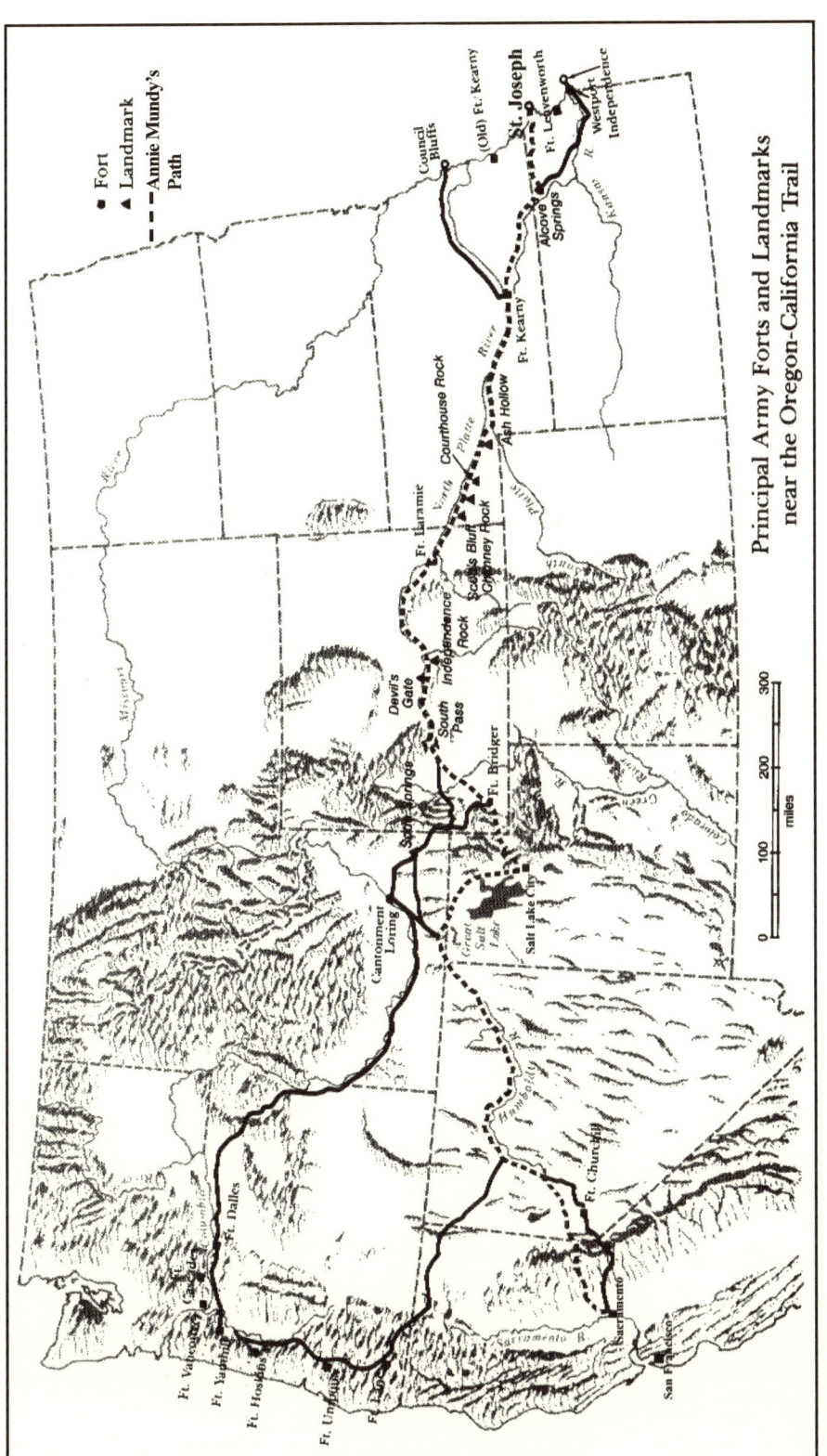

This map is reprinted from John D. Unruh Jr.'s *The Plains Across: The Overland Emigrants and the Trans-Mississippi West, 1840-60.* Copyright 1979 by the Board of Trustees of the University of Illinois. Used with permission of the University of Illinois Press.

Other Books by Robert H. Fowler
Available From Stealth Press

Jim Mundy

To:

Those women who, like the real Anne Eliza Monday, went by wagon train to settle the American West

ACKNOWLEDGEMENTS

A list of the printed sources consulted in doing research for this novel may be found in the back of the book. In this space I want to give credit and offer thanks to the many persons who have assisted me both with my research and my writing.

As with most of my previous historical novels, I owe special thanks to Judy Dillen, chief librarian, and Judith Banks, research librarian, of The New Cumberland PA Public Library, for their help in locating books through the Interlibrary System.

During an unforgettable seventeen-day, 2,500-mile trip following the old Oregon–California wagon trails across the West from St. Joseph, Missouri in 1996, my wife and I talked to dozens of unfailingly helpful local historians, librarians and National Park Service personnel, among them:

Mrs. Robert B. Bristow, docent, and Gary Chilcote, Museum Director, Patee House Museum, St. Joseph, MO; Tamara Daniels, Park Ranger, Scotts Bluff National Monument, Gering, NE; Duane Durst, Site Curator, Hollenberg Pony Express Station, Hanover, KA; Sarah Elder, curator, The St. Joseph Museum, St. Joseph, MO; John Mark Lambertson, director, The National Frontier Trails Center, Independence, MO; Michael N. Landon, Archivist, The Church of Jesus Christ, Latter-Day Saints Historical Department, and Ken Norton, a librarian at the Church's Family History Center in Salt Lake City; Rex Norman, Park Historian, Fort Laramie National Historical Site, Fort Laramie, WY; Ron Valance, operations manager, Ayres National Bridge Park, Douglas WY; and staff members at City of Rocks National Reserve, Almo, ID and at the Empire Mine State Historical Park, Grass Valley, CA.

We are grateful also to the staffs of the St. Joseph Public Library for access to their newspaper files of the 1850's and to other librarians in Sonoma, Santa Rosa and Healdsburg, California; to the Bagaduce Music Lending Library of Blue Hill ME, and the Beinecke Library, Yale University, New Haven CT. Our thanks also go to the Healdsburg Museum and Historical Society and to Ralph Hyde, chief librarian at the Guildhall Library in London.

A Chinese gold miner, Kwong Chung, plays a key role in my novel. I am fortunate in having as a friend and neighbor, Robert Cheung, a native of Hong Kong and former professor of psychology. Now a travel agent, Bob has given me much help in developing my character and in guiding my reading of Chinese literature.

While handing out accolades, I give grudging credit to my wife, Beverly, and my two daughters, The Rev. Dr. Alyce Fowler McKenzie, a professor of theology, and Susanna Fowler, a psychological counselor, whose highly critical readings of the work in progress and equally outspoken and sometimes gratuitous advice guided this often insensitive male author into not only a better understanding of his female protagonist but also served to shape, shorten and, I must confess, improve the story's denouement.

The opinions of my wife and daughters were given further weight by suggestions from two talented editors, Cynthia Vartan and Judith Schnell, who were kind enough to read and comment on an early draft of the story.

The person to whom I owe the biggest thanks, however, is David Allan Comstock, proprietor of the Comstock Bonanza Press, Grass Valley CA, author and publisher of the three-volume work, THE NEVADA COUNTY CHRONICLES, and other books about the historically rich region in which he and his wife, Ardis, live in the Sierras. Not only have I drawn heavily on his published works, I have pestered him with written and telephone requests for information about life in the Gold Fields during the 1850's and 60's. David has never let me down, and I am most grateful to him.

In works of fiction it is usual for the author to disclaim any resemblence of his characters to actual persons, living or dead. I confess that I have taken some liberties with Alonzo Delano, a colorful character, nicknamed "Old Block," who was a banker in Grass Valley, and with the Rev. D.A. Dryden, a Methodist minister.

Then, as those of you who read this book all the way through will discover when you reach my Afterword, there was a real Annie Mundy. And a few of the things that happened to my fictional Annie are patterned on events in her life. But fortunately, as explained in my Afterword, what I know about the real Annie is enough only to inspire my story. Otherwise the Annie of my book is the creature of my imagination.

However, I know enough about the real Annie to understand that she, like my fictional character, was a part of the great migration of some half million persons who crossed the West to California and Oregon by wagon train between 1844 and 1869. I dedicate this novel to her and the other brave women who suffered through childbirth, dust, heat, and the death of family members to reach their promised land in the West.

Robert H. Fowler,
Camp Hill, PA

CAST OF CHARACTERS
(in order of appearance)

Annie Mundy
Her father, Squire Francis Asbury Mundy
Her mother, Lucretia Shelton Mundy
Dessie and Ike, Mundy slaves
Dr. John Mundy, Annie's uncle
Billie Joe Duncan, boyfriend of Annie
Ralph and Myrtle Mae Hixon, emigrants to Oregon
Ralph Jr., their son
Mr and Mrs. Osborne Hixon, Missouri settlers
Elmer Hixon, their son
Zebulon McGee, mountain man turned trail guide
Chester Peebles III, his cousin, also a guide
Mr. and Mrs. Courtenay, English actors
Simeon and Heather Courtenay, their children
Lester and Opal, runaway slaves, servants of Courtenays
Bret Corbett, professional gambler
Kentucky Pete, his side kick
Mr. and Mrs. Herman Mueller, emigrants to Oregon
Jacob, their son
Will Tremelling, Cornish-born miner
Running Wolf, Shoshone renegade
Dr. Horace Dormsby, English Mormon emigrant
Clarence Goodall, frontier trader
Paddy Finnegan, Irish-born ex-49er turned merchant
Evelyn Harmer, madam of Grass Valley's House of Joy brothel
Mildred, Madeline, and Francine, House of Joy prostitutes
Bull Duchamps, French-Canadian miner
Alonzo Delano, Grass Valley banker and author
Soohoo Kwong Chung, Chinese gold miner and scholar
Rev. D.A. Dryden, Methodist minister

My story begins in Oldham County, North Carolina shortly before the War Between the States. I am a Mundy, the eldest, only daughter of a justice of the peace and former state legislator by the name of Francis Asbury Mundy, a proud, prosperous and pious man who married his pretty little first cousin, once removed, Lucretia Shelton, when he was 30 and she, only 14.

They produced three children, myself, born early in their marriage, followed much later by my brothers Thomas and Charles.

Soon after my birth, while my father still represented Oldham County in the Legislature, he sold half of the two hundred acres he had inherited from his father and used the proceeds to buy a slave couple at the auction of a widow's estate. Their names were Dessie and Ike. With Ike soon learning to farm the family's remaining acres and Dessie, to run the Mundy household, my father was freed up to live by his wits rather than physical labor, and my mother to sew and knit and worship her much older husband.

When he was at home, my father was a strict presence who piled his children into a buggy on Sundays to be hauled off to the local Methodist Episcopal Church South and then to be quizzed on the way home about what they had got from the sermon. Everyone in his family, even my mother, called him Papa.

When I was 6, Papa enrolled me in the village school which was conducted six months a year by a purse-mouthed, gray-haired spinster, Miss Daisy Richardson, who smelled of camphor and taught with a ruler in one hand and a copy of McGuffey's ECLECTIC READER in the other.

I was a good student, Miss Richardson's best, she told my parents. By the time my own formal education had ended I was able to teach my little brothers to read and write even before they entered the school. And thanks to an aunt who lent me popular novels of the day, I developed a love of literature that has lasted throughout my life.

I grew up desperately hoping that a better fate awaited me than that endured by my mother. At night I would stare out the window at a moon I knew shined on faraway places I had read about in novels. I yearned, even prayed, for freedom, for adventure, and for love.

We should be careful what we pray for lest we get more of it than we bargain for. Looking back over my life so far, I see that my prayers were indeed answered, both for better and worse.

At least I have rarely suffered from the boredom of my early years.

PART ONE

1

Dessie was the first to guess my secret. She always talked too much. I winced when I heard her saying to Mama in the kitchen, "Something funny about Annie, Miz Lucretia. She be done miss her time of month twice now."

I put down the book I was reading and tried to catch Dessie's eye to shut her up, but she plowed right on with, "You knows I been washing that child's clothes since she was born just about and she been as regular as a clock since she was twelve."

Mama, who was sewing buttons on a shirt, stared at Dessie, attempting to digest the meaning of her words. She looked away, her eyes squinting as she threaded her needle, spit on her finger, then rolled and knotted the thread.

"Dessie, you must be imagining things," she said at last.

"That ain't all. I noticed she hardly touched her breakfast this morning. And I sho didn't just imagine seeing her throw up in the back yard."

I was so angry at Dessie, I started up the narrow steps to get away from the sound of her big mouth, but Mama stopped me with, "Annie, are you sick, baby? Is there something wrong with you?"

Poor, poor Mama. Still so innocent. How could I answer? I burst out crying and ran up the stairs and flung myself across my bed.

My room was cold, for it was February. I had dreaded this moment for weeks now, and with good reason. I had been hoping against hope that my fears were unfounded, Now, on that dreadful morning, I knew that my life would never be the same again.

You see, our family has been staunch Methodists ever since my grandfather, Hosea Mundy, came down to North Carolina from Virginia to take up his pension lands for serving in the Revolution. He died before my time but I grew up on tales of his heroic deeds as a soldier and as a preacher. There had never been a scandal among his descendants, which were and still are thick as fleas on a cur dog's back in Oldham County.

Mama waited a long while before she came up the stairs. At times since, I have harbored a lot of bitterness against her. Now that I have borne and raised daughters of my own, I can appreciate what was going through her heart and mind. I don't know if I can ever forgive Papa for what he did, but that is getting ahead of my story.

Anyhow, Mama opened my door and stood there, hands on hips, just looking at me with watery blue eyes in her anxious way.

"You aren't in some kind of trouble, are you, Annie?"

What does a girl say when she suspects a truth she knows would break her mother's heart?

"Oh, Mama, my nerves are just on edge."

She wouldn't come right out and ask what I might have done that would have stopped my menstrual periods. So finally she said, "When Papa gets home I'll have him take you to Brother John and let him see what is wrong with you."

John Mundy, Papa's younger brother, was the doctor in our part of Oldham County.

I shrank at the sound of Papa's buggy out front. Mama intercepted him before he could go to the barn and unhitch his horse. They came into the house. I got out of bed and leaned over the hole cut in the floor to admit heat from the downstairs stove.

"You aren't saying she has gone and got herself in the family way?" I overheard Papa saying.

"I have told you all I know."

"What does she say?"

"It's just her nerves, according to her."

"I've a good notion to beat the truth out of her."

"No, Papa. That wouldn't be right. Annie has always been a good girl and a smart girl, too. She is headstrong, true, but she is your daughter. She comes by it naturally."

"Somebody has got to talk to her."

"Not yet, Papa, please. Just let me take her to see Brother John."

There was some back and forth conversation, and for once Mama got her way. Papa wouldn't even look at me as I got in the buggy. Leaving Dessie to tend to little Thomas and Charles, who had come home from school by then, Mama climbed in beside me. The distance to where Uncle John and Aunt Mamie lived in Dover's Crossroads was only a mile but I swear it seemed like a thousand as we rode along in silence under a dismal late winter sky.

Once there, Mama made Papa stay outside in the cold while she took me in the little one-story brick house in which Uncle John and Aunt Mamie lived and where he practiced medicine.

I always liked my Uncle John. He had a better sense of humor than Papa who was full of self-importance as a justice of the peace and a former state legislator. Mama spoke to Uncle John in private and then told me to go into his little office "and tell him everything."

Uncle John listened to my story of being on edge from nerves, then asked, with evident embarrassment, about my periods.

After doing some gentle probing of my abdomen, he looked me right in the eye and said, "Annie, you must tell the truth. If you are going to have a baby, as I think you are, you must tell your folks who the father is."

"I can't do that," I said.

"Then maybe you would prefer me to ask them. Come on, Annie. My guess is that whatever happened, it was around Christmas. Am I right?"

Unable to speak, I merely nodded.

"And it was someone your family knows?"

Again I nodded.

His face clouded. "Not anyone in the family?"

Shocked, I blurted out, "Of course not, Uncle John."

"Do you love the man or boy, whoever he is?"

"With all my heart," I said.

"Would you like to marry him?"

"If he'd have me. But he is young."

"How young?"

"Younger than me by a year, I reckon."

"And you are 16, I believe."

"Nearly 17."

"That is mighty young for a husband."

He sat rubbing his chin, never taking his eyes off me.

"Now we come to the big question. I will handle this with your parents, but you had better tell me right out who the man, I mean boy, is."

I took a deep breath and whispered, "Billy Joe Duncan."

* * *

On the ride home Papa never said a word to me or Mama. I went up to my room. Soon I heard Papa drive his buggy out of the yard. He did not return until long after supper. Again I listened at the hole in my bedroom floor.

"It's no use. They say the boy is far too young."

"Did you mention a dowry?"

"Indeed I did. Offered to buy them a hundred acres along Mead's Creek. Good bottom land. Even promised to help them build a house there. Never trust a Presbyterian, Lucretia. Duncan says the boy is just too young. Besides which, he doesn't want him to be a farmer. Family has their heads set on him going to the University and becoming a doctor or lawyer."

"What about Billy Joe? Did you talk to him?"

"Duncan wouldn't let me see him. Only concession he would make was to promise they would keep quiet about this. They act like they are as ashamed as us."

"What will we do, Papa?"

"I got an idea but I'll have to work out the details. We'll talk about this after I eat. Where is she?"

"In bed. Wouldn't touch her supper."

"You talk to her anymore?"

"I don't know what to say to her. This is the worst thing ever to happen in our family. I just dread it when this gets out."

"It's not going to get out."

"But Dessie already knows. She's bound to have told Ike."

"I know how to keep them from breathing a word to anyone, white or colored. And Brother John will respect our confidence. As for the Duncans, they are just as mortified as us. You ought to have kept closer watch over her. She should have been reading her Bible instead of all those novels Mamie keeps feeding her. When did this happen anyway?"

"I remember her talking a lot to Billy Joe last August during camp meeting. I wondered why he was hanging around a Methodist camp ground and him from such a Presbyterian family. Then, you may remember, he spent part of Christmas at Brother Robert's house. He and young Jim are great friends at Professor Mead's Academy. She was over there a lot. And he came by here several times, once with Jim and then without him. I have tried to keep her a good girl, but you know how willful she has always been."

* * *

Yes, all my life I have been headstrong. It's my nature. From my experiences of the next few days, weeks and months, I also became self-reliant and realistic in my attitude toward life, or, to use a bigger word, pragmatic.

That long, awful first night after my secret came out, I wallowed in self pity and in apprehension over just what sort of scheme Papa was working on. The only thing that kept me from utter despair was the love I truly did bear for Billy Joe Duncan; that and my refusal to accept the possibility that my feelings were not reciprocated.

He was so handsome that my heart went out to him the first time we met, which was the previous August at camp meeting. My cousin Jim Mundy, who was then only fourteen, introduced him as a classmate at Professor Mead's Academy, where the smarter lads of the county went on to school.

Billy Joe was big for his age with dark, curly hair, large, light brown eyes and a fair complexion. But it was his shy grin that charmed me most.

For my part, I always had a good figure, with trim legs, slender waist and full bosom. But my hair is mousy brown and straight as a stick. My eyes are a hazel-gray, a sort of compromise between Mama's blue and Papa's fiercely dark eyes. I always hated my acquiline nose which is too pronounced for my roundish face. So I must say he was more handsome than I was pretty.

During our annual camp meeting that previous August, I saw right off he was interested in me but that if anything was ever to come of our mutual attraction it would be up to me to take the initiative. So, I asked Billy Joe to walk with me to the spring to get a bucket of water for our "tent" which was what we called the huts that circled the preaching arbor.

I bragged on how strong he was and drew him out with questions about his school and his family. There is nothing like acting interested in a boy or man to win him over, I long ago discovered and have often used that trick to my advantage.

By the end of camp meeting week, he was holding my hand when we got out of sight of my family. He promised to write and then said, "How would it be if I was to come visit Jim over Christmas? Would I be able to see you again?"

Whereupon I stood on my tiptoes and gave him a big kiss right on the lips. Whereupon he put his arms around me and kissed and hugged me real hard.

It happened at Christmas time. He would come over from Uncle Robert's house where he was visiting Cousin Jim and sit around the kitchen fire and help me with the chores, then steal kisses when we were alone. On one of these visits, I asked if he'd like to help me gather eggs in the barn. And that is where it happened, the first time, in Papa's hay loft.

Oh, that boy had the sweetest, strongest young body. Mama never told me anything about such matters, but from observing farm animals and once from spying in the window of Ike and Dessie's cabin on a Sunday afternoon, I knew about sexual congress. However, nothing prepared me for how we got carried away. I had never imagined the thrill: the delicious, mysterious feeling of closeness that came over me during that and several other episodes during the next few days.

Brought up strictly as I was, I knew that what we were doing probably was wrong, but it seemed so right and natural that in my heart, I could not consider it a sin.

When it came time for Billy Joe to return to school, I made him promise he would come back at Eastertime and that he would write. I told him I loved him and asked if he felt the same toward me. He replied, "I have never loved anyone else like this."

"Like this!" Like what? Often have I pondered just what he really meant.

2

During that long, anxious night after the truth came out, I clung to the belief that the love Billy Joe and I felt for each other ran too strong for family disapproval to thwart. I was confident that, given time, he would come and whisk me away across the state line into South Carolina where it was easy to get married. I was putting those sentiments in a letter to Billy Joe the next afternoon when I heard a wagon pull up in the yard. Papa kept a little office beside the house where he conducted his justice of the peace duties. Looking out my window, I saw a swarthy fellow with a hook nose and a fat, blond woman about twice his size with a little pale boy. They went into Papa's office, and I returned to writing my letter.

Just as I was finishing it, Mama came upstairs, her eyes all red and puffy, to say, "Papa wants to see you in his office."

"What about?"

"He'll have to tell you himself."

Not once had Papa spoken to me since the previous day. Even now he didn't look at me. He just said, "Annie, this is Mr. and Mrs. Ralph Hixon from over in Goose Creek township."

"And this is, Ralph Junior," the woman said as she put her hand on the boy's shoulder and fixed her squinty eyes on me.

Papa continued, "The Hixons are selling their farm and aim to take the trains out to Missouri...well, you tell what your plans are, Mr. Hixon."

"I been reading the past few years about the opportunities that exist out in Oregon," the man said. "Lots of good, rich land out there. Mild climate. Myrtle Mae and me want to go out to Missouri first. I got a brother that has a farm on the Missouri River, near St. Joseph. He has promised to help us buy a wagon, some supplies, and livestock. Then we aim to set out for the West around the first of May when they say the grass starts growing across the plains. It's going to be a real adventure."

"That's right," Mrs. Hixon chimed in. "We're pulling up stakes here. But we are taking our religion with us. We're strong Baptists, you see. By the way, Miss Mundy, have you been baptized?"

"When I was a baby. Why?"

"We'd feel better if at some point you was to be baptized as we do in our church. By total immersion."

"Now, Myrtle Mae," her husband said. "The Mundys is strong Methodists. We don't want to go imposing our ways on..."

She cut him off with, "If we are going to entrust little Ralph Junior and any other of our children that God may send..."

This time I interrupted, saying, "I don't understand."

"Didn't Squire Mundy explain?" she said. "You're going west with us. We're offering you the opportunity of a lifetime."

I got up and ran out of the office and into the house. For the next half hour, with Dessie cowering in the pantry, I railed at Mama who just sat there with her apron over her face and weeping at the harshness of my words. Even now I blush to think of the vituperation I heaped upon her poor prematurely gray head.

"I can't believe that my own mother would let him do this."

"I can't stop him, Annie. His mind is made up. The boy won't marry you. This way we will avoid the shame."

"Other girls have had babies and raised them."

"Poor white trash and darkies. Not Sheltons or Mundys."

The Hixons having left, Papa came in as my tirade was running down and said, "You might as well accept this, Annie. It's the best we can do in a bad situation."

"But I am your daughter, your own flesh and blood. And you want to pack me off like a stray cat with those dreadful people and their wormy-looking little boy?"

"You were our daughter. You should have thought of that before you forgot your upbringing."

All my life I had feared my father. But I could not hold my tongue.

"What monstrous, hypocritical nonsense. Look at all the seven-month babies that have been baptized right in our church."

He answered me in a flat, cold-blooded manner with no trace of compassion: "Yes, and yours could be one of them, but the Duncans won't agree. The boy is too young. Now look, Annie, I am not exactly casting you out into the wilderness. I am taking out a mortgage to raise the three hundred dollars I have promised the Hixons to cover the cost of your expenses on the trip. And I have scraped together a hundred dollars for yourself, to help you get settled in Oregon after the Hixons are established out there. They are good, steady people. All you have to do is help them look after their little boy for a while."

"I can't stand them."

"You'll get used to them. Let's hear no more shouting, Annie. The quicker we get this over with, the better. I will not have our shame published in this community."

I have known some mean-spirited men in my life, but I swear not one of them could match my father, Squire Francis Asbury Mundy, when it comes to hardness of heart.

Too angry for tears, I went back upstairs and tore up my letter to Billy Joe. I wrote a new one in which I told him of what Papa planned for me. I told them about the $100 that would be mine and proposed that he slip away from school so we could borrow Papa's horse and take off for South Carolina. I promised to make him a good wife and help him through the University, if that was what he wanted. Never before or since have I poured out my soul into a letter like that one.

Although Dessie obviously was contrite at having touched off such an upset, I made a point of refusing to speak to her. Her husband, Ike, was a kindly soul who was devoted to our family. I took him aside and begged him to deliver my letter to Billy Joe, who lived with his family near the academy.

"Oh, Miss Annie, that do be a good five mile from here. How I gonna get away without Master Frank to know about it?"

"You slip out tonight. After Papa is asleep, take his horse."

"They don't allow niggers to be out at night without a paper."

"I can write a permission on Papa's stationery. I'll sign his name."

"I don't believe I can do that, Miss Annie."

But in the end, he agreed.

The next morning, Ike looked awful sleepy and worried, too. Papa, noticing how lathered with sweat his horse appeared, feared the animal had taken sick during the night.

On the way to the outhouse, I detoured by the barn where Ike was milking our cow.

"Here you is, Miss Annie," he said, handing me back my own letter.

"Didn't he read it?"

"Yessum, and he writ you something back on the same paper."

As I opened the letter, Ike continued, in a whisper, "Miss Annie, I'm powerful sorry what they is doing to you. It just ain't right. If there was anything Dessie or me could do, we sho would. But Mister Frank do be a hard man and he done make up his mind. I just wants to ax you one favor and that is please don't never let him know what I done for you last night. He be done told me and Dessie he sell us off to a slave trader if we ever opens our mouth about this. So, I am axing you please."

"Of course, I won't tell," I snapped as I opened my letter and turned it over. At the bottom of my plea for him to rescue me and our baby from banishment to the West, Billy Joe had scrawled:

"I'm sorry, Annie. I just can't."

I already had lost my faith in Papa. And now Billy Joe had betrayed me. I have loved more than one man in my life, but since that morning, I have never put my total trust in any of the male species, except for good, old faithful Ike, who risked being sold off to a slave trader to carry my letter to Billy Joe. And that was all in vain.

* * *

We left the very next week. I didn't have the opportunity or desire to say goodby to Aunt Mamie or Cousins Jim and Wesley. Uncle John did drop by to give me some medicines for constipation, diarrhea and other of what he called "travelers' complaints." He also gave me a little handbook for expectant mothers along with some kindly advice.

"Now, Annie," he said. "I think this is a cruel thing my brother is doing. I just wish that Duncan boy were a little older, but facts are facts and we must face them. You are going off to a new land where you can make a fresh beginning. Make the most of your opportunities out there. I do hear it is a marvelous country. Now, is there anything else I can do for you?"

By then I had cried all the tears I had in my system.

"There is one thing. Papa says I am not to write until I have confessed my sins and been received in a church out there and have married a respectable man. Please, could I write to you and Aunt Mamie and would you write back and tell me how Mama and little Thomas and Charles are getting on? Ike and Dessie, too. As for Papa, he can go to hell for all I care."

Uncle John's jaw dropped at that remark, but he recovered and smiled in his kind, understanding way.

"We will be eager to hear from you. And we will keep you up to date on what little happens around here. I don't blame you for feeling bitter toward your father, but don't let this feeling corrode your soul. When the time comes to forgive him, just let go."

"It is easy to give such advice when you are not the victim of the injustice."

"Just bear in mind what I have said. I predict that you not only will survive this experience but in the end you will triumph. I have never said this to you but often I have told Mamie that my niece Annie got all the brains and spirit in her family."

"Thank you, Uncle John," I said as I got up and kissed him. He was such a dear man. I wish he had been my father instead of my self-righteous, hard-hearted Papa. The memory of his use of the word "triumph" was to give me much comfort during the ensuing weeks and months.

* * *

I was allowed to take along two large carpet bags and all that could be crammed into them. Besides copies of IVANHOE, OLIVER TWIST and other favorite novels Aunt Mamie had given me, this included two bonnets, a comb and hair brush, three petticoats, two dresses, an extra pair of shoes, a shawl, extra stockings and under drawers. And, it being late February, I was wearing a long woolen topcoat with hood when the Hixons drove up in a large wagon loaded with two trunks and several valises.

Thomas and Charles had gone off to school at Dover's Crossroads that morning, unaware their big sister was leaving. It really hurt that I didn't get to say goodby properly to my little brothers.

Sent upstairs by Mama to help me finish packing, Dessie spoke with tears in her eyes, "Miss Annie, I wants to apologise for spouting off to your mama instead of talking to you first."

"It's all right, Dessie. They had to find out sometime."

"Well, please don't say nothing to nobody, but me and Ike we been saving back a little money from selling stuff out of our garden. We aimed to try to buy our freedom someday. It ain't much. About twenty dollars. We wants you to have it . . ."

"I couldn't do that, Dessie."

"It can be a loan. You can pay us back when you are able. Maybe you will meet a rich man out there. Maybe he would buy us from your papa and bring us out to work for you."

"You are kind, but Papa has promised to give me a hundred dollars."

"You ain't mad at me no more, then?"

"I am not mad at anyone, except Papa and maybe Billy Joe Duncan."

Mama said her farewell in the kitchen while Papa, who was to drive us the twelve miles to the station, stayed outside talking to the Hixons.

"Try to be a good girl, Annie."

"Yes, Mama."

"Papa says I am not to write to you . . ."

"I know."

"But I do want to hear how you get on."

"Ask Uncle John. He will know."

Papa called from the porch, "Lucretia, it is time for us to be going."

At that Mama threw her arms about me and burst into fresh tears. As I stood there stiffly, not hugging her back, I made a pledge that never would a man dominate and squelch me as she had allowed my father to do to her.

At last she released me to dab her reddened eyes and blow her nose. Before she could embrace me again, I joined Papa and the Hixons.

On the way out of the yard past the mulberry tree where I used to love to play, I looked back at my old home. It was one of those two-story in the front and one in the back frame, unpainted houses so common in the

Piedmont Carolinas. It had a porch across the front and a separate kitchen house in the rear, reached through a covered walkway. Since then I have seen some fine mansions that would make it seem shabby but for many a month I would look back on our home with longing and regret. I still dream about playing in that yard, as an innocent girl.

All the way to the station, Papa never spoke a word to me as Mrs. Hixon chattered on and on. Every time her husband started to talk, she cut in and finished his sentences for him.

From what Papa said, I gathered that he had agreed to buy the wagon in which we rode and the two mules that drew it. At the station, he counted out $300 to Mr. Hixon and then, still without speaking, handed me a leather purse which I later found to contain $100 and a small leather-bound New Testament. Whether he really had to take out a mortgage to raise the money I don't know, but he got a good part of his $300's worth back in the form of an excellent farm wagon and a pair of matched sorrel mules.

But I saw that he was not done with his bargaining when he said, "You understand, Hixon, that you are responsible for train fares and all her living expenses. My daughter has a sum of money but that is for her use when her three years indenture are up."

That was the first I had heard about any three years, but I kept quiet.

"We understand, Squire," Mrs. Hixon said. "Now don't you worry about Miss Annie. We all are going to get along just fine. I am sure we will become good friends in time. By the way, I hear she did well in school."

"She was an excellent scholar."

"Then maybe she can teach Junior to read and write and do his sums on our way out West."

The little two-car train, drawn by a wood-burning locomotive, came huffing into the station before either Papa or I could respond.

After they had put their trunks and the heavier of my two carpet bags into the baggage car, the Hixons shook hands with Papa.

"There now, Miss Annie," Mrs. Hixon said. "Aren't you going to give your pa a goodby kiss?"

"Goodby, Papa," I said without moving.

His jaw tightened and his mouth hardened. He swallowed and, without looking into my face, said, "Goodby, Annie."

"Is that all they are going to say to each other?" Mrs. Hixon remarked to her husband as they mounted the stairs to the train.

I stepped up behind them, then turned to look down into the face of my father.

"Goodby, Papa," I said loudly enough so the Hixons would be sure to hear. "I hope you can live with yourself after doing this to me."

Without waiting for a response, I entered the car and took my seat beside little Ralph Junior. I did not look out the window until the train started moving on its way toward Charlotte.

Papa was standing beside his new wagon and team with a look on his face that I had never seen before.

And that was the last time I ever saw my father.

3

In those days before the Civil War, we didn't have the grand railroad system spanning the country that our nation now boasts. To get from Charlotte out to St. Louis took a week of switching from this line to the next, zig-zagging through the heart of Dixie: across the cotton lands of South Carolina down to Columbia, over Georgia's red clay country up to Atlanta and on through the mountains to Chattanooga and up to Nashville, then north through Kentucky to Louisville where we crossed the Ohio River by ferry, thence eastward, by rail again, over Indiana and Illinois to the Mississippi River opposite St. Louis.

As though my own homesickness and shame were not misery enough, the seats on the trains were hard, the cars heated, if at all, with pot-bellied stoves. You had to be careful where you stepped to avoid the spittoons and their surrounding splatter of tobacco juice. To this day, I cannot abide a man addicted to the filthy habit of chewing tobacco. We spent several nights in rundown hotels and boarding houses along the way. I was sick much of the time, which caused Mrs. Hixon to explain to all who noticed my discomfort, "Poor girl is not used to travelling," as if she had ever been outside of Oldham County herself.

Lord, how I grew to despise that sanctimonious woman and her condescending ways. She never put it in so many words but I could imagine her saying, "We know you have sinned, but good Christians that we are, we do not hold your sin against you. No, we will be the means of redeeming you through making you our servant."

Even now, I have little use for her kind. And, from such experiences, I have observed that persons offering charity in expectation of being rewarded by gratitude often are disappointed.

Mr. Hixon spent most of his time with his nose in an emigrant's guidebook. Now and then, during one of his wife's silences, he would raise his head and say something like, "See here, Myrtle Mae, it says oxen is much more dependable than mules for crossing the West. They is slower but they cost less and they hold up better on the trail, besides being easier to handle. It looks like we ought to have four yoke . . . that's eight steers in all."

"Just don't forget we must have a cow as well. You promised me I could have a cow and a servant girl."

"We have Annie . . ."

They had dropped the "Miss" from their address to me almost as soon as we were out of my father's hearing.

"Yes, but I am not setting foot on the trail without a good Jersey cow as well. By the way, Annie, you know how to milk, I hope."

Through clenched teeth I replied, "At home Ike did all the milking."

"Oh, yes, your father owns slaves, doesn't he? Well, my dear, your days of being waited on hand and foot by darkies are behind you. We are moving to free territory where slavery is not allowed."

Her husband said, "I wrote to Brother Osborne to look out for us a cow and a saddle horse for myself. He'll not let us down."

A few years later, when the news came through from the East about the great Civil War, I often read the names of places I had seen out of those grimy train windows: Kennesaw and Lookout Mountains, Chickamauga Station and the hills outside of Nashville.

Oddly, the farther west we jolted along on those rickety rails, the more I liked or, perhaps, pitied, Mr. Hixon. Although uneducated, he really was a patient, intelligent man. I can't say much for his judgment in choosing a wife, however. And Ralph Junior turned out to be a sweet little boy. To take my mind off my troubles and my homesickness, I began to teach him his A,B,C's. He caught on quickly.

What Papa had told Mrs. Hixon was true. I did do well in our village school. I loved to read, and learning always came easy for me. In fact it had been my dream, before I met Billy Joe Duncan, that I might become a school teacher myself someday. But fate had other plans for me.

*   *   *

After crossing the mighty Mississippi River on a ferry and taking a brief rest in a flea-bag hotel in St. Louis, we booked passage on a palatial side-wheel steamer named The Polar Star which carried us for four days up the muddy Missouri River past Jefferson City, Independence and on to St. Joseph.

Sunk in misery as I had been, I did not catch the spirit of our adventure until we had left St. Louis and entered the mouth of the Missouri. For the first time, I began to feel the pull of the West and to compare the exciting sights I had seen with the constrained life I had led in North Carolina.

Although the state room I shared with Ralph Junior was little more than a closet, it beat the shabby hotel rooms in which we had been staying. And the food was first rate. But the company was what excited the imagination of this backwoods girl. All this happened at the height of the controversy over the Kansas Question, only a few weeks before the little civil war that was to erupt in the Lawrence, Kansas area between slave owners and John Brown's crowd of abolitionists. Tempers were raw. Aboard The Polar Star arguments broke out between those passengers who wished the territory to become a slave state and those determined that it should be free, arguments that sometimes came close to gunplay. High stakes poker games were played far into the night as well.

But the most fascinating of the passengers was a family that occupied the adjoining stateroom, the likes of whom I had never seen or, for that matter, heard.

The husband was an elegantly dressed gentleman with jet black hair down to his shoulders. Although no taller than the average man, his slender build and erect carriage made him appear to be a good six feet tall. His wife, who nearly matched him in height, was a blonde possessed of a classic profile and dressed in clothes far finer than any I had ever seen. With them were two handsome children with carroty red hair: a boy of about 12 and a girl a few years younger. Also in attendance with them were a black man and woman who, I assumed, were slaves they were bringing from Virginia. They remained below deck throughout the trip, so I knew little about them until later.

I soon learned that my neighbors were the Courtenay family of actors on their way to carry culture to California. The husband hailed from London, the wife, from Bristol, England. As a way of working their passage to St. Joseph, they and their children put on nightly performances of short plays or readings from Shakespeare at fifty cents a head. Although Mrs. Hixon disapproved of these shows as "the work of the devil," I slipped out each night and dipped into my cache of money to join the crowd in the boat's dining room. It was the first time I had been exposed to the theater, and I was mightily impressed.

By putting my ear to the thin bulkhead that separated our state rooms, I learned that the Courtenays had come to America a couple of years before to escape some sort of scandal in London, something to do with the husband's relationship with the wife of a theater manager. Finding poor pickings in New York, they had settled for a time in Richmond, Virginia where they performed at a theater managed by the renowned Joseph Jefferson, of whom they spoke with great respect.

Although in public the wife maintained an icy, superior sort of air, speaking in a cultivated voice, once in their stateroom she turned into a regular harridan. In often coarse terms, she berated her husband for their having to perform before "such common yokels." When he tried to defend himself, she cited what seemed to be his many shortcomings.

I gathered that, despite their claims of having been the rave of the London theater, they had always lived a hand-to-mouth existence in their native land and had enjoyed only a middling success in Baltimore and Richmond. Even so, both I and most of the passengers were fascinated by the Courtenays. They gave me my first taste of the theater, a taste I still like to indulge.

4

At St. Joseph, as we stood on the crowded deck of our paddle-wheeler waiting for the gangplank to be lowered, Mr. Hixon pointed to a bluff-looking, red-faced fellow waving from the wharf, and beside him a skinny youth leaning on a cane.

"There's Brother Osborne," Mr. Hixon said.

"Who is that puny chap with him?" his wife asked.

"That would be his son, Elmer. He was just a little bitty boy when they went west."

"I wonder what's wrong with him."

"Don't you remember, Myrtle Mae? They wrote he had come down with scarlet fever. Must have left him crippled."

Elmer Hixon was a thin, dark-looking youth with a great shock of coal-black hair and hazel, almost yellow eyes. The sole of one shoe was built up to accommodate a shortened leg.

"Now, Annie," Mrs. Hixon said. "There is no need for us to reveal your condition. Mr. Hixon and I have talked this over, and we agree to say nothing on the subject, seeing as how you haven't begun to show yet. As far as they are concerned, you are just the daughter of a dear neighbor friend who wants to see the West and is willing to work your passage with our family."

"I don't recall that our families were exactly friends."

"Everyone in Oldham County is friends of Squire Mundy. And Osborne will be impressed that he has entrusted his own daughter to our care."

"Won't he also know that we weren't even neighbors seeing that you lived a good way off from Dover's Crossroads?" I continued in my churlish vein.

She flared up at that, saying, "Now don't you go giving me any back talk, young lady. I am just trying to make things easy for you."

She nudged her husband and, thus prompted, he spoke up, "Yes, as far as Osborne and his family is concerned, you are a family friend. Now, come on Myrtle Mae, Ralph Junior. The gang plank is down."

* * *

St. Joseph turned out to be a bustling town of several thousand souls with many substantial buildings and houses, both brick and frame, set on lovely hills that sloped down to low bluffs along the Missouri. Chief among the buildings was an exquisite little courthouse set high above the town, like a Greek temple with its domed belfry and columns across the front.

Having outstripped Independence as a staging center in recent years, the town was filled with all kinds of hardware stores. Wheelwrights, wagon-makers, and stockyards catered to the considerable numbers of people already collecting there to start for the far West as soon as the weather and grass permitted them to begin their journey. The rich muckamucks who had been fattening off the emigrant trade for several years lived in fine houses up on "the Devil's Backbone" overlooking the dwellings of lesser folk nearer the river. Although fewer in number than in some previous years, during that March of 1856 hundreds of emigrants' tents and wagons already thronged a stretch of meadowland just south of the city, called Patee's Town after the owner of the land.

Osborne Hixon lived a short wagon ride beyond Patee's Town on 60 acres of rich Missouri farmland on the edge of a section called "Little Dixie" because of all the southern families settled there. He and his wife, a sallow kind of a woman who looked to be part Indian, lived in a long, low log cabin they had gussied up with porches and extra rooms through the years. Besides Elmer, their oldest, they had four other children, two girls (with whom I roomed) and two boys, whose ages and names are fuzzy in my memory. But, as events developed, I could never forget Elmer.

As I had observed from the boat deck, he was not a healthy young man, of little use around the farm. Perhaps not as bright as he and his mother thought, he was clever all the same. Like many young men not suited by natural ability or inclination to do hard, physical labor, and having a strong streak of avarice, he was drawn to the legal profession. In fact, he had started reading for the law in the offices of a St. Joseph attorney by day while spending his evenings poring over his law books and showing off his learning to his family.

From the first I couldn't bear the sight of him. He kept staring at me with those yellowish eyes until he got on my nerves so bad one day I said to him, "Didn't anybody ever tell you it is rude to stare? Even little Ralph Junior knows better than that."

His reply nearly bowled me over.

"I can't help myself, Miss Annie. You are so pretty."

Not even Billy Joe Duncan had told me I was pretty, although many a man has pretended to think so in later years. I wasn't ugly by a long shot, but pretty? That's another matter.

Anyway, Elmer's comment took me aback. All I could think to say was, "Nobody ever called me that before."

"Maybe that's because nobody ever took a good look at you."

"You sure have taken a good enough look yourself, and I wish you would stop it. You embarrass me."

"I'll try, but I'm not sure I can succeed."

No matter what we say, it is a rare woman who doesn't appreciate a compliment. But my heart still belonged to Billy Joe Duncan. And, fine, strapping fellow that he was, he made Elmer Hixon look like a feeble excuse for a man.

Elmer's wits were another matter. He read all the newspapers he could get his hands on and enjoyed arguing with his parents and the Ralph Hixon's about anything, especially politics (he was anti-slavery) and religion (a professed agnostic).

This happened the year James Buchanan was elected president and the Republican Party was being created; also the last election before our great country got caught up in the Civil War that nearly spelled its doom; indeed did so for my native Southland.

Looking back, I realize that Elmer argued more to impress me than out of conviction, for every time he made one of his points, he would cut those cat eyes around to see if I had heard.

My mind was not on politics. It was on what my fate in Oregon would be as an unmarried mother tied down for three years of servitude to a woman I despised. By Ralph Hixon's calculations, we would be lucky to reach the Oregon Territory in time for my baby to be born. Although my morning sickness had become only an unpleasant memory, my waist was just beginning to thicken. I would be lucky if we started west before my condition became obvious. And, tired of sleeping in a tiny room with two little girls, one of them a bed wetter, I was looking forward to getting on the trail.

Elmer honored my request to stop his staring, leaving me to simmer in my homesickness and resentment of my father. Curiously though— call it one of my few virtues, if you will—I have never felt sorry for myself for long at a time. I have always figured that no matter how bad a fix you get into, there is generally a way to get out of it. So, I squelched my self pity and began to dream of finding myself a more mature but equally handsome Billy Joe Duncan, a strong fellow who could be bent to my will. The papers were full of talk about the scarcity of young women in both Oregon Territory and the new state of California. Surely somewhere out there I could find myself a man who suited me, somebody as unlike my father as possible but with more backbone than Billy Joe.

One evening as we huddled around the fire, listening to a late March wind howl around the cabin, all of us eating peanuts and throwing the hulls in the fire and the two Hixon brothers spitting tobacco juice into the flames, the talk turned as it usually did to the new world waiting in Oregon.

"I been thinking about this a lot," Elmer announced. "It is time to tell you all something."

"What?" his father asked, as we braced ourselves for another of his son's political pronouncements.

"I hear tell there is a great shortage of lawyers out in Oregon."

"There is a great shortage of everybody," his father replied. "Oregon ain't even a state yet."

"What are you getting at, Elmer dear?" asked his mother, who stood in the door of the kitchen drying a supper plate.

"I have decided to go to Oregon with Uncle Ralph's family."

His mother let out a shriek and wailed, "No, no. You are not strong enough."

His father spat his quid into the fire, and stood up, saying, "Look a'here, Elmer. Don't talk such damn foolishness. You got a great future right here in Missouri."

"I beg to disagree. This is a slave state. I want to go off to a free country where young men with gumption can help them form a new state, where there is no slavery. So how about it, Uncle Ralph, Aunt Myrtle Mae? Can I join your party?"

But his father was not done with his protests.

"Now, Elmer, it will be a long, hard journey, and seeing as how your health is not the strongest . . ."

Mrs. Ralph Hixon as usual could not keep her mouth closed.

"You'd have to have a horse and . . ."

"I got a fine little mare. Pa gave it to me to ride to Lawyer Jones' office. So how about it, Uncle Ralph?"

"I don't like to mention your affliction, but you would have to walk a lot."

At first it amused me to see how Ralph Hixon squirmed to get out of taking his smart-alecky, know-it-all nephew along to Oregon. My amusement turned to alarm as I saw how Elmer, as though cross-examining a witness in court, wore away at his uncle's resolve.

"I have been practicing without my cane. By the end of April, I will be able to walk well enough to keep up. Anyway, I will have my little mare."

"Then there is the question of supplies. Everything I have read says it takes at least 500 pounds of your basic commodities and such to get one person across the plains. And with the four of us, we already got as much weight as one wagon and four yoke of oxen can haul."

"That has been true in the past," Elmer said. "Only now you can buy supplies at Fort Kearny and Fort Laramie."

Then before his uncle could speak again, he added, "Besides which, I could buy a light wagon and two strong mules to haul what I need, which is not much besides my law books."

As Osborne Hixon bit a fresh chew from his twist of tobacco and searched for fresh arguments, his wife broke into fresh sobs.

"Oh, my dear son. You can practice law here in St. Joe."

Elmer drew himself up straight with a superior sort of smirk spread across his irregular features.

"Mama, if I stay here, nobody will ever take me seriously. I will be just the crippled son of a dirt farmer. Whereas, out in Oregon, where no one will know me, there will be no limits to what I can achieve. How would you like it if your son became governor of Oregon or maybe even came back as a U.S. Senator?"

His mother smiled through her tears but finally his father spoke. "This is foolish talk. I am not going to allow you to go."

A mean look came over Elmer's face.

"How can you stop me, seeing as how I am free, white and now turned 21?"

"You ain't got any money. And you ain't getting a penny more out of me. Howsomever, I am willing to finish paying Lawyer Jones for his instruction and to set you up in practice."

"I don't need a penny from you."

This prompted Myrtle Mae to chime in with, "You needn't think your Uncle Ralph and me is going to finance you. We have taken on all the responsibility we can in bringing along Annie. We will have only one cow and it will take all her milk for ourselves."

"I don't like milk all that much, Aunt Myrtle Mae. Even if I did, I could buy a cow for myself, if I was so minded."

"What would you use for money?" his father demanded.

"The seven hundred dollars I happen to have on deposit with Mister Armstrong Beattie's bank in St. Joe."

"Seven hundred dollars? How did you come by such a sum?"
"Pa, did you ever hear of the game called poker?"

*   *   *

It took a while and a change in my circumstances before I learned the full story of how Elmer Hixon won $700 in a single game of late night poker at the Buffalo Saloon in St. Joseph. When I did, I gained not only a measure of respect for Elmer's gumption and brains but also a clearer understanding of why he was so eager to leave Missouri.

It seemed that he had borrowed $90 from a friend, using his little mare as collateral, and after standing by a poker table as an observer, inquired whether anyone else could join the game.

Sensing that here was an easy mark, the players let him take a chair. So, seated with a judge, two senior members of the local bar, a cattle dealer, a steamboat captain, and a professional gambler—of whom far more anon—this callow youth proceeded to ask dumb questions about the rules of the game, as though he had not read several books on the subject. He bluffed when he held bad cards and played timidly with stronger hands, all deliberately, to hear him tell it.

Within half an hour, he had lost over half of his $90 and faced the prospect of having to walk home in the dark and explain to his father what happened to his mare.

I have since learned to play an adequate game of poker myself but I have never pulled off such a coup as did Elmer Hixon.

He won an occasional pot, built his pile up to its original size, then lost half again on an extravagant bet when he held only two pair. Then he hit, or perhaps was allowed to hit, a fresh streak of wins that had nearly made up for his losses.

At that point, he said, "Look a'here, gentlemen, it is getting late and my family will be wondering where I am."

The professional gambler, scornful of Elmer's erratic playing, and desirous of cleaning him out before proceeding with the lawyers and the judge, said, "Well, young man, if you are afraid of what your mama might think, you should not sit down to play poker with grown men such as my friends here assembled."

At that, Elmer said, "I ain't afraid of anybody, let alone a fellow that wears a fancy vest and a four-in-hand tie with a diamond stick pin."

Then before the gambler's gorge could rise further, Elmer said to the judge, "If you are willing, your honor, I'll play just another hand or two before taking my leave."

As I got the story, he drew a pair of sevens, the ace of clubs and two other cards, got a disgusted look on his face, discarded two cards, keeping only the ace and the pair, and then concealed his suprise when he was dealt another seven and the ace of spades.

"I reckon I should have got out when I could," he muttered, just loud enough for the gambler to hear.

"Too late for that, sonny boy."

Elmer could and did drag his story out, but to get to the point, the pot got built up to more than $800. One by one, the lawyers and the cattle dealer dropped out, until finally only Elmer, the judge and the gambler remained.

By this time a considerable crowd of onlookers circled the table. When the time came to show hands, the judge held three eights, the gambler, the two red aces and a pair of fives.

Certain that he held the winning hand, with his three of a kind, according to Elmer, the judge reached out to claim the pot. As he told it, Elmer said, "Not so fast, your honor. I hold not only three of a kind, but also a pair of aces."

Showing his full house, Elmer raked in the money. Over the protests of the other players, he quit the game, went to his friend and repaid his $90 plus $10 interest, and quickly rode out of town.

The drawback to his coup was that the judge had taken a dislike to Elmer and had told Lawyer Jones he could not wait to get the upstart before him in his court.

"My goose is cooked here in Buchanan County," was the way Elmer put it later.

So that is one reason Elmer Hixon cast an ambitious eye toward Oregon. The other, and to hear him tell it, the more compelling reason was yours truly, Anne Eliza Mundy.

5

It has often struck me how a person's attitude toward another changes when that other person reveals the possession of wealth, exalted social position, or other marks of distinction. That is not to say that my feelings, or lack of same, changed all that much toward Elmer Hixon when I learned of his $700. But I have to admit that even I now regarded him with less scorn. Arrogant little know-it-all that he was, the fellow did have grit to match his perhaps unjustified ambition. And anyone truly human would have been touched by his speech to his family about his poor prospects for advancement as the crippled son of a dirt farmer. I have learned the hard way that you really do have to get away from home to be judged fairly for your own qualities rather than who your parents are and other considerations beyond your control.

Myrtle Mae Hixon's opposition to Elmer's coming along with us weakened after his revelation. As I overheard her say to her husband, "Now, Ralph, maybe we ought to consider what it would mean to ourselves to have a nephew out there who is a lawyer. Or just think if he really did become an official of some sort."

"I'd think better of him if he could help on the trail with the oxen, chop wood, fix a broken axle or such. He would just slow us down. Besides which he talks too much for my taste."

"Let's at least think about it."

As for myself, despite my new sympathy for Elmer, the last thing I wanted was to have to look at him every day for five months. He had given up his blatant staring, but now and then, when my back was turned, I could feel those cat eyes fixed upon my person.

A period of strained silence fell over the Osborne Hixon household before the family became reconciled to Elmer's decision. The two Hixon brothers spent several days visiting stock yards around St. Joe. True to his promise, Ralph Senior's first purchase was a young Jersey cow just separated from her first-born calf. He decided against buying a saddle horse, however.

Mrs. Hixon lost no time in setting me to the task of milking the cow, and doing so in a high-handed way calculated to arouse my resentment.

"Let's pull no long faces here, Annie. It is your job to milk Miss Mollie and you might as well get used to it."

The cow, missing her calf, refused to stand still. She lashed me with her tail and twice kicked over the bucket while I was trying to get the hang of milking. I often put my face against Miss Mollie's warm flank and wept at the ignominy of my exile.

Elmer found me one morning as I sat on the stool, shedding tears into a pail of milk.

"What is the matter, Miss Annie?"

"It is none of your business. Go away."

"You are not used to milking, are you?"

"Does it look like I am?"

"Here, let me show you."

He took my place on the stool and, with an air of superiority, quickly produced streams of milk.

"See. You start at the top of the teat, up next to the udder, and squeeze down like this."

When he was done, he stood up and smirked.

"For how long are you indentured to Uncle Ralph and Aunt Myrtle Mae?"

"Three years, if it is any of your business."

"That is a long time. I wonder if it is legal."

"My Pa is a justice of the peace and he gave them a signed paper."

"And you are under age. Sounds like they got you there. However, if you were married, I don't believe the thing could be enforced. Or if it couldn't, I reckon your husband could buy you out of it."

"I am not married."

"You could easily become so."

"Don't be silly. Who to?"

"To me. I will need a wife to help me set up in Oregon. You will need a husband to protect you."

I squelched the impulse to laugh and said, "My heart is already spoken for."

"Why isn't the fellow with you then?"

"None of your beeswax."

"I say you are fibbing. Here I am, free, white and twenty one and well fixed to look after you."

He should have left the matter there, but that was not Elmer Hixon's way. He took my hand and knelt beside me in the milking stall, ignoring the fact that his knee rested in a fresh cow dab.

"Please marry me, Miss Annie. I adore you."

At that I snatched my hand free, picked up the pail and poured the milk over his head.

Knowing men as I now do, I shudder at what I did. They say that hell hath no fury like a woman scorned; let me tell you that goes doubled in spades for men. Often have I seen the dreadful consequences of wounding male pride. The better policy is to let them down gently.

Only Elmer Hixon was not your normal male. Far from backing off, he told his Aunt Myrtle Mae the cow had kicked over the pail and that it was his fault. "I should not have set the milk behind her."

He did not explain the smear of cow dung on his knee.

Thereafter, every time I went to the barn to milk, morning or evening, he showed up to take my place on the stool and plead his case for my hand as he milked.

"We were made for each other, Miss Annie. I am going to distinguish myself out west. Never mind my condition. Look at all the great men of history who were afflicted: Demosthenes, Julius Caesar, Frederick the Great . . ."

"But I don't love you, Elmer. Can't you get that through your head?"

"You don't have to love me. That will come later."

Finally, worn out by his protestations, I took a deep breath and said, "There is a very good reason why I should not marry you, even if I did love you."

And, without going into detail, I told him the truth.

He blinked hard a few times, rubbed his chin in embarrassment, and said, "I had no idea. No, no, of course I won't say anything to my folks." Then he arose and walked out of the barn leaving me to finish milking Miss Mollie myself.

So much for the steadfastness of male love, I was thinking, when there he came limping back to the milking stall.

"You have shared a secret with me, Miss Annie. Now let me tell you mine." He went on to explain that his case of the scarlet fever three years before was not his only health problem. "I also had the mumps."

"Lots of people get the mumps. Both my little brothers and I had them."

"Mine were serious. They went down on me."

"What do you mean?"

"The doctor said I can never sire children. So marry me and I will raise your child as if it were my own. No one will ever know the truth out in Oregon."

"What about your Uncle Ralph and your Aunt Myrtle Mae? You know what a big mouth she has."

"I know something that can keep her quiet. Don't worry."

"But they are sure to tell your ma and pa the real reason I am going west. What would they say about your marrying a disgraced girl like me?"

"There is a way around that problem, as well. So how about it, Miss Annie?"

"I don't need to think about it. The answer is no."

To prove his point about the legality of an underage female's breaking a bond of indenture upon marriage, Elmer gave me one of his law books to read. Sure enough, a case was cited therein that proved he was on sound ground.

However, the law was based on the assumption that a girl became the property of her husband, which set poorly with me. I was not about to chain myself to a nincompoop for life to get out of three years of servitude to his aunt and uncle. It would be like hopping from a temporary frying pan into a permanent fire.

I was ready to tell Elmer to stop pestering me until I read on in the law book to a section that dealt with "conjugal relations." There were listed a lot of things I had never seen in print about the things men and women did, or did not do to each other in marriage. A lot about grounds for divorce, such as adultery or abandonment or cruelty and so. And then I read how a marriage that had not been consummated could be annulled.

It was while pondering on this section that I felt my child—mine and Billy Joe Duncan's—stir in my womb for the first time. Likewise, an idea stirred in my mind. By the next day, when I returned his law book to Elmer, it—the idea or, if you will, scheme—had taken firm root. Looking back, I realize that my plan was as cold-blooded as it was ill-conceived but, at the time, it seemed an ingenious way out of my situation.

"You see what I mean about marrying me and getting out of your indenture?" Elmer asked with a knowing grin.

"It would appear that you are correct."

"Then you will marry me?"

"I just might . . ." I began.

In an instant he was back on his knees, both of them, this time avoiding Miss Mollie's droppings.

"Oh, Miss Annie."

"Don't act like such a fool. Get up."

"You might? Really?"

"There are conditions."

"Anything. Just name them."

"There can be no sexual congress between us."

His face fell at that and he stammered, "But we will be man and wife. It is only natural."

"I mean not until well after my baby is born."

"Our baby. It will be our baby."

"Whose ever. You must promise not to touch me in that way until I say you can."

He thought for a moment, argued a bit, then said, "Oh, well, that is only what, six or seven months?"

"Plus a decent interval for me to recover my health."

"I reckon you are worth waiting that long for."

"There are other conditions."

"Name them."

"On the trail, you will milk the cow in my place and relieve me of all other chores that you are able to do."

"That was my intention anyway."

"Finally, I think we had better keep this to ourselves until we are well on our way. Your Aunt Myrtle Mae is sure to tell your folks of my condition."

"There's a fellow the other side of Contrary Creek, near St. Joe, that will marry us without them knowing a thing. We can wait until we are well on the trail to reveal our relationship. Oh, Miss Annie, you have made me the happiest fellow in Missouri."

He held out his arms, causing me to back away.

"Don't I get a kiss to seal our bargain?"

Reluctantly I let him put his arms around me.

"Just one kiss," I said. "And please don't squeeze me so hard. You might hurt my baby."

"Our baby," he said as he lowered his lips to mine.

* * *

On the pretext that he needed to pick up some supplies from a store in St. Joseph, Elmer borrowed his father's wagon one afternoon. As though it was an afterthought, he said to his aunt, "By the way, would Miss Annie like to come along and get some fresh air?"

I tossed my head saying, "I get enough fresh air, thank you."

Mrs. Hixon frowned at my rudeness to her nephew and said, "That is a good idea, Annie. I need some things myself. Of course she will ride along with you, Elmer. Just be sure she is back in time to do the milking."

We stopped before a wooden bungalow surrounded by cottonwood and walnut trees. A fat woman, wearing an apron, told us to wait in the living room until her husband finished his supper. The walls and ceiling were covered by the same narrow, beaded boards painted a nauseating blue. The odor of fried fish from the kitchen made me so queasy I had to stand in the front doorway. The J.P. emerged in his shirtsleeves, wiping his mouth and appraising us coldly.

He asked our ages and places of residence, then went down the hall and returned wearing a long black jacket.

"Just stand over here."

He brought out a music stand and placed a Bible on it.

"Martha! Need a witness."

Wearing her apron, Mrs. J.P. came from the kitchen, followed by two little boys who plopped themselves onto a couch to watch.

The ceremony took only a few minutes. The J.P. sucked his teeth while we signed papers and Elmer paid him his two dollars.

"I reckon this is as good an investment as I will ever make," he said with a wink.

The magistrate acted as though the joke was inappropriate.

"Ya'll got no ring," Mrs. J.P. said. "Might need one."

She drew a display case of gold-plated wedding bands from under the couch. Elmer, looking ever so proud of himself, nodded. Out of spite, I chose the most expensive one and tucked it into my coat pocket.

The couple followed us out the door and stood on the porch as we drove out of the driveway. Once out of their sight, Elmer pulled over and put his arms around me.

"My wife."

I permitted him a hasty kiss and then reminded him that we had to hurry if we were to visit the store and return in time for the milking.

However, by way of celebration, I did allow Elmer to take me into a restaurant in St. Joe and buy me a dish of ice cream. I had never had ice cream before. It was the only bright spot in that otherwise dismal day.

Lying on a straw-shuck mattress with the two little Hixon girls that night, I dreamed of being in Billy Joe Duncan's arms.

6

That April, St. Joseph's two newspapers were full of news items containing the names of this or that company of emigrants newly arrived from various states with the intent of going west. In amongst the advertisements touting wagon makers, livestock dealers, harness shops and such there appeared a peculiar sort of paid notice offering the services of a certain Zebulon McGee and Chester Peebles III for guiding a large party to the West. According to the advertisement, the two men would shepherd settlers together as far as Fort Bridger in Wyoming Country at which point, after resupplying their train, one of the partners would lead those aiming for Oregon northward to that territory, while the other would guide those who wished to settle in California across the Nevada desert.

In the same paper, I noted that "The renowned Courtenays, late of London" were performing "A Mid-Summer Night's Dream" at a local theater. I ached to attend but, of course, it was out of the question.

A week later, the five of us—Mr. and Mrs. Ralph Hixon, Elmer, Ralph Junior, and I—crowded into a German society's large meeting hall with about two hundred other persons to meet Zebulon McGee and Chester Peebles and hear their proposition.

What a mixed accumulation of humanity was gathered in that hall: mostly men but a goodly number of women as well as a few children. Some of the men wore fine clothing: long-tailed coats and stovepipe hats as if to proclaim their superior standing. They sat or stood elbow to elbow with chaps wearing rough trousers and jackets, their heads covered with cloth caps.

From their conversations, you could tell that many were farmers with a sprinkling of carpenters and such, plus one party of miners from Cornwall in England. You heard mainly the flat accents of Illinois, Indiana and other such western states, with an occasional southern drawl or New England brogue.

Soon every chair and bench in the hall was taken, and folks were standing around the walls, all eyes fixed on the two men who sat on the stage sizing up their audience much like cattle dealers appraising a herd.

Chester Peebles III, a fellow in his late twenties, did most of the talking. With blondish hair already going thin, he was of medium height and square-shouldered. The first two words out of his mouth gave him away as a New Englander. He was well spoken, however, and with good reason, for it turned out he had spent a year at Harvard University before running off to fight in the Mexican War.

I assumed that was how he had met the other fellow, Zebulon McGee, for they had fought together and then joined in the gold rush in California. Later I would learn the story was not that simple.

They made an unlikely team. Where Peebles was a handsome, pleasant chap, with an open face and manner, always grinning, McGee looked like the last man in the world you would want to cross. He could have been anywhere from 35 to 45. Standing well over six feet tall, he was broad of shoulder and lean of flank, with dark hair and a stern, weathered face. Later it would occur to me that he resembled Abraham Lincoln. As it turned out, he had grown up in the same section of Indiana as had old Abe. And he was as taciturn as Peebles was talkative. At McGee's feet lay a dung-colored dog that, I swear, looked as large as a pony.

Peebles introduced first himself and then his partner, saying, "Cousin Zeb here was once a mountain man, buying furs from the Indians, before the war with Mexico and the rush to California. He knows the country out there like the palm of his hand. I have made the trip west three times but Zeb has done it, how many times?"

"Six," was his partner's laconic reply.

"Right. So between us we know the best trails to take and what is required in the way of equipment, supplies and organization to get yourself across the plains and over the mountains and deserts to California or Oregon."

He went on and on, explaining how the party would be organized, what he and his companion would charge for their services, and some general rules of behavior on the trail. He paused to ask if there were any questions,

Myrtle Mae Hixon, to her husband's embarrassment, raised her hand and asked, "I hope that you do not propose to travel on the sabbath."

Peebles grinned. "You know the parable of the ox in the ditch. There will be a lot of oxen on this trip and a lot of ditches. So there may be occasions when Zeb and I will find it necessary to keep us moving even on a Sunday."

A man with a Southern accent asked, "What about Indians?"

"We will encounter plenty. Most will be friendly enough. Just don't wander from the party and don't give them liquor. Some will try to bully you into giving them gifts. Our best bet is to let Zeb deal with them. He will be in overall charge until we reach Fort Bridger. And he knows their lingo. Right, Zeb?"

McGee merely nodded.

On the far side of the hall, a fellow with a polished English accent asked, "Would there be a problem if one were to bring along a horse-drawn carriage as well as a wagon?"

To my amazement, it was the father of the theatrical family, the Courtenays, who had so enthralled me aboard The Polar Star.

"As long as you have good horses and don't try to load the carriage too heavy, we have no objection, do we, Zeb?"

McGee shook his head.

At that, Elmer arose and limped to the front of the hall where he stationed himself in front of the two men as though he were a lawyer cross-examining a witness.

"I was under the impression that such parties as this elected their leaders in a democratic manner. I assumed you two gentlemen were to be our guides, not, as you call it, our leaders."

As he spoke, I thought to myself, "Annie Mundy, what have you got yourself in for, even going through the motions of marrying such an idiot?"

Before Peebles could respond, without standing, McGee said, "Assume what you want, young fellow, but democracy's got nothing to do with this business. If you can't accept my authority or Chester's, you'd better sign up with somebody else or stay home."

But Elmer was not so easily put down.

"Should we pay your fees, which seem pretty steep to me, and accept your dictatorship for five months, is it not reasonable to ask why you are directing us clear down to Fort Bridger instead of taking Sublette's Shortcut from the South Pass over to Fort Hall? Seems to me you are dragging out the trip."

"Look, sonny," McGee said. "I was making this trip when you was in diapers. There's too many women and children such as yourself in this party to take so-called short cuts across rough country where there is no water and little grass. Now why don't you sit down and let us get on with this business?"

Peebles held up his hand to stop the confrontation. The meeting went on for more than an hour, during which Peebles made it clear that he and his partner would allow only such livestock as was needed to pull the wagons and sustain life. "We will make better time if we don't have to herd a lot of cattle or sheep. Also we aim to get a jump on the crowd by starting early and carrying enough dry feed to do us until we reach Fort Kearny."

This announcement caused some grumbling, but when Peebles announced that he was now available to accept the names and signatures of those wishing to accompany him and his strange partner on "an early start" across the West, nearly everyone remained.

Mr. Hixon asked, "What do you think, Myrtle Mae?"

"I like the New England gentleman. I don't know about the other fellow."

"It will be Peebles who will lead our section from Fort Bridger north to Oregon."

"Also, I don't like the looks of some of the gang going to California. They appear to be a rowdy lot."

"All the better to have a tough fellow like McGee in general charge."

"I suppose you have a point there. Did you notice that flashy English couple everyone was talking about on the boat, the actors?"

"The Courtenays," I supplied.

"I hope they are not going to Oregon."

"They aren't," I said. "They are headed for California."

"Good," she said, then frowned, and added, "How do you know so much about those people?"

I wasn't about to confess to slipping out at night for their performances, in which they had announced their intent to "carry culture to the West," or my eavesdropping on their conversations.

"I heard talk of them on the boat," I said.

For his part, Elmer seemed not at all abashed by the way he had been put down by the fearsome-looking mountain man. He stood in line with the rest of us to sign up with the outfit.

* * *

Perhaps in a last ditch hope of dissuading his son from leaving, Osborne Hixon expressed dire warnings about the dangers of the trip, beginning with crossing the various rivers we would encounter. He pointed out that back in 1850, '52 and '54, wagons and teams had stood in lines a mile or more long waiting to be shuttled across the Missouri.

"Takes only five or ten minutes to get over on them two steam ferries they got now, but a hell of a lot longer just to load and unload. And they charge five dollars a wagon, plus extra for every animal, not to mention every person. You can remain in line for two or three days just to work your way up to the landing. And God help the fellow that tries to jump in ahead. There has been many a fight and even some killing over line jumping. And once you leave St. Joe, you'll find lots of rivers but no more steam ferries."

Elmer rolled his eyes as his father went on relating the story of the outbreaks of cholera that had wiped out hundreds of emigrants in previous years.

"Hits them mainly in the first few weeks of the trip. They tell me the way up to Fort Kearny is lined with the graves of men, women and children. And I hear it gets worse between Kearny and Fort Laramie."

He was right about the danger of cholera. Today we know that the disease is caused by germs in drinking water. That fact was not scientifically established until after the Civil War, although some suspected it at the time.

All this grim talk did nothing to improve my morale. There was Myrtle Mae Hixon bossing me about. She even put me to doing the washing. And there was Elmer, sneaking little possessive glances at me. What's more, to divert suspicion, he had given up helping me do the milking.

Then there was the matter of my thickening waistline. Even though I bound my belly up tight and wore bulky clothing, I saw no hope of concealing my condition from the Osborne Hixons until the first of May, which was the traditional date for the start of the annual trek across the prairies.

I was saved from this humiliation, however, by the appearance of a notice in the St. Joseph Gazette announcing the formation of the McGee–Peebles party and serving notice on those signed up that they should present themselves, their wagons and stock for inspection on the following Monday in Patee Town near where work had begun on the foundation for a proposed grand new hotel.

This led to a scramble on Ralph Hixon's part to finish breaking his eight steers to the yoke and mastering the intricacies of working the enormous bull whip he had bought.

Elmer had showed the good sense to trade his mare for a pair of well-broken mules, so he spent his time packing his light wagon with provisions, law books and a tent "large enough for two," as he whispered to me.

Myrtle Mae Hixon busied herself and me with treating onansburg cloth with linseed oil to serve as a waterproof cover for our wagon, and with packing and unpacking the two trunks to which her husband limited her.

By agreement with Elmer, I had taken to treating him with such disdain that Myrtle Mae had rebuked me for my rudeness. So, neither she nor the Osborne Hixons had any inkling of our marriage when, on a bright Sunday morning just after the middle of April, we said our goodbyes to the latter and set forth in our two wagons for St. Joseph.

It was easy to spot our party. The guide named McGee, walking with a slight limp, led a tall, gray horse around the hotel construction site. Followed by his enormous dog, McGee ran his eagle eyes over every wagon and team as they drew up around the encampment.

No matter what the owner's social status, he got a tongue lashing if his wagon's iron tires were not tightly fitted, or if there were no evidence of a grease bucket to keep the axles lubricated or other equipment and tools deemed necessary for the long months ahead.

His partner, Peebles, was more diplomatic, but none-the-less strict. It was plain this pair meant to run an efficient operation. They had even brought in blacksmiths and sutlers to provide the needed goods or services on the spot. And, to their credit, they oversaw the transactions to make sure their party's members were charged fair prices, including that for the dry food on which our animals would be largely fed until we reached Fort Kearny and the grass would be high enough for grazing. This was the cost of getting a two-week jump on the other emigrant parties.

We spent that night, as we would for many another, in our tents: Mr. and Mrs. Hixon in one, Ralph Junior and yours truly in a smaller one, and Elmer in his own. We slept on blankets with an oil cloth underneath to keep out the dampness. Some of the richer pilgrims remained that night in their hotel rooms, but they along with us lesser folk were required, before retiring, to gather for a final inspection of our wagons and gear and to be told the good news that we would not have to wait in line with other parties to cross the Missouri on one of the two steam ferries operating from the foot of Francis Street.

Through bribes, threats, or God knows what, McGee and Peebles had persuaded the captain of a St. Louis-based steamboat to delay his downstream return trip by twenty four hours and to devote the following day to transporting our party of sixty-odd wagons and 200 or so people across the Missouri.

I crawled under our pup tent beside little Ralph Junior, full of both dread and a curious sort of exhilaration.

"Annie," Junior said as I settled myself for the night. "Are you scared?"
"No. Why? Are you?"
"Yes."
"What of? Indians?"
"No. That man that rides the tall horse and looks mad all the time. Him and that big dog scares me. Don't they you?"
"Ralph Junior, they are here to protect, not harm us. Now let's hear you run through your A, B, C's. Then say your prayers and go to sleep."

* * *

According to Osborne Hixon, in the old days, before steam ferries came on duty, emigrants used to swim their livestock across the Missouri and convey themselves and their wagons in oar-powered flat boats. By comparison, our crossing was tame. With McGee on one side of the river and Peebles on the other, we loaded about a dozen wagons at a time. The passage itself took only a few minutes, but the loading and unloading meant that the boat did well to complete a round trip in less than an hour, despite such cursing and agitation as I have never experienced.

It was early afternoon before we all got over and started moving west across the marshy, forested land beyond the Missouri.

Two, maybe three versions of Annie Mundy began that westward trek. The first sat with closed eyes on the rear of the Hixons' wagon, longing to be back in her North Carolina home, once again an innocent girl who had not yet met Billy Joe Duncan. Then that girl opened her eyes and looked back toward the town of St. Joseph rising up the slopes from the high eastern bank of the Missouri. A second Annie Mundy thought what a pleasant, bustling place it would have been to live with a young husband such as Billy Joe Duncan and how stultifying it would have been to remain stuck in her native section of North Carolina even if she could have done so without causing her family shame.

Then some waggish fellow broke her reverie by singing out, "Well, folks, we are on our way to see the elephant."

Whereupon a third Annie Mundy dismissed vain, nostalgic longings from her head, jumped down from the wagon, turned her back on St. Joe and her old life in North Carolina, and started walking, as she would for many another day, west.

PART TWO

1

In general, we could not have picked a better year to make our trip across the West. Traffic was lighter than most years. Except for one episode, which I will get to later, we had no serious troubles with Indians. True, we saw no steam ferries beyond the Missouri, but most of the more difficult streams either could be crossed on flat-boat ferries or, in some cases, even bridges, operated mainly by tame Indians or Mormons, many charging exorbitant tolls, or trying to, until "Captain McGee," as we began to call him, "reasoned" with them.

Looking at a map of Kansas today, you might think that our long train of wagons would find it a simple matter to get from St. Joe to Fort Kearny up on the Platte River in Nebraska. Just set your compass for North-Northwest and proceed in a straight line. Actually, the St. Joseph Trail, by then well established through several years of emigration, curved north, then south and north again across the rolling Kansas prairies, in general following the high, dry terrain that lay between various rivers and ravines, trying to avoid the danger of fords on the one hand or the expense of toll ferries or bridges on the other until it connected with the old Independence Trail beyond the Big Blue River.

The first few days went well enough. The weather was warm by day and pleasantly cool by night. Our guides did not push us hard, giving both humans and livestock time to adjust to the trail.

"The California gang" and "us Oregonians," as we started calling the two sections of our train, took turns in the van, and within our contingents we rotated the positions of our wagons, with yesterday's lead rig falling back to the tail of the train and the next fellow in line taking his place. We started early each day, with the men dry feeding the stock and yoking the oxen and harnessing the mules while the women milked and prepared breakfast. We "nooned," that is we took a mid-day break, for an hour or so, then pressed on until just before dark when it became time to unyoke and unharness the animals, milk the cows, build campfires, pitch the tents and so forth.

I was beginning to wonder why people made such a fuss about the trip west when the first trouble came. It appeared in the form of a fancy-looking fellow on a fine bay horse who overtook us as we were setting up camp for the night on the wooded banks of the Wolf River.

His face was shaded by a flat-topped, wide-brimmed hat. He wore a shiny black coat over a flowery vest and a blue, silk cravat from which glimmered a large diamond stick pin. A mane of brown hair reached to his beefy shoulders.

Elmer and his Uncle Ralph had gone down to the river to water their stock. At that point in our journey we had not started drawing up our wagons in circles at night as we would later in wild Indian country. I was helping Mrs. Hixon build a fire with wood we had picked up that morning when this fellow tipped his hat and inquired where he might find "the party headed for California."

I pointed toward the river and returned to my chores.

When Mr. Hixon and Elmer returned with the stock, I could tell from the look on the latter's face that something was amiss.

As agreed, he and I had been acting aloof toward each other since we had gone through that charade of a wedding before the J.P. Now he sat beside me as I ate my beans and cornbread and whispered, "Annie. Did you see the fellow on the bay horse?"

"How could you miss such an outlandish man? Why?"

"He is the gambler I won all that money off of back in St. Joe. His name is Bart Corbett. He is the last man I want to see."

"You won the game fair and square, didn't you?"

"Yes, but he has a reputation as a sore loser. Oh, Annie, what am I going to do? He has friends with the California gang. McGee has given him permission to accompany them clear out to the gold fields."

"How is that of any concern to me?"

"Why, Annie, you are my wife. A husband is supposed to share his worries with his wife."

That was a poor way to excite my sympathies, but I said, "Keep your voice down." Then, "Are you afraid of him?"

Elmer's face hardened and he sat up straight.

"I fear no man. I just don't want anything unpleasant to happen with you at my side."

"Then go and shake his hand and welcome him to our expedition. That will disarm him. Anyway, we will part company with the California gang at Fort Bridger."

"That will be three months from now. You really think I should do that?"

"Wouldn't have said it otherwise."

I did feel a little sorry for Elmer for I could see that beneath his bravado he was terrified, but my sympathy was dampened by his reminder of our secret and unconsummated marriage.

To my amazement, Elmer took my advice. That evening, as Corbett walked past our campfire, leading his horse, he—Elmer—called out, "Don't I know you?"

The gambler squinted to see who spoke.

"Wouldn't surprise me if you did. Lots of people do. Who are you?"

"I am Elmer Hixon, attorney at law. I am the chap you played poker with at the Buffalo Saloon in St. Joe."

Corbett stepped closer and said, "So you are the crippled son of a bitch who got so lucky? This is a surprise. We'll just have to play ourselves another game in a day or so."

"Nothing would please me more, but Mister Peebles and Captain McGee have forbidden any gambling in their parties while on the trail. Says it leads to trouble."

"Then let's wait until we stop over at Fort Kearny. I hear there is a settlement there where a fellow can get anything he wants, from women, to liquor, to a good game of poker. We can see if your luck holds out when we get there."

Of course Elmer could not let well enough alone.

"You call it luck. Some might say it was skill."

"My, my, ain't the little law clerk a cocky chap? I am glad you introduced yourself. Was afraid this trip would be tiresome. With you along, I know that it will not be. Not at all."

When the fellow was out of hearing, Elmer's uncle said, "If it had of been me, I don't believe I would have spoke to that man in such a saucy way."

"What can he do to me?"

"Maybe nothing, but I would steer clear of him."

"If he don't bother me, I won't bother him."

However, I noted that thereafter Elmer took to wearing his Colt navy revolver strapped about his skinny hips. And he avoided further contact with the gambler.

*　　*　　*

That was our first difficulty. The second came the next afternoon as we plodded on a northwesterly course toward what our guides called the Cedar Creek Campground. Throughout the morning, the sky to the north had been obscured by gray-blue clouds. We nooned near a Presbyterian mission for tame Indians, then yoked up our beasts and set out again.

By mid-afternoon there was no doubt what we were in for. The sky turned darker, and lightning such as I had never seen in North Carolina split the heavens. As though sensing what was to come, the animals tossed their heads and balked, reluctant to venture into the approaching storm.

The rain started falling, slowly at first. Then lightning flashed and thunder boomed around us like an artillery bombardment. Next the rain began falling in sheets. Mrs. Hixon, Junior and I huddled under the wagon cover while Mr. Hixon, on foot, an Indian rubber coat over his shoulders, urged his poor oxen forward.

Our job of waterproofing the wagon cover proved unequal to the task of keeping out such a downpour. Water ran down my neck. Mrs. Hixon put her face in her hands and wept. Ralph Junior cried too and buried his face in my lap rather than his mother's, which did not endear me to her.

Finally Chester Peebles rode past and told us it was no use trying to press on in such a storm.

We spent a miserable night, forced to eat stale biscuits and sleep in sodden tents.

I was seeing the elephant, all right, and wasn't at all sure that I wished any further acquaintance with the beast.

* * *

It took all the next day for our clothing, blankets and tents to dry out but after a bright afternoon of rolling on due west across the undulating prairie, void of trees except along stream beds, my spirits began to recover. I marvelled at the vastness of the Great American West. And to think that we were penetrating just the eastern rim of that territory.

Back in 1856, except for a farm here and there, it was just so much empty country to be got through in our search for new beginnings in Oregon or, in the case of the other party, for treasure in California.

Friendships among the others in our Oregon-bound group soon developed. There were a good many families with children, most from

Missouri and the upper states of what we now call the Mid-West. For the most part, they were good-hearted folks and their children were well behaved.

I particularly liked a large family hailing from near Cincinnati, Ohio, the Muellers, who spoke with German accents. Mr. Mueller was a cheerful fellow who hoped to set up a blacksmith shop in Oregon. His wife was a no-nonsense woman who in time would prove to be one of my best friends. They had five sons, ranging in age from 14 down to 3.

Along with my duties of milking Miss Mollie and helping Mrs. Hixon cook, I continued to work with Ralph Junior on his lessons. I became increasingly fond of the little fellow. He was bright as a dollar. And after a couple of weeks on the trail, he seemed much healthier than when I first had laid eyes on him.

During our noon times of rest I would sit him down in the shade of the wagon and put him through his lessons. Mrs. Mueller, observing this, inquired whether "Miss Mundy" might instruct her children, too. She was joined in her petition by several other mothers, including, to my amazement, Mrs. Courtenay, the haughty British-born actress I had first seen on The Polar Star delivering Lady MacBeth's "out, out, damned spot" speech. Troubled by the fact that hers were the only children among the California gang, which included some pretty rough characters, she persuaded Captain McGee to allow her family to travel with us Oregonians as far as Fort Bridger.

The Courtenays travelled in far grander style than any other family. She and the children rode in a carriage drawn by two black horses and driven by Mr. Courtenay. Wearing an outlandish hat with a feather stuck in the crown and a cape over his shoulders, he cut quite a figure among the emigrants. Their three yoke of oxen were driven by their man slave, Lester, while their cooking was done largely by Lester's wife, Opal. The Negroes carried their own possessions in a large cart drawn by two donkeys. Despite their different mode of dress and speech and his wife's haughty airs, Mister Courtenay made himself so agreeable with his tales of life in London that he quickly became popular with us all.

Myrtle Mae Hixon first objected to my turning school teacher on the grounds it might interfere with my chores but after being buttered up by Mrs. Mueller and the others, she finally and grudgingly agreed to allow me to add other children to my circle.

To my surprise, Mrs. Courtenay came down off her high horse to ask if her own son and daughter, Simeon and Heather, might participate in my school. Objects of curiosity to the other children, they kept very quiet at first. It took awhile before they became as boisterous as the others.

So there I sat in a circle of youngsters of various ages, running them through their exercises and reading to them from OLIVER TWIST. They took to calling me Miss Annie, as did many of the adults in our company.

By this time my body had adjusted to the life fast growing inside me. The fresh air and exercise seemed to agree with me. And, when I looked in a hand mirror, I recognized that glow that many women get during the first half of their pregnancies, the Almighty's way of compensating us for imposing such a burden on our sex.

Elmer's health also seemed to be improving. His normal pallor had been replaced by a healthy tan. Although he generally rode on the jockey box across the front of his wagon, now and then he would hop down and lead his mules, whom he took to calling Peter and Paul, to the annoyance of his aunt who pointed out that these were the names of the two great Christian apostles, as if Elmer, an avowed agnostic, did not know this.

I realized that my condition could not be concealed much longer, indeed felt that some of our fellow emigrants already suspected. Still I dreaded the time when Elmer and I would have to reveal our marriage. Meanwhile, I was oddly happy, enjoying the company of my little students and the peace that had come over me.

Elmer was always finding excuses to busy himself nearby as I conducted my classes. He was keeping a diary in which he wrote each noon, beaming at me with pride from time to time and, I was sure, looking forward to sharing his tent with me. If I had had my druthers, we would have postponed the announcement of our marriage at least until we reached Fort Kearny, but, it was not to be.

At first, we Oregonians had little to do with the California gang, which included a lot of unmarried young men, among them three young Cornish men on their way to take jobs in the gold mines. They were high-spirited lads, all the sons and grandsons of tin miners back in their homeland. At night, around their campfires, they often demonstrated their sport of "Cornish wrestling." Some of us liked to wander over and admire the agility with which they grappled.

To Elmer's irritation, they also began flirting with me. One tall, rosy-cheeked "Cousin Jack," even approached me one noon and asked if he might join my circle of students.

"Don't be ridiculous," I said.

"No harm in asking, Miss. . . . What did you say your name was?"

"I did not say. And my students can only be children."

"I'm Will Tremelling. Thanks anyway."

I found him amusing, but Myrtle Mae criticized my speaking to him, saying, "You shouldn't encourage such attentions, Annie. I would think you learned your lesson about such things."

Swallowing my anger, I said, "The only lesson I have learned is that I like to teach."

"Perhaps when your three years are up with us, you can devote yourself to that occupation. Meanwhile, you are in our care and charge. Mr. Hixon and I will not put up with your carrying on with foreigners or other such riff raff."

Still, the Cornishmen would flirt with me. For my part, I had had a belly full of the lust of males, but I was irritated both by her remarks and by Elmer's possessiveness.

"I aim to tell those fellows off," he muttered to me out of the Hixons' hearing.

"Oh, don't blow this out of proportion."

"You are my wife. It is my duty to protect you."

It was all I could do not to laugh.

"Nobody knows that."

"Then perhaps it is time to tell them."

"When we reach Fort Kearny. Until then keep your mouth shut."

"I just don't like other men flirting with you. Even Peebles is always grinning at you like a possum. I don't like him hanging about our fire at night trying to strike up a conversation with you. And it galls me the way Aunt Myrtle Mae orders you about as if you were a servant girl."

"Not half as much as it galls me. As for Mister Peebles, I don't care two cents for such a pushy Yankee. Besides which, according to him he is engaged to a girl back in Boston. He expects her to join him to be married in Oregon when he gets settled there."

And, in truth I would have found our Oregon guide far too smooth and ingratiating for my taste even if I had not been pregnant and secretly married, and he had not been engaged himself.

Noticing Peebles' occasionally referring to Captain McGee as "Cousin Zeb," I asked the reason. To my amazement, he explained that they actually were second cousins.

"We had the same great-grandparents, Jason and Katie McGee their names were. They lived in Pennsylvania. My paternal grandmother, whom I never knew, and his grandfather were brother and sister. She ended up in Philadelphia and he went west first to Ohio and then Indiana after the Revolution. When time came to settle the McGee estate, the lawyers had to search out their heirs. My own parents having died in New York where I was born, I was reared by my mother's parents in Boston. Grandfather is a Unitarian minister."

Thinking of the disparity in the cousins' way of talking and apparent education, I asked, "How did you ever find each other?"

"It's a long story. I'll tell you when we have more time."

"What about that strange dog? I never saw such a creature."

"Boris is part Russian wolfhound. Zeb bought him as a pup off a sea captain in San Francisco four years ago. He not only keeps wolves away from your stock, he has a fine nose for locating water. He looks fierce but he really is as gentle as a lamb."

* * *

About ten days after leaving St. Joe, we crossed the Big Blue River via a ferry near the newly established village of Marysville and soon struck the old trail leading up from Independence. At that point the Oregonians were in the lead and our wagon near the front of it. I marveled at the long line of animals and vehicles creaking along behind us from the east, heading for the promised land far beyond the horizon.

It was on this stretch that I saw the first of the many graves of the victims of cholera and other diseases that lined the trail all the way up to the Platte and beyond to the Rocky Mountains.

From that junction with the other trail, we followed the long established ruts that led northward toward Nebraska, keeping to the east of the Little Blue River. My daily school sessions were going well. The grass was beginning to turn green enough so that soon our livestock could graze. Feeling healthy and strong and strangely hopeful, I saw no reason why Elmer and I could not delay the announcement of our so-called marriage until mid-May when we were to reach Fort Kearny. But as has often happened in my life, fate—this time in the form of Myrtle Mae Hixon—would have it otherwise.

2

Things came to a head one evening after we had made camp in a lush meadow beyond the first of many Cottonwood Creeks we were to encounter, this one near the border of the Nebraska territory. Mr. Hixon was off letting his oxen graze. I had just finished milking the cow and was about to go and gather firewood along the creek bank when Mrs. Hixon said to Elmer in my plain hearing, "Look at her. She acts like she is too good to gather wood. Just wait until she has to collect buffalo chips."

I stopped and asked, "What do you mean?"

"Haven't you heard? Trees will be few and far between after this. We will have to burn dried buffalo droppings and it will be your duty to gather them each day. Mr. Hixon bought a large tow sack for that very purpose."

I made a face. "You expect me to pick up animal dung?"

"Someone will have to do it. I just hope that we haven't spoiled you by letting you pretend to be a school teacher."

"What do you mean, pretend? The children are learning very well, in case you haven't noticed."

"We will have none of your sass, young lady. Don't forget the kindness Mister Hixon and I are doing by bringing you along."

"If the way you have treated me is kindness, I hate to think what your unkindness would be like."

"Look here, young lady, don't you get uppity with me."

And, then, Elmer would put his mouth into the growing row.

"I don't like the way you are talking to Annie."

"It is none of your business. She is our servant. I will speak to her as I please."

"Not anymore. We will put a stop to that right now."

"I fail to see what business this is of yours, Elmer."

That remark was just too much for Elmer. With a look of the cat that swallowed the proverbial canary, he declared, "Annie is my wife."

Oh, the shock that showed in that woman's face. Her mouth dropped open, then she turned red, frowned and spoke in disbelief.

"Don't be silly. It is obvious that the girl despises you."

"That is just an act we agreed to put on. We got married the week before we left St. Joe."

"You are lying."

"Shall I show you the marriage certificate?"

She turned her outraged gaze on me.

"What about this? Is it true?"

"We did go through a marriage ceremony before a justice of the peace."

She advanced on Elmer as if to strike him, but he stood his ground and said, "So there it is, Aunt Myrtle Mae. Annie is my wife and if she takes orders from anyone it will be from me, her husband."

Of course that set very poorly with yours truly but even more so with Mrs. Hixon.

"I could tell you something about this wicked girl that . . ."

"No need to tell me anything, Aunt Myrtle Mae. Annie informed me of her condition. And I married her anyway. So don't you go calling her wicked in my hearing."

"But why? I don't understand."

"Because I need a wife. And she needs a husband. Besides which I love her with all my heart."

She looked over her shoulder to make sure the Muellers, at the next campfire, would not hear and said in a vehement whisper, "So, she brought shame to her family in North Carolina and now has done the same with ours. What will your parents say when I write from Fort Kearny and tell them of all this? And you needn't think I will not inform the good Christian people who are travelling with us about this sinful arrangement."

"Come down off your high horse, Aunt Myrtle Mae. I left a letter with Mister Armstrong Beattie, my banker, explaining everything to my folks. He promised to send it to them on May 1. Also let me inform you that I know a bit about your own family background in North Carolina, things I will keep to myself unless you start blackguarding Annie and me with our fellow travelers."

That took the wind out of her sails. Her face turn so red I feared (or perhaps hoped) she would suffer a stroke of apoplexy.

"What do you know of my family?"

"Little pitchers have big ears."

"That was all lies. My pa never took that man's horse."

"Perhaps so, but do you want to have to convince the others that the reports are untrue?"

It took a few moments for her to regain her power of speech.

"Annie is behind all this. She is a conniver, and you have let her trap you into giving her bastard child a name."

Now Elmer advanced on her, brandishing his cane as he did.

"Never, never utter that word again or you will regret it to your dying day. Annie's child will be my child. Have you got that through your self-righteous brain?"

The woman now looked frightened.

"You dare to threaten me? Wait until I tell your uncle."

"No, I will tell Uncle Ralph. And Annie henceforth will sleep in my tent. You will no longer order her about like a servant."

"But she is under contract to us. We can take this matter to court and we will if we have to."

Elmer laughed and said, "Dear Aunt Myrtle Mae, have you not heard how the law is like a sieve?"

"What are you talking about?"

"You may think you can see through a sieve, but you will be considerably reduced before you can get through it. It is the same with a law suit. Save your money. That contract is null and void, now that she is married. I can show you the law to that effect."

I had heard enough. Leaving them locked in argument, I walked off to the trees along the creek bank to gather my firewood along with my feverish thoughts.

When I returned with an armload of sticks, Mr. Hixon was busy laying a campfire. His wife was strangely quiet. Elmer was strutting about looking awfully pleased with himself. After we had eaten our bait of slam johns and boiled potatoes and drunk our coffee, we joined the circle where Chester Peebles was delivering his usual evening talk to his Oregon-bound contingent.

"I calculate we covered a good eighteen miles today," he said in his rasping New England accent. "If we get another good clear day, we should cross into Nebraska territory by noon tomorrow and make camp at Rock Springs in the evening. Any questions?"

Elmer raised his hand. "I would like to say something."

"I hope you don't want to make one of your speeches."

"Not a speech; an announcement. Annie's name really isn't Mundy. She is a Hixon. We are married. We have kept our wedding a secret but the time has come to let the cat out of the bag."

I could have died from embarrassment. Several women nudged their husbands as if to say, "I told you the girl was pregnant."

Ralph Hixon looked like he was going to choke on his tobacco quid.

Peebles got a puzzled look on his face then recovered and said, "I suppose congratulations are in order. What do you say, folks?"

A murmer of good wishes arose from the crowd. Ralph Hixon tried to move closer to Elmer, but his wife motioned for him to keep quiet.

Then Mr. Courtenay, the actor. called out in his rich baritone, "By the Almighty, this calls for a celebration."

Turning to his black servant, he said, "Lester, get your banjo."

Another fellow ran to get his fiddle. Several others piled fresh wood on the fire. Peebles gave up trying to restrain the fast-growing celebration. The sound of music and singing attracted people from the California gang. Soon Elmer and I were surrounded by a crowd all singing and cheering. Oh, I could have died. But I stood there, a false smile on my face while Elmer, clutching my hand, grinned.

The celebration went on until Captain McGee came and ordered his lot to get back to their camp. But the Cornish lads insisted on kissing me and, before I knew it, I was being bussed by so many bearded ruffians that my face was raw the next day and my dress stank of male sweat and tobacco fumes. Men really do turn into filthy beasts when not controlled by civilized womenfolk.

Finally, the celebration ran out of steam. Elmer gathered my carpet bags from the Hixon's wagon. I followed him into his tent with about as much enthusiasm as a prisoner mounting the steps to the gallows.

I lay down atop the oil cloth floor of the tent and wrapped my blanket tightly about me, dreading the night. He came in and tried to crawl under my blanket but gave up and covered himself with his own.

"Dear, Annie. You have made me the happiest man in the world."

He leaned over and tried to kiss me but I pushed him away.

"Remember our bargain," I said.

"We said nothing about kissing."

"Well, I am not in the mood for any such goings on. This has been a very upsetting experience. Did you have to shoot off your mouth that way?"

"I figured it was time to bring this to a head. Didn't you like the way I put Aunt Myrtle Mae in her place?"

"I suppose."

"Then don't I at least deserve one little kiss on our wedding night?"

"No. You made me feel like a fool."

"Can I at least hold your hand?"

"I suppose."

He clung to my hand as a child would clutch its blanket, while babbling on about what a great life we would lead in Oregon and of his determination to gain wealth and prestige there for "you and our baby."

Finally, I asked him to shut up and release my hand so I could sleep. But just as I was about to drift off, I heard a chorus of long, ghostly howls from beyond Cottonwood Creek.

"What's that?"

"Wolves," my bridegroom said. "But don't worry, Annie. I am here to protect you against all dangers, whatever they be."

* * *

Thereafter I walked beside Elmer's wagon, drawn by his faithful Peter and Paul. In a compromise with his uncle, Elmer took over milking the cow and I continued to help his aunt with the cooking. Also I took charge of producing butter, which was done by dangling buckets of leftover milk from our wagon's tailgate. And, as I had become fond of little Junior, I continued to teach him and the other youngsters in our wagon train at nooning time.

So onward rolled our caravan northwesterly toward Fort Kearny and the Platte River. Each night I allowed Elmer to hold my hand as I listened to his grandiose schemes for our life together in Oregon. As he babbled on and on, I lay there wishing that it was Billy Joe Duncan with whom I shared that tent. And yet, I was not unhappy. Perhaps resigned would be a better word.

As we approached Fort Kearny, where there would be a postal station, I considered writing a letter to Uncle John and Aunt Mamie in which I would tell them of my marriage to "a promising young lawyer" and of the joy I felt as I contemplated a new life in Oregon. Then I discarded the idea. It would be better to wait to see how things played out between Elmer and me.

* * *

The rich grassland and undulating prairie terrain that lay between St. Joe and the border of the Nebraska territory was nothing like the wooded red-clay land of my native North Carolina Piedmont. Flowers, the like of which I had never seen, began to appear amidst the quickly greening grass. I did not like the sound of wolves howling at night but enjoyed seeing the occasional antelope watching our caravan from distant low hills.

The trail followed the rim of the valley of the Little Blue River into Nebraska, toward the Great Platte River. Now the soil became sandier and, as the trail climbed gently toward the ridge line of the Platte Valley, our oxen and mules had to pull harder.

During our big blow-up with Mrs. Hixon and the hubbub that greeted Elmer's announcement of our marriage, I had forgotten about Bart Corbett, the gambler who had joined the California gang. He and one of the more unsavory fellows in his mess, a tall, gaunt, one-eyed chap known as Kentucky Pete, intercepted me one evening as I was filling a bucket at a spring near our camp ground.

"Well, if it ain't the new Mrs. Hixon," Corbett said as he raised his fancy hat.

"So it is."

"How is your young bridegroom?"

"You can ask him for yourself."

"I would, but he seems to be avoiding me."

"I can't think what business he might have with you."

"But we do have some business . . . unfinished business."

"Then take it up with him direct. Now I must get this water back to camp."

"May I carry the bucket for you? It is not good for a lady in your condition to strain herself."

"You may not carry my bucket. As for my condition, that is none of your concern. Now please get out of my way."

"Oh, my, she is as saucy as her husband, isn't she?"

"Hey, Bart," Kentucky Pete said. "Leave Miss Fancy Pants alone. It is plain she thinks herself too good to talk to the likes of us."

"There is no harm in me asking her to give her husband a message," he said as he stepped out of my path.

"What message?" I asked.

"Just remind him that I will be ready and willing to meet him at the poker table when we get to Fort Kearny. I hear tell we will lay over there for a day or two, so there will be an opportunity to get over to Dobytown for a game."

I swept past the odious pair without replying. When I got back to our camp and told Elmer what had transpired, he first turned pale, then grew so angry that I had to calm him down by assuring him that Corbett had not really offended me.

"Anyway," I said. "You surely aren't going to play cards with him again, are you?"

"No matter what you think, I am not a complete fool, Annie. We will need our money to set up housekeeping in Oregon."

"I hope you have it in a safe place."

"As safe a place as there is and that's the gospel."

I might have asked him what he meant by that statement, but was too proud to inquire. I still had nearly all of the hundred dollars Pa had given me and assumed that with that sum and my developing skills as a teacher, I could support myself and my baby in Oregon. At that point, I still clung to the notion that, once in Oregon, it would be a simple matter to have my marriage to Elmer annulled on the grounds it had never been consummated. Therefore, I figured, Elmer's cache of money was none of my concern.

Meanwhile, I began feeling more than a little smug at how things were working out for the former Miss Annie Mundy who was no longer under the thumb of Myrtle Mae Hixon, enjoying her new profession of school teacher, and, despite the way he irritated her, benefiting from the protection of her bogus bridegroom. Only, of course, he did not realize my intentions. God forgive me, it would not be the last time that I would use a man to my advantage. We women have to employ such gifts as the Almighty has seen fit to bestow on us to get along in this male-dominated world.

3

While I had "seen the elephant," in a figurative sense, we did not spot our first buffalo until we had left the lovely valley of the Little Blue and were headed for the Platte River. Later we would see bigger herds, but this one, even at a couple of miles distance, was large enough to cause our wagon train to halt so that we could gaze at the wonder of a hillside covered by the great, humped creatures.

Some of the bolder fellows were all for riding out to do some hunting but Captain McGee quickly put a stop to that notion.

"You'll see plenty of buffalo this side of the mountains. Even if you got lucky and shot one, you'd wear out your horses trying to overtake them. Then you'd have to butcher your kill and haul it back while we wait for you. Nothing doing."

"But we can use the fresh meat."

"Wait until we get to Kearny and you can buy all the buffalo meat your belly can hold. Now let's get this train moving."

It is hard to believe that the buffalo have just about been wiped out since those days. At the time, it seemed the supply of the animals was inexhaustible.

A little later that day we found the land along the trail littered with huge dabs of buffalo dung. I could tell that Myrtle Mae was dying to suggest that I start gathering the chips for our camp fire that night, but I ignored her hints and she didn't dare broach the subject openly, not in Elmer's presence.

My so-called husband broke the tension by saying to her with that sly way he had, "Aunt Myrtle Mae, did you not say you had brought a sack to collect buffalo chips?"

With eyes full of suspicion, she nodded.

"If you will give me the sack, Ralph Junior and I will gather enough for our fire tonight. I have read that they make a better blaze than wood and that there is no odor."

Ralph Junior turned into an eager fuel gatherer. Eventually, with much praise from Elmer, the dear little fellow took over the chore for the entire Hixon tribe.

So that day on which we saw our first buffalo and gathered the first of their droppings ended on a happy note. And that evening, for the first time, Captain McGee ordered our caravan to park our wagons in two circles, one for each contingent. By now the grass had turned green and had grown high enough for our livestock to subsist on it, which was good, for our dry feed had been exhausted. And now McGee and Peebles ordered the men in the two parties to start standing two-hour watches during the night to keep our oxen, cows, mules and horses from wandering and to guard them against predatory Indians or wolves. There was much grumbling about the military way in which Captain McGee gave his orders, but no one, not even Elmer, dared confront him on the issue.

The next day, after our noon rest beside a feeble spring Boris had located, we found the trail blocked by a small army of Indians on horseback and foot. I had seen plenty of tame Indians both in St. Joe and along the trail, but you could tell these were the real article just from the wild, proud look in their eyes.

Some of the braves who sat on their scrawny ponies in a line across the trail carried old flintlock muskets; others, steel-tipped lances and bows and arrows. Behind them the squaws, papooses strapped to their backs, were on foot, holding the halters of ponies laden with teepee poles and buffalo robes. Dogs swarmed about the party. Some even dragged travois.

The braves wore fierce expressions and little else to hide their nakedness. I would have felt more fear at their appearance had the oldest of their crew, their spokesman, not been wearing a ludicrous stove pipe hat, far the worse for use, and an ill-fitting swallow-tailed coat.

They were Pawnees and, since this was their country, they demanded whisky and gunpowder in exchange for our right of passage.

At first Chester Peebles conferred with them but in a few minutes up rode Captain McGee on his big gray gelding, in company with his wolfhound and a dozen of his roughest Californians, among them Bart Corbett and Kentucky Pete. McGee wore both his huge revolvers on his waist, plus a Hawkins rifle in a scabbard on his horse's right side and a double-barrelled shotgun on his left.

The conference that followed was short but apparently far from sweet, at least from the Indians' viewpoint, judging from the way the braves glowered at us as they sullenly stood aside for our wagons to proceed.

As we rolled past the dispirited women and children I spotted a pretty young squaw in a more advanced state of pregnancy than my own. I smiled at her and patted my midriff. Her face broke into a grin and she raised a hand in acknowledgment of our sisterhood. I have often thought of her, wondering what happened to her and her baby in the turbulent times that later swept over the West.

That night, around our campfire, Peebles explained that the Pawnee once had been a feared presence in these parts but, bullied by the Sioux and Cheyenne to the north and weakened by the white man's small pox and measles, they had fallen to a lower estate.

"Used to be they'd cut a fellow's throat for his boots. They still are a long way from being tamed. And they hate and fear the Sioux. That is how Cousin Zeb got rid of them. Told them where they can find that herd of buffalo we saw yesterday, then promised he would say nothing of where they were headed to any Sioux we may see along the trail beyond Fort Kearny. Sort of an implied threat. Zeb knows just how to deal with Indians. You never want to insult one in front of his friends, but on the other hand, you can't show any sign of fear or they will take advantage of you."

So, onward we pressed away from the pleasant valley of the Little Blue across the sandy prairies toward the Platte, which we came in sight of just three weeks after having crossed the Missouri.

For me they had been the most exciting and, in many ways, the most satisfying three weeks of my life. I was free of the more onerous aspects of travel, under the protection of a so-called husband who was proving surprisingly useful. Except in the eyes of the resentful Myrtle Mae Hixon, I was free of the stigma of bearing an illegitimate child. And, I thought I had found my vocation in life, as a teacher.

So my spirits ran pretty high when we came in sight of the broad, multi-channelled and shallow Platte and the distant line of low hills beyond, the celebrated "Nebraska Coast." We would be looking at one stretch or another of that river for the next several weeks.

The flag that flew from the top of Fort Kearny's high flagpole could be seen many miles distant as we followed the treeless south bank of the Platte. Fort Kearny turned out to be a collection of unpainted wooden buildings two and three stories high plus a flock of long, low sod huts and sheds, all grouped around a parade ground nearly a mile south of the Platte which at that point divided into several channels, separated by wooded islands. Except for a few artillery pieces here and there and that big American flag, to my eyes, it wasn't a very military looking establishment.

While our two parties had got the jump on other emigrants who had congregated at Fort Joseph, we found the grasslands near the fort already thronged with wagons of early-bird trekkers who had set out from Nebraska City, nearly 100 miles farther up the westward curving Missouri from St. Joe. Also in evidence were a few Indian teepees.

It was here that we saw the first of the prairie dog towns so common in the Platte Valley. Scores of these little rodents popped out of their burrows to scrutinize our train. Captain McGee warned the men against riding through their villages lest their horses step in a prairie dog hole and break a leg.

The trail passed between the fort and the river. Near a sutler's capacious frame store on the edge of the fort, our train was halted by a sentry who notified McGee and Peebles that captains of all emigrant trains had to report to the commanding officer. While they rode off to the officers' quarters to comply, members of our train thronged to see the wares the sutler was offering for sale at exorbitant prices. But Elmer stayed behind to engage the sentry in conversation, peppering him with questions.

The soldier, a scrawny little Irishman, spoke highly of the fort's commanding officer, "Captain Wharton. From Philadelphia, he is, and a real gentleman."

Elmer inquired why there were no Sioux about, as we had been led to expect by our guides.

"You'll see naught but Pawnee this side of the river these days. The Sioux have made themselves scarce hereabouts ever since we kicked their asses last year near to two hundred miles up the North Platte at Blue Water Creek. Pardon my English, miss."

"It's not miss," Elmer said. "She's my wife. But what about the fight?"

I was annoyed by the delay in visiting the sutler's establishment, but soon became first fascinated, then horrified, by the soldier's account of a battle in which he and several hundred other soldiers had fought with the Brule Sioux the previous September. This, of course, was the famous battle of Ash Hollow, in which the army trapped and nearly wiped out a band of Indians they held responsible for the massacre of a small group of soldiers the previous year near Fort Laramie.

Back in North Carolina, I had heard nothing of either affair, but judging from Elmer's questions, the Missouri newspapers must have been full of the subject.

Personally I was appalled by the soldier's graphic description of how his expedition had killed "near to a hundred of the savages" and had destroyed all their possessions and carried off many of their women and children. He seemed more than a little proud of having "taught them a lesson."

His recitation was interrupted by the return of Captain McGee and Peebles to notify us that we would have to move on a half mile to camp, as the army reserved the pastures near the fort for their own livestock. This put us in the midst of other camping emigrant parties and close to a ragtag collection of sod and adobe huts called Dobytown, and that much nearer to serious troubles.

* * *

Captain McGee had been right about the availability at Kearny not only of buffalo meat but also hides, spare wagon wheels, flour and corn meal (although weevily) and dozens of other necessities. Pawnee squaws swarmed over our camp offering moccasins for sale until Captain McGee shooed them away. You could even buy steers and mules but at that stage of our trip our livestock did not yet need replacing.

Anyway it was a great relief to be given the remainder of that day and all the next to rest and refresh ourselves before beginning our big push up the Platte Valley some 300 miles to Fort Laramie.

* * *

I had put Bart Corbett out of my mind for the past several days, caught up as I was in the excitement of seeing buffalo and real wild Indians. So when I saw him, at a distance, talking to Elmer, I was too engrossed in washing clothes and rearranging the gear in our little wagon to pay any attention.

By now many friendships had been forged among us Oregonians. Nobody much liked Myrtle Mae but her husband got along well with everyone. Several of the older women befriended me, offering all kinds of advice about my condition. I knew they all thought my marriage to Elmer had been a shotgun affair. They had felt sorry for me earlier when I appeared to be the Hixon's servant girl. Now they seemed to pity me for being married to a callow cripple who did not know when to keep his mouth shut.

The establishments of Dobytown offered not only a vile brand of whisky but also the services of a variety of brazen women. Being mainly God-fearing family folk with wives keeping a close eye on them, the men in our section avoided this Sodom-on-the-Platte but I noted a stream of those from the California gang passing between their camp and Dobytown which was already thronged with bull-whackers from a freight wagon train carrying corn and oats for Ft. Laramie.

Every morning and evening, the soldiers at the fort fired off a cannon. It was a comforting sound, a sort of reminder that the United States Government was there to protect us.

At the close of that day of rest, as the sound of the evening gun echoed over our camp, Elmer seemed distracted. After our supper of buffalo stew, while I helped Myrtle Mae wash our plates, he paced around the camp, looking worried.

"What could be bothering Elmer?" Myrtle Mae asked.

"I haven't the slightest idea."

"A good wife knows what is on the mind of her husband."

"If she ever gives him the opportunity to speak for himself," I replied.

She looked at me, started to reply in kind, but thought better of it and took herself off to ready their tent for the night.

I considered writing a letter to tell Uncle John in confidence of my married state but then reflected on how embarrassing it would be later to announce the annulment. So, instead, I used the remaining light of day to transform one of my skirts into trouserlike bloomers as many of the other women had done since leaving St. Joe. These garments were far more practical than skirts for walking fifteen or more miles a day in dust and mud alongside a wagon and team of oxen.

That job done, I was just getting drowsy when Elmer joined me in our tent. For once he did not take my hand after he had settled in beside me, for which I was grateful. My stomach was full of nourishing stew. Besides fashioning my bloomers, I had got my clothes washed and had bought a pair of combs from the sutler's store. Looking forward to the next day, I dropped off into a dreamless sleep.

4

After the sound of the fort's morning gun had awakened me, I lay quietly, asking myself what I was doing in a tent halfway across the continent from my home and married to a man I did not love. Failing to see Elmer beside me, I assumed that he had risen early to milk the cow, but, no, when I looked outside, Miss Mollie lay nearby chewing her cud.

I was at the point of asking the Hixons where Elmer might be when Will Tremelling, one of the Cornish lads from the California gang, came running up, out of breath, to say, "Miss Annie, you had better do something about your husband. He is in big trouble."

"What kind of trouble?"

"Come and see for yourself."

I followed Will at a trot beyond our camp toward the bank of the Platte. As we drew near I saw a group of rough-looking men both from the California gang and from among the inhabitants of Dobytown in a line facing the river. I pushed through this wall of ruffians and, lo and behold, there was Elmer, his revolver in hand, standing back-to-back with Bart Corbett, likewise armed.

One of the California gang was conferring with the pair.

"What is going on?" I asked my Cornish guide.

"Your husband called Bart Corbett out."

"You mean it's a duel?"

Kentucky Pete, Corbett's crony, laughed and said, "Duel, hell. It's more like a suicide. Bart is a dead shot."

Now the referee was backing away from Elmer and Corbett. When he was out of their line of fire, he halted and announced, "Gentlemen, when I give the word each of you take twenty paces, then turn and face each other. You each get just one shot. Hold your fire until I say the word. All right, begin."

For a moment I feared I would faint. Then a deep anger swept over me, an anger directed at Elmer for putting himself in such a ridiculous and dangerous situation. God forgive me, but for a second the thought also flitted through my head that by making me a widow, he would set me free of our hopeless marriage, saving me the trouble of going through an annulment proceeding.

The referee wore an enormous pistol at his hip. By now Elmer and Corbett had walked their twenty paces and had turned to face each other.

Elmer looked pathetic standing there with his Colt in his hand and a frozen look of terror on his face. Corbett's face bore an expression of contempt and confidence.

"Are you ready, gentlemen?" the referee called out.

That is when I did something which to this day, I cannot explain.

"Wait!" I cried, and before anyone could stop me I dashed up to the referee and snatched his pistol from its holster. Using both hands to hold it out front, I advanced toward Corbett.

"What the hell are you doing?" he demanded.

"You shoot my husband and I will shoot you."

"Get her out of here," Corbett yelled at the referee.

I looked over my shoulder at that worthy and said, "You come near me and you are a dead man."

The fellow must have been a natural-born coward, for his face turned white.

"Now young woman, you be careful with that gun. It's got a hair trigger."

"Just keep away from me and you won't get hurt," I said, turning my attention back to Corbett.

Today I am a pretty fair shot with a pistol or a rifle but at that time I had never held a firearm.

Corbett's face no longer looked so confident as he again asked the referee to remove me.

Finally, Elmer found his voice, saying "Annie, you keep out of this."

"I am not going to let this happen. Corbett, you are a low life scoundrel."

"It was your sorry little excuse for a husband that challenged me," Corbett said. "Oh, I see his game now. He put you up to intervene."

"Say that again and I'll shoot you for lying."

So there we stood in a sort of triangle, Elmer, Corbett and me, all holding pistols. The crowd, some cat calling and laughing, fell back to get out of the way in case there was a shootout. Elmer and Corbett still faced each other. The referee continued to implore me to step out of the way and return his weapon.

I was turning back to confront Corbett, when a shot rang out behind me, and Elmer pitched forward on his face. Corbett turned toward me. Thinking he had shot Elmer and now meant to shoot me, I tried in vain to cock the referee's revolver. As I was struggling to do this, a huge hand appeared over my shoulder and snatched the gun away. I looked up into the angry face of Captain McGee, who held his own smoking revolver in his right hand and the referee's in his left.

"What in the hell is going on here?"

Instead of answering him, I ran to Elmer and turned him over onto his back, looking for his wound.

"He ain't shot," Corbett said. "The little piss ant just passed out. I didn't think he had any grit."

"Corbett, what in the hell is all this about?"

Captain McGee was looking down at us as Elmer's eyelids began to flutter.

"This little namby-pamby took offense at something I said in jest and he challenged me to a duel. So I accommodated him. But then his little bride here interfered, otherwise he'd be dead meat now. He should have known better than to mess with Bart Corbett."

McGee's big dog began licking Elmer's face, causing him to raise his arms to fend off the animal and then scramble to his feet.

"You started this, Corbett. You insulted my wife in front of your friends. So I still challenge you. Stand aside, Annie, Captain McGee. We'll see who is the better man."

"Shut up, both of you," McGee roared. "There ain't going to be any duels in my party. So little Mister Hixon, just keep your mouth shut. You talk too much for your own good. As for you, Corbett, I should have known you for trouble the minute I laid eyes on you. If you want to travel with my party, you will lay off pestering this young couple."

Some of the gang of spectators seemed disappointed by the interruption of the duel while others appeared to be relieved.

Once back at our camp, I gave Elmer a tongue lashing which I concluded with, "Why do you have to play the fool every chance you get?"

Tears in his eyes, he replied, "He insulted you, Annie. I couldn't let him get away with that."

"How could that man insult me?"

"He pestered me to play cards with him. I refused. Told him I didn't want to risk the money which is to be our grubstake in Oregon. He said he would let me play without financial risk. When I said I didn't take his meaning, he said I could use you as my stake."

"What did he mean by that?"

"He said he would put up a hundred dollars against spending a night with you. I told him he had better mind his tongue. He asked me if I was afraid for you to learn what a real man was like. I threw a dipper of water in his face and challenged him."

"That was a foolhardy thing to do, Elmer."

"I couldn't let such an insult pass. Can't you see that, Annie? I still wish you hadn't interfered. It makes me look like I am hiding behind your skirts."

"Elmer, you idiot, you need some skirts to hide behind."

He got a funny look on his face, then said, "Would you really have shot Corbett?"

"I would have, but I couldn't manage to pull the hammer back on that fellow's pistol."

He doubled up with nervous laughter and, before I could stop him, put his arms around me.

"I believe I have gone and got myself a wife it doesn't pay to mess around with."

"Yes, and that goes for you as well as the likes of Bart Corbett."

5

The emigrants reacted to the aborted duel in different ways. Some, including himself, felt that Elmer had shown commendable courage in challenging a fellow like Bart Corbett who, so it was reported by his crony, Kentucky Pete, had killed a man in a bar room brawl back in St. Louis the year before. Others were of the opinion that Corbett had solidified his reputation as a man to be feared and that Elmer was lucky that his wife had interfered. In the eyes of still others, I stood out as the heroine of the piece, a woman who not only had saved the life of her young husband but who also had prevented a criminal blot on the record of our expedition.

Elmer confided to me that he wished he had shot Corbett and still would do so if he ever again insulted "my precious Annie."

"Stop talking such nonsense, Elmer. And let me make it clear that if you get into any more such scrapes, you can get yourself out of them."

Anyway, I noticed that Elmer went about his chores the rest of that layover day at Fort Kearny with a fresh bearing. He strode about like a bantam rooster, without the aid of his cane. He insisted on taking me to a sutler's hut and offering to buy "whatever suits your fancy."

During our layover, the men watered our livestock in the muddy Platte but we drew water for washing dishes and making coffee from shallow wells around the camping and grazing areas.

Elmer went to post a letter back to his folks in Missouri. He returned with a letter that had arrived for me from Uncle John with the previous week's mail.

I blessed that good man's heart as I broke the seal and then read that all was well in Oldham County. My little brother Charles had caught the chicken pox. Papa was busy out talking up the Know Nothings now that his old Whig Party had fallen apart. Although Papa owned only Ike and Dessie, he was a strong pro-slavery man and, in the bargain, an ardent anti-Catholic and hater of foreigners, neither of which group was represented in Oldham County.

Uncle John also reported that the word had passed around the community that I had insisted on going west and my parents had agreed reluctantly to let me go.

For a few minutes after reading this news, I felt a stab of homesickness, but the mood passed quickly as I reflected again on the events of that early morning. Corbett really had feared my shooting him more than Elmer's doing so, it occurred to me. I had placed him in double jeopardy. First there was the slight chance that Elmer might have made a lucky shot. But even if he, Corbett, had lived up to his reputation and had killed Elmer, there had stood this bold little pregnant girl ready to fire on him and, of course, he would not have dared shoot her.

I reflected, too, on what my circumstances would have been if Will Tremelling had not summoned me. We might be burying Elmer about now. Everyone would commiserate with the little pregnant widow. Although the problem of dissolving my marriage to Elmer would have been solved, what would I have done about handling a wagon and two mules across the hundreds of miles that lay ahead?

As I was mulling over all this, Elmer walked up and handed me a bunch of flowers he had picked along the bank of the Platte.

"For my brave Annie," he said.

"Why thank you, Elmer. That was sweet of you."

He grinned and said, "Guess what Mister Courtenay has asked me to do tonight."

"I hope it was not to fight another duel."

"Seriously, Annie, he and his family plan to put on a minstrel show after supper. They need someone to serve as their end man."

"What is that?"

"Didn't you ever see a minstrel show?"

"They don't have such entertainments in Oldham County."

"I have been to several in St. Joe. Anyway, the end man makes the announcements to the crowd and he sets up the actors for their jokes and such. Mr. Courtenay says he has been impressed by the way I speak up in public. Thinks I have the makings of an actor. And he called me a valiant fellow for standing up to Corbett as I did."

I shook my head and said, "I just hope you aren't going to make a fool of yourself again."

But in truth I thought that maybe Elmer wasn't so much a fool as he was just immature. I had to admit he had grit to match his ambition. Some men are considered courageous because they are too stupid or too cocksure to feel fear. Elmer had been afraid but had not let his fear stop him from defending my honor, or maybe it was his own. But all that is beside the point of what happened later that night.

* * *

Elmer, along with his uncle and other men had gone down to the Platte that afternoon to have a swim and a much-needed bath in the cold, muddy water. Using a screen of blankets strung on ropes stretched between our wagons, Myrtle Mae and I took a sponge bath in a tub of well water. She looked at my swollen middle and said, "I reckon you think it is a good thing after all that you and Elmer got married and not just because it got you out of your legal obligations."

"Why do you say that?"

"Otherwise there would be no hiding your shame from other folks."

Now here is a big difference between women and men. This was not the first time this obnoxious woman had insulted me. But instead of challenging her to a duel as a man might have done, I used my tongue.

"Mrs. Hixon," I said, "When we are finally judged at the end of our lives, whose shame do you think will be the greater, mine or my father's for exiling me into the care of second-rate people, or your own for using your advantage to humiliate and exploit me?"

"Oh, you are a saucy piece of goods aren't you? How dare you speak to me in such a way?"

"You have forced me to be bold. Suppose we leave it at that."

She started to reply, but I headed her off with, "So don't you speak of my shame and I will not mention your own family's."

That hit the mark, for she turned red and clamped her mouth shut. I made a mental note to ask Elmer more about what her father had done back in North Carolina.

*   *   *

While the Hixons and I ate another good, filling supper of antelope meat, rice and fried apple pies, using ingredients bought from a sutler, Elmer busied himself with helping the Courtenays set up their theater, that and learning his lines.

By nightfall, they had created a rickety stage of borrowed wagon sideboards laid across boxes. Behind this structure, they had erected a tent through whose flap the players made their entrances. At either end of the makeshift stage, to provide lighting, there burned bonfires.

Although most of the California gang were seeking less cultural entertainments in Dobytown, more than a hundred other persons, some soldiers from the fort and a handful of awe-struck Pawnees, gathered to see the show.

First Mister Courtenay, his face blackened and wearing a wooly wig and white gloves, mounted the stage and announced that he and "my lady wife" had considered offering "a truncated version of a play in which we each acted various roles during its long run at the great Lyceum Theater in London. But we decided that 'The Happy Land' might not be suited to New World tastes and so we have, after much debate, settled upon a peculiarly American art form, a minstrel show. Now, making his debut on this or any other stage, I give you our interlocutor for the evening, from St. Joseph, Missouri, your own, your very, very own Elmer Hixon, Esquire."

To a fanfare of banjo music provided by Lester, the Hixon's slave, Elmer, his face all rouged and wearing a fake moustache, leaped from the tent, onto the stage and made a fool of himself all over again.

After the traditional walk around of the players, which included the two Courtenay children and Opal, their slave woman, Elmer cried out in a loud voice, "Gentlemen, be seated!"

The jokes might have been old hat to habitual theater goers, but most of our crowd had never heard them. Soon their laughter rang across the campground. Their delighted faces shone in the light of the bonfires. At times the men, weary of three weeks on the trail, rolled about on the ground, convulsed with laughter. The women, too, shrieked at the rough humor. At one point, Mrs. Mueller said to her husband in a voice loud enough for me to hear, "Mine Gott, Herman, I have gone and pissed my britches."

Then came several lively songs, sung by Mrs. Courtenay, who really did have a magnificent alto voice. Later in the program, she also delivered several soliloquies from Shakespearean plays. Her husband did a fine job of Marc Antony's "We have come to bury Caesar, not to praise him" speech.

The two Courtenay children, shedding their usual shyness, sang several sweet little duets.

To tell the truth, though, the Courtenay's two slaves outshone their owners. Lester played the violin even better than the banjo. The program ended with Opal's doing a "jump Jim Crow" dance to her husband's accompaniment that brought down the house,

Elmer passed a hat for a free-will offering of "those who have enjoyed the performance."

The crowd applauded until their hands ached. Mister Courtenay gave them one encore and would have offered another but Captain McGee interrupted the show to announce that we would be roused early the next morning and that we would be crossing later in the day to the north bank of the Platte.

Elmer, emboldened by his stage success, demanded the reason for this, saying, "I thought only Mormons followed that route."

"You thought wrong. From what the soldiers tell us, there is a flock of wagon trains already on the trail out of Nebraska City. That will mean jam-ups ahead at fords and bridges. We will have fewer streams to cross on the north side of the Platte anyway. The grazing is better, too. And you will find about as many gentiles as Mormons north of the river, although it is true that the so-called saints prefer that route."

So Elmer and I went to bed, both of us freshly bathed, and under our newly clean, separate blankets.

Elmer did not try to take my hand. I thought he was going to sleep without first talking my ear off for once.

But no, after a long silence he said gently, "Annie, can I ask you something?"

"I wouldn't know how to stop you."

"Why did you do what you did this morning?"

"Just seemed the thing to do. I hate Corbett. I hate the way he looks at me and how he tries to bully you. But it was stupid of you to challenge him."

"If I had not, he would have made me a laughing stock."

"Elmer, sometimes you make yourself a laughing stock. You should have seen yourself passed out on your back, with that big dog licking your face."

"Maybe you are right. I can't help it. Don't you see, if I don't speak out and assert myself, I will not amount to anything in this life."

"You came close to losing your life."

"Would it have mattered to you if I had?"

"It would have made things very awkward for me."

"Yes, but would you have grieved for me?"

"Oh, Elmer, it is over. Let's not dwell on such things."

"If anything was to happen to you, Annie, it would kill me."

"That is just empty talk."

"I am serious. You have become my reason for living."

"That is sweet of you to say. Now let's go to sleep."

"I know you don't love me, not yet. But let me tell you something: Before this trip is done, you are going to learn to love me. You might as well accept that."

"I don't exactly hate you, Elmer."

"It would kill me if I thought you did. Oh, Annie, I do love you so . . ."

It may have been just his overwrought nerves finally giving way, but suddenly he broke into such violent sobs that I feared the others would hear. Without thinking what I was doing, I put my arms about him and held his head against my bosom.

Gradually his sobs subsided, and with them my resolve never to let our marriage be consummated. Maybe it was pity or a grudging admiration for the courage he had shown in facing up to Corbett. Perhaps it was because he really had done a fine job as the end man for the minstrel show, good enough so that Mr. Courtenay asked him to repeat his performance when we reached Fort Laramie. Maybe it was the freshness of his smell and the cool of the prairie night. But when he raised my blanket and slid his lame leg over my thighs, I did not resist.

The thing happened so quickly that I scarcely had time to protest, even if I had been so minded. It was nothing like my experiences with Billy Joe Duncan, but it happened nonetheless, almost like a rooster feathering a hen.

Afterwards, he kissed me and said he hoped he had not been too rough. I assured him he had not and urged him to get some sleep.

I lay awake long into the night, thinking what a fool I had been to let my sympathy run away with my better judgment.

Well, I thought, unless I wanted to perjure myself, there went my grounds for annulling our marriage. Looking back, I realize what an ill-formed scheme it had been in the first place. Now, for better or worse, I was married, if not to a fool, at least to a foolish man.

Ah well, I must make the best of my situation. Maybe, with guidance from me, he would gain some wisdom in time. And, who knew, maybe he might become a governor or senator some day, whether I learned to love him or not. Besides, he really had proved to be a very funny end man for the minstrel show. Once I got over my embarrassment, I had enjoyed his performance almost as much as he had himself.

6

On the way up from the valley of the Little Blue, we had seen numerous graves of emigrants who had fallen ill with cholera during the great migrations of the early 1850's. Today, we know the cause of these sad and sudden deaths was drinking water infected by human wastes. The only reason even more did not die was the universal habit of drinking coffee and tea, made, of course, with boiled water.

The ailment had not been such a problem the year before, in 1855, probably because of the relatively light traffic during that period of widely reported Indian troubles along the Platte between Forts Kearny and Laramie.

And so as we set out early the next morning, the California gang in the lead, past Dobytown, my thoughts were on my much changed circumstances on the trail and new prospects in Oregon, not on diseases that had cost previous expeditions so many lives.

Judging from the way he whistled and occasionally winked at me as he urged our two mules forward, Elmer likewise had his mind on the near future, not the past.

Captain McGee led us several miles west, following the main trail along the south bank of the Platte. We soon overtook a train of some two dozen enormous freight wagons owned by Russell & Majors out of Ft. Leavenworth. Drawn by six yoke of oxen, each of the Conestoga wagons was laden with 6,000 or 7,000 pounds of corn, oats and such. These huge vehicles were herded along by some of the most profane and filthy men it was ever my misfortune to encounter. They wielded their long bull whips with amazing accuracy, causing them to crack just close enough to their patient animals' ears to keep them plodding in the right direction.

I quickly saw the wisdom of Captain McGee's decision for us to cross to the north side of the Platte to avoid such cumbersome traffic. After eating the dust and enduring the blasphemous banter of the bullwhackers for a mile or so, he ordered us to halt while he and Peebles rode their horses into the broad, shallow river and criss-crossed back and forth to the other side, feeling out the best route for our wagons to ford the treacherous stream.

Peebles gathered us Oregonians to explain that because of the clinging sand in the river and the current, it would be necessary to double team our wagons, that is use six or eight yoke of oxen to draw our vehicles over to the north bank, the number of animals depending on the sizes and weights of the wagons.

He urged us to secure all tools and goods in case our wagons tipped over. And he cautioned us against falling into the water.

At the conclusion of his talk, he paused to say quietly to me, "Miss Annie, or should I say, Mrs. Hixon, I did not see that incident that occurred yesterday, but if I had known of their intentions, I would have put a stop to it, just as Zeb did."

"I don't doubt that you would have."

"Anyway, I just wanted to say how much I admire your pluck. That was a rare act of heroism on your part."

"You are kind to say so."

"Your husband is a lucky fellow to have won the hand of such a wife as yourself . . ."

He paused as though to say more in this vein, but then put his hat back on and ended with, "If there is ever anything I can do to help you, anything at all, please don't hesitate to ask."

"I can't think what that might be. As you can see, I am very well provided for. Nonetheless, thank you for saying so."

Curious fellow, I thought, as he walked away. I wondered, distant cousin or not, what could account for such a smooth, well-educated chap to be hooked up with a rough-cut customer like Zebulon McGee. Peebles belonged back in Boston with a soft job in a shipping office rather than serving as guide and wagon master for a gang of emigrants headed for Oregon.

"What was Peebles saying to you?" Elmer demanded.

"Just offered to help us if we run into more difficulties."

"He should stick to guiding and leave the rest to me. I don't like the way he acts around you, anyhow. Seems to be trying to charm you."

"Don't be silly. Who would waste their charms on me?"

"Me. In fact I can't wait until tonight."

"I meant anyone with good sense," I replied, with just enough of a smile to take the sting out of my words.

* * *

It was not nearly as easy or quick to get across the Platte as we had thought. The water came up to the bellies of the livestock and, in places, even higher so they had to swim here and there. And the water slopped up into the bottoms of our wagon beds. A wheel ran off of one wagon and had to be replaced on the other shore. The Muellers got their overloaded wagon stuck in a bed of sand. Elmer would try to play the hero, plunging into the cold water to seize the nose ring of the lead ox and steer it and its fellows to firmer footing.

Our mules, being tall and sure footed, hauled our light wagon across with little trouble. Elmer got us over, then waded and swam back to help his uncle by leading their cow across. By the time our party had all reached the other shore, he was exhausted. His lips had turned blue and his teeth were chattering.

Our guides allowed us to take our noon break after the crossing so we could dry out around fires and fortify ourselves with hot coffee.

When time came to get started, Elmer asked if I would mind driving the mules while he rode in the back of the wagon.

"Nothing wrong, is there?"

"I am just a little weary."

So I climbed onto our wagon's jockey box and slapped the reins against the mules' rumps.

It is said that the grass always grows greener on the other side of the fence. In the case of the Platte, this turned out to be true. Far more buffalo chips lay about. And the grass was more lush.

So we made close to ten miles before halting that evening near a small clump of wagons already drawn up beside the trail ahead.

Until that evening, I had never laid eyes on a Mormon, had only read or heard about what seemed their bizarre ways of thinking and acting. The notion I had of them was one of large polygamous families who shunned us ordinary Christians. Since then, I have known scores of Mormons and, while I am unconvinced by some points of their theology, I must confess that, with a few exceptions which I will touch on later, they were industrious, fair-minded folk.

It was one of their parties that was camped out that evening after we had crossed the Platte. As we were to learn, they were an advance guard their leader, Brigham Young, had asked to come out from Council Bluffs. This was in anticipation of a horde of British and Danish converts on their way to settle in the State of Deseret which Young had created near the Great Salt Lake in what is now Utah. This was a short while before all those zealots set out late in the season from the East pushing hand carts, only to suffer great privations in the early snows in the mountains. But that has nothing to do with my story.

These Mormons were well-equipped, with sound wagons and excellent livestock. And, like us, they had got a jump on the season. Peebles advised us to have little to do with them, in particular those in our party from Missouri and Illinois as "the saints bear a particular animosity for persons from those states because of the persecutions they have endured there."

Peebles came back to our camp fire to tell how well-organized the Mormons were and to note that "they even have a doctor and his wife travelling with them. We have agreed that they should hit the trail first tomorrow. They will not hold us up as some trains would do."

During all this, Elmer sat beside our camp fire with his blanket wrapped around his shoulders. The connubial ice having been broken between us, I was dreading that night. However, Elmer, complaining of the cold and his weariness, was content to cuddle and tell me through chattering teeth how much he loved me.

The next morning he felt feverish but managed to milk the cow and harness up our mules. Seeing how tired he looked, I suggested that he ride and let me drive again. I was not that worried about him. I just enjoyed driving the mules.

With the Mormon party setting a brisk pace ahead of us, we made excellent time that day, a bit more than twenty miles, according to Peebles. But when time came to unharness the mules, set up the tent, and milk the cow, Elmer said he felt too weak. So I pitched our tent and ordered him to bed.

Ralph Hixon, seeing my fumbling efforts to unhitch the mules, took pity and finished the job while I milked the cow and Myrtle Mae lit a fire, using buffalo chips gathered by Ralph Junior.

Leaving Elmer in our tent, we ate a hearty stew and big bait of slam johns and drank our coffee under an increasingly cloudy sky. I carried a bowl of stew and cup of coffee into our tent, but Elmer shook his head. I felt of his forehead and found it alarmingly hot.

By now a drizzle had started falling. I reported Elmer's condition to his uncle who seconded my diagosis that he was seriously ill.

"Besides which, he don't make sense when he talks," Ralph reported.

Peebles came by to inspect Elmer and took me aside to ask if he had drunk any unboiled water recently. I recalled that he had drunk from a pail of water drawn from a well back at Fort Kearny.

"He is seriously ill, I would say."

"That seems obvious. What shall we do?"

At my urging, he rode over to the Mormon camp to ask their doctor to come look at Elmer.

The doctor turned out to be a strange sort of fellow with side whiskers who spoke in an English accent. Had it not been for his thick spectacles and his mournful expression, he would have been handsome, for a middle-aged man.

By this time Elmer's raging diarrhea had turned the atmosphere in our tent foul, but the doctor went about poking and probing him as though he were immune to the stench.

Since Elmer seemed not to comprehend, I told the doctor about his, Elmer's, drinking the well water and of his exertions in crossing the Platte.

"You are his wife?"

I acknowledged that this was the case.

"How long have you two been married?"

"Several months now," I replied, thinking it was none of his business.

The doctor squinted at me through his spectacles, then enlisted my help in forcing Elmer's mouth open to receive a draught of laudunum.

"Give him the rest of this when he awakens. Not much to be done for him except to let this thing run its course. Keep him warm and quiet. He is young. That is in his favor. There will be a crisis in a few hours. By dawn you should know whether he will recover."

Refusing my offer to pay, this curious man took his leave.

There followed for me, the longest night of my life. From time to time, to escape the foul atmosphere of our tent, I would draw on Elmer's India rubber cape and walk out into the unrelenting rain.

Although I did not love Elmer and doubted that I ever would, he had gained my grudging respect. And to be quite frank, I was curious to see how he would turn out, driven as he was by his furious ambition.

Around midnight, the laudanum having worn off, Elmer began moving his head from side to side and babbling nonsense. He called for his mother. He spoke to people of whom I had never heard as though they were present, people such as his grandparents back in North Carolina. Once, he laughed and said, "There you are, gentlemen. I have a full house. I win the pot." Then he rambled on and on, asking for a Bible, which made no sense to me seeing as Elmer regarded himself as an agnostic.

"Seek and ye shall find," he kept saying over and over. To stop his ranting, I gave him the rest of the laudanum, and that eased him off into unconsciousness.

The rain let up near morning and a fresh wind swept the clouds away to reveal a sky full of stars brighter than any I had ever seen. I looked up and said a prayer for the odd man who was, for better or worse, my husband.

As the sun was just about to break over the horizon, I re-entered the tent. His eyes were open.

"Annie? Is that you?"

"Yes, Elmer."

"Am I going to die?"

"No one has said so."

"I have never felt so weak. Don't think I can go on."

"Then we will remain here until you are well."

"You know I love you, don't you, Annie?"

"Yes."

"But do you love me?"

I took a deep breath. There was no harm in telling him a lie, surely. So I said, "Of course I do, Elmer. After all, you are my husband."

He smiled, then coughed, and fell silent. A look of great peace came over his irregular features so that for the first time he appeared handsome to me. I congratulated myself on having wrought a miracle with my comforting lie. It took me several minutes to realize that he was dead.

7

Back home in North Carolina, when someone died, neighbors would flock in with all kinds of food and promises to do anything they could for the family. There wasn't the time or wherewithal for offerings of food, but the kindness of my fellow emigrants was touching.

Mrs. Mueller dismissed me from the tent and took charge of washing Elmer's body. She removed his watch, pocket knife and a handful of coins from his pockets and gave his fetid clothing to her husband to be burned.

Other women came by to assure me that they and their husbands would look after me.

Chester Peebles announced that the party would delay its departure for two hours while a grave was dug.

"I reckon we ought to have a funeral," I said. "What will we do for a preacher?"

"If you will permit me, I will say a few words and offer a prayer."

"You?" I said.

"Yes. At one time I meant to be a Unitarian minister, as was my grandfather. Studied theology for a year at Harvard before the wanderlust got to me."

Ralph Hixon patted my arm and assured me that "as a family member you are entitled to the protection of Myrtle Mae and I."

His wife agreed rather stiffly, but would add "although naturally we will expect you to carry out your obligations as we agreed with your father."

I was too weary from a sleepless night and too numb to react to the implication of her words.

After Mrs. Mueller had finished her ministrations, she led me into the tent where I found Elmer lying on a borrowed wagon tailgate, wrapped in a blanket like a baby in its bunting, with only his head showing. Mrs. Mueller had combed his usually unkempt hair. His face still wore its peaceful expression.

"What do you think? Don't he look good?"

"You have done a fine job. Thank you."

She put a powerful arm around my shoulders and said, "You chust look here. It is all right if you want to cry. Better not to bottle it up."

"I don't want to cry."

"Then it will come later. You want to be alone with him?"

"That is not necessary."

She looked at me oddly, and said, "Then I will let the others come and see."

Beaming at the compliments for her laying out skills, Mrs. Mueller stood by the raised sides of the tent while all of our Oregonians and a goodly number of the California gang filed past to gaze upon Elmer's corpse and mumble their condolences.

The last to appear was Captain McGee. I noticed that his face was sweaty and that he was breathing hard.

"We have got his grave dug now. We dug it good and deep so the wolves and coyotes can't get to him. I am sorry about this, but we got to keep our wagons moving."

"I am ready," I said and fell in with the Ralph Hixons to follow him to the grave which had been dug between the ruts of the trail. A large pile of stones lay beside it.

Mr. Mueller, his sons and several other men carried Elmer's remains on the tailgate and set him on the ground.

I felt too confused to remember exactly what Peebles said, but from what others told me he spoke eloquently about the shortness of our days and the comfort that could be taken from a life that had been lived with courage.

I do remember, however, that Mr. Courtenay volunteered to recite the 23rd Psalm, doing so from memory in his rich English accent that gave the words a fresh meaning. After that, Peebles led us in reciting the Lord's Prayer.

The man who had lent his tailgate wanted it back. So they lowered Elmer, shrouded in his blanket, into the grave and covered his body with a layer of stones. As they shoveled in the dirt, Mrs. Mueller led me away to pack my belongings into our wagon.

Later I looked back to see Captain McGee driving a team and wagon back and forth over the grave. Noting my surprise, Peebles explained that "Here along the Platte, the Indians have a habit of digging up bodies to steal the clothing. This will conceal the grave."

So the death and burial in an unmarked grave of Elmer Hixon, would-be governor of Oregon, delayed our departure that morning for only two hours.

Before we took off, Captain McGee rode back to tip his hat and say, "Little lady, if you don't want to continue all the way, you could turn back when we reach Fort Laramie. There is a mail coach that runs between there and St. Joe every month. Goes along the regular trail south of the Platte. They could find room to take you back to your family, I reckon."

"Thank you, Captain," I said. "I will keep that in mind."

Myrtle Mae was listening to this exchange. She chimed in with, "She can't go back. She has an obligation to our family."

I let the remark pass, but Captain McGee looked at her in the way he had of putting people in their place and said, "I would think that the little lady might have something to say about that."

Before she could reply, he put his spurs into the flanks of his great, gray horse, and, followed by his dog, cantered to the head of our column. The assurance of this strong, taciturn man that the choice of returning east or remaining with the party would be mine, gave me a sense of comfort.

* * *

Judging from the map, the spot where Elmer was buried lies near the present day town of Lexington, Nebraska. It would be impossible to find the exact location but I have considered hiring someone to erect a memorial there, someday. Good intentions may be sufficient to pave the road to Hell but they don't get monuments erected.

Anyhow, it took us the next three weeks to reach Fort Laramie, which lay close to 300 miles up the Platte and North Platte Valleys. My recollection of the first week of that stretch is blurred. I recall the complete absence of trees except along the river banks and on the numerous islands, the long line of low hills, studded with outcroppings of rock, which paralleled our course and that of the river, hordes of mosquitoes and horse flies, clouds of choking dust, and the great supply of buffalo chips that lay about. We saw several herds of buffalo in the distance, but Captain McGee stuck to his rule against chasing off to hunt them.

To the obvious displeasure of Myrtle Mae, various men in our party took pity on me. They pitched my tent at night and took it down in the morning. They vied for the privilege of hitching and unhitching my mules.

The oldest son of the Muellers, 14-year-old Jacob, was assigned by his parents to graze Peter and Paul and would have milked Miss Molly, but I would not permit this. The chore proved to be a comfort. I liked leaning my forehead against the cow's warm flank and smelling the fresh milk.

Toward the end of the first week after Elmer's death, about the time we reached the point where the two branches of the Platte River came together, I noticed some of the women looking at me strangely and sensed they were talking about me. Normally I don't waste much time worrying what people may say, but this seemed so curious that I spoke to Mrs. Mueller about it.

That good woman gave it to me straight. "Vell now, you see, Annie, they are chust wondering why you don't act more grieved about your husband. Ain't you sad at losing him?"

"To tell you the truth, I don't know how I feel. Confused, I suppose."

"Like I told you before, it is no sin to cry. Do you good."

Perhaps I should not have told that good, earnest woman that I really had not loved Elmer Hixon, that, indeed, I never expected to do so; that I had used him to free myself from both the shame of a pregnancy and the domination of Myrtle Mae Hixon, not to mention enduring three years of servitude in Oregon. But tell her, I did, and, once started, poured out my soul to her.

She listened to every word, her blue eyes never leaving my face as I explained that my confusion sprang from my uncertainty about my fate. Captain McGee had offered to find me safe passage back to the East from Fort Laramie, but what would await me there? I missed my home in North Carolina but could not bear the thoughts of returning to the domination of my father. I liked St. Joe, but there I would be caught up by Elmer's family who would wonder at my pregnancy. Yet to continue West would mean falling increasingly back under the thumb of Myrtle Mae Hixon, who continued to hint that "in due course" I would be expected to resume my place as her personal servant, something I had no intention of doing.

"That explains a lot," Mrs. Mueller said when I finished. "It ain't easy being a woman, is it, Annie? Tell you what you do while making up your mind. You chust wear this black cloth around your arm as a proper widow should. And try to look sad. Everything will work out for you. No, no, I don't say nothing to nobody."

She paused, looked shrewdly at me, and laughed.

"Maybe it will help you to know that Jacob was well on his way before Herman and me got married. At first Herman didn't want to take responsibility, but my papa and my brothers took him aside and had a talk with him. He took their meaning and today I couldn't ask for a better husband. Chust between you and me, I can't swear whether Jacob is Herman's son or a certain Irish fellow's. You may of noticed he is the only one that ain't got blond hair. So there, now. Don't you tell my secret and I won't tell yours."

I leaned over and gave her a hug.

"Another thing," she said. "You should count your blessings. These here mules and the wagon, they are all yours aren't they?"

"I suppose."

"And then what about your husband's money?"

"What money?"

"Everyone says Elmer was rich. Some thinks that is the only reason a smart, pretty girl like you would marry such an eesel."

"Why, Mrs. Mueller, his folks are just dirt farmers."

"Ja, but there was something about him winning a lot of money from that fancy fellow he had the trouble with."

"Oh, that? I expect he spent most of it on this wagon and the mules. I never saw any signs of great money."

Still, her inquiry set me to thinking. So that night, by candle light, I went through all of Elmer's possessions. There was a set of law books, a dictionary, a Bible with a clasp lock, and the small ledger in which he had written during our noon breaks.

I searched everything, but found no money. As I was at the point of extinguishing my candle, I flipped open the ledger, and out fell our marriage certificate. Then I saw that Elmer had been keeping his diary since the first day of the year, 1856.

At first the entries were rambling records of his political views and his determination "to make something of myself."

Impatiently, I flipped through this sort of thing and notations about the weather until I came to the entry in which he described meeting me on the dock at St. Joe. He rhapsodized about meeting "this lovely flower from North Carolina who has been cast upon our Missouri shore."

From that point on, I was fascinated as I deciphered his scrawling account of what he seemed to regard as a great love story. I am only sorry that I no longer have that diary. Yet many parts are etched in my memory.

He noted his decision to accompany his uncle to Oregon "to be near her whose presence is dearer to me than all I ever have known."

Concerning my repeated refusals of his proposals, he wrote, "I think I shall do away with myself if she should never accept me."

With trembling hands, I turned to the page on which he recorded that morning when I told him of my "condition." He did not say exactly what that condition was, noting only, "At first, I was filled with disillusionment, cast down and shocked, but upon reflection, I saw that her secret offered me a chance to claim her as my own."

Regarding my finally agreeing to marry him, he wrote of "the joy that consumes my very soul, although she has attached conditions to our being wed in secret."

Only then did I fully realize how deeply and truly that lame, seemingly arrogant young misfit had loved me. A sense of guilt swept over me, not because I belatedly reciprocated his love, but because of my regret at my insensitive treatment of him. And so, at last, I wept, quietly at first, but with increasing volume until, Myrtle Mae, hearing my sobs, came to investigate.

"What are you crying about?"

"Elmer," I sobbed.

"It is about time you showed some decent sorrow," she said.

I must have wept for a good hour or so. Afterwards, despite the howling of wolves, I slept peacefully and awoke the next morning, purged of my confusion and my numbness. I had found no trace of the grand wealth Elmer was reputed to have left, but I had discovered something that gave me great comfort: a belated appreciation of having been truly loved. Yes, someday I must have that marker put up near the grave of my young, first husband, Elmer Hixon.

PART THREE

1

Although I was far from certain whether I would continue on our Western trek or would defy the Hixons and accept Captain McGee's offer to find me safe passage east, that stretch of the trip from the forks of the Platte to Fort Laramie in many ways proved to be the most enjoyable part of my journey.

The nights grew cooler. During the day, the trail swarmed with insects and dust. The grass was not so green or lush, but there was enough of it to nourish our livestock. At least good old Peter and Paul offered no complaints. We weren't conscious of it, but we were slowly ascending toward the foothills of the Rockies.

Now that I wore my black arm band and word had passed of my belated outburst of grief, the other women treated me with great warmth. I resumed gathering their children every noon for an hour of lessons and stories. Except for the chore of milking the cow every morning and evening, I hardly had to lift a finger, so attentive were the men in our party to my needs. The Cornish lads and others from the California gang even came by to bring me gifts of jack rabbits or prairie hens which Captain McGee allowed them to shoot so long as they did not stray too far off the trail.

Noting with disapproval the way they hung about to talk in the evenings, Myrtle Mae suggested that I resume sleeping in the pup tent with Ralph Junior, who had been sharing his parents' tent. Although she professed to be concerned for my reputation and safety, I suspect her real motive was to regain her privacy with her husband. And, actually, I was finding it lonely in my own tent. But, rather than moving back in with Ralph Junior, I suggested that he join me in mine.

The boy was delighted by this arrangement and so, I judged, was his father, although how any man could have found that bossy wife of his desirable was beyond me.

Myrtle Mae may have thought she had won the battle to re-enslave yours truly, but the war between us was far from over.

So our train plodded on, following the north bank of the North Platte, making an average fifteen to eighteen miles a day, under the superb discipline of Captain McGee and Chester Peebles. I had my admiring band of students who dutifully called me Miss Annie. The other women, Mrs. Mueller in particular, showed me many kindnesses and offered a great deal of unasked advice.

Noticing how often and long Peebles lingered to talk to me during our noon breaks and in the evening, Mrs. Mueller asked if I found him a nuisance.

"He means no harm, I reckon."

"All the same, if I was you, Annie, I wouldn't encourage him."

"I don't encourage him. In fact, I can't stand him."

"I am glad to hear that. His kind of fellow is all talk. He wouldn't amount to anything without that Captain McGee to give him some backbone. Now, for my money, there is a real man. I wish he was guiding our party to Oregon instead of Peebles."

*   *   *

I have never believed in ghosts except for a brief period on the trail to Fort Laramie. We stopped to camp near the point where the Blue Water Creek meanders from a bluff-lined valley and empties into the North Platte River from the north. Get your map out and you will see that Ash Hollow lies on the opposite bank of the river. Overlooking that spot is the legendary Windlass Hill, the steep decline which caused so many broken axles and overturned wagons for parties following the regular Oregon–California trail. We couldn't make them out from our camp across the Platte but we were told that over the years the locked wheels of countless wagons sliding down that precipitous slope had worn deep troughs in the underlying rock. So mark up another advantage for following the north, or Mormon, side of the Platte.

It had been a long, hard day and I was tired. After helping Myrtle Mae clean our supper dishes, I settled down in my tent, told Ralph Junior a bedtime story, and fell quickly asleep.

I was awakened by Junior's hand on my shoulder.

"What's the matter?"

"I have been hearing babies cry. They woke me up."

"It was probably just some creatures."

"No, it was babies. Some even screamed."

I listened, but heard nothing except a rising wind coming down the valley of the Blue Water.

"I'll hold your hand. Now stop talking and get some sleep."

Thus assured, the boy drifted back to sleep, leaving me wide awake for the rest of the night. I heard no babies crying, but there did seem to be something ghostly in the air. I felt the presence of somebody or something out in the dark that I could not identify.

The next morning as I was milking Miss Mollie, I told Mrs. Mueller of my sleepless night.

"Why, my little Fritz woke me up saying the same thing. I agree with you. This place gives me the shivers."

Chester Peebles came by during this conversation and Mrs. Mueller told him that she disliked the place and why.

"If you were a Sioux, you would dislike it even more. From what I hear . . ." And he went on telling virtually the same story I had heard the sergeant tell Elmer back at Fort Kearny, about the so-called Battle of Ash Hollow.

He concluded by saying, "They buried six of our soldiers nearby. Perhaps you would like to see the graves, Miss Annie."

"What about the graves of the Indians they slaughtered?"

"They generally carry their dead and wounded away."

He paused and gave that possum grin, then added, "You sound like you might be an Indian lover, Miss Annie."

"I don't hold with mistreating people. After all this is, or was, their land."

"Would you feel better if we kidnapped them and took them back home to serve us?"

"I fail to take your meaning."

"I hear you are from North Carolina, although I could have told that from your drawl. Now, don't you have a considerable number of black slaves in your native state?"

"Some people do. My family owns only two. We treat them almost like family."

That was a lie, but in truth, Dessie and Ike did have a far better life than most members of their race at that time.

"Hear that. They owned but two fellow human beings. I suppose this fortunate pair volunteered to travel from Africa for the privilege of being treated almost like members of your family."

All the while he was making this sarcastic remark, he kept up that irritating grin.

"I think this conversation has gone on long enough. As for my drawl, you are fortunate in not having to listen to that grating accent of yours as others do. At least I don't talk through my nose."

At that Peebles burst out laughing.

"My apologies, Miss Annie. Anyway you must understand now why we have naught to fear from the Sioux, at least in this area. It will be a long time before they pull off another Grattan massacre.

"The fellow has more spunk than what I gave him credit for," Mrs. Mueller said when he had gone about his business.

"I regard him as just another of those self-righteous New England abolitionists," I replied, not stopping to think how much I must have sounded like my father.

Twenty years later, when news of the Battle of the Little Big Horn came in, I thought back to the so-called Battle of Ash Hollow and how wrong Chester Peebles, not to mention General Custer, had been in thinking the spirits of the Sioux had been broken.

Actually Peebles had to eat his words that very morning for no sooner were we all on the trail again than we came upon a village of a score or more of Indian wigwams. In the matter of minutes, our trail was blocked by some of the finest specimens of Indian or indeed of any other men I had ever seen.

I have written of the wild, fierce look in the eyes of the Pawnees we met south of the Platte. These had equally fierce looks but, in addition, projected an air of expecting to dominate whomever they encountered. They surely dominated, or anyway intimidated, Chester Peebles.

"Run back and tell Captain McGee we got big trouble here," he said to Jacob Mueller.

As the boy scampered back to the head of the California gang, Peebles tried in vain to make conversation with the only one of the Indians who was mounted. The others lined up with muskets at the ready, but this fellow simply sat astride his pony with arms folded across his muscular chest. His face could have been that of a Roman senator cast in bronze.

Even I, in my ignorance of Indian ways, could see that his outfit would not be so easily dealt with as had the Pawnees.

Behind the line of stalwart braves, the women and children of the village collected to watch the proceedings.

I expected Captain McGee to come rushing up with his gang of Californian cut-throats, all armed to the teeth to clear our path. But this time he rode up alone, except for his dog Boris, stopped in front of the Indians, and took off his hat.

To my amazement, the Sioux chief broke into a smile and gave a joyous whoop. Both he and Captain McGee leaped from their horses and ran toward each other. Laughing like two village idiots, the two men threw their arms around each other and began dancing about and jabbering away in Indian lingo.

The story did not come out all at once, but eventually we learned that the chief and McGee were, or had been, brothers-in-law. Seems that some years before, McGee had married this fellow's younger sister, a beauty named Yellow Moon, and had lived with her tribe for two years, until she died of small pox. Heart-broken at his loss, McGee had refused offers of other braves for him to marry their daughters and had wandered off to California, where he and his cousin Chester Peebles got involved in the Mexican War and so on.

While the two men squatted Indian fashion, bringing each other up to date, the women and children of the village flocked around our wagons, imploring us to trade coffee, sugar and whisky for moccasins, buffalo meat and hides, and, even, children's bows and arrows.

Some of the young braves wandered among us as well. One of them, a tall, slender fellow with the physique of an ancient Greek athlete, kept walking around my wagon and staring at me. By now I was in the sixth month of my pregnancy, so I took umbrage at what I regarded as his rude curiosity and withdrew beneath my wagon cover.

He was gone when I looked out. Now a flock of Indian women were admiring the flaxen hair of the younger Mueller boys. This went on until they frightened the lads with their touching, and Mrs. Mueller shooed the squaws away.

At last the family reunion between Captain McGee and the Sioux chief ended and we hit the trail again.

A couple of days later, McGee stopped by our campfire to say, "Little lady, I understand that you heard ghost babies crying back at the Blue Water camp."

"Not me. The Hixon's son heard them. And the Mueller boy, too."

"Let me put your mind at rest. That was some of the young braves having a little sport. I heard them too, by the way. Spooky sound."

"Why did they do that?"

"They were mocking us as baby killers. They haven't forgot what the army did to their cousins back there last year. I don't expect they ever will. Indians never do."

He paused and said with one of his rare smiles, "By the way, one of them braves wanted to know who owned you."

"Nobody owns me," I said hotly. "Why did he ask?"

"He wanted to trade his pony and three buffalo robes for you and didn't know who to make the offer to."

"That is preposterous."

"I know, but there ain't no Sioux word for preposterous and anyway I didn't want to hurt his feelings, seeing as he is the chief's son. So I lied and told him you had a husband waiting for you in California."

With that this curious man put his hat back on and went about his business. It was many a day before Mrs. Mueller stopped teasing me about turning down the chance to become the wife of the son of a Sioux chief.

2

Despite what I have written about Ralph Hixon, the poor man did occasionally get an edgewise word in. And, in defense of his wife, the woman was a good cook who took pride in her work.

Getting back to Ralph Senior, after our encounter with the Sioux, he got out his guide books and refreshed his memory of what they said about this stretch of the trail.

"Remember, this here is not the prairie anymore," he said. "My books calls this 'the upland plains.' And this book was written for folks following the main trail across the river. Therefore the Courthouse may look different from over here on this side, if we can see it at all."

"The Courthouse?" I asked, thinking it strange that such a building could have been built so far from any established town.

He smiled slyly and said, "Oh, yes. If you see it, you will know what I mean."

At that time, still miffed at his sarcastic remarks about the South, I was not speaking to Peebles, or he would have explained just what Ralph Senior was talking about.

It must have been a good thirty miles off when I saw, on the western horizon, what appeared to be the top of a vast building looming over the cloud of dust our wagon wheels created. As we pressed on over the now sandy soil, I could see more and more of the structure, standing as it did above the relatively flat terrain. Toward evening, however, the formation seemed to divide. A separate, smaller "building" appeared to the east.

That evening I asked Mr. Hixon what were these great monoliths jutting up from the plains south of the Platte.

"Annie, you have seen the elephant way back down the road and now you have seen the Courthouse," he said with a laugh.

"You were teasing me. It does look like a big courthouse or maybe even a castle. What about that other big rock?"

"The guide book calls it the Jail House. Here, read it for yourself."

Since then I have seen dozens of accounts of travelers sighting these strange, out-of-place rock formations, which remained in view for the next couple of days, until they disappeared to the east behind us.

By that time, another great landmark loomed across the river, the famous Chimney Rock whose summit, Mr. Hixon's guide book claimed, reared 400 feet above its dome-shaped base.

Mrs. Mueller and I gaped at the long, slender rock shaft.

"It don't look all that much like a chimney to me," I said.

"Me neither. Peebles told my Herman its real name, the one the fur traders gave it years ago."

She leaned closer and said, "They called it 'the elk's penis,' you know, the elk's thing."

"I know what penis means, Mrs. Mueller. But I never knew what an elk's would look like."

She laughed and said, "Me, neither. I have seen plenty of others . . . animals that is, for the most part."

I joined in her merriment, causing Myrtle Mae, who had been driving me with a light rein since Elmer's death, to frown and say, "Annie, I sure could use a hand with the churning."

"In a moment, Mrs. Hixon," I called back and then muttered to Mrs. Mueller, "I don't think I can stand that woman much longer."

"Can't blame you. Look, Annie, Herman and me been talking. If you don't want to go home from Ft. Laramie, we would chust love to have you travel with us. I always wanted a daughter, but I keep turning out boys."

"That is good of you, but if I go on to Oregon, the Hixons will try to enforce the agreement my father made with them, and I won't have Elmer to get me out of it."

"Can't you buy your way out?"

"What with? It would take three hundred dollars plus the hire of a lawyer."

"As much as that? My, my. I expect they plan to take it easy on you until we get to Fort Bridger and Captain McGee goes off with the California gang. That is why she ain't yelling to get over there and do the churning, much as she'd like to. They are afraid of Captain McGee. They know that agreement or no agreement, he won't let them stop you from turning back if you want to. Now then, a word to the wise is sufficient."

"Many thanks, Mrs. Mueller," I said. And before Myrtle Mae could call me again, I went and churned the milk left over from Miss Mollie's production of the previous day.

There were many other interesting rock formations to be seen the next day or so along that increasingly arid and sandy stretch of the trail but nothing worth recording until we sighted Scott's Bluff which, like the Courthouse and Jail, lay on the south side of the North Platte. Many times bulkier and much higher, this massive formation marked the true beginning of the West for me.

Some of the livelier men, the Cornish lads among them, took advantage of a half-day layover to ford the river, patronize a trader's post at the base, and climb to the 800-foot summit of Scott's Bluff. While they were doing that, Captain McGee led a hunting party to the north to try its luck on a huge herd of buffalo. They managed to shoot two cows. The party, including an ecstatic Jacob Mueller and his father, returned, laden with great chunks of bloody meat across their saddles and all marvelling at the skill Captain McGee showed in stalking their prey without prematurely stampeding the herd.

In Mr. Mueller's words, "He made us stop downwind of the critters and tie our horses, while he led us close enough to start shooting. Of course once we done that, the whole herd took off. They don't run in a straight line like cattle. They zig zag so's it's hard to overtake them. And it takes more than one shot to bring them down."

As I watched the men joyously returning from the hunt, I thought how different they were from women. I felt a sadness at the fate of the great, stupid beasts, for some reportedly had been hit by bullets but had escaped, probably to die.

Yet, hypocrite that I was, I did enjoy the great chunk of charred buffalo hump that I ate that night. I sat by the fire, wrapped in my blanket, listening to the Cornish lads exult about the glorious views they had seen from atop Scott's Bluff.

"We could look back over the way we have come clear to the Chimney Rock and beyond," Will Tremelling said.

"Yes," said another. "And we could see west even farther."

"And what did you see?" I asked.

"More of the same, I am afraid. Except way off we could make out a big mountain peak. Looked to be white at the top. Could that be in the Rockies?"

"According to my guide book that would be Mount Laramie," Mr. Hixon said. "It lies a good hundred miles west of here."

After the Cornish lads had left I, sated with buffalo steak and staring into the flames, became aware that someone had come and sat down beside me.

"Miss Annie, I want to apologize," Chester Peebles said in a gentle voice. "I should not have said what I did back at Blue Water. Actually I think your accent is charming. And I know all Southerners are not like Simon Legree."

"Simon who?"

"Haven't you read Mrs. Stowe's book? It's called UNCLE TOM'S CABIN. Tells all about slave life. I will lend you my copy. Read it and you will understand my feelings about slavery."

"You don't need to apologize. I just considered the source and have dismissed it from my mind. As for reading material, I have plenty of my own. Now, if you will pardon me, I must retire."

Without half trying, I could really be a bitch in those days.

*   *   *

Refreshed from our half day of rest near Scott's Bluff, with loose tire rims chinked to tighten them against the dry air, with our clothes washed and our spirits renewed, we got an early start for the three-day trek that would carry us up to Fort Laramie where I would have to decide whether to continue or turn back.

As we plodded along past a line of low, brown hills, I debated whether to take my chances and press on to a new life in Oregon or to turn back to resume a semblance of my old existence in the East. If I chose the latter course, there might be a great ruckus with the Hixons, but they could not stop me. And I did have nearly all of the $100 tucked away in a corner of one of my carpet bags. That surely would be enough to get me back to St. Joe where I could take refuge with Elmer's family. Yet I did not relish the idea of relying on their charity. Nor was it a promising prospect to return to North Carolina, pregnant and armed with what might be considered a spurious marriage license.

Although Oregon sounded appealing, I did not want to make that long trip as the indentured servant of the Hixons. I was faced with a difficult choice. What would be best, not only for me but even more important, for the child I carried in my womb?

Otherwise, the trip up to the point on the North Platte opposite Fort Laramie went smoothly. It was there that the Mormon would join the main trail to follow it to Fort Bridger.

Captain McGee was considerably put out to find a jam up of wagons that had set out early from Council Bluffs waiting to be ferried across the Platte on two boats owned by army officers and operated by soldiers. At $2 per wagon, these paid servants of the U.S. Government were enriching themselves at our expense. But we had come nearly 300 miles from Fort Kearny, plus another 230 from St. Joe to Kearny. Our oxen were showing the strain of dragging 2,000-pound wagons. Their sides were gaunt and some of their hooves were worn down by the increasingly sandy soil. Everyone was anxious to refit their wagons and livestock, so rather than trying to ford the river, all we did was grumble at the cost and wait our turn at the ferry.

Although it did not conform to my notion of a fort, Laramie did present a more military appearance to my naive eyes than had Fort Kearny. Situated on a flat stretch of grassland, it lay in a loop of the fast-flowing little Laramie River, a bit over a mile from where that stream emptied into the North Platte. The post boasted a grand, newly-built two-story building that doubled as officers' quarters and as the office of the post commandant. Along an imposing parade ground there stood also one barracks for the infantry and another for the cavalry, as well as stables and various storehouses and a brig, or jail. Except for the ruins of an older fort on the very edge of the river and some rudimentary earthworks, I saw no real fortifications.

The fort was ringed with the workshops of blacksmiths and wheelwrights as well as several sutler's stores where you could find even more goods than back at Kearny. And all around the area were dotted the wigwams of Indians, mainly Sioux but some Cheyenne, all making great pests of themselves, trying to cadge coffee and sugar from our fellow travelers.

Also doing a brisk business were livestock dealers willing to buy weary animals at knock-down prices and to sell theirs at inflated rates. A few in our party did trade in their trail-worn oxen but more, including Ralph Hixon, went to the lesser expense of having their beasts shod.

It had never occurred to me that bovines, with their cloven hooves, could be clad with metal shoes, like horses and mules, but these Laramie smiths knew how it was done. They would tie the oxen's legs, topple them onto their sides, and roll them onto their backs in a sort of trough built into the earth. In that helpless fix, the beasts became docile, suffering themselves to have their hooves trimmed and fitted with a separate metal shoe covering each section of their feet.

As I watched this process, Mr. Hixon said, "How about you, Annie? Don't you want to get new shoes for your mules?"

Actually my mind was on deciding whether to turn back, in which case I would sell the animals and the wagon and use the proceeds to help pay my way back to the East.

Seeing my hesitation, he added, "I'd be glad to advance the money for the work to be done."

To buy time, I said, "Let me go look at their hooves and see how they are holding up."

"I have looked, and I doubt they'll make it clear down to Fort Bridger which is the next place you can get such work done. And Mr. Peebles says the roughest part of the trip lies ahead."

I returned to my wagon to count my remaining money and to collect my thoughts. I was thankful to see that there was no one around at the time, except for Mrs. Mueller who was napping against her wagon wheel.

As soon as I had climbed aboard my parked wagon, I realized that something was amiss. My carpet bags, lying open, were not in their usual corner. Elmer's law books and his Bible had been scrambled. And both his colt revolver and the ledger in which he had kept his diary were missing.

Frantically, I groped through my larger carpet bag for the leather pouch in which I carried the money and the New Testament given me by my father.

At first I was shocked, then outraged. I shook Mrs. Mueller awake and told her of my loss.

"With all these filthy savages about, it is no wonder. You had better report this to Captain McGee."

I found our leader overseeing the work of a wheelwright in tightening the rims on a set of wagon wheels.

Without changing his expression, he listened to my story, then said flatly, "You ought to have had better sense than to leave your money in your wagon."

His unsympathetic tone brought tears to my eyes.

"It had been there all along. And Mrs. Mueller was supposed to be keeping watch, but she went to sleep."

"Not much I can do to help you, little lady. The Indians figure the white man has took so much from them, they got a right to get some of it back."

"This leaves me in the lurch," I said.

"You mean you don't want a ride back early with the mail stage?"

"I don't know what I want."

"It's none of my business, but you ought to think of your child. It is a question of whether you want it to grow up back East or in Oregon. You got until tomorrow to decide what you want to do. As for getting your money back, I'll see what I can do, but I make you no promises."

This cold comfort came just as I had begun to think the man was human after all.

The last people I wanted to know of my loss were the Hixons. So I approached a seedy-looking livestock dealer who was wandering through our camp looking for trading opportunities.

Would he be interested in buying a pair of fine matched mules and a first-class wagon with all necessary equipment?

He allowed as how he might. He first examined the wagon and volunteered that it was too light to carry much on the trail. The tent might be worth a few dollars. As for the law books, who would want those for anything unless it would be to burn for a cook fire?

He went over the mules more carefully, looking in their mouths and declaring them to be several years older than Elmer had been led to think. He examined their legs and opined that Peter was developing splints and likely would go lame before many more miles. Paul had a spot on one eye that led him to fear the animal would soon lose his sight. And he confirmed my diagnosis that both mules needed new shoes "which will cost somebody a good twenty dollars."

"How much will you pay?" I asked with sinking hopes.

"For everything, except for your personal effects, I'd be stretching myself to pay fifty dollars."

Nowadays, I would know how to deal with such a skinflint but, green girl that I was in those days, I thought at first I might faint.

"There it is, Miss . . ."

"Mrs.," I corrected him. "Mrs. Elmer Hixon."

"Whoever. That is my best offer. Take it or leave it."

"I will have to let you know."

"Don't wait too long. I only got so much money to invest. By the way, I notice you are wearing a black armband. Lose a member of your family?"

"Yes, my husband."

He removed his sweat-stained hat in mock sympathy and said, "I am powerful sorry to hear it. Shame your wagons and mules ain't worth more."

"Perhaps they are worth more to me than they are to you."

I turned away, leaving him to go try to fleece someone else.

Despite my show of bravado, I felt about as hopeless and friendless as I had when my father packed me off to come west with the Hixons.

Speaking of whom, they had heard from one of the Mueller children of my robbery. Myrtle Mae, hiding her undoubted pleasure of my increased dependence, made a great display of sympathy. Her husband renewed his offer to advance the money to have my mules shod.

"How could I repay you?"

"I reckon we could start your period of indenture when we get to Oregon rather than from the time we signed it."

"Let me sleep on it."

Like everyone else, including myself, they assumed that one of the Indians had stolen my money and that recovery of it would be impossible.

Only later did I wonder why the thief or thieves had taken Elmer's ledger as well as the money, but had not touched my supply of sugar and coffee.

* * *

It did not take long for people in both of our camps to hear not only of my loss but also the dilemma I faced as to whether to continue to Oregon or turn back.

While the Hixons acted as if they were not aware of the choice I had to make, the Mueller children begged me to remain. Chester Peebles offered to take up a collection on my behalf, and I told him I was not interested in charity. The Cornish lads showed up with the suggestion that I forget about either returning east or going on to Oregon.

"Come to California with us, Miss Annie," the eldest said.

"Don't be silly, boys. I have no one to go to there."

"You don't need anyone. You'd have us. We'd look after you and your baby in time."

Captain McGee came by to say that he had reported Elmer's death to the commandant of Fort Laramie and had elicited from that gentleman a promise to have the wife of one of his officers look after me until the next mail stage was ready to depart.

"So what do you want to do, little lady? Continue on or turn back?"

"I don't know."

"You're going to have to decide by morning. I aim to get an early start."

With that he left me to stew in my indecision.

That night I waited until I thought Ralph Junior was asleep before I retired. But no, the little fellow was wide awake.

"Annie, you're not going to leave us, are you?"

"What makes you think I'd do that?"

"I heard Papa tell Mama she had to be extra nice to you so you won't try to leave us."

"You go to sleep and don't worry about such things. Whatever happens will be for the best."

That was an idiotic thing to say, for things often don't happen for the best, not unless you have the gumption to take events by the scruff of the neck and turn them to your advantage, something I was not as skillful at in those days as I have become in later years.

Honestly, as I lay there for hours, I did not know what I would do on the morrow. There were plusses and minuses to either turning back or continuing on to Oregon. I went to sleep, however, with the parting words of Captain McGee echoing in my head: "you ought to think of your child. Maybe it is a question of whether you want it to grow up back east or in Oregon."

Throughout the rest of the night, I was plagued by troubling dreams, one of which remains as vivid in my mind as when it occurred back in that June night of 1856. I was back in the tent with Elmer. He was lying there dead, with that peaceful look on his face, his eyes closed. As I felt for his pulse, suddenly his eyes opened and he grasped my wrist.

"We must go on," he said.

"Where?"

"To the Promised Land."

"How?"

"Seek, and ye shall find," he said, and then first his face and then the rest of him dissolved.

I can't say what finally decided me—Captain McGee's observation, Ralph Junior's plea, or that dream—but by the time Fort Laramie's morning gun boomed the next day, I was already milking Miss Mollie, having made no effort to stop Jacob Mueller from stowing my tent in the wagon and hitching up my still unshod mules.

3

With refitted wagons and refreshed animals, we covered a good twenty miles that first day out of Fort Laramie, following the regular Oregon Trail along a deeply rutted route which paralleled the North Platte several miles to the north.

At the end of the day we had reached the bank of yet another Cottonwood Creek where we found the camp of the same band of western-bound Mormons we had encountered the night of Elmer's death.

The near-sighted doctor who had visited Elmer came over to pay his respects. He introduced himself as Dr. Horace Dormsby and went on to explain that he had "joined the company of the saints" in Birmingham, England two years earlier and now was headed "for our new Zion in a new promised land."

He inquired as to my plans "now that your husband is no more."

Although I regarded this as none of his business, I bit my tongue and replied that I felt certain all would be well, surrounded as I was by loyal friends.

"All is well with them that trust in the Lord," he replied in an oily tone, then, after a moment's pause, added, "Don't hesitate to call on me for assistance if there should be anything you require on the trail or at Fort Bridger where we will remain for a few days. Anything at all."

I could think of nothing I would want from this unctuous zealot but thanked him for his concern nonetheless.

The following morning, instead of crossing Cottonwood Creek near our overnight camp site, Captain McGee led us several miles along the south bank to a less-crowded, easier crossing.

There we met two families, who we soon learned, were disgruntled Mormon converts returning to their homes in the East. Disillusioned by life in Salt Lake City, they were full of bitter stories of what they regarded as Brigham Young's dictatorial regime.

"It was like being a slave," one of the men said. "They work you for next to nothing on the wall they are putting around the town and they expect you to do their every bidding. I tell you, I rue the day we let them come into our kitchen with their book of Mormon and their talk of Joseph Smith. The whole thing is a bunch of humbug. I wish we had never left Ohio."

One of the women confided in Mrs. Mueller and me that she wanted to return east before her husband got it in his head to take on another wife.

Later we would meet other such small groups of ex-Mormons, some who had left Utah of their own volition and others "under denunciation" for failing to live up to the rules of the Latter Day Saints.

By the end of the next day, we had encountered two more lesser creeks and had passed over increasingly rough sage-brush country known as the Black Hills. On the following day, we crossed two more streams and found ourselves on a high plateau with fairly good grazing.

Although we had spent only three days out of Fort Laramie, the trail had proved difficult west of Cottonwood Creek, leading as it did across numerous small streams and following rocky, gullied terrain. So, on the fourth day, a Sunday, when Captain McGee called an early halt to rest our teams and recreate ourselves, no one contested his decision.

There was much talk of a nearby natural wonder which could not be seen from the trail. According to Chester Peebles, it was a natural bridge through which flowed a gorgeous stream, the little La Prele River. As we were all coated with dust and sweaty from our travel and eager to see this so-called bridge, he arranged that the men should descend the bluff overlooking the stream to swim while we womenfolk prepared a dinner, after which it would be our time to visit the creek.

In answer to queries as to whether the womenfolk would be safe bathing by themselves in Indian country, Peebles assured us we would be in no danger.

"Indians never go there, I understand. Seems that years ago a hunting party got hit by lightning down at the natural bridge and, being the superstitious savages that they are, they think there is a curse on the place." He added with that crooked grin, "Besides, I expect you would be a lot safer without menfolk about."

Speaking of whom, they soon returned to our camp, refreshed by their swim, ravenously hungry and full of praise for the beauty of the spot they had just visited.

After they had eaten and we had cleaned the dishes, Captain McGee and others organized an antelope hunt off toward the Platte which lay about ten miles north of the trail at that point. With the other females, I walked to the top of the bluff overlooking the creek and descended with them to one of the most lovely spots we had seen. The natural bridge was merely an abutment of the rocky bluff past which the little river flowed. My disappointment at its appearance was more than compensated by the picturesque wooded meadow along the river bottom.

Because of my condition, I was chary of bathing but not so the other women. So I withdrew to prop myself against a box elder tree while first one and then another of our women and girls disrobed and, squealing at the chill of the water, waded into the creek. It was amusing to watch these women, with whom I had travelled for six weeks, stark naked, shedding their modesty almost as quickly as they had their dresses, petticoats, bonnets and the bloomers many had fashioned from skirts. Some, most notably Mrs. Mueller, sported enormous breasts, while those of others hung like half-empty sacks.

What did men see in our sex that so excited them, I wondered as they splashed water and laughed like school girls.

It was delightful sitting in that idyllic spot, weary from the descent down the little bluff and drowsy from our large mid-day meal. Before many minutes passed, I had fallen asleep.

I awoke, perhaps an hour later, to the sound only of the water rushing under the arch of the natural bridge and the twittering of birds in the bushes that lined the stream. The women were all gone. The sun was still high in the afternoon sky. And that water looked so inviting.

No one to see me now, I thought, and rash girl that I was, I stripped off my dress and my undergarments, and put them in a pile under a bush, then waded into the creek, first up to my ankles, then my knees and finally, in a pool near the middle, I lowered my swollen belly into the icy water and sat down.

With the water now up to my shoulders, I luxuriated in the delicious coolness. I turned my face up to a cloudless sky and let my hair cascade back into the current. I was caught up in a rare feeling of freedom from concern over my future or that of the baby in my womb. The water seemed to wash away my resentment of my father and of Myrtle Mae Hixon alike. Life was good, after all. And, although it might be irksome to be indentured for three years, young as I was, surely there would be time ahead for me to find the right man to marry and to pick up my life as a school teacher in a land far removed from my native country.

Covered with goose pimples, but feeling like a new woman, I eased myself to my feet and headed for the bush where I had concealed my clothing.

As I scrambled over the smooth rocks, my head down the better to find secure footing, a man's voice called out from the bank, "Did we enjoy our little swim, Mrs. Hixon?"

Aghast, I looked up to see Bart Corbett standing on the bank. Holding my clothing, he said, "Looking for this, perhaps?"

4

To this day, when I think back across the years to that awful moment, my blood runs cold. I came very near to fainting, then recovered and put one arm over my breasts and the hand of the other over my private parts. Then, to further conceal my nakedness, I sat down in the water.

"It won't do you any good to try to hide. Besides I have seen everything you got from up on the bluff."

He was a big man to begin with, but he seemed a giant standing on the bank with booted feet wide set and a truly evil grin on his face.

"What do you want?" I managed through chattering teeth.

"Where is the money?"

"What money?"

"Don't play dumb with me. I want the money that little bastard you called a husband took off me back in St. Joe."

"There isn't any money."

"Oh, but there has got to be at least several hundred dollars of it left."

"All the money I know about was that given me by my father. And it was stolen from my wagon back at Fort Laramie."

"You mean this?"

From one of his vest pockets he removed the leather pouch my father had given me.

"You low-life scoundrel," I said. "You were the thief."

"I was only looking for what was rightfully mine. When I couldn't find it, I took this as a down payment."

"Just wait until Captain McGee hears of this."

"He ain't going to hear about it. I can keep you quiet."

"Don't be silly. Now put my clothes down and go away or I will scream for help."

"A lot of good that will do you. Everybody is either back at camp or off hunting miles from here. So let's stick to the subject. Where is the rest of the money? I know you hid it somewhere. I didn't have time to look as careful as I wished."

"I swear to God, I have no idea where Elmer's money went. Please just put my clothes down and go away."

"Nobody makes a fool of Bart Corbett and gets away with it. Your husband and you have heaped insult on injury upon me and I aim to square accounts here and now."

"How can I square accounts when you already have taken away every penny I owned?"

"Ah, 'this lovely flower from North Carolina who has been cast upon our Missouri shore' there may be a way to set things right between us, besides the money."

Recognizing the passage from Elmer's diary, I half rose from the water in my indignation, then, remembering my nakedness, sat back down.

"You took his ledger, too. Why?"

"I figured he might have made a record about the money. Sure enough, he wrote he had withdrawn it from the bank. It was the day before you left St. Joe. And you are trying to tell me you don't know where it is? You must take me for a fool."

"I take you for a blackguard. This has gone on long enough. So, once more I implore you to go away and leave me in peace. If you do so promptly, I will say nothing of this to Captain McGee or anyone else."

"So now we are imploring. First don't you want to know what you can do to help square up the matter of the missing money?"

"What more can you want of me?"

"Anybody that would give it to a little wormy fellow with a gimpy leg, surely wouldn't mind a go with a real man."

He paused and said with a smile, "I would never tell any one. And we could set the matter of the money aside for the time being, anyway. So how about it, my little flower from North Carolina?"

"I would rather die."

"Refuse me and you just might do that."

He drew a narrow-bladed knife from his belt.

"There is no getting out of this for you. Either you come out of the creek and let me show you what a real man is like, or they'll find you here in the morning with your throat cut."

"They would hang you for murder."

"First they would have to find me. I left my horse up on the top of the bluff, saddled and ready to ride. By tomorrow morning I can be miles away."

Only then did I begin to weep, but stopped when, through my tears, I saw the look of satisfaction that had come over his face. In a very sensual way, this wicked man was savoring his power over me.

"You don't really have much choice, do you?"

Desperately I cast about for what to do. I considered screaming but that would simply cause him to come into the water with his knife. Besides, he probably was right in saying nobody would hear my cries. I considered also the possibility of fleeing to the opposite bank, but he could easily overtake me if he cared to get his fancy boots wet.

"What about it? Just give me a few minutes of your time, and I guarantee you will thank me for what I can show you."

"You have the advantage of me."

"Of course, I do. So you might as well come on out and let's get on with it."

"What I meant was I am naked but you still have on your clothes."

"You want to see what you have to look forward to, is that it?"

"You said you were a real man. Prove it."

"No harm in that I reckon."

Whereupon, he threw my clothing on the ground, and removed his snakeskin boots, then his coat, vest, and shirt and, finally, his trousers and underdrawers. Still wearing his broad-brimmed hat and holding that knife, but otherwise naked, he waited for me to come out of the water.

Looking back, I marvel at the recklessness of what I was doing, not with any definite plan in mind but just to gain time. Apparently Corbett had been sexually stimulated either by seeing me naked or, more likely, by his sense of power over me. At any rate, his male member was standing upright. It was a fat, stubby thing protruding from the bottom of a forest of hair that began across his chest and ran clear down his belly into his crotch.

My legs trembling, I crawled onto the bank and looked up into that evil face.

"Ready to get on with it?"

"Not on the ground, please."

"There ain't no bed. Look, I'll show you how it's done dog fashion, if you don't already know."

"At least spread my dress out on the ground."

Still holding his knife, he said, "Spread it yourself and be quick about it. We ain't got all day."

I flapped my dress out over the stony bank and then, still playing for time, said, "Wait a minute. I have to pee."

"For God's sake, go ahead and pee."

"Not here. In the bushes."

"Behind that bush then, but no tricks."

If only I could get his knife, I thought, as I headed for the bush. In doing so I stepped, inadvertently, on Corbett's vest which lay across his jacket. It felt to my bare foot as though there were a rock under it.

"Mind where you step, you little bitch, and get on with your piss. You are trying my patience."

He was standing between me and the creek now, facing west, his nasty thing still stiffly elevated. He had lowered his hat brim against the rays of the afternoon sun which reflected off his stilletto.

As I moved away, the gleam of mother of pearl protruding from his vest pocket caught my eye. In less time than it takes to write this, I stooped and snatched up his derringer pistol.

"Hey, what are you doing?"

As he started toward me, I cocked the little weapon and pointed it at him.

"What in the hell do you think you are doing?"

"Stop, or I will shoot."

He laughed. "We are playing that game again, are we? The joke is on you this time. That gun can't fire. There ain't no cap on it."

Yet, he did not come nearer, just held out his hand.

"So why don't you hand it over and let's get down to our business?"

"Keep away from me," I said.

"Don't make me hurt you. Give me the gun."

He took a step forward and I, one backward, still holding the little weapon in front of me. That was when I noticed that his member no longer was standing at attention, so to speak.

"You are wasting your time pointing that thing at me. I never carry a capped pistol. It is too dangerous."

"It looks to me like you are no longer up to the business you had in mind anymore, Mister Real Man. Let's forget the whole thing, shall we?"

That was a foolish thing to say. If I had not done so, he might have backed away and left me be, but my remark seemed to inflame his male pride, about which I knew far less then than I do today.

He growled like a wounded bear and lunged for me, one hand brandishing his knife and the other outstretched, reaching for the gun he claimed would not shoot.

I closed my eyes and pulled the trigger. Instead of a futile click, the little derringer seemed to explode in my hand. I could not believe that so small a device could produce such a deafening blast.

Opening my eyes, I saw that Corbett had halted in his tracks less than a yard away, his face frozen in an expression which I took to be one of amazement.

I dropped the pistol and backed away, expecting him to descend on me with his knife. After a moment, he took a half step toward me and gurgled "Why . . . Why did you . . ."

Only then did I see a red hole gleaming through the thick brown fur covering his upper abdomen.

He did not fall. He just dropped his knife and clutched both hands over the wound and sagged, first down on one knee, then the other. Finally, to both my horror and relief, he slumped forward onto his face, his legs doubled up under his torso and his milky white buttocks pointing skyward.

5

Without pausing to look further at the crumpled form, I scooped up my clothing and shoes and ran toward the path that led up the little bluff overlooking the creek.

Once out of sight of the spot where I had left Corbett, I stopped and hurriedly dressed. Then, with my damp hair bundled up under my bonnet, my breath coming in gasps and my heart pounding so I feared it would burst, I climbed to the top of the bluff. Across the rough, rocky plateau, I could see our wagons drawn up in two circles. Plumes of smoke already rose from the camp fires in preparation for an early supper.

Off to my right, I saw two horses. One was Corbett's roan. The other I recognized as the gray gelding of Captain McGee. A moment later, McGee himself arose from his squatting position. Apparently he had been examining the hobbles on Corbett's horse.

He waved his hat at me, mounted his horse and cantered over to where I stood.

"What in hell's name are you doing out here all alone, little lady?"

The only answer I could make was to burst into hysterical sobs, so violent that my body shook and my bonnet fell off to reveal my wet hair.

He dismounted and put his hands on my shoulders.

"What is wrong with you?"

"C . . . C . . . Corbett," I stammered.

"What about him?"

"Down there. He, he tried to . . . to . . ." I said, then knelt and put my face in my hands.

McGee left me kneeling while he fumbled in his saddle bag and produced a flask.

"Take a swallow of this and get control of yourself."

That was the first time I had ever tasted ardent spirits. The brandy burned my throat, making me gasp.

"Take a deep breath. Relax and talk slow. Now what about Corbett?"

It took several minutes more for me to calm down enough haltingly to pour out my story. The longer I spoke, the darker McGee's face grew. When, at last, I had told him everything, he said, "So the son-of-a-bitch tried to violate you?"

"He said he would cut my throat if I did not submit."

"And you shot him with his own pistol?"

"He claimed it wouldn't fire."

"Think you killed him?"

"I didn't stay to see."

"Excuse my language, but I should never have let that bastard join our party. Well, if he ain't dead, he'll wish he was when I get through with him."

"What shall I do? What will the others say when they hear of this?"

"We'll cross that bridge when we come to it. What I want you to do is pull yourself together. Go back to camp like nothing happened. Stop and gather some flowers on the way. Tell them you been wandering about and lost track of the time. But whatever you do, don't mention Corbett's name. You understand?"

I nodded and asked, "What are you going to do?"

"Don't know yet. Whatever, don't say a word to anyone about this. Can you keep your mouth shut?"

"I think so."

"Don't just think so. Say absolutely nothing unless I ask you to. Now, you want another shot of this snake bite medicine?"

I shook my head. He put his big hands under my arms, lifted me to my feet and turned me toward our camp.

"Don't walk too fast. Keep calm. Just gather flowers while I go and investigate this here situation."

Between that draught of brandy and the confident manner of Captain

McGee, I recovered a measure of my composure, enough to do his bidding.

Myrtle Mae, who was one of the few women who had declined to visit the creek, demanded, "Where in heaven's name have you been? The others said you left them long ago."

"I thought the family might enjoy these," I said as I thrust my clump of flowers into her hand.

"Flowers are pretty but they don't get cows milked. Besides, you ought to be more careful. You could have got into trouble out there by yourself."

"I suppose you are right. I could have."

Before she could say more, I went to milk Miss Mollie. I needed to lean my head against her warm flank for comfort and to try to make sense out of the horrible thing that had occurred down on the bank of that pretty creek.

As my mind went back and forth, it occurred to me how stupid I had been not to have taken back my purse when I had the opportunity. Well, no use crying over spilt milk, I thought. I had been lucky to escape with my life.

How I managed to keep my air of calm during our supper, I don't know. We were eating our slam johns and stew when I saw Captain McGee riding across the plain, not from the direction of the creek, as I would have expected, but from the east. From the pommel of his saddle there hung two jack rabbits. As he passed our camp, I tried to catch his eye for some sign of what he had found, but he continued back to the camp of the California gang without a glance at me.

I had already gone to bed in my tent when I heard Chester Peebles talking to the Hixons and the Muellers, telling them of Corbett's failure to return to camp.

"His friends are worried about him. For my part, I hope he has decided to ride off and join another train. That fellow is nothing but bad news."

"Anybody going to look for him?" Mr. Mueller asked.

"Too dark now. If he isn't back by morning, Zeb will have to decide what is to be done about it."

I slept not a wink that night, reliving the experience by the creek over and over, stewing over what I might have done differently, blaming myself, as females are wont to do, for separating myself from the other women and for being foolish enough to stay and swim alone.

Then, I thought, if it had not happened there, something equally bad might have occurred later on the trail. Obviously the man had a festering grudge against me. Then came the chilling fear that he might not have been that seriously wounded, that he might recover.

At dawn Corbett's horse, despite its hobbles, managed to make its awkward way back to our camp. Captain McGee immediately ordered search parties to fan out in all directions.

It seemed curious to me that he directed Corbett's cronies and the Cornish lads to go and search the creek bottom near the natural bridge, while Peebles was ordered to lead a search party toward the North Platte, and he himself led a group back over the trail we had come the previous day.

Myrtle Mae was indignant that so much trouble was being taken for so dissolute a man and asked Mrs. Mueller if she did not agree.

"He is a human being, after all," that good woman replied.

It did not take long for his friends to find Corbett. They announced their discovery by firing their guns from atop the bluff as a signal to the other search parties.

A bit later, one of them galloped up to our camp to report, "Found him lying beside the creek, stripped of his clothes. It was horrible. Looks like it was murder."

My blood really ran cold at that remark. Foolishly I blurted out "Who do you think shot him?"

"Oh, he wasn't shot. He was killed with an arrow and it had to be Indians. And the worst part was they cut his throat and scalped him as well. Must have stole his clothes while they was at it. It's a wonder they didn't take his horse, too."

"Scalped him?" I asked in puzzlement.

"Lifted his hair right off his head. Awful sight. There poor Bart was lying on his back with that arrow sticking right out of his chest and most of his scalp missing. Where is McGee so's I can tell him?"

A further fusillade of shots into the air attracted the other search parties to return. The expression on Captain McGee's face did not change as he listened to the report, but Peebles looked puzzled.

"You say it was Indians that killed him?" he asked.

"Come see for yourself. Who else would kill a man with a bow and arrow, scalp him and steal his clothes?"

"Indians are supposed to be afraid of that spot," Peebles said.

Captain McGee interrupted to say, "Maybe the word ain't got around to all of them. Anyhow, let's get shovels and go take care of the mess."

This will have to be reported back to Fort Laramie, but Chester, you can take depositions from them that found him later. We are wasting daylight here when we should be back on the trail. You stay here, Chester, and make sure everybody is ready to set out when we are done with this business."

6

There remained some 300 miles to be covered before we reached Fort Bridger where the California gang, under Captain McGee, and our party, under Chester Peebles, were to part company for our respective destinations.

Those 300 miles would have been the most interesting of the trip for me had it not been for the awful memory that weighed on my mind and heart of having killed a fellow human being, however despicable he may have been. During the Civil War a few years later, men were slain in droves, among them many of my relatives back in North Carolina. As horrible as that slaughter was, I doubt that any soldier, Yankee or Rebel, experienced the strange mixture of remorse and relief that I felt. Had there been anything else I could have done? Yes, I could have submitted to Corbett and allowed him to ravish me, but then I would have felt a different kind of remorse and shame. Or, I might have merely wounded him, but then all would have known the circumstances and some would have questioned my virtue, as folks often do in such cases. And Corbett was capable of claiming that I had trapped him into a rendezvous, yes, and would have produced friends who would support his lies.

Each night I slept fitfully, often awakening in a cold sweat from the same nightmare in which Corbett stood, naked, towering above me and demanding that I submit. My heart pounding, I would lie still, forcing myself to breathe quietly and give thanks that I had been spared from physical harm and to pray that the true circumstances of Corbett's death would remain unknown to anyone but Captain McGee.

Not once during the next two and a half weeks before we reached Fort Bridger, did he speak to me. Rather than reassuring me, his silence preyed on my mind, making me wonder whether he felt that the encounter with Corbett might have been my fault; that somehow I was not as innocent as I had claimed.

It was plain to me that Peebles had been puzzled by the reported circumstances of Corbett's death. He did interview the men who had found the nude, mutilated corpse and had written a record of their accounts to be posted back to Fort Laramie. I knew this because the Cornish lads talked of the interviews, describing over and over the sight upon which they had stumbled back there beside that beautiful creek.

"Mister Peebles, he must have asked us a hundred times if we seen any hoof prints or signs of a fight and so on, like he thought we was lying. But all we could do was tell what we seen. And in truth, we had little time to go poking about. Captain McGee set us straightway to getting him deep under ground."

So, even though he was dead, the spirit of Bart Corbett still hung over our party as we passed up to the point where we were to cross the North Platte, on a bridge owned by a pair of brothers who were getting filthy rich off the traffic going in both directions.

A booming little community had sprung up around the bridge. Occupying the several log buildings were a grocery store, wagon outfitters, blacksmith shops and so on. A small company of the U.S. Cavalry was stationed there to keep an eye on the Crow and Sioux Indians of the area.

While waiting our turn to cross the bridge, I gave in to Ralph Hixon's renewed offer to have the paper-thin shoes of my two mules replaced by a nearby blacksmith. At that point penniless, I saw no alternative to my continuing on to Oregon and thought what did it matter whether I served three years as their servant or a month or so more.

So, onward we plodded, leaving the Platte River behind and passing over a steep, sandy divide aptly named Prospect Hill, and down into the valley of the Sweetwater River. Now we were in clear sight of snow-capped mountains off to the northwest. Captain McGee reissued his stern warning not to water our stock from any spring unless he or Peebles declared it to be free of alkali, which was especially deadly for oxen.

His warning was given extra weight by the scores of skeletons of oxen that lay alongside the trail. Also littering the landscape were heavy items: cast iron stoves, anvils, oaken bureaus, bedsteads, etc., relics of wagon trains from the great treks of 1850 to '54. At one point we came upon a party of Mormons gathering up metal items to be hauled back to Salt Lake City to be refashioned into tools and such.

At the famed Independence Rock, that great rounded lump of stone overlooking the trail, all the men, even Mr. Mueller and Ralph Hixon, took the time to scramble up its side and carve or paint their names alongside those of hundreds of previous emigrants.

Ralph Hixon explained that the formation had been given its name because some earlier emigrants had celebrated the Fourth of July here and that subsequent parties sought to reach this point no later than that same date.

"And here we are a good two weeks ahead of schedule," he pointed out. "Didn't I tell you we were hooking up with the right folks, Myrtle Mae? Ain't this all wonderful. And the book says we are to see even greater wonders before we reach Fort Bridger."

He, or his guide book, were right. Even I, in my befuddled, fearful state of mind over the Corbett incident, marvelled at the cleft called Devil's Gate through which the Sweetwater flowed, but which the trail bypassed. And a few miles farther, we camped near a marshy area beneath whose surface leftover winter ice still lay. And off to the northwest loomed the snow-capped mountain peaks which represented to me the true West.

So we plodded onward, the trail mounting so gradually that we were not concious of the increasing altitude, on toward the Continental Divide and the famed South Pass. No longer did we see huge herds of buffalo, prairie dog villages or Indian teepees. Now we depended on the branches of greasewood and sage brush for fires. And water left in buckets developed a skim of ice overnight, although the days were warm enough. Nosebleeds became common, a side effect of the higher elevation of the trail.

Some in our party wanted to pause on July 4 to celebrate Independence Day, but Captain McGee decreed otherwise, and so we pressed on to the South Pass. Like many emigrants before me, I was disappointed by its appearance. Far from a spectacular gash in the Rockies, it was simply a thirty-mile wide saddle in an unimpressive mountain range.

As I shivered around our evening fire, Ralph Hixon consulted his guide book and announced, "Says here if you was to pour a barrel of water on the ground, half would end up in the Mississippi and the Gulf of Mexico while the other half would end up in the Colorado River and the Pacific Ocean. We are near to a mile and a half above sea level here. Ain't that something, Myrtle Mae?"

She replied, "I think that would be a great waste of water."

How could I listen to that woman's stupid remarks and put up with her bossiness for three more years?

However, my mood began to improve once we were beyond the South Pass and had made our way over barren country down to the Big Sandy River. Like the Sweetwater and the Platte, it served as a highway for the settlement of the West. With the Continental Divide behind us, I thought of it as a barrier protecting me from any evil consequences of my having killed Bart Corbett.

* * *

The Green River was the last great water barrier we were all to pass over as one group. Soon half of us would head for Oregon and the others, for California. Fed by lesser streams that flowed down from the snow-capped mountains to the north and east, the Green River was swift and icy cold.

After some spirited haggling with the operators of a ferry at the Lombard Crossing, we paid our tolls and after several hours of waiting in line, crossed to the other side and pressed on toward Fort Bridger, sixty-odd miles to the southwest.

Chester Peebles warned us against giving offense to the Mormons who had taken control of Fort Bridger the previous year from the founder and longtime proprietor, the legendary mountain man, Jim Bridger.

"Cousin Zeb and old Bridger used to be as thick as thieves. There was some sort of conflict between Bridger and Brigham Young. The Mormons twisted the arms of Bridger and his partner, Vasquez, to sell them the fort and about twenty square miles of land around it. Zeb thinks Bridger was hornswaggled in the deal but he is not exactly an objective observer. Anyway, mind your p's and q's when we get there. Don't get on the wrong side of the Mormon militia."

The beautiful country through which we passed from the Green River down to Ft. Bridger, populated mainly by members of the Shoshone or Snake tribe, was also the home of dozens of old mountain men who, after the collapse of the beaver trade, had settled down with Indian wives. As we were to learn, a great deal of animosity existed between these old fur traders and the Mormons Brigham Young was sending east from Salt Lake City to colonize the lands they had procured from Jim Bridger.

As I got it from further listening to Peebles, Bridger, fearful of meeting foul play from the Mormons, had left matters in the hands of Vasquez and had settled with his Indian wife somewhere in Missouri, from whence he had ventured to Washington to lobby the government for the recovery of his lands around the fort which he had established way back in 1843 (when it then was in Mexican territory) to capitalize on the emigrant trade.

I asked Peebles about Bridger's partner, Vasquez. He explained that whereas Bridger was illiterate, Vasquez not only was well educated but also enjoyed the trust of Brigham Young and other Mormon leaders.

"Fact is, although he lives in St. Louis just now, Vasquez still owns an interest in a mercantile establishment in Salt Lake City. I wouldn't tell you this if you weren't going with me to Oregon, but one reason Cousin Zeb plans to go through Salt Lake City on his way to California is that he is carrying some messages from Bridger, something about the rest of the money the Saints owe him for his land. Otherwise Zeb would conduct his gang up to Soda Springs or Fort Hall with us before heading west for California. Now don't you go talking about this. Zeb doesn't want the Mormons to know what he is about."

At last we reached Ft. Bridger. The fort itself, now manned by members of the Mormon militia, looked to be a far more military establishment than either of those maintained by the U.S. Army at Fort Laramie and Kearney. A wooden palisade of about 100 feet square, plus a large enclosed corral, occupied the center of a richly grassed meadow through which several swift little streams flowed. There was the usual conglomeration of sutlers, huts and blacksmith shops surrounding the fort and, as usual, the grounds beyond were dotted with Indian teepees, mostly those of the dominant Shoshones but with a sprinkling of Utes and Arapaho.

Once again, you could buy just about anything you had the money to afford, except, as far as I could see, the services of prostitutes. The Mormons would not tolerate that line of work. Since we were well ahead of our schedule, Captain McGee decreed that we should have a three-day layover at Ft. Bridger. I expected this to be a three-day period of rest and relief from the anxiety that had followed me like a dark cloud since my killing of Corbett the previous month.

But as the poet wrote, "The best laid plans of mice and men gang aft agley."

7

Up to now, I have said little of the new life taking form in my womb. Even though its conception had upset my life, I nurtured the kindliest of feelings for my baby. At night, to take my mind off the Bart Corbett episode and the ignominy of having to remain with the Hixons for three years of servitude, I let my imagination wander to what my child might be like.

If it was a girl, I would name her Mamie, after Uncle John's sweet wife. She would be reared as a lady and be given as good an education as I could provide.

If it was a boy, his name should be Walter, after my favorite author, Sir Walter Scott. I would expect him to be strong and handsome like Billy Joe Duncan. And in either case, I reckoned that I could find myself a suitable husband to help me rear my child. After all, everyone except the Hixons and Mrs. Mueller assumed that the baby I was carrying within me had been fathered by Elmer Hixon.

That first evening outside of Ft. Bridger, as I was milking Miss Mollie, I was startled by an English voice saying behind me, "Mrs. Hixon, pardon me for intruding, but I wonder if I might have a word with you in private."

Turning my head, I look up into the solemn, but handsome face of Dr. Dormsby, the Mormon doctor who had attended Elmer the night before he died.

"It is a free country. What do you want to say to me?"

"As you know, I am a member of the Church of the Latter Day Saints. And, as you might have observed, I have a wife who shares my faith."

"I have seen Mrs. Dormsby," I said, thinking as I did what a browbeaten, sad little woman she appeared.

"And you may have observed that we have no children."

"I had not given that fact any thought. What has that to do with me?"

He pushed his spectacles back against the bridge of his nose and looked about as if to see whether we might be overheard, then continued, saying, "I have noted that you are a young woman of spirit and enterprise. No, no, let me finish. Through inquiries, I have learned also that you are in some way indentured to the family with whom you travel. Please, let me continue. It is obvious that you, a young widow, are with child and therefore in need of protection. If reports in your camp are true, you are less than happy with your circumstances and prospects."

Beginning to get his drift, I stood up and looked him squarely in the eyes which, magnified by his glasses, seemed enormous.

"My circumstances are my business. What have they to do with you?"

"I have discussed the situation with Mrs. Dormsby and she has amiably agreed that we would like very much for you to join our family."

"You mean leave the service of the Hixons and enter into your own?"

"You misundertand, dear Mrs. Hixon. We do not wish you to become our servant. Dear me, no. We wish you and your unborn child to join our family. To become a Dormsby."

"You mean adopt me as a daughter?"

"No, no, not a daughter. Let me explain. Our faith, as revealed to the prophet Joseph Smith, permits, nay in some cases even encourages that in certain circumstances, our members take second and even third wives."

Ever the one with a sharp tongue, I replied, "How about women? Does your faith allow them to have more than one husband?"

He let a faint smile flicker across his face before continuing in a serious vein, "No, it is a responsibility . . . note that I do not say privilege . . . a responsibility, you might even say a burden, that is laid upon our masculine members, we being the stronger of the sexes."

"I have heard that your religion has some unusual beliefs and practices, but fail to see what concern this should be to me."

"I propose that you be sealed to me as my wife. Hear me out. Mrs. Dormsby has had three miscarriages in our ten years of marriage, so we have no hopes of children of our own. Your baby and any subsequent offspring we might produce would bear the family name, and I would rear them as my own. Ah, do not turn away. I am serious."

For a moment I was tempted to empty my pail of milk over his head as I had done to Elmer, but restrained myself and replied, "But I am a Methodist. We do not believe in polygamy."

"As a matter of fact, Mrs. Dormbsy and I were members of a Wesleyan congregation ourselves, until we were converted."

"Be that as it may, Doctor Dormsby, the last thing on earth I would want to become is a second wife, Mormon or no Mormon."

"I apologise for bringing up the matter so abruptly. Please do not be hasty in your response. I understand that your party will remain here for a day or so. While you are pondering the matter, please let me lend you this copy of the Book of Mormon."

Without thinking, I accepted the proffered volume.

"Read for yourself the grand message it contains. Then, if you like, tomorrow, we can talk together with Mrs. Dormsby."

"Have I not made it clear. . . ."

"That you are under bond to the Hixons? Don't give that a second thought. I have more than ample means to compensate them for the loss of your service. Here in the midst of so many of my brethren, they will be helpless to refuse a reasonable offer. I really think you would make a fine wife and I flatter myself that you would not find me an unsuitable husband."

Too taken aback to reply, I clasped the Book of Mormon and, in disbelief, stared at him.

Without waiting for a further response, he turned and strode back to his own camp.

*   *   *

As I carried the pail of milk back to our camp site, I did not know whether to laugh or to become angry. Dormsby had to be in his late thirties, twice my age at least. If he had been a few years younger, were not already married, and would have shaved off those ridiculous side whiskers, oh yes, and if he had remained a Methodist, he might have won me over. After all I was not in a position to be choosy. And he would have been an improvement over Elmer Hixon.

By that time, Mrs. Mueller and I had grown so close that she could read my moods. After supper that evening, she drew me aside to inquire if something were troubling me.

"I'll tell you if you promise not to laugh."

Despite her pledge, that good, hearty woman had to clamp her hand over her mouth to choke back her mirth as I related Doctor Dormsby's marriage proposal.

"And he was serious?" she asked as she wiped the tears from her eyes.

"Dead serious."

"Then that explains why he came around asking questions about you."

"I hope you did not tell him everything."

"About the father of your baby? Oh, dear Annie. Not even my Herman have I told of that. Your secret is safe with me."

"How did he know that I am unhappy about my arrangement with the Hixons?"

"I was not the only one he spoke to. I saw him talking with Mrs. Courtenay. She took her nose out of the air long enough for a long chat."

"Who else?"

"He spoke to Mrs. Hixon, but only briefly. No, I expect it was the high and mighty English acting woman that informed on you."

She paused, tried to compose herself, but then gave up and broke into hearty laughter.

"You promised not to laugh."

"Can't help myself. First an Indian chief's son and now a Mormon doctor. I wonder who it will be next. Oh, dear, Annie, you have made me wet my drawers again."

"It serves you right for making fun of me."

She was still laughing when I left her to walk over to the Courtenay's campfire, where Opal was frying bacon.

"Mrs. Courtenay be in the tent laying down. Said she don't want to be disturbed."

"Who is it, Opal?" Mrs. Courtenay's voice sounded from the tent.

Her long, blond tresses hanging down around her shoulders, the actress opened the flap of her tent.

"It's me, Mrs. Courtenay. I wish to speak to you."

"I can see that it is you. Come in and let's hear what you have to say."

I have read how ornately Bedouin sheiks furnish their tents on the Arabian desert. The actors' tent put me in mind of such. The earth was covered by a rug. There were two large canvas cots, and the walls were adorned by wigs and various costumes.

She took one camp stool and pointed me to the other.

"Homer has taken the children fishing. I have been trying, without success, to rest. He insists on our staging another of those vulgar minstrel shows tomorrow night. You can't imagine how demeaning I find it to take part in such awful things. Our old friends in London would be appalled if they knew. But Homer thinks that is the only fare this crowd would appreciate. I can't wait until we reach San Francisco where the audiences are said to be more sophisticated. Ah well, enough of my complaints. What did you wish to say to me, my dear girl?"

"It is about Doctor Dormsby," I began and then, as quietly and as calmly as I could, I told about his proposal.

She listened with a half smile on her face. When I paused, getting up my courage to demand to hear just what she had said to the man, she spoke.

"So that is why that odious little quacksalver was after, with his inquiries."

"Yes, and I want to know just what you told him."

"My dear girl, I told him simply that you struck my husband and me as a young woman of considerable spirit and, judging from your success with your open air classes, a person of above average intellect. I am not a gossip, child. I did not put him up to his proposal."

"How did he know of my indenture with the Hixons and my dissatisfaction with my circumstances?"

"Anyone could have told him that. You are unhappy, are you not? And not just because of the unfortunate death of your young husband."

This was said with a knowing gleam in her brilliant gray eyes.

"I have little cause to be happy, Mrs. Courtenay. However, I did not realize that you had taken any notice of me."

"Actually I noticed you in the audience aboard the steamboat from St. Louis to St. Joseph. And I recognized you later at the meeting hall, when your husband spoke up so readily to that uncouth Captain McGee. Or was he then your husband?"

"He was, but no one knew it."

"And how about on the boat? Were you married to him then?"

"I did not meet Elmer until we reached St. Joe, but what is the purpose of your questions?"

She looked at me, again in that knowing way.

"And that was in March. Your baby is due . . . when?"

"I am not certain, and besides, I don't think it has anything to do with this matter."

"This matter being?"

"That Mormon doctor's wanting to take me on as his second wife. That is preposterous, and I want to know how he came to such a notion."

"So you prefer to proceed to Oregon as a bond servant of that dreadful woman with whom you are traveling. You poor, naive girl. Are you sure those are your only choices?"

"What others could there be?"

"I will see what my husband thinks. Forgive me, but what is the amount of your indenture?"

"I am not certain. I have never seen the document. It was drawn up by my father. He is a justice of the peace."

"Why would he do such a thing? Were you terribly unhappy at home?"

"It was not my idea."

She raised her eyebrows, seemed about to ask another question, then paused before saying, "Curious. So go about your business and give me time to talk to my husband. Now I must study my lines for that dreadful minstrel show. By the way, your husband displayed a genuine flair for the theatrical, setting aside his strange accent. He was a curious young man. Did you love him very much?"

"I was beginning to a little," I said, and, to head off more questions, thanked her for her time and returned to my own tent.

* * *

Ever since Captain McGee, following Elmer's death, had broached the possibility of my returning to the East, Myrtle Mae Hixon had been riding me with a light rein, so to speak. I realized that once our parties had divided and we were headed north to Fort Hall and thence on to Oregon, minus the California gang and Captain McGee, that she probably would try to reassert her old authority over me.

I felt helpless. Bart Corbett had stolen my little cache of money and, I presumed, had spent it on drink or gambling. The value of my wagon and mules was low anyway. If I sold them, I would be thrown more completely back upon dependence on the Hixons. By now I had grown so large about the middle that I waddled rather than walked with my former girlish gait.

The departure of the California gang for Salt Lake City would deprive me of the services of the Cornish lads, leaving me to depend on Jacob Mueller alone.

Despite my bleak prospects, however, I had no intention of accepting Doctor Dormsby's offer to become his number two wife.

I did take time to browse through the Book of Mormon he had forced upon me. In fact I was turning through its pages the next morning when Chester Peebles passed. In his usual nosey Yankee way, he inquired how I had come by the volume.

"Doctor Dormsby lent it to me."

"What do you think of it?"

"I was happy with my New Testament, but it was stolen along with my money back at Fort Laramie. Have you read it?"

He squatted on the ground Indian fashion and took the book from my hand, which at first annoyed me.

"I have dipped about in it, myself," he said. "Strikes me as being awfully full of 'And it came to passes' and names made up to sound

Biblical. Besides that, if there once was a great latter day Christian civilization in North America, where are the relics? We know mastodons once roamed this land. We have found their bones. The Indians have occupied North America since long before the time of Jesus, I should think. None of them, as far as I know, has ever spoken of an early Christian empire as the Mormons believe. As a Unitarian, I have my own doubts about the divinity of Jesus and all that business of the Trinity, although I would be the last to deny Christ's role as a messenger of the Almighty. But this Mormon theology strains all credulity."

It has always been my nature to challenge strongly expressed, dogmatic statements such as Peebles was making. So I countered with, "Yet they are industrious, intelligent people and they not only are convinced of the truth of their religion, but their numbers are growing. And I find it inspiring the way they sacrifice for their faith and how they care for each other."

"They do stick together, that is true. And they have achieved something of a miracle in the Salt Lake Valley. Now they are creating a chain of stations clear back to the East to aid the thousands of converts who want to emigrate out here. Their latest scheme is to organize parties of converts who will convey their belongings in push carts. But then think of the great pyramids that were built by people who believed the world to be flat."

He paused and continued with, "What will you do when you reach Oregon, if it is any of my business?"

"It seems to be no secret that I am indentured to the Hixons for some time. Afterwards, I hope to find employment as a teacher and to rear my child."

I wasn't about to tell this pushy New Englander of my desire some day to have a real marriage.

"A worthy ambition. And if you will allow me to say so, I think you would make a first class teacher."

Ignoring his flattery, to deflect further questions, I asked, "What of your own ambitions, Mister Peebles?"

"Please call me Chester. As for myself, I have so many interests I hardly know where to begin. I considered the ministry but became a soldier instead, not that I was very good at it. Then I tried panning for gold and found little success at that. I think I might enjoy owning a newspaper, for I like to write. Or I may go into business, or maybe even politics."

"You seem to be somewhat at loose ends."

"That is true. I envy Cousin Zeb. He sets his mind to something and the Devil himself can't deter him."

"Is he really your cousin? You seem so different."

"That may be why we are drawn to each other. We complement each other. But yes, we are descended from the same great grandparents. They were pioneers back in Pennsylvania. My grandfather, the first Chester Peebles, was a New Englander who moved south and chose the wrong side in the Revolution. A school master, he was killed down in your neck of the woods, at Kings Mountain. My branch of the family drifted back north to Philadelphia. Then after the War of 1812, my parents moved to New York, had me rather late in their lives and died soon after. I was reared in Boston by my maternal grandparents. I hope all this does not bore you."

"Not at all," I said. "What about Captain McGee?"

"His grandfather was one of George Washington's Life Guards. After the Revolution, he moved first to Ohio and then Indiana."

"How did you two get together?"

"Our great grandfather, one Jason McGee, left many descendants, mainly in Pennsylvania. The summer after my first year at Harvard, some kinfolks hosted a family reunion back at Jason's homestead near Harrisburg. I attended as the only member of my branch. Zeb had just returned to Indiana from the Far West, so he came to the reunion. The long and short of it was I was so taken with his experiences that I persuaded him to let me accompany him to California. This was in 1845. We got out there in time to sign up together for the Mexican War. You may notice that Zeb limps when the weather is bad. He was wounded in the leg at San Pasqual and came near to bleeding to death. Anyway, that is the story. We have been together ever since."

"Only now you are separating. Why is that?"

"I think Oregon may be a more suitable place than California to rear a family. As you may have heard, I am engaged to be married. Amy is a fine girl from a good family. Here is her portrait."

He removed the locket that hung from a chain around his neck and opened it to show me the daguerrotype.

"Very pretty, but young, too," I said.

"Yes. She is only 17. Her father will not give his consent until I have settled down and proved my ability to care for her. Once I can convince him of that, she will join me in Oregon."

Returning the locket, I said, "So, let us hope that we both realize our ambitions in Oregon. By the way, what are Captain McGee's ambitions?"

"I can't really say. Zeb keeps his thoughts to himself. He thinks I talk too much for my own good. Perhaps I do."

"Would you do me a favor, Mister Peebles, I mean Chester? Would you return this Mormon Bible to Dr. Dormsby for me?"

He looked puzzled, then said, "Anything for a lady, Annie."

8

That was the longest and frankest conversation Chester Peebles III and I had ever had. Before then, I had marked him down as just a cocksure Yankee adventurer. Now I saw him as a man who, with his youth beginning to fade, still was floundering about, trying to find his place in the world.

Although I liked him better now, I began to doubt whether one so indecisive had the grit and gumption to lead us up to Oregon without his tough, older cousin to guide him and us. And Ralph Hixon's guide books indicated that the most difficult part of our journey still lay ahead. North of Fort Hall, the mountains would be formidable, and there were many rivers to be forded, not to mention some unpredictable Indian tribes to be dealt with.

But my more immediate problem was how to inform Doctor Dormsby in no uncertain terms that he would have to look elsewhere to find himself a second wife. I hoped that by having Peebles return that copy of the Book of Mormon, I would make it plain to Dormsby that I was not at all interested. I did not reckon on the man's tenacity.

The next day, as I was dismissing my students from their daily class and was about to help Myrtle Mae prepare our noon meal, he came striding in his purposeful way right up to me.

In Myrtle Mae's plain hearing, he addressed me without preamble.

"You have had time to consider my proposition, I presume."

"More than enough time, Doctor Dormsby."

"And I trust you see the wisdom of your joining our family."

Before I could respond, Myrtle Mae came over. Hands on her hips, she demanded, "What is this about joining your family?"

"I was not addressing you, Mrs. Hixon."

"Yes, but you were addressing our indentured servant. What is the meaning of this, Annie?"

Again, before I could reply, Doctor Dormsby said, "I have asked the young Mrs. Hixon to become my wife."

I wish I had a photograph of the expression that came over Myrtle Mae's face.

"Don't be a fool. You have a wife already."

He started in to explain the Mormon position on polygamy, but I headed him off, saying, "Don't waste your breath. I don't want to marry you."

Instead of backing away and apologizing, he grasped the lapels of his coat and lowered his head like an angry bull.

"You should consider the consequences to yourself and your unborn child if you refuse me. Surely you do not want to end up in a strange country with no husband and under the thumb of this overbearing woman who seems to think she owns you, whereas, as my wife, you would hold a place of honor in a grand new city not many miles from here. You and your child and those of ours that will follow will never want for material goods."

"Who are you calling overbearing?" Myrtle Mae demanded. "And who gave you the right to try to lure away our servant?"

For once, Dormsby's face broke into a smile, revealing a set of beautiful white, even teeth.

"There you are, Annie, if I may make so bold as to address you so. She only wants you for a servant to be exploited. Whereas I desire you for a wife to be cherished and protected to the end of your days. I would rear your child as our own, whereas this rude woman, who cannot control her tongue, would regard it as a nuisance."

By now Myrtle Mae looked as though she would suffer a stroke.

"That is a damnable lie. We don't regard the baby as a nuisance. We may want it for ourselves. It is in the contract her own father drew up. We have the right to keep the baby as our own, if it turns out to be healthy and . . ."

She must have seen the look of horror on my face for she halted in mid-sentence. That was the first time I had been given any inkling that the Hixons felt they had the right to claim my baby. And my own father had made such an arrangement?

"Wait!" I fairly screamed. "You can't have my baby!"

"You should have told that to your father before he drew up the papers. He thought it would be in your best interest not to have to rear an illegitimate child."

Doctor Dormsby, now frowning, turned to me.

"There seems to be more to this situation than I had thought. At any rate, you, Mrs. Hixon, should understand that you are in a territory administered by the Church of the Latter Day Saints. I have but to say the word to the right person and we can force you to produce this document you claim to have and test its validity before a local court. We could prohibit you from dragging off this helpless young widow to Oregon against her will."

Suddenly, the brilliant blue of the Wyoming sky turned white. The grassy earth began to spin under my feet. The last thing I recall was seeing the face of Doctor Dormsby smiling in triumph. Then everything went black.

When I came to, I was lying in my own tent. Mrs. Mueller and Mrs. Courtenay were looking down at me.

"What happened?" Then, remembering, I said, "Has he gone?"

"If you are speaking of Doctor Dormsby, yes. Mrs. Courtenay here gave him a good piece of her mind and sent him away with a flea in his ear."

"And Myrtle Mae?"

"She has gone off to find her husband. She looked to be considerably upset."

"Keep her away from me. Keep them both away. Make them leave me alone. They can't have my baby . . ."

On and on I babbled, until Mrs. Courtenay seized my shoulders and shook me out of my hysterics.

"Pull yourself together, girl. Tell us what they did to put you in such a state."

As I sobbed out my story of the confrontation between Myrtle Mae and Doctor Dormsby, the faces of the two women made a sharp contrast, the one cool and aristocratic; the other, earthy, peasantlike. But the longer I talked the more alike their expressions became, ranging from disbelief to indignation.

"They made me feel like they were fighting over the rights to a mare and her foal. They can't have my baby. Neither one. I don't want to see either of them again."

"We must find a way to guarantee just that," Mrs. Courtenay said. "Now, Annie, let's give up our pretenses here. Mrs. Mueller has told me the truth of your circumstances."

"That is not how it was," Mrs. Mueller replied, hotly. "You acted like you already knew."

"As you wish. I suspected that your husband was not the father of your child. Mrs. Mueller merely confirmed my suspicions."

"We talked this over while waiting for you to come around," Mrs. Mueller said. "She and her husband can help you."

"That is enough for the present," Mrs. Courtenay said. "Now, Mrs. Mueller, I shall ask Opal to fetch this girl a cup of good strong English tea. Meanwhile, would you be good enough to stand guard to keep anyone from further upsetting her?"

Mrs. Mueller set up a camp stool in front of my tent. It was not long before I heard Ralph and Myrtle Mae Hixon demanding to see me.

"Poor girl is sleeping. I will tell her you came around. No, I said she was sleeping. If you disturb her it will be over my dead body."

I don't know which comforted me more, the cup of Opal's strong sweet tea or the knowledge that a stalwart friend, Mrs. Mueller, was shielding me while an unlikely new-found ally, Mrs. Courtenay, was considering how to get me out of my sorry fix. Unless they happen to be competing for some male, women often form such strange sisterhoods.

As I sipped my tea, I reflected on what seemed to be my only two choices: continue on to Oregon with the Hixons or accept Doctor Dormsby's proposal. Had Myrtle Mae not let it slip about my father's signing over to them the option of keeping my baby for themselves, I would have chosen continuing on to Oregon as the lesser of two evils. But the other choice was equally intolerable for me. I would have died rather than become the second wife of a fanatical Mormon doctor.

My mother liked to say that it often is darkest just before dawn. Failing to see any possibility of a dawn, in my despair, I did something I had not done since before being exiled. I got down on my knees in the privacy of my tent and prayed for a way out of my dilemma. I confessed to the Almighty that I had been a willful person. I asked for forgiveness for having seduced Billy Joe Duncan and, while in this vein, even prayed for the soul of Bart Corbett. Then while at it, I asked forgiveness for having callously used Elmer Hixon as a way to escape the consequences of my sinning with Billy Joe.

Then my father entered my thoughts. There I was, on my knees, struggling without success to do as Uncle John had counselled me to, that is forgive my father, when I heard the voice of Captain McGee outside the tent asking Mrs. Mueller if I was about.

"She is but can't be disturbed."

"I got to see her before she leaves for Oregon."

"Well, you can't. The girl is too upset to talk to anyone."

Glad of an excuse to dodge facing up to the question of forgiving my father, I interrupted my prayers to say, "It's all right, Mrs. Mueller. I will see the captain."

I sat up on my pallet as he stooped to enter the tent, removed his hat and squatted, Indian fashion, beside me.

In a low voice, he said, "Little lady, my crowd is heading west for Salt Lake in the morning, and yours is starting for Fort Hall. Before we split up, there is something you should have."

To my amazement, he held out a wad of bank notes.

"I am not looking for charity, Captain McGee."

He bent his craggy face nearer and said in a still lower voice, "This ain't charity, little lady. I think it is rightfully yours. Go ahead and count it. You'll see."

I took the money and found that it came to ninety two dollars.

"Is that how much was stolen from your wagon back at Laramie?" he whispered.

"Exactly. But I don't understand."

"Don't ask questions. Just take the money. It has to be yours."

I started to protest, but he put his finger to his lips and sat back on his buttocks like a white man, so that his eyes were level with mine.

"Corbett had this on him. I didn't dare give it to you before lest folks started putting two and two together. The money was in a little velvet pouch, but I threw that away. Now, I want you to remember: Nobody knows about what happened back at that natural bridge. Let's keep it that way."

"Chester Peebles did not appear to be satisfied with the report he got from that search party you sent down to the creek. He said Indians shunned that spot."

"Chester never keeps his mind on anything for long. Don't worry about him. Only I notice he likes to talk to you. Just don't go letting the cat out of the bag on your way up to Oregon."

"I am not a fool, Captain McGee. I will keep silent."

"What about her?" he asked, nodding toward the tent flap where Mrs. Mueller still stood guard. "I see you two talking to each other all the time. She got any idea of what happened?"

"Believe me, Captain, I have never revealed anything to a living soul. Nor will I."

"All right. I believe you, little lady."

He arose and said in a voice loud enough for Mrs. Mueller to hear, "I just wanted to tell you I am sorry you ain't feeling good and I want to wish you well on your new life in Oregon."

Without further ado, he clapped on his hat and walked past Mrs. Mueller, pausing just long enough to say, "Hope you and all your family get to Oregon safe and you have a good life there. It has been a pleasure guiding you this far."

When he was gone, Mrs. Mueller put her head through the tent flap to inquire, "What was he after?"

Taking care to conceal the banknotes, I said, "He just wanted to wish me well for the rest of the trip."

"He didn't say anything about the Dormsby business?"

"No. What made you think he did?"

"All that whispering so I couldn't hear a word. I thought maybe he was putting in his own bid for your hand. That would be something: first a Sioux Indian and then a Mormon doctor. Why not a big, strong old mountain man as well?"

Seeing the disturbed look on my face, she said, "I'm sorry, Annie. It wouldn't have surprised me, though. For that matter, it is a good thing Peebles is engaged to be married. He seems to like you, more maybe than he should. Here you have all these men after you, and my pa and brothers had to force Herman to marry me. Count your blessings."

"Some blessings," I replied. "Oh, Mrs. Mueller, what am I going to do?"

*   *   *

One of the advantages men have over women is that when they find themselves in a tight spot, they are freer to take some initiative to get themselves out of it. Usually lacking that freedom themselves, members of our sex have to rely on men to work their wills. In my case, Homer Courtenay was working on my behalf, as his wife came around to explain.

"His mind is much occupied by this minstrel show he insists on our producing this evening, but he has promised to come and consult with you afterwards."

"I only have until tomorrow morning."

"I know. Meanwhile, Homer has asked me to see into certain matters."

"Such as?"

"Your financial means. Have you any money?"

Not daring to reveal Captain McGee's return of my stolen cash, I shook my head.

"Your mules and that little wagon. Are they not rightfully yours?"

"I assume so, but they were judged to be of little value by a livestock dealer back at Laramie."

"What about your personal effects?"

"Beyond this tent and my clothing, I own nothing beyond a few novels and Elmer's set of law books. What are you getting at?"

"You will see. Just remain quietly here in your tent while we ascertain what can be done."

Later that afternoon, the Hixons came to talk to me and, once more, Mrs. Mueller would not let them enter my tent.

"Why not?" Myrtle Mae demanded.

"You have upset the poor girl."

"It wasn't me. It was that nasty little Mormon doctor."

"According to Annie, you said you have the right to keep her baby."

"Did you tell her that, Myrtle Mae?" her husband asked.

"I told Dormsby and she heard me. Now don't you go questioning me, Ralph. We have got to talk to that silly girl and straighten this out."

"For once in your life, Myrtle Mae, let me do the talking."

"What has got into you, Ralph? Have you been drinking?"

"Just shut up. Shut your mouth and keep it shut."

Then, before she could recover, he said to Mrs. Mueller, "Would you allow me to speak to Annie?"

"Nobody is to see her until she feels better."

I called out, "He can come in, but she must go away."

"No, Annie," Mrs. Mueller said. "You mustn't let yourself be upset again. You could lose your baby."

"Then you come in with him, Mrs. Mueller. I'd like a witness present anyway."

A muttered conversation followed outside, ending with Hixon's shouting, "God damned it, Myrtle Mae. Clear out and leave this to me."

In a moment, Mrs. Mueller opened the tent flap for Ralph Hixon to enter and followed him with her tent stool. After I explained that Mrs. Mueller knew my entire story, he took off his hat and swallowed hard, trying to find the right words.

"Annie, I am sorry for what Myrtle Mae went and done."

"She told the truth, didn't she? My father signed over the rights to my baby."

"That ain't the whole story. Look, I know how you feel toward your pa, and I don't blame you. But he was trying to protect you from being stranded in a strange country and saddled with a fatherless child. So he drew up a paper binding us to adopt your baby. That is the long and short of it. He paid us for the trouble we would be put to."

"And he indentured me to you for three years. Why would you agree to keeping my baby?"

"We needed the money as a grubstake. Besides, he told us who the father is. The Duncans is good stock and so is the Mundys."

"Your wife made it sound like you would take the baby only if it was healthy."

"That is just her notion. You know I am a fair-minded man."

There were tears in his eyes as he continued, "And I realize Myrtle Mae has not been as kind to you as she should of. Myself, I have come to look on you as a daughter. I didn't think Elmer was good enough for you, to tell the truth, but I liked the idea of us becoming kin folks, so to speak."

"And our marriage got you off the hook so far as caring for the baby," then, before he could respond, I added, "I have never seen the document you say my father drew up."

"I can go get it if you want."

"No matter what it may say, Doctor Dormsby threatened to have it challenged here by a Mormon court."

"Oh, Annie, you got to be careful about involving him in this. We just can't let you go throwing yourself away on him. What would your Pa think when it got back to him we let you run off and marry a Mormon?"

"Knowing my Pa, he might enter a suit to recover his three hundred dollars. He hates to be cheated."

That was a shot in the dark, but I saw at once that it had hit its mark. He gulped, ducked his head and fumbled for words.

"That thought never entered my head," he finally said. "But if it was to come to that, we have gone to considerable expense paying your train and boat fares. And there has been hotel expenses, not to mention a month's lodging at my brother Osborne's."

Realizing my sudden advantage, I turned the screws tighter by pointing out the labor I had provided in milking, cooking and looking after Ralph Junior.

"Yes, and I appreciate it. But look, Annie. You ain't going to marry Dormsby, are you?"

Why not make him sweat a bit more, I thought.

"I don't know what I shall do. I will let you know in the morning."

"It would ruin your life."

"My life has been pretty well ruined anyway. You had better go now and make up with your wife. She is not used to your talking back to her as you did."

After informing Hixon that I was too distraught to share my tent with little Ralph Junior that night, Mrs. Mueller congratulated me on my handling of the interview. "As my Herman would say, 'you got him by the short hairs.'"

9

Young and naive as I was, still I realized that any advantage I held over the Hixons could only be temporary. Once on the road north with them, my pregnancy advancing rapidly, the Cornish lads no longer handy to help me, I would be thrown back on the Hixons' doubtful charity more and more.

Although I did not doubt the sincerity of Ralph Hixon's apologies, for he was not a mean man, his wife was a different matter. She had been made to look like a fool by Doctor Dormsby. She had been humiliated by her husband in my hearing and that of Mrs. Mueller's. How could I trust myself and my unborn child to that vengeful woman's control?

I have read that long-term convicts often grow to value the shelter and care afforded them above the uncertainty of the outside world. I was beginning to develop some of that same attitude. I loved Mrs. Mueller like a mother. Her children and others, including sweet little Ralph Junior, had won their ways into my heart. Belatedly, almost reluctantly, I had grown to enjoy the company of Chester Peebles, for all his faults.

In a way, I felt toward my fellow travellers as a headstrong child feels toward a troublesome family. At that stage they were all that I had to rely on, or so I thought as nightfall came over Fort Bridger.

As I prayed and fretted in my tent, from across the campground there came the sound of the minstrel show beginning. I recognized the rich voice of Mr. Courtenay without being able to make out his words. Soon Lester's banjo music rang out as did more voices and roars of laughter. Then the sweet, melodic alto of Mrs. Courtenay singing "Old Folks At Home" wafted over the campground. More jokes and laughter echoed. A clamor from the audience was rewarded with Lester's singing "Oh Susannah" in a powerful baritone. A duet by the two Courtenay children and a final solo by Mrs. Courtenay, "Hark, I Hear an Angel Sing," ended the program.

After the applause had finally stopped, although I could not make out their words, I recognized the voices of first Peebles and then Captain McGee. It appeared that they were saying their goodbyes to each other, for their remarks were greeted with "Hip, Hip, Hurray" and the singing of "For He's a Jolly Good Fellow."

A wave of regret swept over me at the thought of no longer enjoying the company of the high-spirited Cornish lads or seeing the bright, eager faces of the two Courtenay children, or, for that matter, feeling the sense of security the leadership of Captain McGee inspired.

Again, I went down on my knees, weeping and praying for a release from my difficulties. Again, I promised my Methodist God henceforth to lead a pure and blameless life, devoting it to the rearing of my baby and to the teaching of other children, anything if only He would show me a way out of my slough of despond.

When I was very young, for a time I believed the stories my mother told me about angels. I really did think that God sent heavenly, winged creatures to assist those who trusted and prayed to Him.

Of course, as I grew older, I shed this childish belief. But as I knelt in prayer that night, I heard my tent flap open, and looked up to see the figure of a person with golden, shoulder-length hair and a lily white face that shone in a strange glow. This figure stepped into my tent, raised a lantern, and I swear, I saw wings growing from her shoulders.

I was at the point of fainting when, I heard, "Annie, am I disturbing you?"

"No, no, Mrs. Courtenay. You just startled me. Why are you dressed like that?"

"It was Homer's idea for me to get myself up so to sing *'Hark, I Hear an Angel Sing'.*" It is a ridiculous new song, but that lot out there seemed to enjoy it. Well, everyone is saying their goodbyes. We are to set out at dawn. So get up off your knees and hear what we have worked out for you."

* * *

If some observant person, unacquainted with our party or my circumstances and blessed with keen eyesight, had wandered through our camp shortly before dawn the next morning, he would have seen some curious goings on.

He might have seen a tall, blond woman and a slender, dark-haired man carrying a blanket and clothing as well as a theatrical makeup kit enter my tent. He might have seen the light of a lantern glowing through my canvas, then be extinguished.

The man and woman would have been seen emerging from the tent and leading a young Indian squaw with long, jet black braids, a blanket over her shoulders, rawhide breeches covering her lower half and moccasins on her feet. These three persons disappeared into a large tent across the camp ground.

Soon after, the observer would have seen a stout woman and a slender youth enter my tent. A few minutes later, the woman would emerge leading what appeared to be a younger female, with a thick waistline, wearing a long skirt and a bonnet that obscured her face. The stout woman led this person to a small wagon to which a man was hitching a pair of mules. The large woman and the other person climbed into the little wagon and busied themselves in creating a bed of buffalo hides.

While this was going on, the man, having completed hitching the mules, then hobbled them, and went to the tent, took it down, and carried it to the little wagon.

After that, he took an armload of books and two carpet bags from the little wagon and delivered them across the campground to where the blond woman and her husband had escorted the Indian squaw.

"So far, so good," Mr. Mueller said as he handed me my novels and carpet bags.

"Wonderful, Mr. Mueller. I don't know how to thank you for what you are doing."

"We are going to miss you, Annie, but you are doing the right thing."

"Of course she is," Mrs. Courtenay said. "Annie will have a far better life in California."

"At least I will be shed of Myrtle Mae Hixon," I said. "Mr. Mueller, when the cat is out of the bag, please hand out these letters. One is for Ralph Hixon, one for your wife, one for Chester Peebles, and one for Jacob. I want to thank him for pretending to be me. Also I have enclosed a few dollars to reward him for all his help on the trail."

"What about your wagon and the mules?"

"They are to be yours . . ."

"Aw, I can't accept that, Annie."

"Of course you can. They will be of greater use to you homesteading in Oregon than to me in California. My letter will verify your rights to them."

"What about the Hixons?"

"In my letter I list every cent they paid for train fares, ferry tolls, and lodging . . . even for having my mules shod. And I have enclosed enough to cover their outlay. Although they will not be getting their hands on my baby, they can keep the money my father advanced to them."

I paused and looked out across the camp ground to where Myrtle Mae Hixon was talking to Mrs. Mueller. It was plain to see that they were arguing and that Mrs. Mueller emerged as the victor, for Myrtle Mae turned away and stalked back to her own wagon where her husband and little Ralph Junior were taking down their tent.

"What were you saying, Mister Mueller?"

"There is a passel of books in your wagon. What should we do about them?"

"They are Elmer's law books. It would rouse suspicions to haul them over here, besides which I have no use for them. Just dump them somewhere along the trail."

"There is a large Bible, too."

I almost told him to dump that too, but remembering my pledges to lead a more Godly life, said, "It was Elmer's. I suppose I should keep some memento of him. So if it is not too much trouble and if Mrs. Courtenay does not object . . ."

"We'll find room for your Bible."

At first I regarded it as a silly business to make me up as a squaw. Why not just hustle me over to the Courtenay's wagon in the dark and cover me with a blanket until we were well out of sight of Fort Bridger?

But no, Mr. Courtenay insisted on adding this dramatic touch to my getaway, and his wife said it was easier just to indulge him.

While Lester and Opal started taking down the Courtenay's tent, I took refuge in the family's large wagon. I was sitting there Indian fashion, blanket over my shoulders, as the Cornish lads walked by. Will Tremelling was complaining about "that cow of a German woman" whom, he said, had forbidden them to see "our lovely lass."

"If you had of got up your nerve to ask her to marry you, maybe we wouldn't have to part company with her," one of the others was saying.

As their voices trailed off, I peeked out the back of the wagon and saw Doctor Dormsby striding past. He halted beside a small stream that separated the California from the Oregonian campsite. He was joined there by two bearded men on horseback. Wearing shotguns slung over their shoulders and wide-brimmed hats, they looked to be members of the Mormon militia.

The two men dismounted and stood holding their horse's reins while Dormsby marched toward my little wagon. There, I could see, he was barred by Mrs. Mueller. A great waving of arms followed, but Mrs. Mueller remained firmly planted in his path.

I would love to have heard the words that passed between those two determined individuals.

Dormsby turned away, shaking his head. He halted beside the little creek and held a brief conference with the militia men. Still dismounted, they and their mounts accompanied him back past the Courtenay's wagon. Terrified that Dormsby would recognize me, despite my disguise, I lay down and drew the blanket over my head.

Dormsby was saying, "I'd rather it was done legally, but the family won't show me the papers. Told me it was none of my business. And now this other woman won't let me talk to the girl. One way or the other though, I will be sealed in marriage with her. Will you two help?"

"We told you we would. Just let them set out this morning and leave the rest to us."

When Mrs. Courtenay came by to check on me, I told her of what I had overheard. She promptly walked over to the Muellers to warn them, then returned to report, "She says not to worry. They will remain alert. Just to be on the safe side, Homer feels you ought to slip away and start walking. We will pick you up once we are clear of the camp."

"What will Captain McGee say when he finds out?"

"We will tell him you have become a member of our family, and so you will be. What's more, we'll not expect you to milk cows or do any work until we reach California. This will make a grand story to tell your grandchildren some day." Although far advanced in my pregnancy and left with only a few dollars, I felt the greatest sense of freedom and joy I had experienced since making love with Billy Joe Duncan back in my father's barn the previous Christmas.

PART FOUR

1

The Courtenays kept me concealed in the back of their wagon until I heard Captain McGee calling out for our noon break, by which time we had come a good ten or twelve miles west of Bridger, the trail being fairly smooth.

If I had had my way in the matter, I would have slipped out of my Indian garb, discarded the black-braided wig, and scrubbed the reddish brown stain from my face before revealing myself but, no, Mr. Courtenay, ever the showman, had to have his fun, so he announced in a voice loud enough to be heard by our entire company, "Come quick and see. We have a stowaway."

Of course this drew a crowd around the Courtenay wagon in a minute.

I peered out of the wagon to see Captain McGee holding the reins of his horse and demanding, "What in the hell is going on here?"

I could have died of embarrassment as Mr. Courtenay helped me disembark from his wagon and whispered in my ear, "Now, Annie, keep quiet and let's see if they recognize you."

He turned to the mostly male circle and announced, "She says her name is Minehaha, which is Shoshone for Running Doe."

He bent over me again and whispered, "See, Annie. What did I tell you? They don't recognize you."

He straightened up to continue his charade with, "She says she is the daughter of Washakie, the great Shoshone chief."

By now Captain McGee's face had become a study in puzzlement.

He said, "I never heard Washakie had such a daughter. Why has she took up with you folks, anyway?"

Courtenay bent over me again and whispered, "Oh, this is delicious. Don't give the game away yet."

Then, to the crowd, he said, "She says she wants to join her lover who is a Mormon living in Salt Lake City."

"What a lie," I hissed just loudly enough for him to hear.

Before Courtenay could say more, Captain McGee said, "She can't stay with us. I don't want trouble with the Shoshone. Besides, if she is Old Washakie's daughter, which with a name like that, I doubt, he would bear me a grudge if he found out I was a party to her running away."

I don't know how much longer our deception would have held up if Will Tremelling had not have stepped out from the crowd and looked closely into my face.

"That is no squaw. It is our very own Annie."

At that Courtenay, with a theatrical flourish, pulled the blanket from over my head and shoulders, and removed my wig.

"So it is. Our very own Annie, and she is going to California with us."

A general jubilation followed, which Captain McGee was helpless to prevent.

While most of the California gang thronged around me, Courtenay took Captain McGee aside and acquainted him with pretty much all my story, leaving out, I was to learn, only the paternity of my baby.

Having been so briefed, McGee shooed the Cornish lads aside and stood before me with a half-smile on his face.

"You know what you are doing, I hope, little lady."

"Indeed I do. May I stay with your party?"

"As long as you are acting of your own free will and these English folks are going to be responsible for you."

Mr. Courtenay spoke up, saying, "We shall treat her as if she were our own daughter."

"Then I reckon it is all right."

"Oh, Captain," I said. "Thank you from the bottom of my heart."

He laughed and shook his head. "You are just about the beatingest girl I ever ran across. I see now why Chester was always talking about you."

"Truly, I do thank you."

"You already said that."

He took my elbow and drew me out of earshot of the others.

"Just don't go blabbing our little secret. Corbett has some friends among us I would just as soon did not get suspicious."

"I am not in the habit of blabbing. And did I not already promise you I'd keep quiet?"

He frowned at the archness of my tone, turned his back on me, and yelled for all of the party to gather around.

There followed the longest speech I had yet heard from that strange, aloof man.

"Listen up, all of you. If you think this has been a hard trip, let me tell you, you ain't seen nothing yet. So far you have had pretty much even ground to pass over. As the crow flies, Salt Lake City lies only a bit over a hundred miles from here. Only we ain't crows. We got two fair-sized rivers to cross and mountains such as you have not yet seen. There will be some tough climbs to be made. There will be places where we will have to double team our oxen. We may even have to unload our wagons and haul our stuff a ways by hand. We will be going down slopes where we will have to chain lock our rear wheels and hold back the wagons with ropes. There will be no more twenty-mile days between here and Salt Lake. Most days, we'll be lucky to make five miles. But hang together and I will get you through. Once we are in Salt Lake City, you and your stock can take a good rest before we push on across the desert to California. Any questions?"

Kentucky Pete, the tall, sardonic friend of Bart Corbett, raised his hand.

"If the trail to Salt Lake is so Goddamned rough, why didn't we stick with the other gang up to Soda Springs? Indian fellow back at Fort Bridger said the trail is a lot easier that way."

"We are saving quite a few miles this way."

"Yes, but we will be moving slow. And you say we are to spend time in Salt Lake City. This way don't make sense to me."

"You should have raised that question at Fort Bridger before we split. You are welcome to turn back if you don't like it."

"I was indisposed back there."

"I think you mean you drank too much with that Ute I seen you consorting with, that rogue, Running Wolf. I remind you all there is to be no drinking and no giving liquor to any Indians."

He turned his attention back to Kentucky Pete. "So how about it, mister gambling man? Are you staying with us or going back?"

"You can kiss my ass, McGee. I have had a bellyfull of your bossing everyone. I am heading back to Fort Bridger."

With great relief I watched that sinister man with the eye patch mount his horse and turn back to the east. Every time I saw him, I had been reminded of his crony, Bart Corbett.

* * *

What Captain McGee told us regarding the difficulty of the terrain that lay ahead was, if anything, an understatement. Once we had reached and forded the picturesque Bear River, an adventure in itself, we found the going increasingly difficult.

No longer were the mountains great, austere snow-capped peaks looming far in the distance. Though lower than the Rockies, these pressed in closely upon us. One stretch of our trail led us through a narrow canyon where our gang entertained themselves by shouting and singing just to hear their voices reverberate back to our ears. We crossed one stream at least a dozen times and rough crossings they were, over great rounded boulders.

The hooves of our oxen became so worn that many left bloody hoof prints on the stony soil. Lacking time or resource to replace their shoes, some made leather moccasins for the poor beasts.

I was glad to be under the guidance of Captain McGee rather than Chester Peebles. This formidable man ranged back and forth on his horse along our column, urging laggards to keep up and cautioning those in the vanguard to take care in getting over patches of boulders.

Oddly, however, while our travel grew more arduous each day, the state of my own spirits steadily improved. Except for reading to the two Courtenay children and teaching them their sums, I was free of all duties.

Opal and Lester attended to the cooking for our party. And as the Courtenays had stocked their larder with more luxurious foods than either the Hixons or Muellers, I ate better than any time since leaving home. Hearing they could replenish their hoard at Salt Lake City, they made free use of their canned oysters and sardines. And here and there along the rugged trail, we came upon the cabins of Mormon families who were eager to sell us milk, butter and eggs.

Several times we encountered small bands of former Mormons who had become disillusioned with their new religion and were returning to the East, full of bitterness toward Brigham Young and his regime.

I felt sorry for these dispirited former pioneers. There is much to be admired in the faith of zealous Mormons. As the New Testament says, a tree should be judged by the fruits it bears. Now that the Mormons have officially disowned the practice of polygamy, I must say that they do produce fine crops of earnest, industrious and honest citizens. Today I make it a rule always to treat their young missionaries who come to my door with courtesy and respect.

But, to return to my story, I did enjoy the trek across the Wasatch Mountains, through first Echo and then Emigrant canyons. Initially, I rode like a princess in the carriage with the Courtenays. That privilege ended when the way became so rough that we found it more comfortable and less dangerous to walk.

To ease the burden of their poor, footsore oxen, the Courtenays shifted part of their wagon's load into their carriage. Meanwhile, the patient donkeys of Opal and Lester continued to drag their cart without complaint.

I have said little about those two because, to tell the truth, I had been too absorbed in my own affairs and because I was not close enough to the Courtenays to ask nosy questions. Opal was a stout, brown-skinned woman whom I judged to be in her late thirties. The darker, graying Lester seemed somewhat older.

The Courtenays had never bothered to explain the status of the pair. Everyone assumed them to have been slaves.

Around the fire one night, as we partook of a rich oyster stew Opal had made, Mr. Courtenay inquired about my family. I told him of my father's political prominence and of my Uncle John's status as a physician, seeking to impress him.

"And slaves? Did your family own any?"

I told him about Dessie and Ike, pointing out that since my father lived by his wits rather than farming, we needed no more help than that.

"What is your view of slavery?" he asked.

"As long as we don't mistreat them, I don't see anything wrong with it. Living in America surely is better for them than remaining in Africa."

Overhearing me, Mrs. Courtenay fairly snorted.

"Hear the dear, naive girl," she said. "Doesn't she see what a blot slavery is on the very soul of America? It gives the lie to their Declaration of Independence and the precious Constitution they are always arguing about." Without giving me a chance to reply she walked away.

Taken aback by the vehemance of her remarks, I said to her husband, "But you own Opal and Lester and they seem happy enough to me."

He looked around to make sure no one was in earshot before saying, "They are not our slaves. We are helping them escape from slavery."

He went on to explain that the pair had been house servants of a family near Richmond. They had heard Lester playing his banjo and singing at a plantation festival for slaves

"I took pains to investigate and found that the family were thinking of selling the couple to a slave trader because they had become uppity. The owner reckoned he could get two thousand dollars for them. We did not have that much money but I could not rest until we found a way to set them on the road to freedom."

"You mean you are helping two runaway slaves?" I said. "That is against the law, you know, to take slaves you don't own across state lines."

"The infamous Fugitive Slave Law itself is a violation of the laws of humanity."

Unable to think of any counter argument, I said only, "Chester Peebles was a great one for abolition, too. I am surprised he did not object to allowing you to join his Oregonians for the journey as far as Fort Bridger."

"He was opposed until I swore him to secrecy and told him the circumstances. What did you think of Peebles?"

"He has no grit. Can't decide what to do with himself."

"I don't know what you mean by grit, but I found him to be a young man of principle. Now you must keep our secret about Opal and Lester, until we reach California where one hears there are settlements of free Negroes who would never permit one of their race to be carried back to slavery against his will."

"Of course, Mr. Courtenay."

Thereafter, my attitude changed toward Opal and Lester. As I observed them going about their tasks without complaint, I no longer saw them as human chattel, born to do the will of white masters, but rather as proud, courageous persons worth far more than the likes of Kentucky Pete and such riffraff.

2

I have read various accounts of how in 1847 Brigham Young, at the end of an even more arduous journey than ours through the Wasatch Mountains, looked out over the great Salt Lake Valley and declared, "This is the place."

Nine years later, that same vista awed this backwoods girl. Great gray mountains stretched to my left and right. Far in the western distance, across the treeless valley, loomed a range of other, less lofty mountains. To the northwest, the briny waters of the Great Salt Lake shimmered in the July heat.

Closer to hand, the raw young city the Mormons had created, and were in fact still creating on land deemed by the Indians as useless, seemed to be welcoming us.

This was the first settlement we had encountered since leaving St. Joseph that could be called a town. The population of this New Zion was about the same as St. Joe's, but the similarities ended there. Missing the natural growth of trees, the saints had diverted streams so that water flowed down to irrigate the saplings they had set out along their broad streets. Four square miles were enclosed by an earth-and-adobe wall ranging in height from three to twelve feet, meant, I suppose, as a fortification although Mr. Courtenay scoffed at its likely efficacy.

At the center of the town, the saints were busy laying the foundation for what was to become their temple. And occupying a commanding little hill was the white mansion where Brigham Young lived with several of his forty odd wives.

Many of the renegade Mormons we had met heading back east had complained of the hard, ill-paid labor they had been expected to perform on these public works. Well, it has been said that there is no gain without sacrifice. Now, of course, Salt Lake City has become an orderly, attractive place, with its magnificent Temple and great Tabernacle, all built with donated labor.

In that summer of 1856, however, it was a raw, unfinished town. Yet it offered many amenities. There were more than twenty stores, some owned by Gentiles as the saints called those of a different religious persuasion, to the amusement of Mr. Courtenay. In his words, "Here is a place where a Jew can legitimately call himself a Gentile."

Despite their reputation for close dealing, however, no Hebrew could match some of the Mormon settlers around Salt Lake City for greediness. Whereas we had let our oxen and mules graze freely on the way out from St. Joe, here the Mormons exacted a fee of five cents per day to graze each head of livestock. There was much grumbling over this, although perhaps I should not blame land owners who had animals of their own to tend.

Mr. Courtenay was all for putting on a minstrel show during our layover in the Mormon stronghold, but on the advice of Captain McGee discarded the idea. Weary from our slow, tedious crossing of the Wasatch Mountains, the Courtenays took two rooms in the largest of the city's hotels, one for themselves and one for the children and yours truly. Opal and Lester remained in camp outside the city to watch over the family's possessions.

At first I found it hard to adjust to sleeping on a real bed with feathered mattress and soft pillows. Even more strange was the sensation of sitting in the rocking chair of our room and looking out on the comings and goings of the bustling city. As far as I am concerned, nothing can beat a good, old-fashioned rocking chair for sheer comfort.

The Courtenays liked to promenade about the town with their children and me in tow. On one of our strolls we passed the Lion House, as Brigham Young's official mansion was known. Lo and behold, there stood in the doorway of his adjacent office the great man himself.

A tall, sturdily built gentleman in his mid-fifties, he was of dark complexion and hair. Physically, there was nothing special to look at, yet he did exude that aura of power that men of long-accustomed authority develop.

Mr. Courtenay was all for going up and introducing himself, but his wife would not have it.

"He'll try to convert us," she said.

By the time they had finished their bickering, the issue had become moot. Young had disappeared back into his office.

Say what you will of Brigham Young, he was a great man, in my opinion. The history not only of Utah but of the entire Western United States would be a far different story without his strong-willed influence.

However, Captain McGee did not share my opinion of the Mormon leader. This came out in a conversation I overheard between him and Mr. Courtenay in which the latter told of seeing Young and of being thwarted by his wife from shaking the hand that ruled a church and a vast territory.

"I'd sooner shake the paw of a pole cat," McGee said.

Pressed for the reason for his dislike, the captain in a few terse words told of the feud between Young and Jim Bridger and of how he felt the Mormons had forced Bridger and his partner, Louis Vasquez, to sell their land grant for a pittance.

"Old Jim got that land fair and square from the Mexicans in 1843. Young forced him to sell it for eight thousand dollars, and it is worth many times that. Besides which they still owe him half the money."

"Why doesn't your friend Bridger call for his payment?"

"He don't dare come out here in person. He thinks the Mormons want to kill him."

"What for?"

"Aw, they accuse him of stirring up the Utes against them. But that is a damned lie. Anyhow, last I heard, Jim was headed for the Yellowstone country guiding an English lord with more money than brains. Vasquez is back in St. Louis figuring out how to collect the rest of what is owed them."

I almost blurted out what Chester Peebles had told me about McGee's mission from Vasquez, but just in time remembered my promise not to mention it.

So while McGee conducted his mysterious business, we passed three of the pleasantest days of my life there in the New Zion fast springing up in the shadow of the everlasting hills.

*   *   *

By the last day of our stay in Salt Lake City, I was beginning to like the place and the people far better than I had expected. We often saw fashionably dressed women on the broad streets. In the well-stocked and very expensive stores, the clerks were friendly, eagerly discussing their religion and inquiring about ours. There was much talk of the poor crops they were experiencing in the valley due to not enough rainfall and far too many grasshoppers. Yet, we were struck by the general tone of optimism. The soreheads among them were headed east I suppose. And they were preparing for a new flood of push-cart converts to come from Britain and Denmark.

I commented on the get-up-and-go spirit of the people to Mrs. Courtenay. In her arched way, she accused me of harboring second thoughts about refusing Dr. Dormsby's proposal of marriage.

"Oh, Mrs. Courtenay, I couldn't bear playing second fiddle in a marriage even to a man I loved."

"I was only testing you. There was something shady about that little man. He claimed to have studied medicine at 'St. Bart's Hospital in London,' as he put it. That marked him down as an imposter. The proper name is St. Bartholomew's Hospital or just plain Barts, but never St. Bart's. No, I expect he was a barber or more likely a chemist who promoted himself on the way across the Atlantic."

"What makes you think he was a chemist?"

"Did you not notice his stained fingers? And the man told me he hated tobacco as well as alcohol."

"Believe me, Mrs. Courtenay, whether Dr. Dormsby smoked or not is of no interest to me now. I am just glad to be rid of him. He gave me the creeps."

*   *   *

By the time we gathered for our last civilized meal that evening in the hotel dining room, Mr. Courtenay had become the darling of the manager and the entire hotel staff, having gone out of his way to charm them. And what a meal they put on for us: succulent lamb chops and juicy roasted chicken, with rice and gravy and a variety of fresh vegetables, ending up with the best deep-dish apple pie I ever tasted.

Although the hotel normally did not serve alcoholic beverages, the manager allowed Mr. Courtenay to provide his own wine which he had procured from a Gentile merchant.

The more wine the two Courtenays drank, the merrier and more animated their banter became. They laughed over recollections of old acting friends back in London, the meanness of some of the theater managers they had known, and the rudeness of some of the audiences. By the end of the meal, everyone in the crowded hotel dining room had become privy to the story of their lives.

Although I had refused their offer of wine, even I felt intoxicated by the general atmosphere of the evening. How fortunate I felt to be in the company, you might even say the family, of such charming people, who had pledged to see me safely established in California. Perhaps, under their tutelage, I too might become a performer. I, a child of the backwoods of North Carolina, was picking up pointers from Mrs. Courtenay.

3

We spent our first night after departing Salt Lake City a few miles north of a village called Bountiful. As we passed through a countryside dotted with prosperous farms, I gained a fresh appreciation for what the Mormon settlers had achieved in less than a decade since Brigham Young had decided "this is the place" there in the Salt Lake Valley, in the shadow of the Wasatch Mountains.

Everywhere, we saw men and women at work around their little adobe houses or in their often irrigated fields. They were eager to sell us melons, milk, eggs or butter. If their women were ill-used as some charged, I saw no evidence of it. They complained only of the long summer drought and a plague of grasshoppers.

Through selling us their produce and charging five cents a night per head to graze our stock and squeezing several dollars for ferrying our wagons across their larger streams, these enterprizing saints realized much profit from trains such as ours.

The Cornish lads were no longer so necessary to my welfare, now that I had no wagon or team of mules to drive, but still they would loiter about at every stop, seeking to do me favors.

Mrs. Courtenay counselled me against encouraging their attention. "The Cornish are Celts. They lack the reserve of the true English. Besides as common miners, they do not recognize the finer points of conduct."

Being part Welsh myself, I did not appreciate her condescending attitude toward persons of Celtic ancestry. Besides which, Will Tremelling was an attractive young man in his unpolished way. He was slender, with dark hair and lively hazel eyes. And he was so earnest that I put up with his attention rather than hurt his feelings.

Like myself, he was full of optimism for the life he expected to lead in California.

"Why, Annie, did you know they pay three dollars a day in wages in the gold country for experienced miners?"

"Yes, but it costs a lot to live out there as well."

"I don't mean to remain a miner for long. It is my intention to work hard and become a foreman at least. Later, I may learn how to run a mine. Americans can't dig like us Cornish."

"Don't you miss England?"

"Cornwall," he corrected me. "Oh, I miss my mother's cooking. She made the best pastries you ever would want to taste. And I miss the good beer. Do you not miss your home back in Carolina?"

"At first I was miserable, but so much has happened the past few months that I no longer am homesick."

"A lass like yourself will get along no matter where. Your husband was a lucky man . . ."

"Considering how he died, I wouldn't call him lucky."

"I mean being married to yourself. Do you miss him?"

Maybe it was a bit of Mrs. Courtenay rubbing off on me, but I decided that Will had got as personal as I would permit.

"I see your friends looking this way, Will. They must have your supper ready."

As he walked back to his own campfire, it occurred to me that I had not thought of Elmer for many days.

The dog Boris, formerly so aloof, also began to pay me brief visits. Long before, I had learned that he was far more gentle than he appeared, yet it was a surprise when he showed up at my side and put his great muzzle close until I patted his head.

*　　*　　*

So we slogged our way northward, through the Mormon settlements Brigham Young had planted between the rugged Wasatch Mountains and the briney shores of the Great Salt Lake. Due to the long drought, the dust on the trail lay so deep that I had to stop often and empty it from my shoes.

We marvelled at the whitish appearance of the salt that lined the shores of the lake and the flocks of sea gulls that squawked overhead. Some of our party clamored to go and dip themselves in the lake to see if, as reported, you could not sink in its dense waters, but Captain McGee would not permit it.

The atmosphere was so dry that I did not mind the heat so long as I had my bonnet to shield my face. Mrs. Courtenay, her English complexion protected by a large parasol, remained in her carriage while Opal and I walked.

Perhaps because I hailed from a slave-holding state, Opal had been stand-offish toward me throughout the trip. Only gradually did she warm up, finally even offering me advice about taking care of myself during my pregnancy.

I explained that my physician uncle back home had given me some medicines and a little handbook for expectant mothers.

"Yes, but he is a man and they don't know what it is like to have a baby."

"For that matter, neither do you."

She merely snorted.

* * *

It took us about ten days to proceed from Salt Lake City up to where the cutoff joined the regular California trail leading out of Soda Springs, the route Kentucky Pete had criticized Captain McGee for not taking.

Captain McGee kept us moving north at a steady pace, up near the point where the Bear River flows into the Great Salt Lake. This was the same Bear River we had crossed far upstream near Fort Bridger. It flows north, to the east of the Wasatch range, then curves back west and through the mountains above Salt Lake City. Here, near its mouth, the stream was not as swift or rocky, but still was deep and wide enough so that Captain McGee suffered us to be bilked of $3 per wagon for the privilege of using a Mormon-owned ferry.

As we awaited our turn to be ferried across, Mr. Courtenay said that Captain McGee told him the ferrymen had dug out nearby natural fords so that no one could avoid their tolls.

I replied that I thought the story improbable.

"Perhaps so. Our esteemed leader has little love for the saints. He mistrusts them. Did you notice how he was reluctant to advertise his own presence in the city? He was conducting some business on the sly. That had to be why he brought us this way."

Remembering what Chester Peebles had told me of the captain's mission on behalf of his old friend, Jim Bridger, I started to speak, but then thought of my promise to keep silent. I was glad when he changed the subject which had to do with his desire to write a book about our experiences.

"If you do, I hope you will not write about my adventure."

"Ah, Annie, you may be sure I would do nothing to embarrass you."

* * *

Beyond the Mormon settlements and the Bear River, the trail veered to the west, passing around the northern shore of the salt lake. A yellow-hued line of hills lay to the north. We camped by a set of springs which stank of sulphur, then pressed on toward a gap in the low-lying Hansel Mountains.

At night sometimes the stirring of the baby in my womb awakened me. Surrounded by people who had become my protectors, I felt safer than at any time so far on the journey. Opal chatted more freely with me. At times Mrs. Courtenay treated me almost like a daughter, at other times like a nuisance. Her two children fawned on me, plaguing me to read to them at every stop. Mr. Courtenay lent me a copy of ROMEO AND JULIET after I had finished reading them IVANHOE.

The Courtenays had never spelled out their intentions for me, and I thought it better not to pin them down.

*   *   *

Along the way we overtook several droves of livestock being driven by Mormons toward California. And parties of merchants bringing goods from Sacramento passed us, headed for Salt Lake City. One of the latter group, headed by a Mormon, warned us of Indians along the trail between City of Rocks and the headwaters of the Humboldt River that flows across the desert.

That night, Captain McGee made one of his rare speeches.

"We soon will enter Indian Hell," he said. "We got to keep our stock from wandering. From sundown to sunup, we got to keep two men at a time on watch. Each watch will be only for two hours so you'll stay alert. Don't want any sleeping on the job."

"What kind of Indians are they?" Mr. Courtenay asked.

"Mostly Utes and a few renegade Shoshone and the occasional white Mormon renegade. So mind what I say and we'll get you through, Boris and me."

*   *   *

Leaving the Mormon settlements far behind, we plodded along at a steady pace over and around some low mountains until we reached a curving canyon that led us to a branch of the Raft River, which we followed to a broad, grassy meadow, called Junction Valley.

I could not help comparing the picturesque setting of this trails crossroads with the junction of the St. Joseph and regular Oregon Trails way back on the Kansas prairie. It was hard to believe that we had come so far in just twelve weeks.

We reached Junction Valley early enough to allow our stock to start grazing before the sun sank behind Granite Mountain looming over the western rim of the valley. The sunlight reflected off two huge, conical stones that lay a couple of miles to the east.

Mr. Courtenay explained that these monoliths were called the Twin Sisters and that beyond them lay a vast area covered with enormous, strangely shaped boulders known as the City of Rocks.

"It is a pity we won't get to see the place," he said. "Our esteemed captain doesn't want to spend the time. Also he fears the possibility of lurking Indians."

I replied, "I don't know why. He has handled the Indians we have met so far pretty well."

"I agree, but he warns these are a greater danger, at least to our livestock. He says the Utes won't bother taking one's scalp but they like nothing better than to steal your livestock, especially your horses. Therefore we are under orders to hobble them tonight and to set extra guards over our steers."

As we set about putting up our tents and building campfires, a line of about twenty mules and one wagon appeared along the trail leading from the Twin Sisters. A grizzled fellow wearing a beaver fur hat and riding a spotted Indian pony led this caravan. A half-dozen shabbily dressed younger men followed him on foot, each leading two mules laden with packs. A light wagon drawn by four mules completed the party.

At the sound of their approach, Captain McGee ordered all the men in our party to stand ready with their weapons and for the women to take cover in the circle of wagons.

Then, with Boris at his side, he waited on horseback as the caravan drew nearer.

When the leader of the mule train got to within about a hundred feet of where Captain McGee waited he let out a whoop and shouted, "Why I'll be a son of a bitch if it ain't old Zeb McGee, himself. Look a'there boys. You have heard me speak of Zeb often enough. Here is the real article."

Captain McGee, an unaccustomed grin on his face, waited until the man drew nearer before saying, "Clarence Goodall, you lousy old bastard, what are you doing out here? You belong to be back at Fort Hall fleecing the emigrants."

"Why, God damn, Zeb, I have done enough of that for a lifetime. Now you might say I am carrying the wool what I have fleeced off them to sell in Californy where I aim to settle. Fort Hall ain't what it used to be since Hudspeth opened the short cut from Soda Springs. Then when my wife and our youngest son died last winter, I decided we'd move to Californy."

By now both men had dismounted and were pounding each other on the shoulders.

"Here now, Clarence, aren't these fellows your sons?"

"Three of them are. Matthew, Mark, Luke, come over here and shake hands with the damnedest fellow that ever I have known."

It was obvious that Goodall's sons were half Indian and that they were not used to shaking hands. After doing so, they stood about waiting for their father and his old friend to finish bringing each other up to date.

"Look here, Clarence, a friend of mine was to have lead a party of emigrants through Fort Hall, headed for Oregon. Chester Peebles is his name. I warned him not to do any business with Clarence Goodall if you were still trading there, but you may have taken notice of him."

"A square-shouldered fellow with blond hair? Talks like a mackerel eater? Shore, he come through about ten days ago. How did you get hooked up with such a green horn?"

"We are cousins. Served in the Mexican War together, too. Were they in good shape?"

"Yes, but they had some sort of trouble back down on the Bear River with three Mormons that came looking for a gal that one of them wanted to marry."

Seeing that I was listening, Captain McGee put his arm around the trader's shoulder and drew him out of earshot. I could have killed him for doing so. After they had run out of insults and questions, Mr. Courtenay, ever ready to meet colorful characters, went over and introduced himself to Goodall.

"You sound like you ain't a American," Goodall said.

Mr. Courtenay acknowledged that this was the case, then insisted on bringing the trader over to be introduced to his family and myself. On closer view, Goodall's sky blue eyes, always moving, gleamed with native intelligence.

"And you say you are all in the acting game? Wisht you had of come through Fort Hall. You could have put on a show for us."

"There is no reason we can't do one for you right here tonight."

Goodall laughed and clapped his hands. "By God, that is the best news I have heard in a long time. Will it cost anything?"

"Normally it would, but see here, I hope someday to write an account of this trip. If you will let me interview you, there will be no charge."

"Put her there, Mr. Englishman. It's a deal."

This deal was struck without Captain McGee's approval. He finally agreed on the understanding that the show would last no more than an hour and that there would be no drinking.

"You got to understand we are in dangerous country now. This ain't the time or place for tomfoolery."

Goodall and his pack mule team moved several hundred yards to the west of our campground for the night. After both parties had eaten supper, they gathered around our camp fire to be captivated by a scaled-down minstrel show.

Afterwards, before we turned in for the night, Mr. Courtenay entertained his wife and me with the information he had gleaned from Goodall.

"He is one of the old mountain men. He was married to a Shoshone woman. After the beaver trade died out, he settled down with his family around Fort Hall. He remembers Captain McGee when he came out as a youth near the end of the fur trade era. He says he wonders why we wanted to come through Salt Lake City but in his words 'Zeb has always been a contrary son of a bitch.'"

"Homer," his wife said, "the children are listening."

"Sorry, my dear. Anyway, he has a great admiration for our captain. Says he is the bravest man he has ever known."

"Did he say anymore about the Mormons who interfered with the other train?" I asked.

"I tried to pump him, but it seems Captain McGee asked him to say no more about that. So I dropped the subject. I wish I had time to talk to him at greater length. He is a gold mine of anecdotes about the days of the fur trade."

"I think you spent quite enough time with such a disreputable character," his wife said. "Now we must get the children to bed. And please, Homer, no more minstrel shows until California."

So, full of a good supper and with Lester's banjo music still ringing in my ears, I retired to my tent with the Courtenay children. I lay awake for a long time, reflecting on the strange turns my young life had taken during the year since I had invited Billy Joe Duncan to help me carry water at our camp meeting. I wondered if he ever thought of me and our baby.

Outside, the mountain air turned cold but inside our tent we were warm and snug under our blankets. My two young companions slept. My baby turned and settled itself in my womb. The guards of the first watch talked in low tones around the camp fire. A lovely sense of well being settled upon me until a wolf howl sounded from one side of the valley to be answered by another from the other side. But I dismissed my momentary unease and soon fell asleep.

4

I awakened shortly before dawn to a great commotion outside. Men were swearing and shouting in the dark, while, from a distance, there sounded Indian whoops, followed by gunshots.

Captain McGee was roaring, "Don't let the stock stampede!"

But from the sound of pounding hoofs, it seemed his warning had come too late.

"Forget your saddles. Grab your weapons and follow me. Here, Boris."

I peered through my tent flap to see the dim outlines of Mr. Courtenay and Lester struggling to loosen the hobbles on the two carriage horses. More shouts and shots sounded from the west, in the direction of Granite Mountain.

Captain McGee yelled. "Come on, men. Ride fast and maybe we can head them off. Sic 'em, Boris."

The sounds of hoof beats and shouts grew dimmer as Mrs. Courtenay, Opal and I stood shivering with fear and cold outside our tents, straining to make sense of what was happening.

The first faint light of dawn was outlining the Twin Sisters when Clarence Goodall rode up to demand what all the fuss was about. When we told him, he said, "Goddamned Utes" and put the spurs to his pony's flanks to gallop off toward the hullabaloo.

Will Tremelling came over to explain that he and Lester had been on guard when the trouble began.

"Everything was quiet except for a pair of wolves that kept howling closer and closer. That made the oxen nervous, you could tell. Then, all of a sudden, two men on horseback came charging out of the dark between the wagons and where the stock was grazing. I feel terrible such a thing happened on my watch."

It was well past dawn when Captain McGee, hatless and riding bareback, appeared, leading seventy-odd steers. Lester, Mr. Courtenay and Clarence Goodall rode beside the herd while Boris brought up the rear.

Apparently the animals feared the dog more than the Indians who had tried to steal them. He trotted behind them, occasionally nipping at the heels of laggards or racing to head off a steer that tried to leave the pack.

Captain McGee halted in front of Will and gave him such a dressing down as I had never heard.

Poor Will denied that he had been sleeping on guard. Lester confirmed this.

"Captain, we was both wide awake. They came in like ghosts."

"Well, we're lucky we lost no more animals than we did."

"Go easy on the boys, Zeb," Goodall said. "They are green horns. The Utes is veterans at the horse-stealing game. You notice they took only horses. They don't care about cattle."

"Where do you reckon they ran with the horses?"

"I'd say up over Granite Mountain, but they could have circled around and gone back into City of Rocks where they must of come from. We'll keep a sharp lookout as we pass through Goose Creek Valley and I would advise you to do the same, Zeb."

After promising to look each other up when they got to Sacramento, he and Goodall said their goodbyes and the mule train proceeded toward Granite Pass.

"There goes the last of a vanishing breed," Mr. Courtenay said.

"I just hope you didn't believe everything he told you," Captain McGee replied.

"He told me some interesting things about you, Captain."

"Then keep them to yourself. Damn it, one of the roughest stretches of the trail lies ahead and here we have wasted half a day."

Once our animals had settled down, a census showed that the rustlers had made off with two horses which had been left unhobbled. But Captain McGee continued to fume at the travel delay.

So, with the sun almost directly overhead, our train again started moving west, heading for a pass that lay high up between two peaks of Granite Mountain.

"One of the roughest stretches of the trail," turned out to be an understatement. It took us the rest of the day to struggle up the deceptively gentle-looking eastern slope to the pass. Mule droppings along the way reminded us that the Goodall caravan had preceded us.

My heart went out to our poor oxen as they strained to draw our wagons up and up. It was out of the question for anyone to ride anymore. Besides the roughness of the trail, the animals needed every ounce of their stampede-depleted strength to haul their loads.

As we inched our way up the eastern face of the mountain, Lester explained how he and the other men had managed to halt the stampede and recover the stock.

"That dog is what done it. He ran ahead of us and got in front of the oxen. They are scared to death of him."

"What about the Indians? Did you see them?" I asked.

"We didn't get a good look. They ran off when they seen the stampede had stopped. I reckon they are afraid of the dog, too."

By the time we reached a spring just before the top of the gap, it was too late to hazard the descent down the other side to the valley of Big Goose Creek. It was not a very good place for a camp, but we made do. It was, however, a grand place from which to gaze back over Junction Valley and beyond, past the Twin Sisters toward the jumble of giant boulders called City of Rocks.

Still in a foul mood, Captain McGee forbade us to build camp fires. So we ate unheated food and spent a miserable night in the bitter cold. Assuming that our trouble with Indians lay behind us, many of the men grumbled at what they considered to be the unnecessary inconvenience.

Awakened before dawn to yet another cold meal, we were treated to a lecture from Captain McGee.

"Some of you complained about the trail through the Wasatches. You ain't seen nothing yet. We are going to have to chain lock our rear wheels for the next few miles. Be ready to help the other fellow hold back their wagons. Be careful not to let them run up against the back legs of your oxen. All right, folks, let's get this over with."

At the top of the gap, Mr. Courtenay declared that we stood nearly 8,000 feet above sea level. As the first wagons were having their wheels chain locked, I looked to the west and was treated to perhaps the grandest panorama of the journey. To our right lay the massive Flatiron Mountain. Directly ahead, we could see range upon range of mountains. And below us, lay the valley of Big Goose Creek, toward which our wagons soon started moving, or perhaps I should say, sliding.

The first leg of the descent led down through a ravine full of wild flowers and, as it turned out, peril. The first upset came in this ravine when a wheel of the Courtenay's carriage struck a small boulder. Over went carriage and contents. First one horse and then the other fell onto their sides, tangled in their harness. The rest of the caravan had to wait while Captain McGee, swearing a blue streak, helped Lester and Mr. Courtenay free the horses, set the carriage upright and reload it.

Some bad scares but no further mishaps occurred until nearer the bottom when the weight of a wagon proved too much for the men trying to hold it back with ropes, and it rammed against the rearmost yoke of oxen. One steer, bawling like a motherless calf, went down with a broken leg. Its workmate had to be unyoked. The injured animal was dragged out of the way and put out of its misery by a shot from Captain McGee's revolver.

Scarcely had we survived this mishap when a rear wheel of yet another wagon dropped into a rut and was snapped off its axle. Captain McGee ordered the other rear wheel to be removed, leaving the wagon bed to be dragged down the slope.

All along the side of the trail there lay broken wheels, wagon tongues and cast-off belongings such as chests of drawers and, in one case, an anvil, all discarded by earlier emigrants. Adding to our gloom, a squall line swept in from the west, bringing heavy rain and lightning.

It was a wet, exhausted lot of men and animals that finally reached the western base of Granite Mountain to pause for repairs on the bank of a feeble stream flowing into Big Goose Creek. By now a steady rain was falling. After a brief, much-needed rest, we pushed on to the banks of Big Goose Creek, which flowed north into the Oregon Territory. There we made camp and spent another miserable night without campfires.

Up early the next morning, under a clear sky, we set out at a brisk pace through the valley in which Big Goose Creek looped back and forth between willow-lined banks.

What dreary country this was. Aside from the grass and small willow trees along the stream banks, only sagebrush, prickly pear plants and dull, dry grass grew in the valley itself. The surrounding mountains, however, were studded with aspen and cedar trees. The only animal life consisted of coyotes, jack rabbits, rattlesnakes and the occasional sage hen.

As if all that were not enough to depress us, the skeletons of oxen whose hearts had given out in previous years littered the creek banks, victims of exhaustion, left behind as food for coyotes. At places, the creek water was rendered foul by the presence of rotting animals. Someone should erect a monument to the thousands of those patient beasts, without whom the trip across the plains and mountains of the West could not have been made.

As we trudged along, Mr. Courtenay, ever the optimist, declared that "surely the worst of the journey now lies behind us."

"I should hope so," his wife said. "It occurred to me when they shot that poor ox, that we would have been spared such experiences had we taken a boat and gone by way of the Isthmus of Panama, as I wished."

"I could never have got a book out of that."

"No, but we would be in California by now."

"There, there, dear, let's have no recriminations. We are entering the home stretch. Should be smooth sailing from here."

*   *   *

And so it was in a sense, smooth sailing, at least our route along the level valley of the Big Goose to that point where the stream was joined in its northward course by the Little Goose. Captain McGee wanted to make up for the time the stampede on the other side of Granite Mountain had cost us. He made no allowances for the weariness of our party or our animals. We circled wagons near a large willow and, again, he ordered that no camp fires be built and that double guards be set.

"This is the very heart of Indian Hell," he announced. "Besides the Utes trying to steal your horses, now you got the Diggers to contend with. And they are the ugliest, dirtiest little set you ever would want to meet. They are cowards, but they love to eat meat and that ain't particular whether it is cow or horse. They like to sneak up at night and shoot arrows into your stock, then lie off in the hills and wait until you pass on through the canyon. Then they run down and carve up the carcass."

"That is dreadful," Mrs. Courtenay said. "When will we be out of all this danger?"

"Tomorrow, with any luck, we will get through that little canyon. Beyond there we will pick up the Thousand Springs Creek and then it will be fairly easy going clear down to the Humboldt. We can refresh ourselves there before we set out across the desert. Any more questions?"

"Excuse me, Captain," Mr. Courtenay said, "but those Indians the other night slipped into our camp even though we had a watch set. What's to prevent them from doing the same tonight?"

"Tonight, we will be ready for them. We will keep Boris untied and standing guard. He can smell an Indian a mile away, maybe two miles for Diggers."

So, for a third night in a row, we retired with only cold rations in our stomachs. But everyone was so weary from the ordeal of descending Granite Mountain and from the long, hurried day through Goose Valley that soon the camp echoed with snores.

I put myself to sleep, thinking of the supposedly easy trail that lay ahead of us. My baby was due in just a few more weeks. Mr. Courtenay assured me that my child would be born "in civilized surroundings." But, of course, he was such an optimist.

Captain McGee had trained Boris not to bark unless he told him to, but we were awakened by the sound of the great dog's growling and whining.

The man on watch said, "Captain, shall we sic the dog on them?"

"All right. Go get 'em, Boris."

I heard the dog's paws scrambling in the dirt as he raced off into the dark toward whatever or whoever had attracted his attention. His barking grew fainter and fainter. Then suddenly a shot sounded from the direction of the canyon's mouth, and the barking ceased.

Captain McGee shouted for all the men to fall out with their guns. He ordered Lester and Will to mount up and follow him and for the others to remain behind to make sure the stock did not again stampede.

A bit later, several gunshots came from the direction of the canyon. A long silence followed. This was broken by the bawling of first one and then another steer.

5

When dawn finally broke over Granite Mountain, we realized what had occurred. While Captain McGee and the others had ridden off to see what had happened to Boris, some Indians, presumably Diggers, had slipped close to our camp and had shot arrows into two of our steers and one horse.

None of the animals was killed, but it was obvious that they should be put out of their misery.

Scarcely had this discovery been made when Captain McGee, Will Tremelling, Lester, and Mr. Courtenay came riding back from the mouth of the canyon. At first I thought the captain was carrying a mountain lion draped over his horse's withers, but, as they drew nearer, I saw to my horror that it was the body of Boris.

From his reddened eyes, I saw that the captain had been weeping. Only now his face bore an expression more resolute than any I had ever seen.

He and the others lowered the body of the great dog from the horse and laid it beside the big willow tree. Without waiting for instructions, Lester got two shovels and he and Will started digging a grave.

While this went on, Captain McGee inspected the wounded stock, but refused the suggestion that they be shot to end their agony.

He walked around and around, smiting the fist of one hand into the palm of the other, muttering to himself like a mad man. No one dared approach him. When the grave had been dug, he squatted down and patted the dog's head, just above the hole left by the rustlers' bullet.

To no one in particular, he said, "I wouldn't have taken a thousand dollars for him. This was my fault. Never should have turned him loose in the dark. God damn it, Diggers generally just have bows and arrows. Stupid, stupid. It was a trick to draw him away. Oh, they will pay for this, they will."

"Captain, we have finished digging the grave," Will said.

My heart went out to that aloof, proud man as he stood up and wiped his eyes, then nodded as a sign for Boris to be lowered into his grave there beside the big willow tree on the bank of Little Goose Creek.

At his direction, the boys gathered heavy stones from the creek bed and covered the dog's body with them to frustrate coyotes. Then they shoveled in the dirt and stamped it down hard.

I was saddened by the slaying of Boris, but my grief was nothing compared to that of our train master's. Yet no one dared offer him comfort.

At the completion of the burial, he called our party together and asked the tallest man among the men, Will Tremelling, to don his sombrero.

"Good, it fits. Now try on my shirt."

The leather hunting jacket was too wide across the shoulders for Will, but the captain said, "I reckon that will do. Now, I tell you what I want you to do."

*   *   *

Anyone keeping watch from the cliffs overlooking the mouth of Little Goose Creek Canyon that morning would have seen a tall fellow wearing a sombrero and riding Captain McGee's big gray, lead our train of wagons into the canyon, headed south. They would have observed two steers and one horse lying down near the big willow tree with arrows bristling from their sides.

They would not have seen Captain McGee, Lester and Mr. Courtenay hiding in a clump of small willows a short distance upstream from where the wounded animals lay.

Acting on the captain's orders, Will led us into the canyon briskly but, once within its narrow walls, he slowed to a snail's pace.

Mrs. Courtenay was beside herself with anxiety for her husband.

"He is always doing rash things like this. There is no call for him to risk himself so. The dog is dead. We can spare the animals. I shall never forgive him if he gets himself killed."

Opal who was leading the pair of donkeys rolled her eyes and whispered to me, "She acts like she is on stage. Don't know how that man puts up with her sometimes."

"Aren't you worried about Lester?"

"Lester is like a cat with nine lives."

"What do you think they mean to do?"

"I reckon they just want to teach them little Indians a lesson. That Captain McGee is as big a fool as any man. Maybe bigger than most. He is full of white man's pride. And his pride has been hurt cause them Indians outfoxed him. Pride goeth before a fall. He is going to find that out some day."

* * *

We had gone little over a mile in the canyon when we heard first one, then another fusillade of shots from our old camp site. A pause was followed by several single shots. Then silence.

Will Tremelling turned Captain McGee's horse around and set off at a gallop toward the sounds. To my amazement, Mrs. Courtenay likewise turned the carriage around.

"Watch the children," Mrs. Courtenay said to Opal as she lashed the rumps of the horses.

Before the carriage gained speed, I ran up beside it and drew myself into the seat beside her.

"This is no concern of yours," she said.

"You are stuck with me now."

By the time we got out of the canyon, Will had reached the willow tree. We could see the gray horse standing with empty saddle beside a group of kneeling men. As we drew near, putting my hand up to shield my eyes from the morning sun, I saw first Captain McGee and then Will stand up. On closer approach, we could make out Mr. Courtenay waving his arms and gesticulating.

"Thank God," his wife said.

At the approach of our carriage, Mr. Courtenay held up his hands to stop us and walked over to say, "You don't want to see this."

His wife thrust the reins in my hand, got out of the carriage, and brushed past him.

"Oh, my God," she shrieked.

Leaving the horses to fend for themselves, I followed her.

Two men lay on the ground. One, face down, was an Indian. The other, lying on his back with open eyes, was Lester. And, sitting against the willow was Kentucky Pete.

His wrists were bound. Blood stained his filthy shirt and his teeth chattered from the pain of his buckshot wounds.

"Who will tell Opal?" Mrs. Courtenay said as she looked down into the face of the man she and her husband had rescued from slavery.

* * *

What had happened, as described over and over by Mr. Courtenay and others, was that Kentucky Pete and his comrade, a Ute named Running

Wolf, had been responsible for stampeding our stock back at Junction Valley, then, as Clarence Goodall surmised, had moved ahead of us up over Granite Pass and into Big Goose Creek Valley. There Running Wolf had recruited a small band of Digger Indians, promising to draw McGee and his dog away so they could wound enough of our stock to fill their bellies after we moved on.

They had been taken in by Captain McGee's ruse of disguising Will Tremelling as himself and had walked into the trap set for them. Only Captain McGee had thought he would be dealing with Diggers armed merely with bows and arrows and perhaps one or two muskets. The Diggers had scampered away but Running Wolf and Kentucky Pete had elected to shoot it out. Running Wolf was killed instantly. Kentucky Pete got a full load of buckshot in his arm and side. And Lester was killed.

Of course, all this did not come out at once. First Captain McGee requested that Mrs. Courtenay drive the carriage back into the canyon to break the news to Opal and fetch her and shovels. Refusing his suggestion that I accompany her, I walked over and looked down at Kentucky Pete. His one eye glittered with defiance.

"So it is little Miss Fancy Pants herself. Never thought I would lay eyes on you again."

I replied, "You mean eye, I think." Seeing he missed my joke, I added, "I am surprised you aren't in jail by now."

"There ain't no law and there ain't no courts out here. Beside which, if anybody is to be tried, it should be you for causing the death of my friend Bart Corbett."

Suddenly, Captain McGee was at my elbow and heard Pete say, "She knows what I mean, and I think you do too. Bart and me seen her down in that creek and he said he was going down to make her cough up the money her husband took off him at St. Joe. I don't think it was Indians that killed him at all."

Before he could say more, Captain McGee's booted foot caught him square on the jaw and, stunned, he fell sideways.

"Really, captain," Mr. Courtenay said. "Is that necessary? After all he is wounded and helpless. We should be merciful."

"Mercy is for human beings, not vermin like him."

"What do you mean to do with him then?"

"First wring the truth out of him."

"What about a trial?"

"You heard him. There ain't no courts or law out here. But that don't mean there can't be justice. Now go off and figure what to say to that poor black woman about Lester when she gets here. No, little lady, you can stay here for a bit. I'll want you as a witness to his confession."

With an offended air, Mr. Courtenay went over to close Lester's eyes and cover his face with a handkerchief.

"What makes you think he will confess?" I asked.

"He'll confess all right. Ah, he's coming around. Now then, Mr. Kentucky Pete, did you ever hear of the game called Russian roulette?"

From the look on his face, it was obvious that he knew exactly what Captain McGee was talking about as he drew his revolver and removed five charges from their chambers. Yet Pete refused to speak even after the captain had spun the cylinder and drawn back the pistol's hammer. He kept his mouth closed even after the captain put the muzzle against his forehead.

"Ready to talk?"

"Go to hell, McGee."

Click! The hammer fell on an empty chamber. The momentary look of apprehension on Kentucky Pete's face was replaced by a grin.

"There, you have played your game, McGee, and I won. So why don't you just let me go about my business? I'll not tell what I suspect about Bart Corbett's death, and you can say nothing of this little affair."

"But the game is not over."

"What do you mean?"

The captain spun the cylinder again and recocked the pistol.

"We are going to keep playing until you tell all about what you and your Indian friend have been up to."

"What Indian friend?"

"Running Wolf," Captain McGee said, "I have knowed the son of a bitch for years. And he's lying over there dead, as you will be sooner or later, if you don't start talking."

"Go to hell, McGee."

This time the click of the hammer made Kentucky Pete jump.

"Every man is entitled to a fair trial," he said, his tone now less belligerant.

Captain McGee spun the cylinder again but before he could cock the weapon, Pete said, "Wait. Maybe we can make a deal. What is it you want to know?"

"Start with how you and Running Wolf got up here ahead of us."

"Do you promise not to shoot me?"

"Only if you answer every question. So start talking."

The ensuing interview went on until we saw the Courtenay's carriage, accompanied by Will Tremelling on the gray horse, approaching from the mouth of the canyon. That is how we learned the details I have related earlier about the stampede and the scheme to dispose of Boris.

Opal leapt from the carriage and ran to where Lester lay. Shrieking with grief, she removed the handkerchief from her husband's face and took his hand.

"Sweet Jesus, why did it have to end like this? Oh, Lester baby, you can't go and leave me like this. You all I got."

While Opal was taking on so, Captain McGee took a shovel and matter of factly began digging a grave near that of Boris. Kentucky Pete watched the activity with a look of triumph, as though he had won some sort of victory.

Perhaps to make up for his earlier rudeness, Captain McGee allowed Mr. Courtenay to take charge of the burial of Lester. With Opal's sobbing as background, the actor did a fine, if impromptu job, quoting the 23rd Psalm and other Bible verses, and praising Lester as "a man of unmatched courage, who, like Moses, escaped from his Egypt only to be denied entrance into the Promised Land."

Once the brief, but touching ceremony was over, they covered Lester's body with a robe from the carriage. The Courtenays had to restrain Opal from leaping into the grave as the men tenderly laid a pavement of heavy, smooth stones atop the shrouded body and then shoveled in the dirt.

When this was done, Captain McGee walked over to Opal and said, "He was as good a man as I ever seen, white, red or black. I am dreadful sorry to lose him. I had got to depend on him."

"Yes," she said bitterly, "I had got to depend on him too."

"Well, folks, I am sorry about this but I reckon we had better get on out of this territory."

"What about him?" Mr. Courtenay asked, pointing to the body of Running Wolf. "Don't we need to bury him?"

"No, leave him lying there as a warning to his Digger friends. The coyotes will save us the trouble of burying him."

"And what about him?" meaning Kentucky Pete.

"I'll ask the Cornishman here to help me deal with him. You folks run on and tell the others we'll be along directly."

The Courtenays helped the sobbing Opal into the carriage. I remained until Captain McGee said, "That applies to you, too, little lady."

I climbed in the carriage beside Opal and put my arm around her shoulders. It was the first time in my life I had ever hugged a Negro but it came as naturally as if she had been my sister.

Opal and I sat facing the rear of the carriage. As we rolled toward the mouth of the canyon where the rest of the wagon train awaited us, I looked back to see Captain McGee and Will lifting Kentucky Pete upon the back of the big gray. The captain, casually it seemed to me, looped one end of a rope loosely over Kentucky Pete's shoulders, then tossed the other end over a limb of the willow and tied it around the trunk.

Naively, I thought he was just trying to wring some fresh confessions out of the prisoner, but, to my horror, saw him slap his hat against the rump of the horse. The startled animal bolted, and there Kentucky Pete dangled, his feet well off the ground as he vainly twisted, trying to raise his bound hands to his throat.

Much as I despised the man, still I was shocked almost to the point of fainting by the sight of the hanging.

Mr. Courtenay was facing away from the scene. Seeing my expression, he asked, "Annie, do you not feel well?"

"I will be all right as soon as we get away from this dreadful place."

Although Opal faced the rear of the carriage as did I, in her grief she had not observed what was happening. She removed her hands from her face to say, "Dreadful place. You said a mouthful there. This is the valley of the shadow of death, if ever there was one."

"Indeed so," replied Mr. Courtenay. "And now let us pray that we will be privileged to be led beside the still waters and lie down in green pastures."

Soon Captain McGee, with Will riding behind him, overtook us. I had come to admire his courage and iron will, but now the man frightened me in a way more than had Kentucky Pete. I had seen him hang a man as casually as he had dispatched that injured ox back at Granite Pass. I dared not look into his face as he passed us. But I could not resist one last glance back toward the willow tree where the body of Kentucky Pete dangled like a straw-filled effigy.

By noon we had cleared the Little Goose Creek Canyon and by nightfall had made our way over fairly even country to a camp site near an excellent spring. Mr. Courtenay tried to comfort Opal with a draught of brandy, but she refused. Mrs. Courtenay told her she need not cook that night, but she replied, "If I don't do it, who will?" and proceeded to prepare us a good meal.

Captain McGee went about his business as if nothing had happened. But Will's face reflected the horror of what he had experienced firsthand.

Although reluctant to discuss it, after I told him what I had seen, he said, "The villain thought the captain was joking at first. When he seen he wasn't, he said that the captain had promised not to kill him if he told the truth. The captain said, 'I promised not to shoot you. I said nothing about hanging you.' Next thing I knew, he drove the horse out from under the man. It was awful, Annie. I seen men die from being hurt in the mines but I never seen anybody hanged like that."

"Nor have I, Will."

"Look now, the captain ordered me not to speak to anyone about this. Don't you let him know what I told you."

"Don't worry. I will keep quiet. But I can't put out of my mind the sight of a man being hanged like that in cold blood."

"Captain McGee is a cold-blooded man, Annie. I'd never want to cross him, you can be sure."

"Nor would I, Will. Oh, I will be so glad when this dreadful journey is over."

"So will I. I can't wait to get to California and start earning that three dollars a day."

6

Once free of the ominous canyon of the Little Goose Creek, we entered an area that was less dangerous but in many ways even more hellish. At noon, the heat grew so intense it sapped the strength of both humans and animals; at night, the cold became equally enervating. The dust, which I had considered intolerable back along the Platte and the Sweetwater, worsened. The same could be said of the insects. Our eyes and those of our stock became caked with dust and the exposed parts of our bodies, covered with bites.

Soon we encountered at first hand specimens of the Digger Indians whom everyone, Indian and white, held in such contempt. Small bands of them stood along the trail or came to our evening camp sites to offer for sale staples of their diet, such as various rodents and roasted insects. One bow-legged, pot-bellied and incredibly ugly fellow offered us a five-foot water snake. He seemed as puzzled by our refusal to trade as we were by his thinking he was offering us a delicacy.

Unlike their proud cousins, the Shosone or Utes, the Diggers had no horses. They travelled on foot and lived by digging up roots and insects, hence their unflattering name.

At least there was no problem finding water on our passage down to the Humboldt. One spring produced copious quantities of warm but sweet water. It was there that we saw a warning inscribed in tar on the sun-bleached skull of a steer. Apparently left by a party that had recently followed the same path we were taking, it read, "Watch out for Indians in Goose Valley. We lost two horses and three oxes." Mr. Courtenay set another skull next to that one and wrote on it, "Now you tell us. Same goes for Junction Valley."

Farther along the trail, we came to an area pock-marked with deep, clear springs, many of them surrounded by old wagon wheels and other debris, including the ubiquitous bones of cattle and horses. Later, we passed through a region marked by spumes of steam rising from hot springs, and there Captain McGee announced that we were in the Valley of Thousand Springs Creek. He warned us again not to let our stock drink any water he had not first ascertained to be free of deadly alkali.

By now, Opal seemingly had accepted the fact of Lester's death. However, I could tell from her look of disapproval when Captain McGee passed our wagon that she held him responsible for putting her husband in danger.

Mr. Courtenay told me that Captain McGee had fired a load of buckshot at Kentucky Pete, whereupon he and Lester stood up from their place of concealment and opened fire. Running Wolf fired back, with a musket, and felled Lester. Captain McGee then fired the second barrel of his shotgun, killing the Ute.

"There were a half dozen other little Indians with bows and arrows. They scampered away, like frightened mice. I emptied my revolver at them, but doubt I hit anyone. Oh, that experience will make a grand chapter in my book."

"A great chapter for you; a very sad one for Opal," I said.

He looked suprised, then frowned at my impertinence, or perhaps at his own lack of sensitivity, and changed the subject.

Men can be such damned fools. I began to understand why the wife of this English actor, with his chequered theatrical career and grand hopes for a new life in Califorinia, questioned his judgment. Yet so far he had been unfailingly kind and courteous to me. For reasons I will get to later, I am reluctant to speak ill of Homer Courtenay.

In the absence of Lester, who had been responsible for caring for and driving their six oxen, Mr. Courtenay pressed his son, Simeon, into service. Although their first efforts were laughable, they soon learned enough to keep up with the rest of the train, although not nearly as well as we had with Lester.

We reached the headwaters of the Humboldt via Bishop Canyon, following a rocky path that crossed the southerly course of Bishop Creek several times, and came at last to the northern bank of the Humboldt River, which we were to follow through the otherwise arid desert for some 300 miles. And every one of those miles was to prove an agony for me, in my seventh month and well-nigh penniless, or for Opal, who had been freed from slavery only to find that her freedom was far from idyllic, or for Mrs. Courtenay who, I could tell, was becoming less and less sanguine about her family's prospects in California.

Still, Will Tremelling and his two Cornish comrades remained cheerful, buoyed by their expectations of escaping from their impoverished homeland to a new Eden where they could earn $3 a day.

What Captain McGee felt, I could not say. He spoke even less frequently. However, one of the men reported hearing him call out in his sleep, "Here Boris. Come back, boy."

Although he never alluded to the fate of Kentucky Pete, it was not long before the details were known to everyone. Mr. Courtenay and Will swore to secrecy each person to whom they told the story, but any fool should have known that once two or more people learn a secret, it no longer is a secret. Men like to say women talk too much. They are the biggest gossips of all.

After all these years, I cannot recall very much about the next two or three weeks as we made our slow way along the Humboldt. Look at your map and you will see how that curious river rises from several small streams in the northeast corner of the present state of Nevada, heads west for about a third of its length, then takes a long loop to the north, turns and runs south by southwest, and finally, near the Trinity Range, peters out, well short of the edge of California.

As we trudged along, mile after tedious mile, my thoughts ran often to our friends now headed for Oregon. I could not help thinking that had I remained with them, at least I would be passing through cooler country, with trees around us. And, whatever else they may have been, the Hixons were good, practical providers, not the feckless dreamers I now perceived the Courtenays to be.

Far from relaxing his vigilance along the Humboldt, Captain McGee took extra precautions. He kept us to the north side of the river, although the grazing would have been better on the south. He said there was a colony of Utes inhabiting the area just below where the river took its great northward swing, who were "as mean a bunch of savages as you'd ever want to meet."

He allowed small camp fires to be built but ordered four guards with loaded weapons to patrol during four-hour watches. As a result, the men in our party grew increasingly testy. I began to wonder if California was a mirage that remained shimmering in the desert air, just out of reach, no matter how many miles we covered?

As the great Nile River provides the land of Egypt with a ribbon of fertile, life-supporting soil, so the Humboldt, although of far more modest proportions, supplied those who crossed the Nevada desert back in those years with a kind of lifeline of water and grazing grounds. Without the Humboldt, the desert would have proved impenetrable even for wagon trains led by men as intrepid and expert as Zebulon McGee.

As we neared the apex of the northern loop of the river, Captain McGee eased up on our nighttime vigilance, declaring us to have passed beyond the reach of the Utes. Now, he said, we would see mainly Paiutes, whom he declared to be "decent fellows who live and let live."

Yet, the August sun and the long physical strain began to take their toll on our animals. More and more we passed wagons that had been abandoned and the skeletons of the oxen who had given out dragging the vehicles. Sometimes, the frames of the abandoned wagons provided us with firewood.

Our passage was made somewhat easier by the occasional trading posts set up along the trail's grazing grounds and offering inferior food staples at inflated prices.

So, onward we plodded, making about twenty miles most days, until we came to that curious region called the Sink, where the Humboldt, instead of emptying into a sea or lake like most rivers, simply petered out into the desert sands, producing a wide swatch of marsh lands. We stopped for a full night and all of the following day to rest our gaunt animals, collect drinking water, and cut bundles of marsh grass to carry in our wagons to sustain our stock for the next day or so when we were to see not a blade of grass.

Today a train can speed across that desert in less than an hour, but, as Captain McGee announced, and Mr. Courtenay's guide book confirmed, the next forty five or fifty miles were considered the deadliest of the journey across the West.

Emigrants had a choice of angling to the south, toward the Carson River or west, toward the Truckee. Each was daunting. The Carson route, although slightly longer, offered the advantage of easier passage through the Sierra Mountains into the interior of California. The Truckee route boasted a set of hot water springs about midway across the desert, but this asset was offset by the very rough mountain travel beyond.

Captain McGee explained our choices, but before anyone could voice an opinion, decreed that we would be taking the Truckee route.

Often since that day have I reflected on the profound difference that seemingly arbitrary decision was to have on my life. Ah well, perhaps it is better for us humans not to see too clearly or far into our futures. Where would the fun and adventure of life then lie? It would be like reading a novel whose ending you have been told.

At any rate, we spent a full twenty four hours resting ourselves and our stock for the approaching ordeal of the desert passage. The moon, although only half full, would cast enough light to make night travel possible, or so Captain McGee said.

Opal silently and sullenly cooked up enough rations to do us for the next day or so. Captain McGee passed through our camp urging us to discard any heavy items not absolutely necessary, warning that we would encounter sand far deeper than any so far and that beyond the desert lay a series of steep climbs and descents through the Sierras. A few Dutch ovens and chairs were left behind by others, but Mr. Courtenay refused to part with any possession from his overloaded wagon or carriage.

Several of our company's steers were ruled by Captain McGee to be unfit for the ordeal. He persuaded the owners to set them free to graze, "Otherwise, they'll end up as skeletons out on the desert."

None of this seemed to dampen the spirit of Mr. Courtenay, however.

"Help me to remember this," he said to his wife. "I want to record what we did, saw and said here as we approach the promised land."

"Oh, do shut up about your stupid book," Mrs. Courtenay said. "And stop parading about making speeches. You haven't collected a keg of water for our animals as McGee instructed."

As soon as the sun had set, we began our passage into the desert. The Truckee and Carson Routes followed the same trail for a short way and then separated. At the forks in the trail, a trader had set up a little store where he sold hot bread and a few vegetables. The odor of his bread was tempting, but we were not allowed to stop.

On and on we rolled over the increasingly sandy trail, following the lantern our leader carried on horseback. Soon the half moon cast a ghostly light over the barren landscape. The white covers of our wagons glowed in the reflected light. The yipping of coyotes rang from the low hills, to be answered by the pitiful bawls of our weary oxen. We moved slowly, often stumbling over stones. The heat of the blazing sun faded so that by midnight our teeth were chattering from the cold.

Opal marched along, leading her two faithful little donkeys. She had spoken only when spoken to for the past few days. Now, without preamble, she surprised me by asking, "What you gonna do when you gets to California, if we gets there?"

"I guess I will have my baby and then see what happens."

"You ain't got no money, have you?"

"Only a few dollars."

"So you are depending on the Courtenays to support you?"

"What choice do I have? Aren't you depending on them, too?"

"Black folks seldom have a choice. You could marry that Will fellow, you know. He is crazy about you."

"He is only a miner. I have my sights set higher than that."

"You didn't set them all that high with your Elmer, if you don't mind my saying so."

"I do mind. And there was more to Elmer than you might have thought."

"How come you to marry him in the first place? It was plain to see you didn't love him."

"Since you are being so nosy, what about Lester? Did you love him?"

"Not at first. The Tollivers put us together like they was mating horses. Then I came to appreciate him after a while. He was a good man. By the way, what did you say was the reason you married your Elmer?"

"I did not say."

"No, but I think I know."

"And I think you are getting nosy."

She laughed, and said, "Don't go putting on airs with me, girl. I am old enough to be your mother. Besides, you are in the same boat as I once was. Only difference is our color and the fact that you can keep your baby. All we got to depend on is an Englishman with big ideas and a big mouth."

"Hush. It would hurt his feelings if he heard you."

"All right, but let me warn you not to put too much faith in him. He likes to talk more than he does to do. Now that Lester ain't here to play his banjo and do all the hard work, they gonna treat me like the slave I used to be. I see it coming. You just watch out they don't try to treat you like that fat woman that used to boss you around."

Oddly, the friendship between Opal and me, previously formal and rather distant, was sealed during our frank exchange on that long, nighttime trek from the Humboldt Sink to the hot springs.

By the early light of the next day, we saw the steam rising from the springs. The oxen, smelling water, began bawling. If they had not been so weary, they would have raced toward the springs. Forewarned by Captain McGee, the men restrained the beasts and went to dip out the scalding water to cool before offering it to our animals.

The water was so hot we could make our coffee without building fires, which was fortunate as there were only a scattering of sage brushes around to be burned.

As eerie and tiring as the night journey had been, it was easy by comparison with the following day. After a two-hour rest at the hot springs, we set out under an increasingly warm morning sun. Soon we were passing over, or rather, through, sand that came halfway up to the axles of the wagons. In places the sand required us to double team the oxen to drag the wagons through beds of the clinging mass.

By noon, with the searing heat of the sun bearing down on us, the first of our oxen began to falter. The train had to stop while Captain McGee inspected the poor creatures to see if a bucket of our precious water would revive them. If not, they were freed of their yokes and turned loose. Generally they simply lay there, panting. Now trunks and other heavy items, that should have been discarded back at the sink, were removed from the wagons to lighten the loads of the remaining oxen.

We did not pause for our usual hour of rest at noon. Instead, we washed down cold rations with water while remaining on our feet.

Mrs. Courtenay, in her carriage, now was the only person not walking. Her husband occasionally made ludicrous attempts to make Lester's old bull whip crack above the ears of his hapless oxen, but he might as well have saved his strength. His poor children stumbled along behind, whimpering at the heat of the sand on their feet.

The trail passed up over a little hill, and it was there that the two lead oxen sank to their knees and refused to rise. Before Captain McGee could ride back to see what was the trouble, one had died.

"I hate to tell you," he said to Mr. Courtenay, "but you ain't going to get this wagon through to the Truckee. Not with just four oxen in their condition. You had better dump everything except for bedding and food."

"But everything we have is in this wagon: props, costumes, play books, all the tools of our trade. We can't leave all that here."

"No, and you sure as hell can't haul it any farther."

After a bit of arguing and vain offers to buy the steers of other parties, with Mrs. Courtenay in tears, they started throwing out their trunks, chairs, tableware, anything to lighten the load.

"Here, Annie," he said. "This Bible is too heavy. I am sorry."

"It was Elmer's. It means nothing to me," I said.

Opal intervened, saying, "Give it to me. I'll put it in my cart."

When I protested, she said, "You gonna need that book someday."

By the time our train drew in sight of a line of trees several miles away, a quarter of our oxen had collapsed and were left behind to join the carcasses and skeletons that lined the gauntlet.

In a kind of stupor, we stumbled on toward the trees, which at first I feared would prove to be a mirage. Then suddenly, our animals began bawling and neighing, and those with sufficient strength, bolted for the water they smelled.

Mrs. Courtenay's pair of horses, resisting her efforts to restrain them, trotted away from the rest of the train.

Soon all of us, animals and humans, were standing up to our knees in the icy cold water of the Truckee River.

7

Although the grassy lands along the Truckee at that point were overgrazed, Captain McGee allowed us to rest beside the stream the next day to recover from the desert passage. Since many of us had discarded our barrels and sacks of food staples, the several traders around the camp ground did a brisk business in selling us weevily flour and nearly rotten vegetables.

By now my girth had swollen so that I had begun to walk with that awkward, reared-back gait of women in the late stages of pregnancy. My back ached and I had become bone weary. Thank goodness the ice had been broken between Opal and me. I don't know how I would have got through the next few weeks without her.

"You getting too big to walk, Annie. But I spect if you was to ride with Mrs. Courtenay in her buggy, all that jostling might bring on the baby early. When did you say it is due?"

"Around the end of September."

"That ain't far off."

"Near or far, all I can do is keep moving with the crowd. But, oh, Opal, I am so tired."

"I know you is, honey. But don't worry. We'll be looking out for you all the way to Sacramento."

It was all I could do to keep back my tears at this unusual show of affection from that stern black woman.

The Truckee flowed east, out of the Sierras, as if it meant to reach the

Humboldt Sink only to change its mind abruptly and head north to empty into Pyramid Lake far off our course. We followed the river west toward its sources in the snow-capped Sierras during the next few days, crossing and recrossing the stream so many times that we soon came to appreciate the more placid Humboldt. The cold, swift water raced over great, slick boulders between which we could see fish swarming.

The trail led ever upward, so that the oxen had to strain to pull even their lightened wagons. It was beautiful country. We passed through forests of great pine trees and often sighted deer running away from the clang of our iron wheel rims on the stony path and the bawling of the emaciated oxen.

We halted for another day of rest on the shore of a majestic lake which Mr. Courtenay declared to be where the famous Donner party had been imprisoned by heavy snows several years before. As he talked about their privations, I looked around our party and wondered whether we, like the Donner group, would be capable of eating the flesh of dead companions if we were similarly trapped and starving.

As we prepared to retire for the night, Captain McGee went among us to caution against allowing our stock to eat the poisonous wild parsnips that grew in the area. He also warned that the next thirty miles could prove the most taxing of all.

"Once we get over the pass, it will be fairly smooth going all the way down to Sacramento."

We had endured the fording of the wide Platte, the long pull up over South Pass, the passage through the Wasatches and over Granite Mountain, and the recent horror of the desert. None of these could quite compare with the next five days, however. It was as if some evil fate had reserved the most arduous part of our journey for the end, when we and our animals were most exhausted, and when this young widow was most pregnant.

We required three days to work our way up the eastern slope of the mountains over a trail that often was a trail in name only. Over and over we had to double team our oxen. Several times the poor beasts had to be unhitched and allowed to scramble over rocky ledges on their own while the men, cursing and swearing, hand carried their loads and then lifted their wagon beds and running gear over these cruel obstructions.

The descent down the western slope was even more daunting. The men had to snub their wagons, one by one, down the steep inclines, doing this by wrapping their restraining ropes around small trees to serve as brakes.

Mr. Courtenay decided this procedure to be unnecessary since he had so lightened his wagon on the desert. The vehicle got away from him and Simeon and rolled down into a boulder, then pitched over on its side with a broken front axle.

Captain McGee inspected the wreckage, looked at Mr. Courtenay with disgust, and declared the wagon beyond repair.

This was more than Mrs. Courtenay could bear. I thought she might be stage acting again, but decided otherwise as she laced into her husband, calling him an "utter fool" for not heeding instructions for descending the slope. She also castigated him for "saddling us with the care of a pregnant girl, against my wishes." Then, loudly enough for everyone to hear, she said she wished she had listened to her father's warning not to marry him.

Normally so jaunty, Mr. Courtenay seemed to shrink physically under the whiplash of her words. Both their children began to cry when she called him "a second rate actor" and "a failure even in the theater." Her tirade grew in intensity and went on so long that Captain McGee made the mistake of intervening, saying, "Now, ma'am, there is no use crying over spilt milk."

She turned her unspent fury upon him.

"There is far more than spilt milk here, you presumptuous idiot. All our stage property has been left out on that desert which you stupidly led us through. Now we have lost our personal belongings as well."

"Why, ma'am, that only means you will be able to travel faster now."

"Why don't you just mind your own business, you uncouth ruffian? You strut about acting like some sort of backwoods God when you are as big a fool as my husband, and that is saying a great deal indeed. If you had not persuaded him to join you in punishing those Indians, we would not have lost our Negro man, who would have had the good sense to get us down this awful hill. And for what? To avenge the death of a stupid dog. Don't deny it! For a half breed dog! What's more, it was you who chose this route rather than the other across the desert. I wish we had never laid eyes on you, you uncivilized boor."

I would never have thought it possible that anyone could get the better of Zebulon McGee, but that outraged English actress rendered him speechless. Like her hapless husband, he, too, seemed to shrink under the weight of her words.

Opal looked at me with wide eyes, saying, "Who-ee, that woman knows how to lay a man out cold with nothing but her mouth. Look at

Mr. High and Mighty Mountain Man. He don't know what to say."

Actually, I felt sorry for the captain, who stood about with reddened face under her verbal onslaught. But I felt even sorrier for the two Courtenay children. I put my arm around Heather's shoulders and took Simeon's hand. Then, I reminded myself of what she had said about being saddled with "a pregnant girl," took a deep breath and yelled, "Mrs. Courtenay! Stop acting like such a damned fool. Get control of yourself. See how you are upsetting your poor children."

I braced myself for a fresh broadside as she turned toward me with flashing eyes. But suddenly she put her face in her hands and sat down on the trail, sobbing hysterically.

Obviously relieved by the respite from her wrath, McGee began recruiting others to help Mr. Courtenay free his four oxen from the wagon wreckage. Heather and Simeon went over to comfort their mother.

Opal looked at me and shook her head.

"You something else, Annie. I didn't have the nerve to do that. Didn't trust myself after I heard her call Lester 'our Negro man' like he was their property. She better not ever call me her 'Negro woman' or she'll find herself doing her own cooking. My slave days is over."

"Yes," I replied without much conviction, "And she had better never refer to me as that 'pregnant girl,' as if I did not have a name and feelings like herself."

The upshot of all this was that Mr. Courtenay, with Will's help, transformed his oxen into pack animals by burdening their backs with the family tent, bedding and other items.

We descended the rest of the downward slope without further serious incident. But I noticed that McGee remained well away from Mrs. Courtenay and that Mr. Courtenay walked with his head down.

Pity us poor women. Sometimes a sharp tongue and a violent temper become our only defenses. And pity the poor men who become the targets of those two deadly weapons.

* * *

With the last great physical barrier of our journey behind us, many in our party, like the Cornish lads, began skylarking and joking as we passed through the western foothills of the Sierras. In general, they had thrived from the exertions and excitements of the journey, not to mention their expectations for good jobs at gold mining. But, of course, they were not females, pregnant, and dependent on a family who no longer seemed so dependable.

Now there was plenty of grass for our played-out stock, and water as well. The sun's rays fell more gently on our backs. The forests through which our trail now led echoed with the songs of birds. As I trudged along, I fantasized about having at my side a strong young husband like Billy Joe Duncan, only older and more responsible, marching with me to begin a new life in this promised land of California.

The Courtenays now spoke to each other only when they could not avoid it. The two children, baffled by the hostility of their parents, clung to me and Opal. When a man and wife stop talking to each other they create a hell for themselves and those around them. It is far better to have your differences out in the open than to let them lie and fester.

Nearly five months had passed since we had crossed the Missouri River and begun our trek of close to 2,000 miles over the plains and through the mountains to this raw new land. I had met more fascinating people during those five months than I would have encountered in five lifetimes back in North Carolina. And I had gone through many more personal dangers than had I allowed myself to be married off to a domineering older cousin, as had my mother. When I died, at least it would not be from boredom.

It had been Captain McGee's intention to pause at Nevada City, in California's busiest gold mining region, but a fellow with a strong Irish brogue who came upon our camp site about twenty miles from the town changed his mind about that. The man was headed east with a team of mules pulling a wagon loaded with empty water kegs and barrels of oats and flour. According to him, a great fire had destroyed most of Nevada City a few weeks before.

"What about the Union Hotel?" McGee asked.

"You'll not find it or any other hotel left, although I hear Bicknell's Block on Broad Street, being brick, survived the blaze. They say it is to be turned into a grand hotel. Nope, your best bet is to continue on to Grass Valley which is only five miles farther. They had a bad fire there more than a year ago, but the town has been built back just fine. You find better grazing there anyway."

After Captain McGee had given the Irishman permission to camp with us that night, the fellow introduced himself as Paddy Finnegan, and explained that he was on his way from Sacramento to set up shop in the desert to succor travelers such as ourselves.

Eager to talk to someone other than his wife or those who had witnessed his humiliation the day before, Mr. Courtenay engaged the man in conversation long into the night. At first, I had little interest in the Irishman's garrulous description of the gold camps, my mind being set on getting to Sacramento, but Mr. Finnegan's colorful talk not only caught my attention but attracted that of the Cornish lads and others.

"I jumped ship in San Francisco in forty nine, with four bits in me pocket and a set of tin cups and dishes in me sea bag. Me and me ship mates stopped off at Sutter's Fort, but finding the claims all taken up there walked up to these parts and took out claims along one of the creeks. Ah, it was bitter cold, wet work, with our feet in water over our shoe tops, scrabbling away in the creek beds, panning out the flakes of gold. Did that for near to a year, during which I collected several thousand dollars worth of gold dust, most of which, it grieves me to confess, I gambled and drank away. Everyone was here for the money, let me tell you. Only women were them come to sell the only commodity their kind had to offer, and I won't say what that was in deference to you ladies. Gambling halls and saloons every few feet. Men quarrelling over claim jumping. Fights and murders every night. Used to be plenty of Indians about but soon those that didn't die of diseases white men brought in ran off into the mountains. Look around at all the tree stumps and you'll see what happened even to the great forests. All cut down for miles around by lumbermen."

Mr. Courtenay interrupted the Irishman's narrative with, "You say you worked for only a year. What happened?"

"One morning I wakes up with a dreadful headache and sick stomach from the last night's carousing and asks meself, 'Patrick John Finnegan, was it for this that ye left County Cork and spent two miserable years aboard the ship of a hateful English captain? Was it for this little sack of gold dust under your mattress that these past twelve months ye have been freezing your hands and arse'...begging your pardon, ladies? So, instead of going to me claim I walked through the streets of first Grass Valley and then Nevada City to see in the cold, sober light of day just who was prospering. Seen it was the fellow that had set up an assaying office, or thrown together a gambling hall or saloon with green lumber and canvas, or that had the gumption and capital to haul in picks and shovels and buckets to sell at outrageous prices to fools such as meself.

Mind you, many such was native born Americans with proper education and friends with money which was denied to a poor Irishman. And being both male and Catholic, I couldn't or wouldn't enter into the business of prostitution. So I sold me claim to a Chinaman and took that money and me bit of gold dust to go down to Sacramento and buys meself a wagon and mule and a load of mining supplies, which I hauled up to Nevada City and sold for twice me investment."

On and on he ran with his tale of his growing success until interrupted again by Mr. Courtenay.

"Then pray tell me, my good man, why you are hauling water and foodstuffs out to sell emigrants in the desert?"

"Trust an Englishman to ask an awkward question. If ye must know, things have changed in the gold fields these past few years. They switched from panning gold out of the streams to sluice mining. None but Chinamen scrabble in the water anymore. Others found they could do better shoveling in the earth from the creek and river banks into these sluices, which is nothing more than long wooden troughs set on rockers. All that took was a claim, a sluice and some shovels, and access to the water. Some even went digging well away from the streams and carried the earth down in wheelbarrows to the sluices. Then back in fifty two the market for gold fell and some son of a bitch, begging your pardon again, ladies, why he came along and discovered hydraulic mining."

"You'll have to explain what that is."

"Why ye gets yourself a great canvas hose such as firemen use with a nozzle on one end and a good source of water high up above your diggings. Then you uses the God-given force of gravity to direct a stream of water against the dirt to wash it down into your ever bigger sluices. All this takes more capital and organization than the old ways. Today ye'll not see one in ten of the fellows such as meself that panned for gold in '49 and '50. And what the bastards are doing with their hoses to this once beautiful land is a crime against nature. Just look around you on your way down to Grass Valley tomorrow. 'Ye'll see whole hillsides being washed away and creek beds filled with their leavings. Now the evil villains fight over who controls the water. They form stock companies and dig ditches to bring the water down from high up in the hills. That takes money. And down in the camps around Grass Valley they've started digging down deep underground to get at the gold ore locked in beds of quartz. That takes big money, mostly from the East to pay for the great machines needed to crush the quartz. Nay, the mining business outgrew this simple son of the old sod. I can do better hauling water out from the Truckee to sell to emigrants such as yourselves. Let the tycoons and foreigners have the gold business."

"Here are three of your foreigners here," Will Tremelling said. "From Cornwall we are."

"Aye, and couldn't I have told ye were Cousin Jacks just by your moustaches and the cut of your clothes, even if your manner of speech didn't give ye away. Well, lads, living costs being so high, ye won't get rich at mining for day wages. Been a bit of a slump lately, but I do hear tell of money being raised for more quartz mining. So be patient and there should be jobs enough to keep ye in beer and pasties if ye know your business."

I do believe the man would have talked until dawn had McGee not come around to order us to turn in for the night, which was to be the last the Cornish lads and others headed for the mines would spend with us.

I was awakened early the next morning by pains such as I had never experienced. They came every ten or fifteen minutes in waves that left me gasping. I concealed my discomfort until after breakfast when Opal noticed my pale color and my sweating.

When I told her what was the matter, she said, "Oh, my God, it do sound like you are beginning your labor."

For once in her life, Mrs. Courtenay sacrificed her own comfort and insisted that I ride in her carriage crammed in between herself and a bundle of her childen's clothing. She had developed into an expert at guiding the horses. The road was smoother now. I was glad to be off my feet at last.

Word of what was happening passed quickly through the train. Captain McGee, like most of the men, seemed too embarrassed to inquire after my health, but he did step up the pace of our passage along the generally downhill road toward Grass Valley.

*   *   *

By early afternoon the pains were coming every five or six minutes, pains so intense that I had to bite my knuckles to keep from crying out. Mrs. Courtenay, her ire at her husband set aside for the moment, relaxed her normal English reserve to apologize for her outburst following the accident and to offer me words of comfort.

"I quite forgot myself back there. You poor, dear girl. We will get you to a place of safety before dark. Just hang on and never fear."

Opal, too, called out words of encouragement.

"Don't fight against the pains, Annie. Try to think of something else."

"That is the silliest advice anybody ever gave me," I replied.

"I reckon you are right, at that."

"You and Opal have grown rather close these past few weeks, haven't you?" Mrs. Courtenay observed.

"She is an unusual woman," I said as I gritted my teeth against a fresh wave of pain.

"Why is it that I perceive a lack of gratitude on her part? After all we have risked in bringing her and her husband out of slavery she has yet to say a simple thank you."

I bit my tongue to keep from suggesting that her own haughty air of superiority might be the reason and said simply, "Perhaps it is just Opal's way."

As we neared Nevada City, between waves of labor pains, I looked about at the land on either side of the ridge along which our road ran. Everywhere you could see the ravages being wrought by hydraulic mining: huge open sores of denuded earth scoured out of mountain sides. And the landscape was further desecrated by the shabby wooden buildings of the mining camps. And this, I thought to myself, was the Promised Land?

About three miles east of Nevada City, where the road began a steep descent from its long ridge route, I gave up trying to stifle my cries. Mr. Courtenay called for Captain McGee to come to our carriage so that his wife could announce that "If we don't get her to a doctor, we will have a baby to deliver here on the road."

McGee took Mrs. Courtenay aside and after a brief consultation told her, "I am turning my horse over to your husband. I have told him of a place between Nevada City and Grass Valley where someone will put her to bed and fetch a doctor."

So it was that Mr. Courtenay mounted the big gray and, with our carriage following, rode rapidly down the hill, leaving Captain McGee behind on foot to drive the family's remaining four oxen. The two children remained with Opal and her donkey cart.

We fairly flew past the burnt-out buildings of Nevada City on to a long, two-story frame building that sat near a stream bordering Grass

Valley. There we waited while Mr. Courtenay knocked at the door. A large woman with reddish hair answered.

I heard him mention the name of Zebulon McGee which resulted in his being invited inside, out of our hearing.

In a moment, he emerged and said, "Very well. She says she can provide a room. And she is sending one of her girls to summon a doctor." Then, to me, he said, "You will be fine now, Annie. Didn't I tell you we would see you through?"

The red-haired woman took my arm as I alighted from the carriage and led me into a room that sported a beat-up piano and an array of chairs. Several young women looked up to see who was entering.

Wondering why Mrs. Courtenay had remained outside without speaking to the woman, I followed my guide down a long hall into which the doors of several small rooms opened. We went back to a kitchen and through it to a little lean-to beyond.

"There is your bed, dearie. Just lie down there. Doctor Jacoby will be here soon, I am sure. What did you say your name was?"

"Annie Mundy," I said, then added, "Mrs. Annie Mundy Hixon, actually."

"And this is your first baby?"

"I am only seventeen."

"And just how long and how well do you know Zeb McGee?"

"Only since last April. He has led our party here from St. Joe. I can't say that I know him all that well though."

"I doubt if anyone could say that of Zeb. I wouldn't do this if I didn't owe him a favor. So you just lay there and try to make yourself comfortable. My, but you are a young thing. And where is your husband?"

"He died of cholera on the trail."

"I see. Don't know why that snooty bitch in the buggy didn't come in with you. Looks like the type that would think herself too good to enter an establishment such as mine."

She turned and yelled down the hall, "Mildred, have you gone to fetch Doctor Jacoby?"

"She is on her way, Mrs. Harmer," a girl's voice sounded.

After that a fresh wave of pain, the worst yet, hit me. I remember very little of what followed.

END OF BOOK ONE

BOOK II

PART ONE

1

When Presbyterians recite the Apostle's Creed, they say that Jesus "descended into hell" following his death on the cross. That is where I was for most of the following night and next morning. I descended not only into a hell of pain such as I had never experienced but one also of utter despair at having been dumped off like an unwanted pregnant cat at a wayside barn.

The doctor, a plump, red-nosed little man who smelled of whisky, examined me, and asked a few questions, some of which I found insulting. Had I ever had any venereal infection, indeed! Then he gave me a sedative that momentarily dulled my agony, and departed after saying he would check on me later, meanwhile I should try to work with rather than against the pains.

I wish every doctor who utters such platitudinous advice would have to bear at least one child himself.

Anyway, I floated in and out of consciousness throughout the night; in and out of periods of mental clarity and of hallucinations, so that I cannot say which of my memories were of real events and which were my drug-induced imaginings.

Someone kept screaming. It was me, of course, but the cries seemed to be coming from some other person. Somehow, I got the notion that if only I could crawl away from the bed I would leave the pain behind. Several pairs of gentle hands constrained me from doing this. From the kitchen next door, I kept hearing the anxious hum of women's voices and, during the early part of the night, the deeper drone of male voices coming from beyond.

By dawn I was so exhausted I wanted to die and have it over with.

Doctor Jacoby appeared again, still stinking of whisky.

"She is dilating but not fast enough to save the baby, I fear."

"You must do something, Doc. She drove our trade away last night with her yelling. I don't want to be stuck with a dead girl on my hands."

"Where are her friends?"

"They figured she would have the baby right off and they would carry her and it on with them to Sacramento today."

"This poor girl would be in no shape to be moved even if the baby came right now."

At that I let out a wail of pain and hopelessness. The doctor's hand stifled my cries. Then, before I could get my breath afresh, he poured a draught of laudunum into my mouth.

"Leave me alone, you quack," I mumbled.

"She really is out of her head, isn't she?"

"Because she called you a quack? Some around Grass Valley might agree with her."

"This is no time for making jokes, Evelyn. Who did you say she is?"

"I told you last night, Doc. I owed this favor . . . "

Their voices and faces faded away as the sedative took effect.

When I came to, it was full daylight. Outside my room I heard voices which I recognized as Captain McGee's and Mr. Courtenay's. I couldn't make out what they were saying, however. They stopped when I began again to yell and moan. Through my pain, I heard the voice of the proprietress telling the men to "shut up and go fetch somebody to take care of her. This is not a hospital, you know."

I don't remember the actual delivery, so much laudunum did the doctor pour into me. As described to me later, it was a messy business, involving much bleeding by myself and swearing by Doctor Jacoby. Nor do I remember saying the shocking things that were attributed to me.

I came out of my drugged stupor to the sound of a baby crying. Opening my eyes, I looked up into the face of Opal.

"There, there, honey," she said. "You ain't going to die like that drunken little doctor said after all, are you?"

"No, but where am I?"

"I would rather not say just yet."

"What are you doing here?'

"They left me to look after you."

"You mean they went on without me?"

"They seen it was taking too long and you wouldn't be able to travel anyway. So they packed up and left."

The baby's cries broke out again.

"What is that?"

"You must still be out of your head. That is your son."

"Oh, my God. Let me see him."

In a moment she was back at my bloodsoaked bed, holding the baby. I tried to raise my arms to take him, but lacked the strength. She laid him on my shoulder.

"He ain't too pretty right now, but give him time. It was a long, hard birth. His head will shape up fine in a few days."

A strange warmth and sense of joy drifted over me as I felt the baby snuggling against my breast.

"Opal, he is all right, isn't he?"

"For a while there it looked like we might lose him and you both, but you came through. And now I am here to look after you."

"Why did they leave you behind?"

"They didn't leave me. It was my idea to stay. Mrs. Courtenay called me a black ingrate. But Mr. Courtenay seen it my way. He may be a fool, but he has a good heart, for a white man, that is."

"Why did you do this, Opal?"

"She just wants someone to cook and wash and for her to boss around. He just wants to strut around and brag about rescuing this poor Negro woman from slavery and make himself look like a hero. He told me they would send for us both soon as they get settled and you are able to travel, but don't count on it. Look at how fast they dropped you off here when they seen how much trouble you would be with a baby."

"Maybe you misjudge them. Else why would they have taken me up in the first place?"

"Oh, Mr. Courtenay gets carried away with ideas and then cools off fast. He calls them adventures. He did help Lester and me get away from them old Tollivers, but we was getting ready to run off north anyway. He talked us into coming with them, pretending to be their slaves."

The baby made a snuffling sound, and I hugged him closer.

"Oh, Opal, he is so tiny. What am I going to do with him?"

"Just raise him up."

"How?"

"The Lord will show us a way. Don't be worrying about that right now. First, you got to give him a name."

"That is easy. I will call him Walter Duncan Hixon."

"How come?"

"Walter Scott is the name of my favorite author. He is a Scotsman. And Duncan is the name of the baby's true father back in North Carolina. It is a Scotch name, too."

"I thought his name was Billy Joe."

"How did you know that? I never told you his name."

"No, but from the way you kept cussing him and calling his name when you was out of your head, I figured that had to be the boy that got you in this fix."

"I called his name out loud?"

"Yeah, and you called him other names that won't bear repeating. Even some of them whores was shocked by your language."

"Whores? Where?"

Opal laughed until tears ran down her face.

"Oh, honey, don't you know where that McGee left you off at? This is a whorehouse. Didn't you see all them girls out there?"

"I don't believe you."

"Child, you got a lot to learn, haven't you? I hate to think what would be your fate if I had not stayed behind. Now, you have talked enough. You need to rest. Here, let me take little . . . what you say you want to call him?"

"Walter Duncan."

"Yeah. Here little Walter Duncan. Your mama needs to rest. We got to make you a sugar-tit to tide you over until she starts to make some milk of her own. Then we got to change these sheets."

*   *   *

The three of us—Opal, little Duncan, and myself—spent the next three months living in that lean-to behind the kitchen of Evelyn Harmer's House of Joy on the outskirts of Grass Valley. After I got over my shock at the nature of the establishment, I began to feel more secure in my surroundings. The several girls of the house, despite my disapproval, could not keep their hands off little Duncan. Ignoring Opal's protests, they insisted on carrying him about the house during the mornings when no patrons were allowed inside. They vied for the honor of bathing him.

At first I resisted their offers of help but my reserve melted the day three of them asked admittance to our lean-to and presented me with a layette made of blue satin together with a rattle and a pacifier. I came very near to crying.

Dr. Jacoby came by every other day for the first few weeks. It was by his decree that I was kept in bed during that time.

At first Evelyn Harmer treated us as though we were nuisances but loosened up when Opal volunteered to take over cooking for the house, a chore which Mrs. Harmer had been doing herself to hold down expenses. She was not what you would call a generous woman, nor a very good cook. The quality of the food at the House of Joy improved immediately and with it everyone's mood.

"That is a handy nigger woman you got there," she said to me. "I was going to have to ask you to start paying room and board, but I reckon we can delay that."

"I am glad we can stay a while, but let me suggest that you never let Opal hear you call her by that name. She is very proud."

"I call it uppity, but I take your meaning."

About three weeks after Duncan's birth, while I was still bed-ridden and very weak, a letter addressed to me in care of Mrs. Harmer arrived. From Mr. Courtenay, it bore the address of a hotel in San Francisco.

He explained that he and his wife had been unable to find "acceptable bookings" for their talents in Sacramento and so had sold their oxen and taken up residence in San Francisco. They were doing minstrel shows there "until roles suitable to our tastes and talents eventuate." Meanwhile, he said, he was starting to write his book about our trip across the West.

He also reported that Zebulon McGee and Clarence Goodall, the old trader squaw man, had found each other in Sacramento and that McGee had asked to be remembered to us when he wrote.

I read on, looking in vain for some word that he would make good on his promise to send for us when I was able to travel.

"I don't know why you thought he would," Opal said. "They was both glad to be shut of you."

"How are we going to get out of this place?"

"The Lord will show us a way."

"But you know Mrs. Harmer will not let us stay here forever."

"That woman does have a heart of stone. Her girls might as well be slaves the way she keeps them tied down. The thing we got to do is make ourselves so useful she won't kick us out before we are ready to go."

"You are making yourself useful enough."

"Yeah, cooking for a bunch of whores. Now you supposed to be so smart, teaching school and all that. And you are white. So why don't you find a way to make yourself useful around here, when you feels stronger, that is?"

"I hope you are not suggesting that I make myself useful in the way her girls do."

"Lord no, honey. But I notice that woman frowning and sweating over her figures. Maybe you can help her. Suppose I mentions to her how you been teaching them children their sums back on the trail."

The upshot was that the next time Mrs. Harmer looked in on me, I volunteered to lend her a hand with her accounts, and she readily accepted.

It was easy to put her income and her expenditures in orderly fashion in her ledger book. Today, many people consider me a good, practical business woman. When they ask me where I learned my skills, I never tell them it was in a brothel in a gold camp.

So, with Opal doing the cooking and me handling the bookkeeping as well as overseeing the purchase of food, towels, etc., and Duncan fast becoming the mascot, we bought ourselves time for me to fully regain my health and for us to get our bearings.

*   *   *

Although I despised what Evelyn Harmer's girls did for a living, I deplored the circumstances that drove them to the so-called earliest profession.

God, themselves and their customers only knew what actually went on in their little cubicles, but in my presence they spoke politely, rarely uttering an oath or making a vulgar remark. And they showed a poignant interest in someday bettering themselves.

Each girl had a story she yearned to tell to a sympathetic female who, unlike Mrs. Harmer, had no wish to exploit her.

Thus Mary, a plump Irish brunette from Dublin's slums, told of being with child by a married man and of abandoning her baby at a nunnery and stowing away on a ship bound for Boston.

Francine, a somewhat older woman, had come out to California in search of her sailor husband who had jumped ship to go panning for gold. She found that he had died in a bar room brawl in Sacramento. Rather than return to her parents' little farm in New Jersey, she had been recruited by Mrs. Harmer to enter what she called "this line of work . . . at least till I get enough money to return home, although I don't know what I would do there."

Mildred was a fat, washed-out blonde, not at all apologetic about her profession. In her words, "We got it and men want it bad enough to pay for it. So what's the harm?"

I was amused to see the disapproving look on Opal's face when this was said in her hearing.

Then there was poor little Madeline, a thin, dark girl from Illinois, not much older than I. With tears in her eyes, she told of how her own father had violated her from the time she was 12 until she ran away to St. Louis at 16.

On and on their pitiful stories ran. And so did their expression of hopes for a better future.

Seeing how her girls were turning to me for sympathy, Mrs. Harmer notified me in her blunt way that I was not to encourage them to talk about their backgrounds.

"They all have tales of woe, and a lot of it just ain't so. They act like they have all been took advantage of when the truth is that they usually was the ones that took the initiative that got them in trouble. So take what they say with a grain of salt."

Thinking of how her harsh observation could have been made of my own case, I changed the subject.

"How about your own situation, Mrs. Harmer? How did a woman of your obvious intelligence come to be in this business?"

"My mother ran such a place in New Orleans. A very good establishment it was, too. But growing up, I was so ashamed I ran away with one of her customers, a shipping clerk who figured he was rescuing me from a life of sin. He married me and we had two children. They all three died in a yellow fever epidemic. A rich older gentleman took me under his wing, so to speak. Set me up in a little house of my own. He died of a heart seizure, in my arms. To hush up the manner of his death, his sons gave me a sum of money and bought me a ticket to come out here to California."

"That is too bad."

"Not really. I run a good, clean establishment. Why do you think Doctor Jacoby came so quick when I sent word about you? I pay him handsomely to keep check on the health of my girls. One of them lets herself catch the pox, and out she goes. One of them fails to tell me of gratuities, which are to be shared by all, and out she goes. I provide them with protection and security and I expect absolute loyalty. Do you understand?"

"Of course," I said, all the while thinking what a hard-hearted woman she was.

"Now consider your own situation. You are young and not bad looking, although some better clothes and a bit of rouge wouldn't hurt. I can't afford to give you and your nigger woman more than room and board, but when you feel well enough . . . "

Before she could complete her sentence, I cut her off with, "Mrs. Harmer, what you seem to be suggesting is out of the question. I would starve to death rather than stoop so low."

"No call to get on your high horse, my dear. I only meant to set your mind at ease, in case . . . "

I stood up, opened the door and said, "You have not set my mind at ease. In fact you have upset me. Now please leave."

She paused in the doorway and said with an affronted air, "You accept my hospitality but you dare to treat me with disrespect. You may find yourself eating humble pie some day."

Opal, working in the kitchen, heard only the tail end of our conversation.

"What was all that about?"

After I had told her, she said, "Honey, we got to get ourselves out of this place. That woman is going to drag us down to her level."

I sat and put my face in my hands.

"What am I going to do, Opal?" I wailed.

"You mean what are we going to do. As long as I got breath in my body, ain't nobody going to turn you into a whore."

"Opal, you are the best thing ever to happen to me. I wish there were some way to repay you."

"There is."

"How?"

"You can teach me to read and write."

"You mean you can't?"

"You from the South. You know it is against the law to teach Negroes back home. But I see you teaching some mighty dumb younguns back on the trail. I reckon I am just as smart as them. So how about it?"

Opal was right, about being smart that is. By the second day of my instruction, she knew her A,B, C's. Within a week I had her signing her name. And, at her request, each morning and evening, I read to her from OLIVER TWIST.

When they were not occupied, Mrs. Harmer's girls liked to gather in the kitchen and hear me read. Sometimes, as I read of the hardship of Dickens' orphans, they even shed tears.

Madeline, the girl from Illinois, shyly inquired if I might teach her to read as I was doing for Opal.

"If it is all right with Mrs. Harmer."

It was not all right with her mistress, however.

"If you want to spend your time teaching your nigger woman, that is your business. Don't go messing with my girls. You will just make them dissatisfied."

So, gradually regaining my strength and confidence, I busied myself with nursing and caring for dear little Duncan, keeping the accounts of the brothel in good shape, and teaching Opal to read, write and do sums.

It galled me to be under the thumb of Evelyn Harmer, but at least, with winter approaching, we had food and shelter. By next spring, I reckoned, Opal and I somehow would find a different way to support ourselves.

It was during this period that the bond between Opal and me was sealed, never to be broken. This happened when I remarked on her skill at child care "when you have never been a mother."

"Who says I ain't?" she replied, and under my prodding proceeded to tell how, when she was no older than I, before she had married Lester, she had borne "a beautiful little girl."

"What happened to the baby?"

"They gave it away before it was weaned, to a free colored family in Richmond. Why? They was ashamed."

"Because you weren't married?"

"No. Because the daddy was married. And what's more he was their nephew, a young so-called gentleman."

Too shocked to speak for a moment, finally, with tears in my eyes, I said, "Oh, Opal, how could you bear such a thing?"

"A slave has to bear things you would know nothing about."

The cold look in her eyes dissuaded this daughter of a slave owner from asking further questions.

2

It is odd what changes motherhood makes even in a headstrong female like yours truly. I awoke every morning and went to bed every night thinking of little Duncan and his welfare. He was a charming baby. Thriving on my plenteous supply of milk, he quickly lost his resemblance to a skinned rabbit and grew quite chubby.

The girls of the house loved to watch him playing with his toes in his basket by the kitchen stove while I worked on Mrs. Harmer's daily accounts. More and more, despite Mrs. Harmer's disapproval, they took me into their confidences, speaking freely of the generally wretched circumstances under which they had grown up. They expressed eloquent hopes for a better future.

Two or three regularly sent money back east to aging parents or handicapped sisters. They often reminisced about this girl or that who had either married a smitten client or who had been infected with a venereal disease and had been kicked out by Mrs. Harmer.

They never divulged to me exactly what they did with their clients behind the closed doors of their cubicles. It was as if they wanted to preserve the innocence of this respectable young widow. I think they saw in me the person they might have been at my age.

Avoiding the knowing stare of Opal, in answer to their questions, I described Elmer as a promising young lawyer who had been destined to become a senator or governor until cholera cruelly struck him down.

As they sat about on chilly autumn mornings, listening to me read from OLIVER TWIST, they reminded me of my little students back on the trail from St. Joe in what now seemed an age ago.

Mrs. Harmer had a strict rule against their discussing their clients among themselves but, out of her hearing, they made sly references to this man or that. For my part, I did not see the men except through the kitchen window as they approached the establishment. The kitchen was off limits for them. The walls of the brothel were only a single plank thick, however, and I could hear their voices, sometimes cheerful, sometimes belligerent or even shy, and often drunken. The heavy clump of their mining boots shook the house. The squeals of the girls mixed with the uproarious cries of the men.

Mrs. Harmer, whatever her lack of bookkeeping knowledge, understood male psychology very well. Although her greetings to her clients sounded hearty, at the first sign of what she called "rambunctuousness," her tone hardened to that of a stern school mistress warning a high-spirited lad to behave himself.

It had been our intention, Opal's and mine, to remain at the brothel through the winter. What was left of the money that had been stolen by Bart Corbett and returned to me by Captain McGee, was hardly enough to set us up in some enterprise such as a school, which remained my dream. That little supply of money became depleted one sunny day in October when Opal and I ventured forth from the House of Joy to shop for fabric and sewing material for baby's clothes and dresses for Opal and myself.

With Opal carrying little Duncan, we crossed Wolf Creek on a wooden bridge and proceeded up Main Street in Grass Valley, then a town of about a thousand souls.

It was a raw sort of settlement. Most of the town, some 300 structures, had been destroyed in a great fire a little more than a year before. Now a number of brick buildings had replaced flammable wooden structures. By that time, I had seen towns from Charlotte to St. Louis, from St. Joseph to Salt Lake City. Grass Valley was unlike any of them. Everything looked as though it had been thrown together in a hurry. Here and there a two-story edifice stood, but most were narrow, one-story affairs. An assayer's office might stand side-by-side with a dry goods or grocery store, a saloon across the street from a hotel. We saw a newspaper office and not one, but two, Methodist churches, one the Methodist Episcopal and the other, the M.E. South.

Oh, yes, there was a considerable contingent of Southerners in the area, mockingly called by other Grass Vallians "chivs" or "the chivalry" for their air of superiority and disdain of hard physical work. We saw also Chinamen and Irishmen.

Higher up the hill from Wolf Creek there were a number of more substantial, even painted, houses, belonging to lawyers, doctors and mine managers.

Opal and I got rather carried away with our shopping, ending up with an armload of cloth and both writing material and a child's primer, the last items to further Opal's schooling.

Back at the House of Joy, we threw ourselves into sewing, one of the few household skills my mother had taught me. With Mrs. Harmer's girls watching every stitch, I fashioned several dresses for Duncan. I made Opal a stout calico skirt and blouse. For myself I cut out a long blue chambray dress such as the mistress of a well-to-do household would have prized.

Our resolve to leave the House of Joy before winter set in, evaporated one morning when we awoke to the sight of several inches of snow on the ground. I was unsettled by the sight for it rarely snowed back in North Carolina.

So Opal and I set aside our half-formed plan to leave. We hunkered down in our lean-to. By now I had Opal reading simple sentences. She was eager to learn to read the Bible for which she had a great reverence, but I dissuaded her. I finished reading OLIVER TWIST and took up IVANHOE which soon had the girls entranced, although Opal thought the story "a lot of nonsense."

*   *   *

We undoubtedly would have remained at the House of Joy until spring had it not been for an incident that occurred on a Saturday night around the first of December. A second snow had fallen on the remains of the first, and it had turned cold. Although the more sophisticated deep pit quartz mines continued to operate, it was too cold for open stream panning, even by the stoical Chinese. And the more prevalent hydraulic mining closed down completely because the water had frozen in the sluices.

All this translated into a boom in the already busy trade in which Mrs. Harmer and her girls were engaged.

I had never showed my face outside the kitchen or lean-to during business hours. And I had learned to make myself especially scarce on Saturday nights. On this particular Saturday, the clients began arriving early. Awaiting their turns, they crowded into the large front room, laughing and drinking. Someone with rudimentary piano playing skills, began banging out barely recognizable tunes by Stephen Foster and such. I could hear Mrs. Harmer as she rapped at doors and called out, "Times up in there. Tell the gentleman he must go now."

Only late on this Saturday night, one decidedly ungentlemanly gentleman was not ready to go. "Bull" Duchamps, a French-Canadian, had taken a great fancy to Madeline, claiming her to be French like himself. Mrs. Harmer forced Madeline to leave her room while she dealt with

Duchamps. Instead of waiting to wash herself and remake her bed, she fled down the hall and knocked at my door.

Her face streaked with tears, she asked, "What will I do, Annie? He wants me to run away with him."

"Do you love him?"

"When he is sober, I like him better than most. But he scares me."

Normally, Mrs. Harmer would have been able to persuade Duchamps to depart peaceably but on this night not only was he raging drunk, he had brought along two roughneck friends from his mining camp. I could hear all three male voices raised against Mrs. Harmer's down the hall.

In one moment, a muffled scream sounded from Madeline's room. In another, our door was thrust open, and there stood Bull himself. He was a stocky, powerful-looking man with dark red whiskers. Behind him loomed a taller, even more menacing-looking chap.

"There you are, mon petite Madeline."

"Where is Mrs. Harmer?" Madeline asked.

"We shut her up in your room. My friend Frank McGinty is holding the door on her. She can't stop you. Come along."

"Come back when you are sober and we'll talk then."

"Too late for talking. Here . . . "

He reached out to seize her arm. Grabbing up a pair of scissors, I blocked his way.

"Take another step and I'll stab your eyes out."

"Who the hell are you?"

His friend stepped into the room and put his hand on Bull's shoulder.

"It's the widow girl. I heard she was kind of pretty. Here, sweetheart, why don't you pack up your things and come along with me?"

These were big men, and with Mrs. Harmer shut away, there was no one to protect us, or so I thought. Judging from the noise coming from the front room, a new batch of miners had arrived. Even if I had screamed, no one would have heard me.

"Keep your voices down," I said. "You'll wake my baby."

By this time Opal had crawled out of her trundle bed. She stood up and said, "Won't you gentlemens kindly step outside to discuss the matter?"

Bull's companion turned upon Opal.

"Ah, yes, and this is the nigger woman I been hearing about. She can come along, too. Frank McGinty is always talking about how much he likes a bit of dark meat now and then."

Opal took her place beside me, shielding Madeline, and as though she had not heard the man's insulting remark said sweetly, "Excuse me, gentlemens. I believe I left a pot of pea soup on the stove. Can't be letting it burn now, can I?"

Reluctantly they stood aside so she could pass.

"What do you think, Bull?"

"About what?"

"The nigger woman. A little long in the tooth, maybe, but you know there ain't nothing like a coon when it comes to . . . "

He never completed his sentence. Suddenly Opal was standing behind him with the pot of boiling water that always stood on the stove top for the girls' use between clients. She hurled its contents squarely upon the back of the man who had insulted her and her race. He cried out in agony. Enough of the water carried past him to splash the legs of Duchamps.

The friend, whose name I never learned, screamed with pain. Bull, cursing in both French and English, turned upon Opal, who backed across the kitchen and took up a poker.

Taking a knife from his belt, Duchamps bellowed, "McGinty. Come here!"

Suddenly there were three of them in the kitchen: one writhing on the floor and shouting for a doctor; one with a knife in hand confronting Opal; and the third, who had been holding Mrs. Harmer's door, trying to make sense of the scene.

I remained in my doorway, still armed with my scissors.

"You take one step toward me with that knife and I will bash your head in," Opal declared.

"Put down the poker or I will cut your throat."

"Oh, this is the nigger woman I been hearing about," the newcomer said.

Brave as Opal was, she didn't stand a chance against those two brawny men. Meanwhile, the fellow who had been scalded, opened the kitchen door to go and roll in the snow.

"Wait!" I cried in my loudest voice. "Leave her alone or I will stab you both."

"Take care of her, McGinty," Bull said.

His friend looked at me with a half smile.

"Now, honey, you are going to hurt your sweet little self with them scissors. Here, give them to me."

How I longed to have Bart Corbett's derringer in my hand instead of a pair of cloth scissors.

"Go ahead, McGinty. Get the scissors away from her. Hey in there, Madeline, baby. Get your things and let's go."

As Madeline darted through the kitchen, McGinty, like a rattlesnake striking, leapt forward and grabbed the arm I raised to protect myself. With my other hand, I plunged the points of the scissors into his shoulder. He cried out but kept his grip on my one arm. Before I could stab him again, he seized my other wrist and made me drop my weapon.

At that Opal advanced on Duchamps and struck at his head with her poker. He warded off the blow with his forearm and struck her with his fist so hard that she was thrown across the floor.

"In here, boys," Mrs. Harmer cried from the hallway.

In less time than it takes me to write this, three lithe young men burst into the kitchen. One seized McGinty from behind, tore him free of his grasp on my arms and sent him spinning into the wall.

The other two pounced upon Duchamps like two terriers besetting a bull dog. One got him around the neck; the other by the legs. The three of them careened about the kitchen, knocking over chairs and tables. At last they brought the powerful French-Canadian down against the stove, knocking it off its base.

Mrs. Harmer was screaming, "For God's sake, don't start a fire." Opal was painfully finding her feet and taking up her poker again. McGinty, stunned from his collision with the wall, sat nursing his head. Outside, the fellow Opal had scalded was pleading for a doctor.

All the girls and their clients were crowding into the hall, gazing upon the shambles of the once peaceful kitchen. In my room, little Duncan had awakened and started crying.

I was at the point of going to him when the fellow who had tackled McGinty, said, "Annie, surely this is not you. What are you doing in a place like this?"

I looked into his earnest face and replied, "Why, Will Tremelling. I might ask you the same thing."

*   *   *

While Mrs. Harmer attempted to repair the damage to her kitchen and after Will had got over his embarrassment at my seeing him in a brothel, he and I quickly brought each other up to date on our respective lives.

He and his two friends had parted company with the wagon train under the impression that I would deliver my baby and proceed with the others to Sacramento. And I had been so absorbed in motherhood that I had hardly thought of the three cheerful young Cornishmen who had been so helpful to me on the trail.

The three of them had found jobs at a new quartz mine and were lodging with several other miners at a camp south of Grass Valley. Will assured me that it had not been his idea to come to The House of Joy, that he was just accompanying his friends. I pretended to believe him.

Peace was gradually being restored to the House of Joy. Bull Duchamps and McGinty, swearing vengeance upon Mrs. Harmer, had departed to haul their scalded friend to a doctor. The remaining clients set the stove back onto its base before a fire could break out. Opal was holding a wet cloth to her swollen jaw. I had got little Duncan calmed down and was showing him off to Will and his friends. All's well that ends well, I was thinking when Mrs. Harmer demanded, "Where is Madeline?"

The girl was not in her room. All her possessions were gone.

Under close questioning, Mrs. Harmer got Mildred to confess that she had seen Madeline packing up.

"She said she was going after Bull."

There followed a howl of anger and frustration.

"After all I have done for that ungrateful little bitch. I took her in and treated her like my own daughter. And this is how she repays me. All of you are silly, stupid bitches, especially you, Mildred. You could have stopped her. I hold you responsible."

At this Mildred started blubbering.

"Shut up! I've half a mind to turn you all out to go with her and her lousy French Canadian."

On and on she ranted like a madwoman. The Cornish lads looked embarrassed by the outburst. Then little Duncan became upset by the noise and started crying again.

Remembering how I had snapped Mrs. Courtenay out of her hysterical tirade following the wagon accident, I spoke up.

"Mrs. Harmer! Get control of yourself. You are acting like a fool. These girls had nothing to do with Madeline's leaving. Besides, this is a free country. Why shouldn't she go if she wants to? Now stop it."

She turned upon me with a fury I had never experienced, at least not from a woman. Speaking in a low, deadly hiss, she said, "I think you may be behind this entire thing. Yes, I am sure of it. That McGee fellow said you would be no trouble. He said your English friends would send for you and the nigger woman. Yet here you have remained, eating up my food and setting my girls to thinking they are better than they are. I should have known you were trouble the minute I laid eyes on you and your uppity black huzzy. Well, I have had a bellyfull of your self-righteous airs, as if you are too good for my establishment. So if you think Madeline did right to leave me on a busy Saturday night, you can just pack up your things, take your squalling brat and your nigger woman and clear out."

Taken aback by the vehemence of both her manner and her words, I could only respond with, "Right now?"

Opal and I looked at each other, then at Mrs. Harmer. I saw nothing but a cold hatred in her eyes as she replied, "Right now."

"Annie," Will said. "You could come and stay with us, if you have no place to go."

"Thanks, Will, but that won't be necessary."

"But it is bitter cold outside. Where will you go?"

"I noticed a nice-looking hotel on this side of Grass Valley, the Pacific, I think it is called. Perhaps you all would help us carry our things over there. Just give us a few minutes to get packed."

3

I had the presence of mind to change into the grand dress I had made for myself but had never worn. With Opal carrying Duncan and all three of us bundled against the cold and with the three Cornish lads lugging our effects, we made our way across the crusted snow to the lobby of the Pacific Hotel.

There I stood in my long, lace-trimmed dress, trying to look like a Southern lady. Behind me, Opal held the baby and did her best to look like a faithful Negro mammy. The three Cornish lads, burdened with our luggage, hung back, letting me do the talking.

The clerk, a bald-headed fellow, had been napping behind the counter when we entered. He rubbed the sleep from his eyes and surveyed the five of us, actually six, counting Duncan.

"I don't think we can accommodate you," he said.

"Why not?"

"There is so many of you and we are short of rooms."

"Perhaps you did not hear me. It is only I, my child, and my servant who require lodging. These gentlemen are neighbors who kindly agreed to transport our belongings."

"It is near to midnight. Why are you . . . "

"Why do we seek lodging? If it is any of your business, there was an accident in our kitchen. The stove was tipped over. We were forced to vacate."

Taken singly, each of these statements was true, of course. It just goes to show how selected truths can add up to what amounts to a lie.

"Well, I wish we could accommodate you, Miss."

"It is Mrs. Mrs. Elmer Hixon. My husband died on the way out here from Missouri. He was a lawyer. Now stop this pretense of not having any rooms available. Do I not see the keys for two hanging from their nails? Perhaps if you were to fetch the manager, I could speak directly to him."

That took the wind out of the fellow's sails for a moment, but he recovered and beckoned for me to join him at the end of the counter.

"We don't normally rent to the colored trade," he whispered.

"That is ridiculous. If you knew anything of our Southern customs, you would understand that it is quite acceptable for hotels to accept the nurses of young children. She will sleep on a pallet on the floor, if that matters."

"How long would you be wanting to stay with us?"

"I would say for a week."

Seeing his face cloud at this, I quickly added, "And naturally I would pay in advance. How much would that be?"

He named a price, apparently setting it high to try to discourage me.

"That would include meals, of course," I said.

"For three people? I think not."

"Why don't you think again? Or go fetch your manager and let's ask his opinion."

The upshot of our exchange was that he agreed to include breakfasts and suppers and I turned over half of my remaining dollars to him. Then I said goodbye to Will and his friends and thanked them for coming to my rescue.

Will assured me once more that it had not been his idea to visit the brothel "but the way things turned out, I am glad we did."

"I am too, Will."

Our unheated room was large and drafty. It did, however, boast a wide bed with a firm, horsehair mattress. Forgetting my assurance that Opal would sleep on the floor, we both piled into the bed with Duncan cuddled between us.

Before we drifted off to sleep, Opal said, "You know, Annie, you are something else. That is what you are."

"Is that a compliment, Opal?"

"I reckon so. But now that we have got ourselves out of that whore house, what is going to happen to us?"

"Nothing is going to happen to us."

"What do you mean by that?"

"It is up to us to make things happen, not just wait until they do. I have learned that much, at least, from our trip across the West."

My last thought before falling asleep was the recollection that it had been almost a year since I had invited Billy Joe Duncan to help me gather eggs in my father's barn. And now his son, his and mine, lay snuggled up against my breast in a California hotel. Knowing what I then knew, if I could turn back time to that previous December, would I have done the same thing all over again?

I fell asleep before I could answer my own question.

*   *   *

We spent all of the next day, a Sunday, in our room, allowing our minds and spirits to recover from the bedlam back at The House of Joy. While Opal nursed her swollen jaw and I nursed Duncan, we discussed what our future might be.

"I think this town might need a school," I said.

"How you expect to bring off something like that?"

"Opal, we are 3,000 miles from where people know anything much about us. We have a grand opportunity to invent a history for ourselves."

"What kind of history?"

"Give me a little time and I will come up with something good. Meanwhile, instead of moping about, would you like to hear a chapter from IVANHOE?"

"I am tired of that silly story. You got anything else by that Dickens fellow?"

"No, but tomorrow we will try to buy another of his novels."

"How about the big old Bible we lugged all across the desert? I told you I want to learn to read it myself. Here, I will fetch it for you."

She dug out the leather-bound Bible which Elmer had brought along and which I had wanted to leave behind at Fort Laramie.

"This Bible has a clasp and it is locked, Opal. We would have to cut the strap, and I hate to do that."

"Where is the key?"

"I don't know. Maybe it was in Elmer's pocket when he died. We burned his clothes. When there is time, we can hire a locksmith to open it for us. So, how about IVANHOE?

"All right. Just remember I want to be able to read the word of God for myself. So don't you be trying to throw that Bible away again."

* * *

On Monday morning, after I had eaten a sumptuous breakfast washed down with coffee in the hotel dining room and had carried up portions for Opal, we set out to pursue my scheme.

A reluctant Opal had learned the role and the lines I had decreed for her to play and speak. I wore my fine gown while she suffered herself to be got up like a Southern mammy, complete with a large bandana handkerchief tied about her head.

"Now, Opal," I cautioned her. "Leave the talking to me. Also, I don't want to see you rolling your eyes or sighing or sucking your teeth while I tell my story."

"I'll do it, but I don't have to like it."

The only bank in town at that time was one on Main Street, started by a former Wells Fargo agent, one Alonzo Delano.

Delano turned out to be a lanky fellow of about 50 with a narrow face, a high forehead and a prodigious Roman nose. He listened with a half grin on his face as I told how my young husband and I had set out from Missouri for Oregon where he meant to practice law and enter politics.

My father, a prominent politician and judge himself back in North Carolina, had insisted that my family nurse, Opal, accompany us. Unfortunately, my dear young husband had died on the trail.

Here I paused and put my handkerchief to my eyes, then straightened up, blew my nose, and told of how I had decided that California might offer better opportunities for a young widow than Oregon. The dates of my departure and arrival and circumstance of travel, I kept hazy. As to the question about my present residence, I mentioned the Pacific Hotel and quickly moved on to my views on the importance of educating the young and of my decision to open a private school.

My credentials for such a career? Crossing my fingers and not daring to look at Opal, I responded, "I don't suppose you ever heard of Professor Mead's Academy in Oldham County, North Carolina?" Then, without ever actually saying I had attended there, I rattled on about the good professor, drawing on things my cousin Jim Mundy and Billy Joe Duncan had told me.

"If I had been a boy, naturally I would have gone on to our state university at Chapel Hill. At any rate, on the trail out here, I organized and conducted regular classes in educational basics for the children in our party. So, you see, sir, I have the education, the experience and the determination. All I lack is a suitable building and sufficient funds to launch my enterprise."

"What collateral can you offer, Mrs. Hixon?"

"All I have to offer are my abilities."

He frowned at that, then launched into a long-winded story of how, leaving his family behind, he had come out to California himself from upstate New York in '49, to mine for gold. Later I would learn that Delano, or "Old Block" as he liked to be called, had written a successful book about his trip across the plains and mountains and his early days in the gold fields.

Aching for him to get to the point, I coughed and said, "Now, regarding my request for a loan."

He leaned across his desk, chuckled and said, "You say you have no collateral. Too bad you're not back in North Carolina. You could put up your slave woman here as collateral. I reckon she would be worth at least three hundred dollars. Right, auntie?"

Opal's eyes flashed and her mouth tightened. I feared that she would lash out at the banker, but she said with exaggerated sweetness, "I reckon you do be right, mister banker man."

Delano nodded and said, "However, slavery has been outlawed here in California, and I am glad of it. So, Mrs. Hixon, much as I sympathize with you, unless you can show me at least some collateral, a loan would be out of the question."

As we arose to leave, he added, "Have you thought of seeking employment at a laundry or boarding house and saving your wages until you have sufficient capital? Your expression tells me that holds no interest for you. Well, good day. I wish you good luck as well."

Outside, on the plank sidewalk, I said, "Some day, Opal, I would like to be rich enough to buy out that bank and discharge that blow hard."

"I'd like to be rich enough to buy him and put him up for collateral for a loan. Bet nobody would lend a penny for him."

Our hopes and spirits deflated, we returned to our hotel and stayed there for most of the remaining days of the week, venturing out only to buy a second hand copy of DAVID COPPERFIELD to be read aloud to Opal. She liked the story far better than IVANHOE but for my part I found it depressing.

By the end of the week, our spirits had fallen. Opal kept saying "The Lord will show us a way" until I said in exasperation, "So far He has shown us nothing but trouble and disappointment."

"That is the trouble with white folks," she muttered. "They think they are gods themselves."

On Saturday, weary of looking at the four walls of our room and fed up with the Dickens story, I led us out onto the streets of Grass Valley, crowded with miners and those who fed on them.

I had never seen such a variety of men, not on the trail, not even in St. Joe, and certainly not back in Oldham County. They came in all sizes, shapes, nationalities and manners of speaking. They milled most densely around the saloons but pretty heavily as well outside the offices of assayers and lawyers.

As I was again wearing my fancy new gown and was closely accompanied by Opal and the baby, generally they stood aside and tipped their hats or caps as I passed. Occasionally I heard remarks such as "There is a looker for you" or "Ah, see the fine lady," but otherwise was not bothered.

All up and down the unpaved streets that ran between the flimsy, hastily constructed buildings, the men of all races and tongues thronged in what seemed one gigantic carnival.

I looked at all those men who produced gold and spent their money freely and thought that surely there was some way for me to find backing for my school.

My euphoria lasted only until we returned to the lobby of our hotel. The desk clerk who had so reluctantly admitted us the previous Saturday night asked for a word in private.

"Mrs. Hixon, you have been with us for a week now."

"Not quite. I call it six and a half days."

"For hotel purposes, that is a week. I was wondering if you propose to remain longer with us."

"We have no plans to move just yet."

"Then we will require payment for another week."

"Have I not established credit with you?"

"It is just our policy."

"Your policy is insulting. I will pay upon departing."

"I am sorry. We must have our payment now."

"I refuse to pay for a full week. Here is enough to cover three nights. That will give me time to find a more accommodating establishment."

"At our daily rate, this will cover only two nights."

"Then two nights it will be. But I shall report your lack of courtesy to your manager and all persons with whom I come in contact. And I would like a receipt for our entire stay."

Up in our room, Opal said, "There is some mean folks in this world. What are we going to do now, Annie?"

"I don't know," I replied, then added with heavy sarcasm, "Maybe God will show us a way."

But then, like the 17-year-old that I remained under my self-confident facade, I sat down and wept bitter tears of despair.

Opal knelt and put her arms around me.

"Oh, poor little Annie. Life has been hard on both of us. But we gonna make it somehow. Don't never give up your faith. Sometimes it is all you have to hang onto. What was it the fellow in that book kept saying about how something will turn up?"

I dried my tears, blew my nose, and said, "If it doesn't turn up by Monday, we will be out on the street without a penny and no place to go except . . . "

"Not back to that whore house."

Only a week before I had been full of vain hopes of gaining a bank loan and starting my school. Now we faced being turned out into a cold world where only money seemed to matter. I grew so despondent that I lost my appetite. I sat staring out the window, ignoring Opal and leaving the care of Duncan to her.

I was startled when suddenly she appeared beside my chair. She held my scissors in one hand and Elmer's Bible in the other.

"You got to read this to me."

"The clasp is locked. I told you that."

"Then let's unlock it," she said, and before I could stop her she cut the leather strap and dumped the Bible into my lap.

"Now, let's hear the word of God."

Without really wanting to, I opened the Bible and began reading, "In the beginning God created the heaven and the earth . . . "

On and on I read through the story of Adam and Eve.

Drawing up a chair and holding Duncan against her breast, she listened with glistening eyes until I reached all the begats.

"Now read me the part about the meek inheriting the earth."

I flipped to the New Testament and turned to the Sermon on the Mount in Matthew. A look of great satisfaction came over her face as I read the powerful message of love and trust. She would not let me stop reading. When I came to the passage, "Take no thought for the morrow . . . ," she interrupted to say, "See there. We got to quit worrying about tomorrow. 'Sufficient unto the day is the evil thereof.' That is powerful stuff."

"All right, Opal. And I think sufficient unto the night is the reading of this Bible. I am getting hoarse."

"Just a little bit more, I beg you."

So, without enthusiasm, onward I ploughed into the seventh chapter of Matthew, wanting nothing more than to go to bed and try to forget my troubles.

At the bottom of a page, I read, "Give not that which is holy unto the dogs," stopped and said, "Really, Opal. That should be enough for one night."

"We ain't got nothing else to do. Let's hear just a little bit more. Please, Annie."

I turned the page to "Ask and it will be given to you; seek and ye shall find."

I thought to myself how little had come of my seeking and knocking the past few days. And that is when I noticed, glued by two corners to the facing page, a sheet of parchment about six or seven inches square.

"Don't stop," Opal said.

"Wait. What is this? Hold the lamp closer."

I detached the document from the page of Matthew and saw that it bore the inscription, "The Armstrong Beattie Bank of St. Joseph, Missouri."

"Oh, my God," I said, letting the Bible slide from my lap.

"What is the matter?"

I stood up, waving the paper, and danced around the room, laughing and crying at the same time.

"Oh, sweet Jesus, she done gone crazy on me like I feared she would."

I flung my arms around her and Duncan and danced them around in a circle, then cried, "The Bible is right, Opal. Knock and it will be opened. Seek and ye shall find. God, or Elmer, or someone has answered our prayers after all."

4

This time leaving Opal and Duncan behind, I set out early the next morning, a Monday, to call on Alonzo Delano again.

"What can I do for you today, Mrs. Hixon?"

"More, I hope, than you did a week ago, Mr. Delano. The name of Armstrong Beattie may not ring a bell with you, but here is a draft for five hundred dollars on his bank in St. Joseph, Missouri."

He accepted the document and said, "Why did you not tell me of this last week?"

"I wanted to evaluate your bank before granting my business to you."

"I am indeed flattered that we passed your test. How shall we proceed?"

The Bible says that the love of money is the root of all evil, but from my experience I would say that the lack of money may cause even greater evil. Money may not bring you happiness but it does bring you respect and what passes for power. It is too bad that more women don't realize that a dollar doesn't give a hoot about the sex of the person who owns it.

So, I left that New Yorker's office with $300 in my purse and a new lilt in my bearing. Before going up to our hotel room, I stopped at the desk and badgered the clerk into a special low rate for the next month.

By the end of the first week, I had made a downpayment on a building that had housed a now-failed grocery store. The front room was large enough for classes. It had a large pot-bellied stove and good exposure to the sunlight. Several small rooms, in which the grocer's family had slept, opened into a hallway running down one side of the building to a kitchen at the rear.

I spent the next week buying lumber and hiring labor for the construction of tables and benches. Only by the middle of the third week did I feel sanguine enough about our progress to insert an advertisement in the Grass Valley Telegraph for "Mrs. Hixon's School" and to place an order with a San Francisco firm for a dozen slates plus chalk and a supply of McGuffey's "eclectic" readers and spellers.

For the next several days, the students and their mothers trickled in for interviews. Although I made it appear that our school would be selective, actually I turned down no one, so that by the end of our fourth week at the Pacific Hotel, I had money in hand for the first month's tuition from fifteen students.

Opal and I moved from the hotel into the rear of our building, and around the first of February, 1857, Mrs. Hixon's school opened with a dozen boys and girls ranging in age from 7 to 14. Teaching such a variety of ages taxed my abilities, but I did enjoy it. I realized that I would never grow rich as a school mistress, but it was an honorable profession and it brought me great satisfaction.

Our school continued through the rest of the winter and into the spring. Looking back, I realize that I was ill-equipped to teach anyone much beyond reading, simple writing and some elementary arithmetic. Knowing nothing of algebra or geometry, and being totally ignorant of Greek or Latin, I could not come even close to imparting the knowledge and skills taught by Professor Meade back in Oldham County. Yet I was successful in teaching my students to enjoy literature. The money I took in from their monthly fees was enough to meet our living expenses but not nearly enough to pay more than the interest on my bank loan. The loan was partly secured by the draft Elmer had concealed in the Bible, but if the bank should ever call it in for repayment, I would be left penniless. But we humans live on hope. Mine was to enjoy such success for the rest of the school term that by the next, in September, I might have so many students that we would have to enlarge our little house or, perhaps, move to a bigger one.

So the banker was happy that I met my interest payments; my students and, more important, their parents, were happy with my instruction; Opal was happy with her responsibilities in running our household and with her monthly wages of $10; and little Duncan was happy to be receiving the doting attention of two women, not to mention that of my students.

Looking back, those few months during 1857 when Mrs. Hixon's Academy was in operation were some of the most tranquil and satisfying of my too often turbulent life. In a single year I had gone from the status of a disgraced exile to that of a respected young widow who had found what seemed to be her calling in life. I had a devoted friend in Opal. I dearly loved my little boy.

Along the streets of Grass Valley, bankers and merchants tipped their hats when I passed their establishments or when they saw me in the doorway of my school. I visited both branches of the Methodist Church, but although I was made to feel welcome, I was not moved to join either congregation just then.

* * *

It did not take Will Tremelling long to hear of my school and to seek me out. He came around one Saturday afternoon to see if I needed any work done. I did not, but he stayed around anyway, drinking my tea and making awkward conversation. On the trail, I had been happy to call upon his services. Now that I was succeeding on my own, I did not need him. I was civil to him, of course, but did nothing to encourage his attentions. After he had left, Opal took me to task for my standoffishness.

"That man is crazy about you."

"Well, I am not crazy about him."

"Think you are too good for him. Is that it?"

"That is not it. I just don't need another man messing up my life, especially one that thinks himself on top of the world because he earns three dollars a day."

"You ought not to forget how he saved us that night back in the whore house."

"I have not forgotten either that or the fact of his presence there as a customer. And please, Opal, I wish you would use another term in speaking of Mrs. Harmer's place, if you must mention it at all."

During that period, I gave little thought to my experiences in Mrs. Harmer's establishment. Apparently knowledge of my residence there the previous year was limited to the girls themselves and to a few of their clients, most of them residents of the mining camps that ringed Grass Valley and therefore not likely to mix with the regular citizens of the town itself. The House of Joy period of my life lay behind me, or so I thought.

* * *

In writing so much about my personal trials and triumphs, I have neglected to note those of the community. Poor Nevada City, the larger, rival town of Grass Valley and county seat of Nevada County, was just getting back on its feet after the ruinous fire of the previous July when, in the winter of 1857, a second disaster struck.

A new dam just constructed on Deer Creek, seven miles upstream from the town, had been touted as absolutely safe. Forty feet high, it was designed to impound 200 acres of water vital to the hydraulic mining industry. Guarantees of its safety notwithstanding, following heavy rains, the flood gate becamed clogged with debris, and the owners, in desperation, ordered their workers to open holes in the structure to allow the backed-up water to escape.

Their efforts were in vain. Near dawn on a Sunday morning, the dam collapsed, and a fifteen-foot high wall of water surged downstream, carrying away trees, houses, bridges and anything else along the creek's banks. Many of the hoteliers and other business owners who had been ruined by the great fire of 1856 were again wiped out. It just goes to show how dangerous it is for mere mortals to monkey about with Mother Nature. The purpose of the dam had been to enable profiteers to gain even more wealth from the sale of water to be used by other greedy men in washing away the hillsides that God had created. And for what? Profit.

Of course, I would not have been so self-righteous if my money had been invested in the water rights companies instead of in a school.

* * *

At the end of our school year, in May of 1857, there was no reason to think that I could not reopen in September with even more students who, now that my reputation seemed to be established, would pay even more for the advantage of young Mrs. Hixon's institution.

Other events occurred that summer to frustrate my plan. First came the bank panic in St. Louis and New York. Like the bursting of the Deer Creek dam, this sent a wall of financial disasters coursing across the nation. I was already in debt to the local bank for more than the amount of Elmer's draft, and, with the cessation of tuition payments for the summer, no fresh income was available to me.

And then there was the appearance of three of Mrs. Harmer's girls at my door one morning.

Led by Mildred, the overweight blonde, they showed up the day after I had endured a most unsatisfactory interview with my banker. No, he was not about to call my loan, but it was out of the question for him to advance me additional funds with which to expand the school. Even so, when Mildred and her two fellow prostitutes came to ask if I would not take them on as students for the rest of the summer, at first I said no.

"How much are the children paying you?" Mildred asked.

When I told her, without hesitation, she replied, "There is five of us as would be interested and we would be willing to pay you twice that amount, wouldn't we, girls?"

Stalling for time, I said, "What about Mrs. Harmer? She wouldn't like it a bit, I should think."

"She needn't know. Besides, we ain't her slaves. We learned that much from Madeline. Our money is ours to spend as we please and so are our mornings. Please, Annie. Just an hour or so on Saturdays only."

I looked across the kitchen at Opal, who frowned and shook her head.

"Excuse me, girls," I said. "I don't want to hurt your feelings, but I have my reputation to think of."

Immediately, I regretted my remark. Mildred's broad face collapsed and tears ran down her cheeks.

"Don't you see," she wailed. "This is the only way out for us. Education. And we'd be glad to slip in by the back door. Please, Annie. Just for the summer."

Now the other two girls were crying as well.

Not daring to look at Opal, I said, "And you really would be willing to pay twice my usual fees?"

I don't claim that they were good students or that I taught them very much. But they were faithful in their attendance and, more important for me at the time, in the payment of their fees. And, despite my protests, they insisted on bringing gifts of clothing or toys for little Duncan.

True to their promise, they came quietly, one by one, to my back door. And they came in simple clothing such as a modest housewife might have worn. Also they wore large bonnets that practically concealed their faces.

Despite their generally low level of intelligence, they were eager to learn. It was not prudent to give them homework to take back to The House of Joy, but two of them did give me money to purchase suitable books. I was able to find a copy of Parson Weems' life of Washington and a book of Mother Goose rhymes for them.

So all was going well for me that summer. Despite the nation's larger financial problems, the bank was not calling my loans. Fees for teaching the prostitutes brought in enough income for us to live on. Duncan, now trying his first stumbling steps, had grown into a ruddy-cheeked, happy little fellow. I had already begun drafting the announcement that I planned to put in the papers to advertise my new school term. In fact, I was in the process of rewriting that announcement one morning as I awaited the arrival of my students, when a loud rapping sounded at our front door. I sent Opal to see who knocked so imperiously and turned my attention back to my announcement.

"We got trouble," Opal said from the hallway.

"What kind of trouble?"

"You go see for yourself. And just remember that I tried to tell you."

Before I could ask what she meant, she had marched back to the kitchen. So I was already apprehensive as I walked out to our large front room. There stood Evelyn Harmer, wearing a long, flowered dress, an enormous hat, and the expression of an angry harpy.

"Why, Mrs. Harmer. What a pleasant surprise. What can I do for you?"

"It has been brought to my attention that you have been trying to educate my girls behind my back."

For an instant, I thought that she might have come to ask me to add her to my students. So in my friendliest tone, I said, "Yes. Why don't you have a seat and I will explain what we are doing."

"I prefer to stand. As for what you are doing, I understand that only too well."

"If you will wait just a few minutes, your employees will be here. You can observe their class to see for yourself."

"They will not be here this morning or any other unless they wish to be turned out of my house and this town. As for what you are trying to do for them, that is obvious."

"I don't take your meaning."

"You are trying to incite them to abandon their profession and myself. You are a troublemaker and I shall not put up with your interference any more. You made enough trouble for me when I took you and your runaway slave woman into my establishment. You shall do me no further injury. You may count on that."

"Mrs. Harmer, your girls sought me out. I was trying to help them, not harm you."

"It comes to the same thing."

I really should not have lost my temper, but as the enormity of her callous remark sank in, I could not restrain myself.

"You really are the most spiteful woman I have ever met. You cruelly exploit those poor, simple-minded girls, and then further injure them by stopping their learning to read and write. I can't prevent you from forbidding them to come here, but I certainly don't have to put up with your hateful presence in my house. So I will ask you to leave."

"Not so fast, my dear little so-called widow. It is not I who will be leaving. It is you."

"What do you mean? This house is mine. How can you make me leave it?"

"I was not referring to this hovel. I meant the town of Grass Valley."

"Don't be silly. I have become well-established here. My school has been enjoying a great success."

"Has been, yes. But will it continue to do so when word gets around that you have been teaching whores?"

"That is a strange remark to come from the madam of a whore house."

"Yes, the whore house where you came to bear your bastard child and where you yourself worked for a good many weeks."

I went to the door and opened it.

"Please leave now, before I tell you in what utter contempt I hold you."

"Don't say I didn't warn you."

"Get out or I will have Opal come to help me eject you."

"Oh, yes, your Opal. There are more than a few Southern gentlemen around here who feel as I do that the Fugitive Slave Law should be enforced even in California. Give some thought to that as well, my little self-righteous Southern belle."

After Mrs. Harmer had flounced out, Opal said, "There goes one more evil woman. Just remember I tried to warn you not to get yourself involved any more with them whores."

"She is just making empty threats. Who would credit anything such a woman might say? I just feel sorry for her poor stupid girls. Now let's put this out of our minds. We can keep body and soul together until the new school term."

So, after drinking my mid-morning cup of tea, I finished rewriting my announcement, put on my best bonnet, and, with Opal and Duncan in tow, took a copy around to *The Telegraph.*

The counter was manned by a tall, gangling young chap with a shock of brown hair and the beginning of a scraggly moustache.

He said, "I been thinking. Your school might be worth a long article. That would save you the cost of an ad and probably would do you a lot more good. When would you have time for me to interview you?"

"What's wrong with right now?" I said without thinking.

I fed him a good line about being left a widow on the trail from St. Joseph the year below, leaving out, of course, my premature pregnancy, the episodes with Bart Corbett and Doctor Dormsby, and the fact that our original destination had been Oregon.

He asked none of the questions I feared he might, such as when I had arrived and where my child had been born. I laid it on thick about conducting classes for the children of our emigrant train and of investing the money left me by my late, beloved husband in my academy for which I now had even higher hopes.

On the street later, Opal said, "If you don't be careful, you going to make me believe all that stuff you told that poor man."

"I told him no lies. Perhaps I glossed over a few points which he did not need for his story. Oh, Opal, if he writes the right kind of article, it will be an enormous help to our school."

5

That newspaperman did write a most satisfactory article. He even brought a copy of the paper to me fresh off the press. He made me sound like a Joan of Arc who was devoting her young life selflessly to the education of Grass Valley's young.

I ached for him to go away so I could savor the article in solitude but, with his foot in the door, he hung about until I offered him a cup of tea and listened to his story of growing up in St. Louis as the son of a Presbyterian missionary and of his dream of someday owning his own newspaper. He was so eager to impress me that he got on my nerves. Someday I should write a handbook of advice for young men seeking to impress a young woman. The trick is not to try too hard. And never show that you are in awe of the girl whose head you hope to turn.

Finally, when it became obvious that we were not going to invite him to stay for supper, he left.

I danced around the kitchen, reading the piece aloud to Opal.

Within the next five days after the appearance of that fulsome article, I had twenty students signed up for the new school term and was considering whether to cut off the reservations.

* * *

My euphoria lasted until the following Tuesday when *The Journal,* a rival paper to *The* Telegraph, came off the press over in Nevada City. Some anonymous person left a copy at our front door that same day. A headline fairly jumped right off the front page.

Reading "SHOCKING DISCLOSURE," it appeared over a letter to the editor, signed "A Concerned Parent." Apparently written in response to the favorable article in the opposition sheet, there in black and white were related such circumstances of my arrival at the House of Joy and the birth of my baby that only Mrs. Harmer could have told the writer. Through innuendo, even my role in the ruckus that occurred the night of Madeline's flight was outlined.

As though the letter was not bad enough, it was accompanied by an editor's note saying that "in the interest of truth" he had investigated the story and confirmed the allegations.

To say I was humiliated would be to understate my feelings. My first impulse was to hire a hack to carry me over the Nevada City so that I could confront the editor, but Opal dissuaded me.

"Is there anything they wrote that ain't true?"

"It is the way they wrote it," I replied. "They make it sound like I was practically one of the girls myself. And this business about . . . how did they put it, 'an on-going relationship with her former associates.' That is carrying things too far."

"You did get pretty thick with them whores. I tried to tell you."

"If you say that one more time, I will scream."

The cancellations started the next day. One by one, either by hand-delivered letter or in person, I was notified that little Johnny or Mary or whoever would not after all be among my students in September. These cancellations were followed by a summons from Alonzo Delano to present myself to discuss my outstanding loan.

He wasted no time getting to the point.

"It would seem that you somewhat misled me when you applied for a loan."

"I told you nothing but the truth, Mr. Delano. And I gave you a valid bank draft as collateral."

"Even so, you owe this bank considerably more than your draft can cover. And in the light of the article in *The Journal* your ability to carry the note would seem to be in doubt."

"This is most unfair. You read the earlier article in *The Telegraph.*"

"By that damned fool editor that nobody takes seriously."

"Fool or not, it was a highly favorable piece and it brought me in twenty students within five days."

"Ah, my dear young Mrs. Hixon, you should realize that ten of what you call favorable articles can be undone by a single unfavorable one. Do you still have those twenty students signed up?"

"No," I admitted. "But give me a little time and I will advertise for new ones. I can more than replace those dropouts."

"I have no time to give you. Circumstances arising from bank failures back east have caused credit problems for us out here. I am afraid we must cash in your draft and take our lumps."

"Which means you will never recover the excess of the loans over the value of the draft. That seems foolish to me."

"We can foreclose on your furniture and other household goods."

"But that would bring you but a pittance. Give me just a week and I will come up with a solution. Please, Mr. Delano."

"What kind of a solution?"

"I will think of something. Surely you can delay for a week."

Delano really was a good-hearted man. And I suppose I did put on a pretty good show for him, complete with tears, I am ashamed to admit. Anyway, he said, "I should not do this, but I suppose it won't hurt to give you one week."

* * *

Those next few days were bleak ones. Not only had I run out of money and credit, but also of reputation. The gentlemen who had been tipping their hats to me now averted their eyes as they passed me on the street, so that I took to staying indoors, even remaining in bed until noon. My other waking hours were spent wandering about our house in a dressing gown.

Opal had the good sense to stop reminding me of how she had warned against trying to help Mrs. Harmer's girls. As for that wicked woman I felt certain that she was behind the article in the Nevada City paper, but I could not prove it. Anyway I was angry at her and the banker, the offending Nevada City editor, and even, the hapless fellow who had written the article that had drawn the attention of the other paper to me.

The frustrating part of all this was that I could see no way either of striking back or of recovering my reputation. Like they say about virginity, once lost, it is hard to regain.

So I was feeling hopeless around midmorning late in the week of grace granted by the bank when Opal knocked at my bedroom door to announce that I had a visitor.

Before I could ask who, Mildred barged past her.

As she removed the shawl from her head, revealing an absence of her usual rouge and lipstick, she blurted out, "I got only a few minutes before I must return. That woman only lets us out of the house one at a time and then only for an hour. And she has forbidden us to come near you anymore."

"Then why are you here?"

"She read us the piece in the Nevada City paper."

"She?"

"Mrs. Harmer. Said there was more to come for you. Said she had connections that would see you run out of town."

"I am beginning to think she may be right. Only I have no place to run to."

Quickly, I explained how I had lost my students and now faced foreclosure by the bank.

"And it is all our fault. But there is a way out."

"I have been fretting and praying for several days and so far I have seen no such way. What do you mean?"

She shut my door in Opal's face and lowered her voice.

"There is seven of us working for Mrs. Harmer. At least five of us would be more than willing to move here with you."

"Why, Mildred, how would that help either me or you?"

"We would go to work for you."

"I have no work for you. In fact, I don't know how I will support myself and my baby anymore."

"Don't you see, Annie? This place is smaller than The House of Joy but it is in a better location. We would much rather work for you than that nasty old woman."

When the impact of what she was proposing finally dawned on me, I didn't know whether to laugh or cry.

"Oh, Mildred, I am not interested in running a brothel."

"Why not? We could make you a rich woman. You'd make far more than you ever would running a school."

"But that would be immoral. I have my reputation to think of."

"What reputation, honey?"

"Self respect then. I just could not be a party to such an enterprise."

"We even took up a collection to pay for buying towels and such furniture as would be required."

"A collection?"

"Yes. I brought along four hundred dollars."

"Oh, Mildred. I couldn't accept your money, not for a brothel."

"They are going to be mighty disappointed. Look, I got to get back or that woman will have my hide. If you change your mind, let us know. You could turn this into a high class place with your brains and style."

I should have known Opal would be listening outside the door. As poor Mildred, drooping with disappointment, turned to leave, in popped Opal, saying, "Wait a minute, Annie. Let's not be hasty about this matter."

"Surely you don't think we should get involved in prostitution."

Ignoring me, she turned her attention to the bewildered Mildred.

"I couldn't help but hear what you been saying. That is sweet, mighty sweet, of you and your friends to want to help us in our hour of need."

"They like Annie and little Duncan. And they liked your cooking, too. That entered into it."

"I do appreciate the compliment. And you say you brought four hundred dollars along to invest with Annie?"

"It is here in my pocketbook. But she says no and I have to get back."

"We could use that money. No, I don't mean as a gift. As a loan."

"I don't know about that. We was hoping to kill two birds with one stone. You know, helping ourselves at the same time we helped Annie."

"Maybe I used the wrong word when I said loan. Maybe I should have said investment. We could put your money to work for you."

"I don't follow your meaning. Look, I will be in big trouble if I am late going back."

"Then just let me see you out. Now, Annie, honey, you go on back to sleep and leave me to say good-by to Mildred."

"Miss Mildred, if you don't mind."

"Whatever. Just come along then, Miss Mildred."

I was too downhearted to get out of bed to do my own eavesdropping. But when Opal returned to my room, I demanded, "What do you think you are up to? We can't take their money. How could I ever pay them back? And, anyway, money alone is not going to help me get my school started again."

"Don't raise a fuss with me. She wouldn't lend us the money. Didn't hurt to try, did it?"

"I reckon not. Oh, Opal, there just doesn't seem to be any hope for us."

"There is always hope except for folks that gives up and stays in bed all day instead of stirring around, yes, and praying and having faith. The least you could do is get out of that bed and show a little gumption. You starting to get me down."

Stung by her words, I did drag myself out of bed and dress. There was nothing to do, however. Opal saw to Duncan's needs. I missed teaching the girls from Mrs. Harmer's place as well as my children. I even began missing my home in North Carolina.

* * *

On the Saturday afternoon before my period of grace expired at the bank, Will Tremelling showed up at our door. He wore a black, obviously new waistcoat, and his usually unruly black hair had been plastered down.

There was nothing to do but admit him. He took Duncan on his knee and dandled him until Opal came and led him away. I am sure she did so to leave me alone with Will.

Will told me all about working in the quartz mine. He was proud of the praise he and his comrades received from the mine manager. He reminisced about our experiences on the trail. Then he seemed to run out of anything to say. I ached for him to leave.

After several minutes of awkward silence, he blurted out, "Annie, we seen what they wrote about you in that newspaper."

"You and everyone else in Nevada County."

"Would you like me and the boys to go over to Nevada City and give that editor a lesson in Cornish wrestling?"

"That would do no good. It would only get you arrested."

"What are you going to do, then?"

"I haven't decided, Will. I am just about at the end of my rope. There is no place left for me to turn. I have even been thinking of going back to North Carolina."

"Do you want to do that?"

"Not really. I like it out here."

"Enough to spend the rest of your life?"

"I thought so when my school was going so well."

"I aim to spend the rest of my life here, too. You couldn't drag me back to Cornwall."

Another long silence followed.

"Annie, how old are you, if I may ask?"

"I will be nineteen my next birthday. Why?"

"I am twenty five myself. You know, I noticed you back at St. Joseph at that meeting hall. Then again on the trail, before we knew you was married."

"Yes, Will. And I remember you and your friends, how you wanted me to include you in my classes."

"I just wanted to be near you."

"That is sweet of you to say."

So abruptly it startled me, he stood up and began pacing around the room, finally stopping to look down into my face.

"Blast it, Annie, what I am trying to say is that I want to marry you."

"Why, Will, that is a great compliment, but . . . "

"Compliment or not, it's what is in my heart. Now I ain't asking for an answer right now. I'm afraid you'd say no, and that would just about kill me. All I want to say is I want you to be my wife. Look, I have already saved up near about a hundred dollars. Don't look at me so, and don't shake your head. Just say you will think about it."

I didn't have the heart to say what I really felt, so I replied, "I will think about it, certainly, Will. But don't get your hopes up."

"Then you aren't saying no."

"I am not saying anything, just that I will think about it."

I suppose that I should have invited him to stay for a meal, but I really just wanted him to leave me alone to think.

When I finally got free of my earnest Cornishman, Opal emerged from the kitchen, laughing, to say, "Which you rather be, the wife of a miner or the madam of a whore house?"

"Neither one," I said.

"I hope you wasn't serious about going back to North Carolina, cause I sure ain't going back to Virginia."

"No, I want to stay here."

"Then we better put our heads together to figure out how we going to do that."

*   *   *

"Annie, I been thinking hard, and praying hard, too."

"So have I, Opal."

"Have you come up with anything we can do?"

"Not so far."

"I know black folks is supposed to sit back and let white folks do all the thinking, but maybe you ought to listen to what I wants to say."

"I wouldn't know how to stop you."

"See, Annie," she said. "The reason them whores has so much money is because out here there is so many more men than women. A man has natural needs, but they got other needs. They think they can't get by for long without a little poon tang every week or so . . . "

"What?"

"You never heard it called that? It is what men and women do."

"Oh," I said. "Get to the point."

"However, men, women and children also has to eat at least two or three times a day. Back home even black men generally had themselves a woman to do their cooking. Out here there ain't enough women to go around for poon tang or cooking."

"I am no more interested in hiring out as a cook than I am in operating a house of ill repute."

"Oh, no," she said with a scornful edge in her voice. "You wants to run a school. Dress up nice and have everybody call you Mrs. Hixon. But that ain't possible anymore. Now you seen how them whores lapped up my cooking. And you seems to enjoy my food even if you don't say so."

"I'm sorry, Opal. I have so much on my mind. You are a good cook. Are you thinking of hiring yourself out?"

"Lord, and white folks thinks themselves to be so smart. No, child, no. Look, we got this house for as long as we can meet the payments. You knows how to keep books and talk to bankers and all that sort of thing. And them whores is got more money than they know what to do with. If I was doing the cooking and you was to take care of the business end, we could turn this place into a restaurant."

"That doesn't appeal to me very much."

"Running a whore house don't appeal to you, either. Or marrying a gold miner. Or going back to North Carolina. How about eating regular? Does that appeal to you?"

"I am not sure I like your tone."

"And I don't like you lying around like a sick puppy. All you got to do is take down that sign and change the words on it. Then we'll let that fat, yellow-headed whore know we wants to talk to her and her friends again."

"I can't. My reputation is ruined after that awful article."

"Ruined for running a school, maybe, which didn't bring in much money anyway. But a hungry man ain't going to care about your reputation. Now has you got a little gumption, or you just going to give up?"

* * *

Three weeks later the house that had been a grocery store, then a school, reopened as "Annie's Place." I considered changing my sign from "Mrs. Hixon's School" to "Mrs. Hixon's Restaurant" but Opal convinced me that "Annie's Place" had a better ring.

At the bank, Delano was dying to know the source of the money I showed him, but I put him off by acting as if I had a mysterious backer who wished to remain anonymous. Mildred was not easily persuaded to back a restaurant rather than a brothel but finally came around when I agreed to accept her as my chief waitress.

"I think it is time I tried earning a living on my feet instead of my back," is how she put it. "I won't make as much but at least I can be around to keep an eye on my investment."

We cleared out a little room for her next door to Opal's. Opal didn't like the arrangement but wisely accepted it.

Will Tremelling passed the word about our establishment to his friends in his mining camp. Mildred's friends also quietly mentioned to their clients that Annie's Place would have good food. I placed a handsome ad in The Telegraph. The upshot was that about on the same day that my school would have reopened, we served our first dinner, at a dollar a head. Our little converted school room was quickly filled and men were standing in line awaiting their places at our tables. Business boomed that day and every day thereafter, except on Mondays, when we remained closed.

PART TWO

1

The next year of my life (and that of Duncan, Opal, and Mildred) passed without further difficulties. Thanks to Opal's excellent cooking and our hard work, Annie's Place flourished so that by the following spring we were able to make a down payment on the larger brick building next door which had housed a dry goods store until the '57 financial panic put it out of business. We transformed the structure into a new and larger restaurant and kept our old grocery store for our living quarters.

The gentlemen who had given up tipping their hats to me during the scandal caused by the newspaper article, began to patronize our restaurant as word of our food and service spread. They sat on benches side-by-side with mine managers and miners, gambling house operators and lawyers, even ministers of the gospel.

I gave up my shallow pretense of being an educated school mistress and took to boldly greeting my patrons by name as they entered, chatting with them about the news of the day as they ate, and thanking them for their business as they departed. Anyone wearing ragged or dirty clothing or under the influence of whisky was politely, but firmly, turned away.

*   *   *

One chilly morning, during that first winter of our operation, there came to our kitchen door a curious little Chinaman. He looked older than the general run of his countrymen. Dressed in a thin tunic and wearing a billess cap, he leaned on a crude crutch as he asked through chattering teeth, "Where store?"

"No more store here," I explained. "This restaurant now."

Seeing that he seemed not to comprehend, I made motions of eating. A grin spread across his weathered face and he nodded.

"Yes. You got food? Velly hungly."

Opal opposed admitting what she called "a heathen" into her kitchen, but I could not turn the poor fellow away. I gave him a bowl of the soup that Opal always kept simmering on the stove and a hunk of her corn bread. I never saw a man eat with such obvious relish.

When he was only half done with the food, little Duncan entered the kitchen, paused in the doorway, and then, before I could stop him, toddled straightway to the odd little man who wore his hair in a queue and whose feet were shod in wooden-soled shoes.

Although his hunger was far from assuaged, the Chinaman set aside his bowl and plate and held out his arms to Duncan, who, without hesitation climbed upon his lap.

An outraged Opal started to snatch him off the heathen's lap, but seeing the smile on the Chinaman's face, I stopped her from interfering.

So when he, in broken English, asked if I had any work for him, I responded with, "What kind of work you do?"

"Washee clothes. Cookee food. Do what missy say."

Then he paused and looked down into Duncan's fascinated face and added, "Takee care baby."

I can't explain how that melted my heart. After that morning, Soohoo Kwong Chung, to use his full name, never left our house except briefly to collect his belongings at the mining camp.

It took a while for me to learn his story. After three years of panning for gold, he had been attacked by a gang of Irish toughs because he refused to sell them his 30' x 30' claim on a creek near Grass Valley. With a broken leg, he could no longer work his claim. Chinamen could not testify against white persons in California's courts. So, Kwong Chung and his friends were powerless to bring their assailants to justice.

He found with us a permanent home and job. Opal never fully accepted him. After Mildred got over her jealousy at Duncan's affection for the Chinaman, she came around.

He was content to sleep on a pallet behind the stove in our kitchen. He accepted Opal's stern authority. There was never a more efficient dish washer or laundryman. I don't think we could have managed the expansion of our business into the brick building next door had fate not delivered Kwong Chung to our doorstep. I will have more to say about him and his place in our lives later.

* * *

In chronicling my own experiences during my first year in Grass Valley, I have neglected to mention the election of 1856 in which James Buchanan of Pennsylvania defeated Fremont for the presidency. As I have noted, there was a vocal colony of Southerners in Nevada County and these "chivs" rejoiced in the fact that Buchanan had carried California in the election.

For my part, I was not much interested in politics, but it was hard to ignore all the debate about whether slavery should be allowed in the territories such as Kansas and Nebraska. The controversy got pretty intense in 1858 when the local newspapers carried long reports of the debates between Lincoln and Douglas back in Illinois. In my restaurant I did my best to discourage political bickering, going so far as to put up a sign over my door, "Park your firearms and your politics here and eat in peace."

During that year I reckon I received at least a dozen proposals of marriage, aside from the standing offer of Will Tremelling. That total does not include those made in jest. Among my potential husbands were the Jewish owner of a dry goods store, a young lawyer newly arrived from New York, a Welsh mining engineer, two Irish saloon keepers, and a Wells Fargo freight agent, just to mention a few.

I turned them all down, doing so gently, with the explanation that I valued my independence too much, and the assurance that if I were interested in matrimony, I could hardly have done better than to accept their proposals . . . no hard feelings, please.

Meanwhile, my bank account kept swelling. Duncan was growing into a fine little lad with dark curls and the same lovely, light brown eyes of Billy Joe Duncan, of whom, I am ashamed to confess, I still dreamed at night.

During this period, letters passed back and forth between Uncle John and me. I told him that although I had found school teaching emotionally rewarding, I had switched to the more remunerative business of running a restaurant.

He reported back that there was much agitation in Oldham County over the presumed threat to the institution of slavery. Papa, he wrote, had helped form a new militia company, The Oldham Rifles, and was talking up secession from the Union if, God forbid, the new Republican Party should ever elect a president.

But these questions seemed unlikely to affect me in far-off California. As we entered 1859, I was far more concerned by the unusually cold and snowy weather that hung on in our area. Snow fell practically every day, piling so high in our streets that our patrons could not reach our restaurant. But, thanks to Kwong Chung, we had a good supply of firewood and, to Opal, plenty of food. I put up a sign in the window of Annie's Place reading "closed due to weather," and we all hunkered down next door to wait until winter released its grip.

* * *

I would not have seen the theatrical notice that appeared in the Nevada City newspaper if Will Tremelling had not called it to my attention. Placed by the manager of the new Metropolitan Theater in Nevada City, the notice announced the coming appearance of "The Courtenay Family Players." According to this advance publicity, the Courtenays were "an acclaimed British theatrical family" who had been playing to packed houses in San Francisco. Now they were venturing up into the gold-mining region to stage a repertoire of scenes from Shakespearean plays, beginning the following Saturday evening.

Will offered to hire a buggy and escort me to see the performance. At first I declined, saying, "They let us down when we were in need. We haven't heard from them in over two years."

Then Will said something that struck a chord with me. "I would think you'd want to dress up in your finest and show them how well you have done without their help."

"He's right," Opal chimed in. "Let them know how we have landed on our feet. Besides that, you needs to get away for a while. Now don't you be worrying about the restaurant. Me and Mildred and the Chinaman can handle things for one night, and I will look after Duncan."

* * *

Will arrived earlier than I expected the following Saturday. He was driving a smart rented rig drawn by a docile mare. He wore a new derby hat and sported an embroidered vest under his coat. Except for his brogans and his calloused hands and black, broken fingernails, he might have been taken for a mine manager rather than a miner.

The five-mile drive to Nevada City, during which he told me more about quartz mining than I really wanted to know, took only an hour, so that we arrived at the Metropolitan Theater a good three hours before the show was to start.

He left me sitting in the buggy while he bought our tickets. I noticed that after he had spoken at length to the ticket seller, that worthy disappeared inside the theater. In a few minutes, out came none other than Homer Courtenay, himself. He seized Will's hand and then strode over to the buggy to greet me.

"Bless my soul, it really is our dear, dear Annie. What a pleasant surprise. Oh, Mrs. Courtenay and the children will be overjoyed to know you will be in the audience tonight. Come, pray dismount and allow me to give you a tour of the theater. Nonsense, there is plenty of time before curtain call. Here, allow me to assist you, my dear."

Upon closer scrutiny, I saw that his moustache was going gray and that his waistcoat needed mending.

The Metropolitan Theater occupied the second floor of a long office building. It could seat several hundred persons. A stage ran across the far end of the steep-roofed auditorium. Behind the stage there were two dressing rooms, one for men and one for women. At the end of the tour, Mr. Courtenay seemed at the point of dismissing us until Will blurted out, "You know, Annie here has become quite the successful business woman. She owns the busiest restaurant in Grass Valley."

"Does she indeed? That hardly surprises me. Always liked her spirit. Done well has she? I would like to know more about this enterprise. Look here, we held our rehearsal this morning. What say I go to our digs and rouse up my lady wife and the children. We have made no dinner plans. We could meet you at the National Hotel say in half an hour. Bring ourselves up to date on each other. I hear they set a good table there. Don't dream of saying no."

Will drove us about Nevada City for a while, giving me a chance to admire the new county courthouse and the many brick buildings that had replaced the wooden structures destroyed in the great fire of 1856. After leaving our rig and mare at a livery stable, we made our way to the National Exchange Hotel.

Formerly a building housing offices and stores, this was the finest structure in Nevada City. The first floor boasted high ceilings and an imposing staircase.

Seeing that Will did not know how to proceed, I stepped up to the head waiter in the commodious dining room and asked for a place for six persons. We were soon seated at a large table with a view of the bustling street.

The calm of the dining room was shattered by the booming voice of Mr. Courtenay greeting the head waiter. In he, his wife, and the two children swept like members of royalty.

Mrs. Courtenay had put on weight since she had left me at the door of the brothel. And as children will do, theirs had grown.

"It is Annie, isn't it?"

"Yes, Mrs. Courtenay."

Then turning to Will, she said, "And you are?"

"You remember Will Tremelling," I said.

"Oh, yes. One of the Cornishmen. Please sit, all of you. Simeon, Heather, you remember your old school mistress."

In the last words they would speak for the next hour, they said they did . . . remember me, that is.

Our conversation was strained at first but became livelier after Mr. Courtenay had drunk his second glass of wine. Just as he had done at the Salt Lake City hotel, he began talking so loudly and vivaciously that soon everyone in the dining room was being treated to an account of the family's alleged success in San Franciso.

"But you wrote that you had difficulties finding suitable roles in Sacramento," I said.

"So I did, but there is a different atmosphere in San Francisco. Now there is a city for you, a city marked for a place alongside the great metropolises of the world, right up there with New York, or even Paris or London, given time."

As he ran on about San Francisco, his wife remained silent.

"And how do you like the city?" I asked during a pause in her husband's talk as he motioned for the waiter to bring more wine.

She was busy frowning and shaking her head at her husband. I repeated my question.

"I find it not nearly so civilized as Homer represents it. Perhaps you have heard of the so-called vigilance committees that until recently handed out rough justice to criminals."

"Yes. But the audiences there. Do you find them receptive to your company?"

Before she could reply, her husband regained his voice.

"Wonderful audiences there. They love us."

"Yes," she muttered. "Too bad their tastes run to minstrel shows."

"Let us not speak disparagingly of that peculiarly American form of entertainment, my dear. Especially since it puts bread and meat upon our table."

"And very little else."

To head off what I feared was the beginnings of a tiff, I veered the talk in a new direction.

"You were at work on a book about our trip across the West. Have you completed it?"

"I got us as far as Fort Laramie, but then the demands of the theater took precedence over those of the literary muse. Never fear, however. I have kept my notes. I shall complete the work in due course. Enough of ourselves now. What's this about you and a restaurant? Trilling here says you have enjoyed great success in that enterprise."

"It's Tremelling," Will said. "And it is true. Annie's Place is one of the most successful restaurants in Grass Valley."

"Will exaggerates," I said, then added with a spiteful thrust, "But like your minstrel shows, it puts bread on the table for myself, my little son and Opal."

That got Mrs. Courtenay's attention.

"That black woman we rescued from slavery? She remains with you? I am surprised to hear that she can be loyal to anyone."

"I owe more to her than any person I ever met," I replied. "She rescued me from the rather awkward position in which I was abandoned when we arrived in this area."

"That was an awkward time for us all," she replied, then turned to her husband and said, "Homer, no more wine, please. No, not another drop. We are due to go on in little more than an hour."

"So we are, my dear. My, how time flies when one is with old friends. One more glass and we must take our leave. You already have purchased your tickets, I believe. Just mention my name at the door, and you will be shown to the best seats in the house."

"We wouldn't like to impose," I said.

"Nonsense. It is little enough for us to do after enjoying such a sumptuous repast as your guests."

It was news to me that the meal was to be my treat, but what could I do?

After they had departed, Will looked up and said, "Let me settle for the bill, Annie."

"No, Will. After all, you paid for the tickets."

"They haven't changed all that much, have they?"

"No. He is still mostly talk. They are not very good about keeping their promises. I learned that the hard way."

However, Homer Courtenay did keep his promise of seeing that we would get choice seats for the performance. We were led down front to two chairs that had cushions and arm rests.

I had not been exposed to much theater and so not only was I awed by the Metropolitan but also by my acquaintance with the actors.

The curtains remained closed as the advertised time came and went. They opened only after the crowd grew restive and began stamping their feet and yelling.

After a few minutes of this, out stepped Mr. Courtenay, clad in a doublet and wearing a short cape. He apologized for the delay ("due to technical difficulties"), then launched into an anecdote about the time at the Drury Lane in London when some practical joker had sewed the curtains shut. He went on from there into a yarn about the family's success on the East Coast and in San Francisco.

"And, now we are ready to bring to you here in this great gold country of California, some of the essence of what we have learned during the long career on the stage we have been privileged to experience."

He really should have taken his wife's advice and stopped drinking after his second glass of wine. As he rambled on about the scenes from Shakespeare to which we were to be treated, someone—an Irishman, judging from his accent—yelled, "Get on with the show, ye bloody Englishman."

This demand was seconded by a chorus of catcalls. An arm, which appeared to be that of Mrs. Courtenay, reached through the curtains and drew him out of sight. Then, in a moment, the curtains were opened and the show began with highlights from The Merchant of Venice.

The audience suffered in silence during Portia's "the quality of mercy" speech as delivered by Mrs. Courtenay. They put up with her husband as Shylock during his "Hath a Jew not feeling" soliloquy delivered with slurred speech. They allowed the two Courtenay children to get through the balcony scene from Romeo and Juliet without interruption, even giving the youngsters a round of perfunctory applause.

The trouble began after a short intermission, when Mr. Courtenay reappeared as King Lear. Since then I have seen Lear done by Edmund Kean himself, who elicited from his audience feelings of pity for an old man losing his powers. This audience of rough miners neither felt pity nor showed any mercy for Mr. Courtenay in his ill-fitting white wig and false beard as he stumbled through his lines. They were respectful of Mrs. Courtenay until her husband nearly dropped her during the scene when he was to carry her from the heath. The theater shook from the rude shouts such as "Need a hand there, old fellow?" or "Get a horse to haul her off stage."

Just as the actor had fortified himself during the intermission with more drink, so it turned out had many in the audience. Hindsight would say that

Mr. Courtenay should have ended his version of Lear at that point, but, no, he would return for the mad scene. He had scarcely begun, when an egg came sailing from the rear of the theater and splashed against the back wall of the stage. He ignored that missile as well as a tomato that came closer to the mark.

Soon the shouts of "shut up" and "give us the young ones again" nearly drowned out the voice of the actor but did not deter him from doggedly continuing. The crowd switched from tomatoes back to eggs, and when Lear showed no disposition to end his lament, they brought out their heavy artillery, in the form of cabbages.

Although splattered with tomato pulp and egg yolks, Mr. Courtenay continued to the end of the scene, then rose unsteadily to his feet and bowed ceremoniously to the audience, some of whom, out of sympathy, I suppose, actually applauded.

We had intended going back stage after the performance but decided that the Courtenays might be further embarrassed if we did. So we rescued the hired horse and gig from the livery stable and tried to leave the ugly memory behind.

"Everybody enjoyed them so back at Laramie and Fort Bridger," Will said as we rode toward Grass Valley.

"They were doing minstrel shows," I replied, and added, "And he was sober then."

"He had to be. Captain McGee would have had his hide if he had caught him with liquor."

"He should have had McGee with him today."

"I often think about the captain. I wonder what happened to him?"

"He probably has gone back to escorting greenhorns across the West," I said. "Can't imagine him doing anything else."

Back in Grass Valley, I thanked Will for taking me to the show but did not encourage him to remain, as I had to help finish cleaning up after the evening meal at Annie's Place.

Opal was dying to hear about the Courtenays. After we had closed the restaurant and Duncan had been put to bed for the night, I told her all about it.

She enjoyed my account of the humiliating performance so much that I embellished the tale to add to her pleasure.

"They should have stuck to what they is good at, which seems to be blacking their faces and making fun of my race."

"Why, Opal, they aren't making fun."

"You'd have to be born black to understand. And they threw tomatoes and cabbages?"

"Enough to stock a grocery store."

"And you got stuck with paying for their dinner? Did they ask about me?"

"Mrs. Courtenay in particular took pains to inquire about you."

"It is about time they showed some appreciation."

I let it go at that.

* * *

But I had not seen the last of the Courtenays. Late one morning of the following week, Mildred came into the kitchen to say, "There is an Englishman outside that wants to see you."

Mr. Courtenay, his wife and two children sat in a hack that contained several trunks.

"Dear Annie," he said as I opened the door. "We are on our way to Sacramento and, as I said to Mrs. Courtenay, we cannot leave this area without paying our respects to Annie Nixon."

"Hixon," I said. "That is thoughtful of you. But I thought you were to remain in Nevada City until next week."

"We have had a change of plans. You witnessed that disgraceful exhibition of audience behavior last Saturday. As I told the manager, such ruffians do not deserve good theater. At any rate, we have decided no longer to cast our pearls before such swine. They were largely Irish, you know, and that race has an antipathy toward the British, blaming us for ills they have brought upon themselves. Too late have we heard that not so long ago the great Hugh McDermott himself was similarly treated when he tried to do Richard III in Nevada City. Water over the dam, as the saying goes. Now then, we have heard such glowing endorsements of your restaurant, we thought why not stop and judge for ourselves, that is if you admit lowly actors to your premises."

Opal refused to serve the family but did condescend to come out of the kitchen and speak to them, doing so with an insolent look on her face and without an iota of civility in her voice.

"Her manners have not improved," Mrs. Courtenay said quietly when she had returned to the kitchen.

The Courtenays remained so busy wolfing down our food that I was spared hearing more lies about their acting experiences. It was just as well. There was no audience in our restaurant for Mr. Courtenay's speeches at that time of day.

After polishing off a dish of apple cobbler, Mr. Courtenay arose and indicated that he wished a private conference.

"I have a small favor to ask of you. Damned embarrassing but you see, the manager of the Metropolitan and I have a conflict of interest. He declines to pay us for our performances. I have left the matter in the hands of a lawyer, but, until the issue is settled, well, we find ourselves in an awkward financial position."

"You would like a loan, I suppose."

"How kind of you to offer."

"How much?"

"Would a hundred dollars be out of the question? I will gladly sign a promissory note."

"How about fifty dollars, and never mind the note."

"God bless you. I always regarded you as a young woman of remarkably good heart."

They left for Sacramento with my fifty dollars and without mention of paying for the meal. Opal said it served me right for letting them in the door in the first place.

It took a while for me to see how the way the Courtenays deprived me of $50 and stuck me for two dinners produced any good result, but bear with me. First, I have more to say about Kwong Chung.

2

Early on during his stay with us, Soohoo Kwong Chung, observing my instruction of Opal and Mildred in their off-duty hours, shyly inquired if "Missy Annie" might teach him to read and write "Melican." Of course I agreed, for I did love to teach.

It took a while for him to master our phonetic alphabet and the peculiarities of English spelling, but once he got the hang of the ABC's, he soon overtook Mildred's level of reading and began to approach that of Opal's. His pronunciation left much to be desired, but once I explained the meaning of words, he never forgot them.

Somewhat patronizingly, I sat him down with slate and chalk to teach him arithmetic, too. He listened to me politely for a bit, then excused himself to dig out an abacus from his knapsack behind the stove.

"What is that thing?" I asked.

"I show Missy."

He took the slate on which I had written a problem. His fingers flew along the rows of beads on his abacus and, in an instant, he had written the correct number on the slate. I made no further efforts to instruct Kwong Chung in mathematics.

We often think of the Chinese as being inscrutable because they do not show their emotions as readily as we, but I soon realized that a very intelligent and sympathetic mind lay behind Kwong Chung's unchanging expression. Nor do they reveal their personal histories with the alacrity that we do. But in time, as his trust in me grew along with his command of the English language, I learned a great deal about him and his family and the history of China itself.

Like many of our Chinese miners, he had been born in the county of Kai Pung, near Canton in South China. Many generations earlier, an ancestor who had held a high post in the Chinese Imperial Court had lost favor with the Emperor and had fled to the south to escape punishment. His grandfather had been a well-to-do rice-and-cooking-oil merchant in his village. The family had encountered hard times after his own father, the eldest son, fell victim to the wave of opium addiction that swept over China and, after losing the business, hanged himself. To preserve its honor, the family sold off its assets to satisfy the many creditors.

Thus, just as the family's only child, Kwong Chung, was completing his study of the classics to prepare himself for the Chinese civil service exams, he was forced to take up a very different life to support his widowed mother and the girl to whom he was betrothed. He borrowed enough money to take a sampan for Canton where he worked for two years as a shipping clerk. The salary was poor, but by being frugal, he saved enough to return to his village and be married. Within a year, a daughter had been born to the couple. By then not only had his savings been depleted, he could find no satisfactory employment in the largely agricultural area.

While working in Canton, he had heard of the Gold Mountain that supposedly existed in California. Again he had borrowed money from relatives, made his way back to Canton and there incurred a fresh debt in exchange for passage on a filthy, crowded ship bound for San Francisco.

With some friends from his native village, he had bought a claim on a creek bank from which the easily-found gold had already been taken. Although the flakes of gold he panned were few, he was able to make additional money by writing letters for his largely illiterate fellow miners, enough to live on and to help support his mother, wife and daughter. His goal, of course, had been to earn enough to enable him to return home and for his family to live on for the rest of their lives. Conscious of the grief addiction had caused his own family, unlike many of his comrades, he had shunned opium dens. The attack by the Irish ruffians destroyed his dream. Perhaps, by giving him shelter and a job, I had saved him from his father's fate.

We—especially Duncan—also helped assuage his homesickness for his family. The affection between my little boy and Kwong Chung deepened each month. Duncan followed him about like a puppy. At night, to the consternation of Opal, Kwong Chung often wrapped him in a blanket and crooned what I took to be Chinese lullabies.

Yes, besides proving enormously useful to our family, Kwong Chung was a man of great intelligence and sensitivity. Only later would I appreciate the depth of his wisdom.

So, with Opal doing the cooking, Mildred, most of the waiting on tables, and Kwong Chung, the heavier work, I had myself a large and busy family, all pulling together to make Annie's Place successful. But as I now know only too well, nothing—good or bad—lasts forever.

* * *

A few weeks after my encounter with the Courtenays, Opal came into the kitchen, where I was going over his English lessons with Kwong Chung, to say, "You won't believe who is out front asking to see you."

"Is it President Buchanan?" I asked.

"Here, he can speak for himself. Come on back, Captain."

I did not recognize Zebulon McGee at first. His hair had been neatly trimmed and he was dressed, not in the buckskins I was used to seeing but in a tailored suit of worsted material that must have cost a fortune. And he had replaced his sombrero with a soft felt hat.

But he was as big and rugged looking as ever.

"Excuse me for intruding, little lady, but I was just passing through to Nevada City and thought I'd look in on you."

Naturally that ended my lesson with Kwong Chung.

The captain accepted my offer of a cup of coffee. After he had settled in a chair, I asked, "What brings you to these parts?"

"Business," he said. "But that English fellow that came west with us. The big talking actor . . . "

"Homer Courtenay?" I said.

"Yes, him. I saw a sign outside a theater in Sacramento last week. That is where my headquarters are these days. And they had put up a sign advertising a minstrel show with his name on it."

"He is not playing Shakespeare?"

"Not unless Shakespeare blacked up his face. Anyway I looked him up, thinking you might still be with the family, you and the Negro woman, and he told me of seeing you here and all about you running a boarding house."

"A restaurant," I corrected him. "But why did you think I might be with him and his family?"

"That was the deal when we left you off with Evelyn Harmer. He was supposed to send for you after he got settled in San Francisco. You and what's her name."

"Opal," I said.

"Yes, Opal. That was what he promised he was going to do as soon as you were able to travel. I reckon he let you down. What happened?"

As briefly and discreetly as possible, I told him of our experience at the House of Joy, and the trouble about my school.

"I am sorry to hear of that. So you had your baby then?"

"Indeed, I did. Kwong Chung, fetch Duncan from next door."

In a few minutes, Duncan had been carried into the kitchen of the restaurant, rubbing the sleep from his eyes. He stood as if in awe at the sight of the big, rangy man holding out his hand, then turned and hid his face in my skirt folds.

"Right likely looking young fellow," McGee said. "Must take after your side of the house though, from the looks of him."

Conversation with the former mountain man did not come easily, but I chattered away with questions, such as why had he given up herding emigrants across the West.

"There was big Indian troubles along the trail in '57 and '58, you know. And there was that business between the Army and the Mormons. For a time there it looked like old Brigham Young was going to burn down his city and take to the hills. Scared off the settlers. Things have settled down in Utah now. So I hooked up with Clarence Goodall. You remember him, I reckon. We went into the business of hauling freight in and out of Sacramento."

"You appear to have done well at it."

"Well enough for me, Clarence and his half-breed sons to live on. We keep a dozen outfits on the road all the time. Now I am thinking of opening up an office here in Nevada County. So, yes, I have done all right, I reckon. And from the looks of this place, so have you, little lady."

"It wasn't easy at first, Captain. Evelyn Harmer, in whose care you and the Courtenays left me, was not as kind as she might have been."

"I am sorry it turned out that way. We didn't expect you to stay at her place more than a couple of weeks. That was all I paid her for."

This was the first time I had heard of Mrs. Harmer's having been paid for taking me in.

"I really should repay you," I said. "And thank you as well." Then, before he could respond, added, "Just how well did you know Mrs. Harmer?"

"She wasn't what you would call a friend. It's just that I saved her from being chased out of town back in '54 when I was passing through to the East. There was a mob of do-gooders gathered to wreck her place. I talked them out of it. Me and Boris, that is. Anyway, she told me anytime I needed a favor, just to ask. You were the favor. As for the money, I would have spent it by now, anyhow. So she treated you bad, did she? Maybe I should drop by and have a word with her about that."

"Please don't. In the long run, she did us a favor."

"Yes. I reckon this beats serving them Courtenays as a family nurse maid, which was all they wanted you for."

To change the subject, I inquired about the fate of the other contingent of our expedition, the one Chester Peebles was to lead to Oregon.

"They got there all right. Chester himself even took up a land claim but soon sold it and started up a newspaper. You know how he likes to talk. It's the same way with writing."

"So you hear from him regularly?"

"Every few months, whether I answer him or not."

"He was engaged to be married, to a Boston girl."

"Still is. Only her daddy won't give his consent until Chester has made a pile of money and built her a house."

"He seemed quite unsettled in his mind, about what to do in Oregon, that is."

"I have offered him a job with our company. In fact I am waiting to hear what he says to my offer. Oh, and by the way, he has taken up politics. Has been preaching the abolitionist line in his newspaper, which is one reason he hasn't done all that well."

"You don't agree with your cousin on that issue?"

"Slavery? I am just as against it as he is, but there is a practical matter to be dealt with. What is going to happen to the slaves once they are free? And how are them that has invested their money in them to be compensated? Now, Chester, he is all for going to war if need be to set them free. In my mind, that is carrying things too far. But, see here, I didn't come by to talk politics. I just wanted to see how you are getting on without me to get you out of your scrapes."

"I am fully capable now of standing up for myself, thank you, Captain. Although you must not think me ungrateful for coming to my rescue as you did."

Not only did he rebuff my attempt to repay the money he had given Mrs. Harmer on my behalf, he even declined to accept my offer of a free meal, saying he had to get on to Nevada City before dark.

Carrying Duncan, I walked him to the door.

"Here," he said. "Take one of my business cards. Don't hesitate to let me know if you get in any more scrapes where you need me to help."

He took first my hand and then Duncan's.

"You got yourself a brave mama, young fellow," he said.

Opal came out on the porch with me to watch him mount his big gray gelding and go riding down the street. Mildred soon joined us.

"Who was that gentleman?" Mildred asked.

"Gentleman, my foot," Opal said. "That man caused the death of my husband. He is still just a dressed-up old squaw man that ain't got the manners to call folks by their right names."

"He sure looks like a real man to me."

"I reckon you would know about that," Opal said.

I looked at the card he had given me. "McGee & Company. We haul anything anywhere." I put the card in my apron pocket and did not look at it again until some weeks afterwards.

* * *

Life went on as usual for the next few weeks after McGee's visit. The only thing out of the ordinary that I did was to pay off the balance on my mortgage on the old exchange office.

My banker friend, Alonzo Delano, did not seem overjoyed at this.

"How can our bank make a profit if nobody wants to rent our money, Annie?"

"And, Mr. Delano, how can my restaurant make a profit if I keep shelling out hard cash for your interest payments?"

"I still think that you should be borrowing more, not depleting your cash to pay down this mortgage. You have proved you have brains as well as grit. Have you thought of building a new hotel? You could tear down your house and put up a good brick building right up against your restaurant."

"When I save up enough capital, I might do that. Meanwhile, I will be content to be out of debt and no longer coughing up interest payments."

"Just don't go resting on your laurels. You know the parable of the talents. Only way to get ahead in this world is to take risks. Don't want to go hiding your talents under a rock."

"I believe I am doing the right thing."

And so I thought at the time. It did not occur to me that I might be taking a risk in freeing myself of debt.

* * *

It also seemed the right thing to do to give refuge to Madeline, the runaway prostitute, when she came to our door with a blackened eye and huge bruises on her arms, and, as the saying goes, "pregnant as a pup."

Sitting in our kitchen with tears running down her cheeks, she told a sad story of Bull Duchamps' increasing violence against her.

"He was nice enough for a long while, except for getting drunk now and then. It was better than working for Mrs. Harmer anyway. No, we never actually got married. He kept promising, then would put me off. When he learnt I was pregnant, I thought that would bring him around, but no, he began to beat me regular. I just took all I could. His friends feel sorry for me but they are afraid of him. You are the only person I know that is kind enough to take me in. Please, Annie, can I stay?"

Not daring to look at Opal, I said, "Of course you can. At least long enough to pull yourself together."

Mildred was not happy about sharing her room but, being a good-hearted soul, agreed to do so. Opal was another matter.

"You must be out of your mind. We don't need no more trouble, and that is what we are in for, trouble."

"Have you forgot how we, or, anyway, I, was in the same situation not so long ago, with child and in need of shelter?"

"It is not the same thing. You didn't have a mean man like that Frenchman thinking he owns you."

"Judging from the way he has been mistreating her, I doubt he will mind that she is gone."

"Lord, girl, I thought you had learned some sense. Didn't you never see how the cruelest masters was the ones that went to the most trouble to catch slaves that ran away?"

"Where I come from, there weren't all that many slaves. Besides this has nothing to do with slavery."

"You just think it don't. See, that Frenchman enjoys having her around to mistreat. He wasn't trying to drive her away. He just needs somebody to kick around and to do for him."

"Like it or not, I will not deny shelter to that poor girl. Really, Opal, your hardness of heart disturbs me."

"Yes, and your softness of head causes me considerable worry. Just don't come whining to me when that Frenchman shows up like he did once before."

"He is a French Canadian. And I can't see why he would cause any trouble. If he loved her all that much, why wouldn't he marry her?"

"Don't ask me. Just remember I told you."

Although I really did not expect any trouble from Bull Duchamps, the next morning, as a precaution, I dipped into our cash box for enough money to buy myself a small-caliber, five-shot revolver. The clerk at the hardware spent a half-hour teaching me how to load the weapon. Then he escorted me behind the store, set up a cracker box, and let me fire off several rounds, none of which struck the target.

"You'd do better, Mrs. Hixon, if you just wouldn't close your eyes. And you should squeeze the trigger gradually so it don't jerk the gun off target. Now, you want me to reload it for you?"

Not wishing to give Opal the satisfaction of knowing I had bought a gun, I put it on the top of the wardrobe in my room.

Within a few days, the swelling and discoloration around Madeline's eye had subsided. She begged to be allowed to wait tables with Mildred, but I relegated her to kitchen work instead.

And so, life went on as usual at Annie's Place.

3

The trouble which Opal had predicted came on a Saturday night after we had finished serving our diners, had cleaned up the kitchen, and retired to our house next door.

Duncan was sound asleep in his little trundle bed. Madeline and Mildred were drinking coffee and playing black jack on our kitchen table while Kwong Chung politely read one of his Chinese scrolls, waiting for them to leave so he could retire to his pallet behind the stove.

I was in my room, already in my night gown and taking down my hair, when there came a great hammering at the front door.

Lantern in hand, Opal padded down the hall, calling out, "All right. We hear you."

The door opened and, deaf to Opal's protests, someone stomped past her and down the hall to the kitchen from which Madeline's screams soon erupted.

"No, Bull. Leave me alone," she cried.

Quickly, I stood on tiptoes and took down my new revolver. Concealing it behind me, I entered the kitchen. Kwong Chung was cowering behind the stove, Mildred behind the table. Duchamps had taken Madeline's arm and was twisting it.

"No woman of mine runs out on me."

"You drove me away."

"I was drunk."

"You are always drunk. And you won't marry me."

"I don't have to marry you. You belong to me. And look at you. Taking up with a chink and a nigger woman."

"All right, Duchamps. That will be enough of that," I said loud and clear in my best school-mistress tone, "Turn that poor girl loose."

He spun around to face me.

"So it's you again? You got none of your damned Cornishmen around this time. So if you don't want to get hurt, just stand aside. This woman is going back where she belongs."

"I don't need anyone to protect me this time," I said.

And with that I produced my nickle-plated little revolver and, holding it in front with both hands, as the hardware clerk had instructed, drew back the hammer.

"Good God," said Opal. "She has got a gun."

"I have killed one man," I said. "You will be the second if you don't turn her loose."

"You don't scare me with that little thing," he said, turning his back as he did so, to resume twisting Madeline's arm.

She sank to the floor and I, forgetting my instructions, closed my eyes and jerked the trigger. The report of the pistol was so loud I feared it had cracked our window panes.

I opened my eyes and for a sickening moment feared I would pass out, as Madeline seemed to have done. There stood Duchamps with that same look of disbelief I had seen on Bart Corbett's face back on the banks of the La Prele River. Only, instead of clutching his chest, he had clapped his hand to the side of his head. Blood was flowing down his neck so that I thought my shot had penetrated his brain.

As I drew back the hammer to recock the pistol, he took his hand away from his mutilated ear and looked at the blood that smeared his fingers.

"You could have killed me," he said.

"I will shoot off your other ear if you don't clear out."

"I'll go, but I'll be back. You can't steal my woman."

With that he gave Madeline a savage kick to her stomach and dashed out the rear door.

Down the hall, little Duncan, awakened by the shot, was crying. So was Mildred. Opal kept saying, "I knowed there was going to be trouble," until I threatened to shoot her if she did not shut up.

With Kwong Chung's help, we carried the still unconcious Madeline to bed and all of us tried to get some sleep. But I was awakened before dawn by Mildred saying, "We got to get a doctor for Madeline. She is bleeding like a stuck pig."

While Opal helped attend to Madeline, I gave Kwong Chung a note to be taken to Doctor Jacoby.

By the time the old sawbones arrived, however, it was too late. Madeline had been carrying a baby girl, not yet well formed enough to have survived even if the doctor had been on hand. We let her cuddle the little creature in one of Duncan's blankets while we sat in the kitchen debating whether a funeral was in order and trying to make sense of the night's events.

Opal, shocked by the miscarriage, had stopped reminding me of her warnings, but she did ask, "What did you mean about killing one man already?"

"I was just bluffing," I lied. "Anyway, now he knows he can't scare us. I don't expect to see any more of Mr. Bull Duchamps."

However, just in case we did, I reloaded my little revolver and placed it back atop my wardrobe.

After seeing to the burial of the baby, we kept poor Madeline in bed all the next week. Enfeebled by the loss of blood and her sorrow at the loss of her baby, she lay there quietly, allowing herself, probably for the first time in her life, to be waited on.

By the following Saturday, she claimed to feel well enough to resume working in the kitchen of the restaurant but I forbade her to stir from her room until Dr. Jacoby had another look at her. And that is how, on what was to prove a fateful night, she came to be in our house with little Duncan, she in her room next to the kitchen, and he in the room we shared toward the front of the house.

It was a busy evening for us next door at Annie's Place. Opal had prepared a tasty beef stew plus her now famous corn meal muffins and apple cobbler. The place was packed. I was busy at my cashier's desk when someone on the street shouted, "Fire!"

Not smelling any smoke, I kept making change until a man poked his head in the door to say, "Your house is on fire, Mrs. Hixon."

I ran out the front door of the restaurant to see the back part of our house which was already in flames. I ran to the front door, only to find it barred from within.

"Duncan is in there," I screamed. "My little boy."

Customers now were boiling out of the restaurant to see what was the matter. Several men began futilely trying to break down the front door, but it was made of solid oak and would not yield.

Then suddenly Kwong Chung appeared. From somewhere, he had found a heavy horse blanket.

"I get him, Missy," he said as he wrapped himself in the blanket and, thus protected from broken glass, crashed into the front window. The panes and frame collapsed, and he fell into the now smoke-filled front room. It took the full strength of two men to restrain me from following him. Later they would tell me that I had acted like a wild woman.

The next thing I remember was Kwong Chung handing a wailing Duncan out the window and into my arms. His, Kwong Chung's, face was as black as Opal's. Before I could prevent his doing so, he re-entered the house and was gone so long I was sure that he had perished. Men now were running from all directions bearing buckets of water, but it was too late to save the tinder dry building. The flames licked high above the roof line, sending out showers of sparks over nearby buildings.

Finally, to my vast relief, Kwong Chung appeared at the window, staggering from the weight of the unconscious Madeline. He handed her through the window to the men who had been restraining me, then crawled through himself and collapsed on the porch. They hauled him and Madeline out into the street, away from the fire, which soon spread into the front of the house.

Although the walls of the old grocery building had been constructed of brick, the roof was covered with cedar shingles. Someone fetched ladders and threw water on the roof but by the time they got organized, it was too late. Too many sparks had landed on the shingles.

So there I stood, with my precious little boy enfolded in my arms as I watched the vain efforts of the crowd to save my restaurant. All that I and Opal and Mildred, yes, and Kwong Chung, too, had labored to create for two years was destroyed in less than an hour. Although, the men in the crowd were able to carry out the benches, tables and most of the kitchen equipment, in the end only the charred brick walls remained of my restaurant and nothing but ashes of my house.

But a sadder thing happened while I was watching the fire complete its destruction of my buildings. I discovered what this was when I went to check on Madeline and to thank Kwong Chung for saving Duncan. Madeline's body now was covered, face and all, by the horse blanket. Mildred was sitting beside the body, crying.

* * *

The full truth about what happened that awful night was slow in coming out. When I learned what it was, I was outraged but helpless to take action.

It was after the funeral for Madeline, conducted at my request by a local Methodist minister, and attended by our "family" and her former co-workers from the House of Joy. We saw her buried in a grave beside that of her still-born daughter. As I stood comforting Mildred and her friends, Kwong Chung touched my sleeve.

"That man over there," he pointed to a figure with a bandage around his head watching from a clump of trees across the graveyard. "You see him?"

"Why yes. It is Bull Duchamps. I reckon he didn't have the nerve to attend the funeral."

"He set fire."

"What do you mean?"

"Girl, she tell me when I carry her. She say 'Bull do this.' She say she see him at window. She bar doors so he no get in."

It took me a moment to catch his meaning. When I looked again, Duchamps was gone.

Suddenly it all made sense, why the doors were barred and who set the fire that wiped me out and caused Madeline's death. My first impulse was to run to the sheriff, but his office was in Nevada City. So I bided my time until I saw Mr. Delano, my banker, that afternoon.

He listened to my story and shook his head.

"There is a good chance the fellow did it, all right, but you have only a hearsay report. And even if your Chinaman had seen him set the fire, which of course he didn't, his testimony would not be considered valid. Yes, of course, you are outraged that he should get away with such a thing, but you would be wasting your time to bring charges against him. Besides, you have more pressing concerns, such as what will you do."

"You did offer to lend me the money to build a hotel."

"So, I did, but that was when you had a building to mortgage. Let us consider your means. For how much was your property insured?"

"Insured?"

"Yes. Surely you took out an insurance policy after you paid off your mortgage."

"I thought about it, then let the matter slip my mind."

"Ah, dear Annie, I wish you had not done so."

There went his offer to finance construction of a new hotel. The best he would do in my new circumstances was to advance me $500 for living expenses, with the lots on which my house and restaurant had stood as collateral.

Thus Opal, Mildred, Duncan and I ended up as guests back at the Pacific Hotel. I bought a tent for Kwong Chung to live in at the rear of the burnt-out former dry goods store building.

*   *   *

We were still living at the Pacific Hotel, nearly out of money and, like Mr. Micawber, waiting for "something to turn up," when my twentieth birthday rolled around that year. Frankly I had forgot the date, but Opal had not. I discovered this after she had told me the manager of the hotel wished to see me downstairs.

"What for?"

"He wouldn't say."

I should have smelled a rat when Opal followed me downstairs, with Duncan in her arms,

"Mrs. Hixon," the manager said. "If you don't mind, please come this way."

He led the way to the smaller of the hotel's two dining rooms, then opened the door and bowed for me to enter. When I did, a cry of "Happy Birthday" rang out.

There with beaming faces stood Will Tremelling, his Cornish friends, Mildred, Kwong Chung and, several of my most loyal restaurant customers.

And I had been thinking that I had no friends. Is it any wonder that I was so touched I cried?

After we had all had a glass or two of wine and were at the point of attacking the buffet of food, I whispered to Opal, "You know I can't afford this."

"You ain't paying. He is," she said, nodding toward Will Tremelling.

"How did he know it was my birthday?"

"I told him."

After we had polished off the birthday cake and the others were taking their leave, Will drew me aside to ask, "What are you going to do now that you are entering your third decade of life?"

"I don't really know, Will. I am tired of fighting against the odds. It seems like every time I climb to my feet, something knocks me down again."

"You need a husband."

"I had one husband. That is enough to do me."

"I mean a real husband. A fellow that would look after you. Look, Annie, you ain't the only one with something to celebrate. I been promoted to assistant mine manager. They have raised my pay to $5 a day. Marry me and we can fix up your old building for a house. The walls remain strong."

"I am pleased you are doing so well, Will, but I am not interested in getting married again."

"If you was to be interested, wouldn't I do well enough?"

I laughed, "Better than most for sure, Will."

"Just keep me in mind. It would kill me if you was to marry somebody else."

Naturally Opal wanted to know what we had talked about and, like a fool, I told her.

"Why don't you take him up on it? He's strong and handy. He could turn that old burnt-out building into a good house. All it needs is a new roof. I'd be glad to stay on to do the cooking. You would even have room to keep that Chinaman around."

"Will is nice, but I don't love him."

"Did you love that little Elmer fellow?"

"I was learning to tolerate him."

"You got to admit the Englishman would be an improvement."

"He is a Cornishman, not an Englishman. There is a difference."

"White folks all look the same to me. Anyway, don't you go throwing away a chance at a man that loves you and is making good money in the bargain."

* * *

Will Tremelling was a good-hearted, steady fellow who earned excellent wages, at least by his standards. I wouldn't call him handsome, but he was slender and well-knit, with kindly eyes and a shy grin.

Although it was flattering to have such a loyal admirer, there were several reasons why I did not jump at Will's repeated pleas to marry him.

While he was ambitious to become a mine manager, his ambitions did not go beyond earning a good salary and living in a neat cottage and siring several children.

Will had attended a dame's school for three years back in Cornwall, so that he could read and write. Yet while by no means stupid, he lacked my interest in literature.

One thing I will say for him: He had a fine, clear, sure tenor singing voice.

"Used to sing in chapel back home," he explained.

I don't remember ever saying flat out, "I shall never marry you. Look elsewhere for a wife." No, I kept the poor fellow on a string, enjoying the knowledge that if my situation should become too desperate, Will Tremelling would be there to take me under his full protection, and with me, Duncan and, even, Opal.

He was not so kindly disposed toward Kwong Chung, however, or to be more precise, toward the Chinese race, fearing an influx of Chinamen willing to work for "coolie wages."

What Kwong Chung thought of Will at that time, I could not say, for he kept his opinions to himself.

As my financial means continued to shrink along with my hopes that something would "turn up," I did much soul searching, not just about Will but about the entire question of marriage. After all, if marriage had been my chief objective, Will was not the only prospect in that community of far more men than women.

I reflected on how, as a matter of convenience, I had consented to be secretly married to Elmer Hixon and how well that had turned out in the long run. Anytime I was willing to swallow my pride and give up my independence, there was more than one possibility. There was Mr. Levy, the dry goods merchant who was well on his way to becoming far richer than Will could ever hope to be. The editor of The Telegraph who, while not wealthy or likely ever to be so, did share my interest in good literature.

There were others, but none stirred my love as had Billy Joe Duncan, damn his lovely, light-brown eyes of which I was daily reminded when I looked into those of my beautiful little son.

Yet, I did like Will better than any of the others. That is for certain. And far more certain was the fact that Opal preferred him immensely over the other possibilities. "He wouldn't have to ask me but once," is how she put it.

* * *

It was my habit every day to take little Duncan to walk to the blackened walls of Annie's Place to chat with Kwong Chung and to stand about rueing my failure to insure my property or to accept the banker's original offer to finance a hotel on the site. Kwong Chung had turned his tent into a dwelling snug enough to do him until winter returned. I knew that he was eking out a living from composing letters for his countrymen to send back to their relatives in China and from reading for them the letters they received but did not learn of another of his activities until about three weeks after our fire.

Duncan and I approached his tent to find him sitting on a box outside, studying the hand of another Chinaman so intently that he did not see me.

I backed away, out of his line of sight, and waited while the two men babbled away in their native language. After their business was done, and the other fellow was leaving, I set Duncan down and allowed him to run to Kwong Chung.

I asked him what he had been doing, looking at the other Chinaman's hands.

With what I took to be embarrassment, he said, "Fortune. I tell him fortune."

"You mean you read palms? Why did you never tell me this?"

"You not ask."

"And they pay you to do this?"

He nodded, apparently embarrassed.

"Could you tell my fortune?"

He motioned me to sit on the box facing him. He took my right hand in his and studied my palm, muttering to himself as he did so. Then he freed my hand and took up a scroll, looked at it a bit, muttered some more, and peered into my face.

"Missy very strong woman. What English word? Stubborn. Yes, been through much trouble."

"Of course I have, Kwong Chung. My house and my restaurant have been destroyed."

"Before that. Many troubles."

"That is all in the past. What about the future?"

"You live many years. Die rich woman."

Growing impatient, I said, "Not the far off future. What will happen soon?"

"What Missy want to know?"

Exasperated with him and embarrassed to have to ask outright, nonetheless I did ask, "Will I marry again?"

"You not know?"

"Don't play games, Kwong Chung. What do you see?"

"I see one, maybe two more husbands. And children, maybe three, maybe four."

"When? Who?"

"That up to Missy. Anytime she want. Whoever she want."

"And that is all you have to say?"

"That all I see. Sorry. How Duncan is? Come to Kwong Chung."

* * *

For all my air of independence and what my mother called my "headstrong nature," I remained a woman, subject to the ups and down moods that beset my sex. And this woman was beginning to grow discouraged by all the hard knocks that had come her way during the last three years.

The last straw came with a summons from the manager of the Pacific Hotel to discuss my in-arrears bill.

I asked for a bit more time, knowing full well that there appeared to be no prospects for my fortune to change.

This fellow in whose mouth butter would not have melted a few weeks earlier at my birthday party, replied without an iota of mercy, "You owe us for nearly a month's room and board already. I am not operating a house of charity, you know."

"Just give me one more week, please."

"On one condition. You must sign this promissory note which will be entered at the courthouse as a judgment against your real estate if it is not satisfied."

So, without informing him that the bank already held a first mortgage on the property, I signed the note, thinking as I did so how much I would enjoy opening a competing hotel and driving him out of business.

* * *

When I told her of my conference with the hotel man, Opal said, "So it is gonna be out in the cold for us again," then added, "Unless you come to your senses."

"It is nearly summer. We won't be in the cold. Maybe we'll just pitch a tent beside Kwong Chung's and live there until winter. And what do you mean 'come to my senses?'"

"All you got to do is say the word and you'd have a man earning $5 a day to build you a house and look after you for the rest of your life."

"I just wish you would mind your own business and keep your nose out of mine."

But unless I missed my guess, she did not mind her own business. It must have been at her instigation that Will showed up just when things looked blackest, when only two days remained before the hotel manager would kick us out and a week before the first interest payment was due on my new bank loan.

All dressed up in his best clothes, he drew me into a corner of the hotel lobby and after some hemming and hawing, came out with, "I am not a rich man, Annie. But I will always earn a decent living. And you'll never find a man that will love you more."

I was touched by his earnestness, but also impatient for him to get on with what I suspected was coming.

Perhaps reading my mind, he stopped in mid-sentence, reached in his pocket, drew out a small box and opened it to reveal a ring set with a tiny diamond.

"This is all I could afford just now but after we have got your place fixed up to live in and I save some more money, I'll buy you a bigger one."

I glanced down at the gold band that the J.P.'s wife had sold Elmer back in Missouri. My finger showed its usual greenish tinge. Will's little diamond ring fit perfectly, but I immediately slipped it off and put it back in its box.

Will's face fell.

"Won't you accept it?"

"Give me just a few more days, Will."

"I have waited this long. I reckon I can wait a little longer."

* * *

Refusing to answer any of Opal's questions and leaving Duncan in her care, I put on my hat and marched to Kwong Chung's tent where I found him reading a scroll while waiting for a small kettle to boil over his camp fire.

"We must talk, Kwong Chung."

"Missy, please sit. Want tea?"

"I will sit, but I don't want to waste time drinking tea. What I want from you is some straight talk. No, I don't want my palms read again or to hear what Confucius said. You know the fix I am in. You know that Will Tremelling wants desperately to marry me. I like him well enough but I don't love him. I did not love or like my first husband either, and I was miserable at first. What do you think I should do?"

Startled by my directness, he began fumbling in his knapsack.

"No, Kwong Chung. Don't read to me from a scroll. Tell me straight out what I should do."

"Missy got too much pride. You too proud to marry this Will even though he give you nice house and save you from poverty."

He held up his hand to stop me from interrupting.

"Please. You ask me for straight talk. I give it to you. If you got to swallow your pride anyhow, you might as well drink deep. Don't sell yourself or your pride too cheap."

"Please be more specific."

"Very well, Missy Annie Hixon. Here is what this humble old Chinaman thinks you should do."

* * *

"Where you been?" Opal demanded upon my return. "That manager wants to see you right away. He is hopping mad. Says his lawyer went to file your note at the Court House and seen you done put a mortgage on your lots."

"He can go to hell. Where did you put my apron? Yes, yes, the one I was wearing the night of the fire. There. Hand it to me."

"Where you going now?" she asked in a moment.

"To the telegraph office. I will explain later."

4

I sent that desperate telegraph message too late to prevent our being evicted from the Pacific Hotel. I had only enough time to persuade Mr. Levy to sell us on credit a large tent and three cots and for Kwong Chung and Opal to set up the shelter between the old foundations of our house and the fire-blackened walls of my old brick building.

It was a commodious tent, as tents go. Kwong Chung managed to scrounge enough boards to lay a wooden floor and enough bricks to form a cooking fire pit outside. So by the following day we had, if not a roof over our heads, at least a shelter that would protect us until winter came.

After a week had passed, my hopes of an answer to my telegraph message began to wane. By the end of a miserable second week, they had evaporated. My situation and my spirits were eroded by Mr. Delano's coming around to inform me that he would have to call my note by the end of the month.

And as if that pressure were not enough, Will Tremelling—emboldened by my straits—stepped up his campaign to persuade me to marry him.

"Between what I have saved and what I can borrow from my friends, we can keep up your payments at the bank, buy lumber and such enough for me to put a new roof on the old building. It would make us a good enough house. So what are you waiting for, Annie? Marry me and you'll never have another worry. I will take care of you and your boy for the rest of your lives."

"I am not ready, Will, not yet."

"When will you be ready?"

"Give me a few more days."

"Would a week be long enough?"

"Perhaps."

"Good. I'll take next Friday off at the mine so we can go over to Nevada City for a license, if you are so minded. We can celebrate with a supper at the National Exchange Hotel and then we can get married the next day. There now. Are you saying no again?"

"Just give me a week to sort out my thoughts and affairs."

*   *   *

As that last week wore on, I became increasingly restless, in part because of the rain that fell off and on. Stuck inside a musty tent, Duncan whined and Opal pouted. The ground outside was so muddy, we had to scrape our shoes after venturing forth for fresh air.

Sensing my mood, Kwong Chung kept to his own small tent, occupying himself with reading his scrolls and telling the occasional fortune of other Chinamen. Occasionally, however, I would catch him looking my way as if trying to divine my intentions. And when I was sure Opal was not looking, I said many a short prayer asking for guidance.

No matter what decision I might make, one thing was for sure: I was not going to remain living in a tent indefinitely.

I awoke early that Saturday morning and thought about my situation. True I did not love Will although I liked him well enough. He was clever with his hands and honest, he wasn't nearly as smart or ambitious as I would have liked. Yet he was offering me a life line.

Opal, thinking I still slept, arose and slipped outside to start a cook fire. As she thus busied herself, I counted on my right fingers, the advantages of becoming Mrs. Will Tremelling and on my left, the disadvantages. The score was pretty much even by the time Opal opened the tent flap.

"Got you some coffee here."

I thanked her and sat up on my cot to receive the steaming cup.

"What are you doing in my trunk, Opal?"

"Picking out your dress for today."

"I am perfectly capable of doing that for myself."

"Let's see if you are."

First she held up a checked everyday dress made of calico, then my best summer garment, a taffeta gown with lace collar and cuffs.

"Which will it be?"

"Does it have to be right now?"

"He is coming at noon. So which dress shall I lay out?"

I drew a deep breath, started to speak, then paused and simply pointed to the taffeta gown.

She grinned and said, "Thought you'd come to your senses. Now we got to get that Chinaman to bring us a keg of water for you to take a bath. And we got to do something about that hair. We can't have you going to that big hotel looking like something the cats drug in."

* * *

As noon approached, I was beset by conflicting emotions. On the one hand, I felt like a doomed criminal awaiting the hour of execution, on the other, like a person about to be freed from the prison of poverty and debt.

Opal was right in saying that I could do a lot worse than marrying Will. Either way, that seemed to be my fate, and I was tired of fighting against it. So I sat passively, allowing Opal to wash and braid my hair and to tie and retie the sash of my fancy dress.

Weary at last of her fussing over me, I stepped out onto the plank sidewalk to survey the ruins of my building and to try to envision what it would look like as a house. I could picture a wide porch across the front and a new tin roof that would be proof against the flying sparks that had set the old shingles afire. I could even imagine our clearing the rubble of our old house next door and turning that space into an attractive side garden.

Lost in my reverie, I paid no attention to the sound of hooves on the street behind me.

"Hey, little lady. You look like you are headed for a party."

I turned to see Zeb McGee astride his big gray gelding. Too surprised to speak, I simply stared at him with my mouth open.

"I just got back to Sacramento from Frisco day before yesterday or I would have been here sooner. Looks like you have got yourself in another predicament. Are you going to tell me what happened, or has the cat got your tongue?"

He dismounted, tied his horse to a sapling and walked with me around the ruins while I told him of our fire and the probable cause. Then we adjourned to my tent. There an apprehensive, resentful Opal grudgingly prepared him a cup of coffee and handed it to him without acknowledging his greeting.

"You ain't forgetting your business today, I hope," she muttered to me.

"Of course not," I snapped. "Now please take Duncan outside."

"Her disposition hasn't improved, has it?" McGee said after she had withdrawn with Duncan in hand.

"It comes and goes. But I don't know what I would have done without her these past three years."

"You haven't had an easy time of it, have you, little lady?"

"No, but please don't think I feel sorry for myself."

"I'd never think that of you. Now tell me again where you stand with this banking fellow . . . "

We were still talking, or rather I talked and he listened for nearly an hour, when Opal interrupted to announce, "Will and another gentleman are outside."

Leaving the captain sitting in the tent, I stepped out to see Will, all decked out in his best suit, and a thin, balding fellow dressed in a long-tailed coat.

"Annie, this is the Reverend Dryden from Nevada City. He will take us over to the county seat in his buggy to get our license and then marry us right there in the National Exchange Hotel."

"Yes," the minister said. "Mr. Tremelling says you are a Methodist and that he himself attended Wesleyan services back in England . . . "

"Cornwall," Will said.

"Quite so. Anyway, I am on my way back to Nevada City. I will be more than glad to kill two birds with one stone. However, we will need to get there before the court house closes."

"I can't do that," I said.

"Why not?" Will demanded.

"I have a visitor and we are in the middle of a discussion."

"Who? What kind of a discussion?"

"It has to do with business."

Just then Captain McGee emerged from the tent. Poor Will looked as though he had seen a ghost, as he accepted the captain's handshake.

"Glad to see you again, Tremelling."

"Likewise, I am sure, Captain. What brings you to these parts?"

"This little lady sent me word three weeks ago that she was in trouble. I just thought I had better come see how I could help her. Would have been here earlier but I was down in Frisco . . . "

"Actually, Captain, she don't need help from anybody but me. Things have changed considerably in the past three weeks. She is in good hands now."

McGee looked at me with a puzzled expression and said, "I don't get your drift."

"Didn't Annie tell you? We're getting married tonight. This is Reverend Dryden."

I said, "Will, you are jumping the gun on me."

"You promised to give me my answer today, and Opal here said . . . "

"Never mind what Opal said. It is impossible for me to marry anyone on such short notice."

"I been asking you for the past two years. Reverend Dryden is here, ready and willing to take us to the courthouse for our license and then marry us. I see you are all dressed up. We can spend our wedding night at that big hotel."

"See here," McGee said. "If I am interfering, I'll be glad to clear out."

"Not meaning to be rude, Captain," Will said, "but you have come at a awkward time for Annie and me."

"Speak for yourself, Will," I said. "The Captain and I have important business to discuss. We can get married anytime."

Before anyone else could speak, the minister said, "Obviously you two have some questions to be settled before you take such a big step as marriage."

And, before Will could stop him, he tipped his hat and walked away.

Will glowered at the Captain and me, then pulled his derby down over his eyes and turned his back.

"Thought you said she was ready," he growled at Opal.

"She was until he had to go and show up."

* * *

As I should have remembered from having followed him across half a continent, Zebulon McGee was not a man for letting grass grow under his feet. Having heard of my earlier conversations with Mr. Delano at the bank, he would not even give me time to change from my taffeta gown to a more sensible dress.

"I know bankers," he said. "They are as bad as Mexicans for taking long siestas. So we better catch him before he closes."

Sure enough, Delano was on the sidewalk, in the act of locking his office door when got there. After I had introduced McGee to him, I said, "We would like to have a word with you."

"As you can see from the sign in my window, the office is closed. However, if you would like to return at two o'clock . . . "

"We can't wait until then," McGee said. "We want to talk now."

Once inside, without exchanging pleasantries, McGee said, "I understand this little lady owes you five hundred dollars."

"So she does. And the sum is secured by a mortgage."

"We are here to clear up that debt."

Since this was news to me, I was taken aback.

"But, Captain . . . "

"No buts about it. You don't want to be beholden to a bank that don't trust you enough to extend personal credit."

"Just a minute, Mister . . . " Delano said. "What did you say your name was?"

"Zebulon McGee. Here is my business card."

Delano studied the card, then said, "Surely, Mr. McGee, Annie has told you of our long-standing banking relationship."

"She sure as hell has and from what she says, you are just another one of them bankers that likes to lend money only to folks that don't need it."

"That is a bit extreme, Mr. McGee."

"Then what is this horseshit . . . Pardon me, little lady . . . this business about foreclosing on her two lots?"

"She no longer can keep up her payments. We are not running a public charity here. This is a business."

"Then let's get down to business."

*   *   *

We resolved nothing that afternoon except to clear up my $500 mortgage and for Delano to turn right around and lend me $300 as "a character loan," meaning without collateral.

I offered to give McGee a lien on my two lots to secure his loan, but he refused.

"Haven't you learned to go slow on signing such things? Now I got to get myself over to Nevada City. I'll come back through here Monday or Tuesday and we'll talk again. By the way, I'm sorry I messed up your wedding plans, but, like you said, you can get married anytime. Does that Cornish fellow make a good living?"

"Yes. He has risen to be an assistant mine manager."

"Good for him, if he can stand to wear another man's collar, which I never could. Guess you had better hold on to him, then."

"Thanks for your advice, Captain. And thank you for all your help."

* * *

Although McGee's visit got me off the hook with the bank, it left me somewhat confused in other areas of my life. Even though my two lots now were unencumbered and I was in no further danger of being evicted, still I felt a new responsibility to repay McGee and a sense of guilt at having hurt Will, a feeling Opal did nothing to mitigate.

"Sometimes I wonder if you got a bit of common sense."

"The bank can't kick us off this property now."

"If you hadn't put off Will and that preacher, you would have yourself a man as well as a house. I don't see how you figure you are any better off than you was before that old squaw man came around sticking his nose into our business."

Opal had not known about the telegraph message I had sent to McGee, so I told her. "There. You see, he was not sticking his nose in my business. I asked for his help."

"The last time I washed your apron I seen that card in the pocket and laid it out. Then put it back later. Now I wish I had of throwed it in the fire."

"If you had, I'd be over in Nevada City getting married even as we speak."

"Yes, and if you ask me, you'd be a lot better off. What you going to do about Will? I'd hate to see him get away from you."

"He'll be there if and when I get ready to tie myself down to another husband. Meanwhile, I am going to get out of this silly dress and let my mind rest for a while. I would appreciate it if you would not burden me with any more of your opinions."

5

I spent the rest of that weekend feeling on the one hand guilty at having hurt Will and on the other relieved at remaining single. I felt so distracted that I had forgot about Zeb McGee's promise to look in on me before returning to Sacramento. Suddenly there he was again on that great gray horse.

"You look peaked, little lady. Hope you're not sick."

"I feel well enough, Captain."

"Good. You ought to feel even better after I tell you my news. Aren't you going to invite me to get off my horse?"

Seated inside my tent, out of Opal's hearing, he proceeded to relate how, acting on information he had gleaned during a poker game in Nevada City, he had just paid another visit to Mr. Delano.

"I picked up the report that some fellows from New York are interested in building a hotel in Grass Valley and that they been talking to Delano. So I just went by and had a little talk with the man. I gather he likes you. Anyway, he is willing to lend us the money instead of the New Yorkers so we can turn your property into a first-class hotel ourselves."

"What do you mean by 'us' and 'we'?"

"You and me."

"But a hotel would take a world of money. I have nothing but that $300 he advanced to me, and that must be repaid."

"Delano will put up the bulk of the money on a mortgage loan."

"But I have no way of securing such a loan."

"I'll put up the down payment and you can pledge your two lots. Nothing to it. So there, little lady. You can go ahead and marry your Cornishman, if that is your desire. You and him can run the hotel together. I'll be your silent partner."

"My Cornishman?"

"Yes. That Tremelling fellow. Strikes me as a dependable chap. You and him would make a good enough team, with you handling the money and him looking after repairs and such."

"Why would you want to do such a thing as that?"

"I have admired your spunk from the time I laid eyes on you. So just consider this as a kind of wedding gift."

"You really are willing to back me in such a venture?"

"You are pretty young, but I have known many women twice your age that don't have half your sense. Here now, let me explain how this thing would work."

When he was done describing how with my lots and a $3,000 investment on his part, the bank would lend us enough to build our hotel, I asked, "And what part would I play in this enterprise?"

"We'll set you a good salary and set aside a one-quarter share of the ownership, plus a bonus based on the profits."

"And what would my risk be?"

"Just the possible loss of your two lots, should the bank be forced to foreclose."

"And I would be in complete charge of running the hotel?"

"As long as you do a good job. I got to get back to Sacramento. Think this proposition over for the next week or so. During that time I will have plans drawn up for how the hotel would look. You can be studying about how to run it. Learn what other hotels charge for rooms and such. We'll put our heads together when I return. If you are still interested, we'll go talk business to that Delano fellow. Agreed?"

He took my hand, gave me one of his rare smiles, and left.

It never occurred to me not to accept the Captain's offer. I turned my attention to studying the management of Grass Valley's several hotels. I even hired a buggy and a driver to go over to Nevada City to study their establishments. And, taking Kwong Chung into my confidence, I put him to work helping me draw up my calculations. But I said nothing of this to Will Tremelling.

* * *

Zebulon McGee returned from Sacramento a day or so earlier than I had expected, so all my calculations were not arranged as completely as I had intended. Yet he seemed impressed by what I showed and told him.

After he was done with glancing over my papers and hearing my report on what I had learned from other hotels, he brought that gray-eyed gaze to bear upon my face and said, "So how about it, little lady. You want to do it?"

"You got yourself a deal, Captain."

He laughed and said, "And a hell of a partner, I'd say. Now I got something to tell you, about another partner I am taking on."

To my amazement he told how his cousin and former trail companion, Chester Peebles, had agreed to move down from Oregon to Sacramento to help him operate his growing freight business.

"I thought you had a partner in that Goodall fellow," I said.

"Old Clarence says he is not cut out for the business end of things. He wants to go back to driving a team. Says he can't sleep at night from worrying about the paper work. Anyway, paper work and talking to customers is right up Chester's alley. And since he hasn't done all that well in Oregon, he has agreed to join me as a junior partner."

"What about his plans to marry that girl in Boston?"

"Last I heard, her pa still won't consent until satisfied Chester can provide for her. Maybe when the old man hears he has become a junior partner in a good business, he'll come around. Chester should arrive in San Francisco sometime next month. That ought to give us—you and me, that is—time to get started on our hotel. Have you thought of a name for it?"

"Kwong Chung says we must be careful what name we choose. The wrong name can bring down evil spirits."

Again McGee laughed. "I have known hotels that served some mighty evil spirits. We'll want none but the best for ours. So what have you and your Chinese assistant settled on?"

"How does The Gold Mountain sound to you? That is what the people back in Kwong Chung's part of China call California."

"If he's sure it will bring us good luck, then The Gold Mountain Hotel it will be."

For the next several days, McGee shuttled back and forth between Grass Valley, where he stayed at the Wisconsin Hotel, and his new freight office in Nevada City. Meanwhile, as Delano looked over my draft of our finances, a Nevada City lawyer was drawing up the papers for our enterprise.

During all this time, I was so caught up in the excitement of our project that I failed to notice the change that had taken place either in McGee's demeanor or in my own reaction to his overpowering personality. During the five months he had led our party across the West, I had been in awe of him. Indeed, after seeing what he had done to Kentucky Pete, I feared him. Now he treated me almost as an equal, seemingly both amused and impressed by my enthusiasm for The Gold Mountain Hotel project. Yet everything between us was business. He made it plain that while he trusted me, still he expected me to do my job.

"We're both taking a risk here, little lady, but you as a lone female are taking the bigger one. If this business fails, you'll be out of both a job and your interest in those two lots."

"Never fear, Captain. It will not fail."

"By God, I like your spirit. I don't think you will fail, either. I just wish Chester had more of your common sense. He does fine as long as he has somebody like you or me around to keep his feet on the ground. And to tell you the truth, I need someone like him, a fellow with imagination. Some folks find me a bit hard, you know. I'm sorry I come across that way, but that is just how I am. I decide what needs to be done and I do it."

"I have noticed that," I said with a sly smile.

"All right then. I have lined up a crew to clear off your lot so we can let the contract on the hotel soon as we get bids and some architectural plans. Before I go back to Sacramento, we got to sign some papers at the lawyer's office over in Nevada City which will call for a celebration. We can have dinner wherever you say."

It had never occurred to me that Zebulon McGee ever would invite me to dinner, but, rising to the occasion, I said, "Since we'll be in Nevada City, how about the National Exchange Hotel? I ate there once and found it acceptable."

* * *

The National Exchange Hotel holds a special place in my heart. As a solid brick building, it had survived the disastrous fire that laid most of Nevada City to waste in July of 1856. The smoky remains had been refurbished and added on to so that now it was the finest hotel and restaurant in the county.

I wondered how a former mountain man and rough-cut trail boss like Zebulon McGee would fit into such surroundings. I was impressed by how smoothly he handled the head waiter, not in the glib, show-offy way of a Mister Courtenay, but in a hearty, man-to-man manner that commanded both respect and the best table in the dining room, one in a corner next to a window overlooking Broad Street.

He ordered a glass of wine for us both. Although as a Methodist, I had been raised to mistrust strong drink, I saw no harm in joining him in toasting our enterprise.

Whether it was due to the influence of the wine or the new and easier side of his personality, I began to relax. There were a dozen things I would like to have asked him, but restrained myself lest he stop talking about how he had built up his freight business during the past three years but, fearing competition from a new railroad between Sacramento and Folsom, he wanted to develop business in Nevada County.

During a pause, after the waiter had removed our soup bowls and we waited for our beef steaks, I ventured, "It is a very different world out here, isn't it, Captain?"

That struck a fresh spark with him.

"I wouldn't want to live anywhere else. This is the right place for people like you and me, folks with get up and go, gumption, grit or whatever you want to call it. I grew up thinking Indiana was a great place. Then for a while I thought the plains or the Rockies were best. Now I know that there is no place like California. Here, now, I have been talking too much. Another glass of wine wouldn't hurt you, would it?"

Without waiting for an answer, he raised his hand to draw the waiter's attention, and pointed to our glasses.

By the time we had eaten our dessert and were drinking our coffee, I felt that while the ice had not been broken between us completely, still a definite thaw had set in. Zebulon McGee would never be the talkative sort but he was turning out to be a far warmer, more understanding fellow than the hard man who had escorted us across the West. Thus, emboldened by the wine, I asked a question which I quickly regretted.

"Remember back in the Nebraska territory, Captain, we met that party of Sioux Indians?"

"What about them?"

"Chester Peebles said the chief was your brother-in-law."

"Chester has a big mouth."

That should have signalled me to drop the subject but—blame it on the wine perhaps—I blundered on with, "He said you were married to the chief's sister. Yellow Moon, I think he called her."

He gave me a look of pain and anger. Without replying, he stood and snapped his fingers for the waiter. Within seconds, he had settled our bill and we were outside waiting for his carriage to be brought around.

We rode back to Grass Valley in a silence I dared not break. When we reached the Pacific Hotel, he helped me down from the carriage and handed me my copies of our agreement.

"I'll be heading back to Sacramento in the morning. I plan to return next week. I'll expect you to have final figures all ready for the banker. Enjoyed the dinner. Good night."

I went to bed that night wishing over and over that I had not asked my nosy question. Well, I thought, I got his message. Keep our relationship on a business basis. Let him take the lead in any conversation that could be construed as being personal.

Yet the question about his Indian wife was only one that nagged at me. Not that it was any of my business, but what other women had there been, or were there, in his life? That awful day when I shot Bart Corbett, what had he found down on that river bank? Could Corbett still have been alive? And what was the mysterious business he had conducted in Salt Lake City, supposedly on behalf of Jim Bridger?

They say still waters run deep. I made a resolution to stifle my curiosity about Zebulon McGee and never again to plumb those depths with unwelcome questions.

PART THREE

1

Captain McGee did not return the following week, nor the week after that, which caused me to fear that my prying questions had so offended him that he had changed his mind about the hotel project.

When he did finally show up, I was amazed to see that he had brought along Chester Peebles. Peebles had lost weight and his face had developed more lines. But he still exhibited that grin I remembered so well.

"Chester got to San Francisco sooner than I expected and he took the boat on up to surprise me in Sacramento," McGee said. "I been checking him out on the freighting business or I would have got back two weeks ago."

Chester squeezed my hand longer and harder than I liked, and said, "Cousin Zeb has brought me up to date about your life out here, Annie. Is that handsome little boy yours? Ah, and there is dear Opal. I was so sorry to hear about Lester, Opal. Makes me wish we had taken the two of you up to Oregon with us."

Only later, after the Captain had finished looking over my final plans and the three of us were eating dinner together in the dining room of the Pacific Hotel, did I have the chance to inquire about my old friends from the Oregonian contingent of our wagon train.

Peebles reported that, after taking up a claim of land, the Muellers not only had built themselves a large cabin but also a blacksmith shop. Jacob, the oldest boy, ran the farm while his father forged plowshares and shoed horses for other settlers.

"Oh, yes, and they had another baby last year, a little girl. And you'll never guess what they named the child."

"Some German name like Gretchen?"

"No. Annie, for you. Mrs. Mueller made me promise to tell you."

"What a compliment. I'd like her address so I can write to her."

"I will have to dig it out for you."

"And what about the Hixons?"

"They took up a claim, too, but they didn't do well, so they sold it and now they operate a crossroads grocery. No, Mrs. Hixon hasn't changed. Bossy as ever. Nobody up there likes the woman. I suppose Zeb told you about them and the Mormon doctor that wanted to marry you."

"I only got a glimmer of the story, second hand through Mr. Goodall."

"Looking back, it was hilarious. Thanks to the warning you passed to us, we were ready for them. They popped out of the bushes just as we were getting ready to stop for noon our first day out from Fort Bridger, two of them on horseback and armed, claiming to have a warrant for your apprehension. While I was listening to their cock-and-bull story, Doctor Dormsby rode up from the rear and looked into your old wagon. Young Jacob Mueller still wore your dress and he was sitting there with a shawl over his head as he had been instructed. You know what bad eyesight Dormsby had. He demanded that she, or rather, he, dismount. Jacob hopped down and Dormsby grabbed his arm. Although he is slight of build, the boy is strong as strong can be. Before Dormsby knew what was happening, he had been flung onto his back and his spectacles had flown off. Jacob set up a shout. Three of my fellows pulled out their shotguns and ordered the militia men to dismount. While they tied up the scoundrels, I went back to find Mr. and Mrs. Mueller sitting on Dormsby and Mrs. Hixon fluttering about demanding to know what was going on. See, she still thought it was you in the wagon . . . "

He told the story far better than I have related it here, so well that soon I was laughing and even Captain McGee was smiling. Wiping the tears from my eyes, I said, "And what did you do with your captives?"

"We confiscated their weapons and tied them to a tree. Some were for taking their horses, but I thought that would be carrying things too far. Then we moved on, leaving them tied up and quarrelling among themselves. The funniest thing was that Dormsby, having lost his glasses in the scuffle, never caught on to the fact that it was not you in the wagon. We heard him tell his companions he had never imagined a woman could be so strong and that maybe it was just as well their attempt had failed."

After I had stopped laughing and had caught my breath, I asked, "What about yourself, Mr. Peebles? Captain McGee said something about a newspaper."

"It's Chester, remember? Yes, I tried my hand at it for a while. Had a devil of a time finding a press and a supply of paper. I took the editorial line that not only should slavery in the territory be outlawed but that anyone trying to enforce the Fugitive Slave Law should be arrested. That did not set well with some of your fellow Southerners who have settled up there. But I stuck to my guns until my money ran out. As you know, Oregon has just become a state. I ran for a seat in the new State Senate as a Republican, but didn't make it. Neither did our candidate for the governorship. So here I am, back on Cousin Zeb's doorstep in a state with better opportunity than I found in Oregon."

As our conversation ran on, McGee acted more and more restive, drumming his fingers on the table and glancing at his watch, but I, eager to hear more from Peebles, ignored him.

"And that pretty girl you were to marry? Are you still engaged? I see you still wear your locket."

Before he could reply, McGee broke in to say, "Now that I have taken him in, he can go back east when the money is right, marry the girl and fetch her out to Sacramento."

With that, he, McGee, arose and said, "There'll be time enough in the future for reminiscing. We got to get an early start for Sacramento in the morning, Chester. So, let's say good night. See you again sometime next week, little lady."

Peebles kept my hand captive in his while he told me how pleased he was to see that I had overcome so many obstacles and to assure me that he stood ever ready to help me "any way I can."

"This little lady don't need your help, Chester," McGee said. "Hurry up and say good night."

As his cousin headed for the door of the dining room, he, McGee, paused as if he wanted to say something more to me, but then appeared to change his mind.

* * *

The next morning, I was having breakfast alone in the hotel dining room when the desk clerk entered and handed me an envelope.

"The porter from the Wisconsin Hotel left this at the counter before daylight."

I wiped my butter knife on my napkin and, using it to open the envelope, read the enclosed letter with a surprise that quickly turned into astonishment.

* * *

Dear Annie,

There was a lot more that I wanted to say to you last night, things that could only be said to you alone, but Cousin Zeb kept hanging about during our conversation and then hustled me away before I could get the opportunity to ask for a private audience. The next best course remaining for me, then, is to write this letter in haste before we leave for Sacramento.

You asked me whether I still intend to marry Amy. There has been a serious change in my attitude as to that question.

You see, Annie, I have become a far different person than I was six years ago when first I asked for Amy's hand in marriage. My experiences of the intervening years, the people I have met, the trials I have faced, the hardships I have endured, all these things have changed and, I trust, have matured me, have made me see myself and life in general in a different light. As the Bible says, the scales have been removed from my eyes.

Speaking of the Bible, I am sure you know the story from the Old Testament of how when Jacob sought the hand of Rachel in marriage, Rachel's father, Laban, required of Jacob seven years of servitude, and then at the end of those seven years gave him Rachel's older sister, Leah, instead.

When first I spoke for Amy's hand she was only 15 and, as you know, her father—like Rachel's—set some very strict conditions to granting his permission. Perhaps he perceived some faults in my character that needed correction. I cannot blame him for that. Perhaps when I have daughters of my own, I will feel the same.

At any rate, as time has passed I have come more and more to realize that a marriage between a man and a woman should be a journey to be taken hand-in-hand together and not a prize to be awarded only after success has already been obtained. Think of how much happier both Jacob and Rachel would have been had her father offered her as a helpmate during those seven years rather than as a reward at the end.

Please do not take offense, but I must confess that I envied your husband Elmer when I saw how the two of you were undertaking a perilous trip together to a new land with few resources beyond his ambition and your fortitude. Although many in our party thought the two of you were mismatched, I saw in Elmer a person of considerable courage despite his affliction. In short, he seemed to me the luckiest of men even before that business about the duel.

My admiration for you, already high, grew stronger after that episode. And as we proceeded along the trail to Fort Bridger, following Elmer's death, affection became mixed with admiration. Not to denigrate Amy in the least, I must confess that often I reflected on the differences between her and you. In truth, I could not imagine her enduring the hardships you accepted without a murmur.

Had that blowup between you and the Hixons not occurred at Fort Bridger and had you continued with our party to Oregon, very likely I would have revealed my feelings for you as I did to Mrs. Mueller on the trail beyond Soda Spring, That good, honest woman, in her frank way, took me to task for not informing you of my feelings before we became separated. But of course there was the matter of my engagement to Amy, who is a dear, sweet girl.

Often since then have I thought about you, wondering what was your fate, thinking—erroneously as it turned out—that you were in safe hands with the Courtenay family or perhaps even remarried.

Then, when word of your presence in Grass Valley came to me in one of Zeb's letters, when I learned that you remained unmarried, I relayed this intelligence to Mrs. Mueller, and spoke of my discouragement at ever winning Amy's hand. She looked at me in that knowing way of hers and said, "Forget that girl in Boston. What are you waiting for? Go get Annie before somebody else beats you to her."

I realized in a flash what I should do. That was to accept Zeb's offer and hurry to California to see for myself how the brave young woman who had crossed a continent fared and whether, just possibly, we might be better suited for each other than would Amy and I be.

Mrs. Mueller minced no words in telling me that it would take "more than pretty words" to win you over. She told me that you had regarded me as rather a feckless fellow who did not know my own mind and who was prone to flitting about between conflicting ambitions. But then she said, "Chust maybe Annie could make a man of you."

So there you are Annie. Zeb does not know of my true motivation for coming to California and I would ask that we keep this knowledge from him.

I understand from Zeb that one of the Cornishmen in your party has been pestering you to marry him. If he is the tall fellow, Will, I think his name was, certainly he would be the best of that lot, but really, Annie, don't you deserve a better fate than to become the wife of a gold miner?

But then perhaps you deserve a better fate than to become the wife of a chap who so far in life has failed at preaching, soldiering, newspapering and politics. So I know that I am not exactly the ideal husband for anyone, but as Mrs. Mueller has said, maybe a person of your fine qualities could make a man of me.

I would not be so bold as to make an outright proposal of marriage in a letter like this, yet I have no compunction in writing a plea for you to discuss with me our joint futures, to explore just how well suited we might be for each other and, if not with each other, for whom?

I had better stop before I say too much. I look forward with trepidation and hope to the time when we can sit down quietly together to open our hearts to each other and see where that exercise might lead us.

Fondly,
Chester Peebles

2

To say that I was flabbergasted by Chester Peeble's letter would be putting it mildly. First I was flattered, as probably any woman would have been, to think that he had come all the way to California in the off chance that I might be willing to marry him.

Then I questioned the reliability of a man who, after making such a point of declaring his devotion for his precious Amy, now seemed ready to switch his affections to me. Was not this yet another indication of an unstable character?

Next, I grew angry. Who was Chester Peebles to make derogatory remarks about Will Tremelling, a man who at least stuck to what he set out to do, a man on whom you could depend? No, that comment was entirely uncalled for. No one had the right to speak of good old Will with disrespect.

But when I reread the letter in the privacy of my hotel room, I began to feel sorry for Peebles. Amy's father really had imposed an impossible burden on him, requiring him to establish himself in an uncertain world before granting permission to marry his daughter. And I was touched by his observations about how marriage should be a partnership between a man and a woman. And, shrewd woman that she was, Mrs. Mueller's observation that I might bring out the best in him could not be taken lightly.

Although by the time we had parted company back at Fort Bridger, I had begun to like Chester more than I would have thought possible at the beginning of our trek across the West. I had never thought of him in romantic terms. He was a handsome enough fellow. He had a wonderful gift of gab. I had been entranced by his account of the episode with Doctor Dormsby. We had many interests in common.

No, what he seemed to be suggesting was ridiculous, and I determined to tell him so to his face. At least that was my conclusion after reading his letter for the third time and then hiding it away in one of my carpet bags.

But then that night, just before retiring, I retrieved the letter and read it over again slowly, pondering the meaning of every word. Afterwards I slept fitfully, dreaming over and over of first Peebles and then Will.

The next morning, Opal, noticing my bedraggled appearance, asked if I had not slept well.

"I shouldn't have drunk so much coffee before retiring."

"Well, you had better pull yourself together because there is a fellow down in the lobby waiting to talk to you."

"Who?"

"Will Tremelling."

Poor Will. He looked as fretted as I felt. At his insistence we walked together to the burnt-out walls of my former restaurant. It did not take him long to get to the point.

"Opal has told me all about this matter of you going into the hotel business."

"Opal talks more than she should."

"Be that as it may, at first I didn't like the idea . . . "

"Look here, now, Will. It is not your place to like or . . . "

"Let me finish. What I really mean was I was jealous. I didn't like thinking of you being dependant on a hard, cruel man such as Captain McGee. I wanted to be the one that would look after you, because you see, Annie. Oh, blast it, I don't know how I can go on living without you."

"Why, Will, you have lived without me well enough for a quarter of a century, haven't you?"

"Annie, you got to let me finish. What I want to say is that if you really want to accept the captain's offer and turn this place into a hotel, why, I am ready to pitch in and help. Opal has told me you will need a man and I am willing to be that man. So how about it, Annie? Ain't it time for us to marry and help each other get through life?"

"You mean you would give up your big new job at the mine to help me run a hotel?"

"That is about the size of it. Will you say yes?"

I think that if I had not been distracted by that letter from Chester Peebles the day before, I might have accepted Will's touching proposal then and there. He was such an honest, steady fellow, handsome in his own way, and so eager to please me. Yes, Opal was right: I could do a lot worse than to marry Will Tremelling and, with him at my side, to plunge into the hotel business.

But I didn't say yes. All I did was to say, as I had said before, "There are too many other things on my mind right now to be thinking of marriage. Give me time to sort things out, Will."

"There ain't anyone else, is there?"

"Don't be silly, Will. Now, take that hurt look off your face and come have breakfast with me at the hotel. You can bring me up to date on what is happening at the mine."

* * *

Throughout that day, my mind restlessly flitted from thoughts about The Gold Mountain, to that strange letter from Chester Peebles, to good old Will's willingness to leave his precious job in the gold mine to help me run a hotel if only I would marry him. Unable to sit still, I wandered back to the ruins of my old restaurant.

Kwong Chung was sitting outside his tent, reading from a scroll. Seeing me pacing about my lots, he invited me to sit with him and enjoy a cup of the green tea he habitually drank.

"Missie Annie look worried," he said as he handed me my little cup of his brew.

"I have a lot on my mind."

"If Missie wish to speak of it, Kwong Chung would be glad to hear. Maybe it help to talk."

I did need to talk to someone other than Opal, so I told him about my letter from Chester.

"This is the man who was here with Captain McGee?"

"Yes. He helped lead our wagon train across the West."

"You think he want to marry you?"

"That is the puzzling thing about his letter. He doesn't propose marriage outright. He just wants to discuss whether we are suited for each other."

"And are you?"

"I may not be suited for anybody. So what do you think?"

"I think this Chester Peebles is a clever man. Is he not?"

"He is very clever, with words, that is."

"And he has a ready wit?"

Remembering Chester's hilarious account of the Dormsby incident, I replied, "A ready wit and a glib tongue."

"Is he also a moral man?"

"I am not sure what you mean. What is your point?"

"The great teacher Confucius once asked a disciple, 'What is the good of a ready wit'? A man who is always ready with his tongue often makes enemies."

"That was true of my husband, Elmer. He had a knack of making enemies with his too-ready tongue. But Chester Peebles is not like Elmer. His wit, if you want to call it that, is more subtle. And he has far better manners."

"Confucius once said, 'With flowery speech and flattering manners will seldom be found moral character.'"

"What has moral character to do with anything?"

"Ah, Missie Annie, it has to do with everything. Nothing is more important in a man, or a husband, or a father or son. As Confucius once said, 'a man without moral character cannot long put up with adversity, nor can he long enjoy prosperity'."

Exasperated by all this Confucius business, I arose, thanked him for my tea, and, without sincerity, for his baffling advice.

Before I could depart, Kwong Chung made one more observation.

"This Chester has tried and failed at many things, has he not? And now he is ready to give up his effort to marry this girl in Boston."

"With good reason, don't you think?"

"Boston is far away, yet not so far as China where my wife and child wait with patience for my return."

"Yes, but you are married. Chester and his Amy are only engaged."

"We have a saying in China that potential marriages a thousand miles apart are linked by a single thread."

"You keep talking nonsense. I must go."

Before he could say more, I turned and strode back to the Pacific Hotel.

* * *

"Something's eating on your mind, I can tell," Opal said later that evening as we were putting Duncan to bed.

"What makes you say such a silly thing?"

"You ain't been the same since that smooth-talking Yankee came here the other day. Before that it was his friend Captain McGee that come and messed things up for us. I wish we had never laid eyes on either one. That pair are nothing but trouble."

"The captain has not messed things up. On the contrary he has made it possible for us to own a hotel."

"You mean part of a hotel. You will do all the work while he rides around like Mr. God Almighty. He is a great one for getting other folks to do his hard work. You seen him bossing people around on the trail, but how much work did he do himself? And then he goes and gets my Lester killed and what for? Because he was mad at somebody for killing his dog."

Remembering how the captain had dug Elmer's grave with his own hands and had come to my rescue in the shooting of Bart Corbett, I ached to defend him but, instead, said, "I understand why you don't care for Captain McGee, but what have you got against Chester Peebles?"

"He has got a mighty smooth tongue and a superior manner. Strikes me as a great one for talking and not so great for doing. A lot like Mr. Courtenay."

"Mr. Courtenay is quite a different matter. He abandoned us when we were in dire need. He went back on his word. Then he came here and sponged off of me. Surely Chester is made of better stuff."

"Seem to me like he might be coming here to sponge off Captain McGee."

"That is not why he has come to California."

"Then why has he come here?"

"I think he wants to marry me."

"What? Oh good God. I hope you got better sense than to do that. Wait a minute. What do you mean you think . . . "

So, I told her about the letter. She listened with slitted eyes, sucking her teeth in that annoying way she had.

"Why you want to mess with him? That man is never going to amount to anything. You got a good man been begging you to marry him."

"Don't start about Will again. Why do you like him so?"

"He puts me in mind of Lester. He don't pretend to be more than he is. He works hard. You can depend on him. He ain't like a lot of white men in this country. He don't pay any attention to the color of a person's skin."

"I like Will, but I am not ready to marry anybody right now. This hotel is the chance of a lifetime for me."

"You going to need some man to help you run that hotel. I sure don't see that Peebles fellow doing it. Why don't you write him back and tell him nothing doing?"

"I have to hear him out, even though I am not interested."

"I don't know why I waste my breath talking to you."

After thinking over Opal's advice, I sat down and started a letter to Chester. I wrote that I was flattered by his proposal, but then stopped, realizing that he had not actually proposed. I tore up that letter and started another. This time I wrote that while I was not actually engaged to Will Tremelling, still if I wanted to marry anyone . . . No, that wouldn't do. I crumpled that sheet, too, and so on until I gave up the game and went to bed.

* * *

Remembering the ignominious way in which Elmer had proposed to me in a cow stall, I arranged for my interview with Chester to take place in a corner of the lobby of the Pacific Hotel, far enough away from the desk so that we would not be overheard, but still public enough to discourage any embarrassing display.

Captain McGee was absent, having gone to inspect the work being done on clearing the debris from around the walls of my old restaurant.

"You got my letter?" Chester began as soon as we were seated.

"Yes."

"And what did you think of it?"

"To tell the truth, I was surprised, and a little flattered though I must confess being somewhat confused."

"In what way, confused?"

"All across the plains you spoke of your engagement to Amy. You wore her locket about your neck and were always showing off her picture."

"Did you not notice that I no longer wear it?"

"No. Why not?"

"I don't have it. Sent it back last week."

"You have broken your engagement? Your letter indicated merely that you were thinking of doing so."

"I decided my best course was to burn my bridges. It wasn't fair to keep up this pretense that her father will ever be satisfied with me. Besides, there was, or is, you."

I frowned and said, "If you will forgive my saying so, that was a very rash thing to do."

"I couldn't help myself, Annie. Anyway, that is water over the dam. Here I am ready, eager even, to discuss you and me and what we could mean to each other. Wait, I know what you think of me. Mrs. Mueller made that clear. But that was the old Chester Peebles. You misjudge me if you still think I lack resolve. Ah, Annie, we must be masters of our own fates. We must seize our opportunities, yours and mine."

"My opportunity has been offered by your cousin, Zeb McGee, with no conditions except that I do a proper job of running our hotel."

"True, but I have heard him say that you will need a man to help you keep the establishment in working order."

"I would remind the Captain that I ran a successful restaurant on my own. If the services of a man should prove necessary, which I doubt, Will Tremelling is more than willing to give up his job and devote himself to the hotel."

"The Cornishman, yes. Not meaning to sound in the least disrespectful, he hardly seems the sort to be your front man."

"I can be my own front man. And I do find your remarks about Will disrespectful and will thank you for not repeating them."

"I apologize. My only point was that being even an assistant manager of a fine hotel would require a certain amount of polish."

"I am not sure just how fine our hotel will be. Anyway, Will would see to repairs, to handling luggage, that sort of thing."

"Oh, Annie, this conversation is not going the way I so desperately wanted it to. Here we are talking about repairs and luggage when I had hoped to speak to you from my heart and in a less public place."

"I prefer that we talk here. And I wish you would get to your point."

"The point is you and me and what sort of relationship we might have together now that I am no longer engaged and you remain a widow about to set forth on a great new enterprise."

He leaned forward and would have taken my hand if I had not drawn it out of his reach.

"You see, Annie, out there on the trail, I recognized what a bright, inquiring mind you have. You like to read, and so do I. You have spunk and imagination. If it had not been for my engagement, I would have spoken for your hand as soon as it was proper to do so, following your husband's death. Would you have accepted if I had?"

"Possibly," I began, but seeing his face brighten, quickly added, "I was desperate back then. I am no longer in such straits. These past three years have taught me how to survive, with or without a man."

"I recognize how you have matured and, dear Annie, that makes you all the more appealing."

"Appealing or not, if marriage were my object in life, I could have wed a dozen or more men since I came to Grass Valley."

"Surely you aren't saying you will never again marry?"

"All I am saying is that I am not yet ready to marry you or anyone else."

"Very well. I shall make you no formal proposal, not yet. But let me warn you. Prepare yourself to be courted as never a woman has been. I intend to lay siege to your heart."

"Don't be ridiculous."

"I am serious. I shall shower you with flowers, with boxes of candy, with invitations to the theater, with gifts of books, with exchanges of opinions."

On and on he ran, all the while grinning, until, against my will, I was laughing. If I were to offer one piece of advice to a man trying to sway a woman, it would be to make her laugh.

At last he stopped and said, "So, you do not forbid my attentions?"

"If they are kept in moderation, perhaps."

"We can be friends, then?"

"We already are friends and can remain so as long as you don't try to force your politics on me."

"Never. Ah, Annie, I am so pleased that at least you have not rejected my friendship."

"I have learned the hard way how important it is to have friends, the right sort of friends, on whom you can depend, such as Opal and Kwong Chung and, in his way, Captain McGee, speaking of whom, there he comes down the street. Does he know that you have broken your engagement?"

"He knows my engagement has been broken but he knows nothing of my intentions toward you and I would prefer that he does not."

"The Captain and I don't discuss personal matters. Besides you haven't said what your real intentions are toward me."

"They are honorable, Annie . . . Ah, Cousin Zeb. Annie and I were just having a cozy chat. Never saw a young woman so enthusiastic as she is about your hotel. Here, pull up a chair and join us."

"Glad to hear she is enthusiastic. Now, Chester, this little lady and I need to talk over some private matters. Why don't you find something else to do for a few minutes?"

Although plainly irritated at being dismissed, Chester asked, "Where would I find Opal?"

"Upstairs, in our rooms."

"And your little boy?"

"They are together."

"Good. I want to become better acquainted with that young fellow."

After he had left, the Captain drew a set of papers from his satchel and spread them before me on a low table.

Atop the pile was an artist's drawing of what The Gold Mountain Hotel would look like together with a floor plan for a new brick building connected to my old restaurant.

"See there, we got space for twenty rooms on the second floors if we knock a doorway through the wall of the old building. Then on the first floor, here is your entrance and lobby with a kitchen in the rear. We'll set another doorway, a big one leading into a first-class saloon next door in the new building and behind that a grand dining room."

"This plan shows a third floor for the new building."

"So it does. I told the architect in Sacramento to provide an apartment for you and your son and rooms for your colored woman, the Chinaman and whoever you may want to live in the premises. Now what do you think?"

"The plans are wonderful, and I am touched at the provision for our living quarters. But I suggest we run the veranda all the way across both buildings. That will make it less obvious that we have married an old building to a new one. Then why not create a sort of terrace on top of the porch roof with a nice railing? Make the area accessible from the second floor and you will have a grand place from which to view parades and such."

"Why, you have got a right good head on your shoulders, for architecture, that is. I'm ready to let the contract. Are you?"

"I see no reason not to press ahead."

"Now we got to consider some personal matters," he said as he looked at me with that disconcerting gaze. "Have you talked to your Cornish fellow about our hotel plans?"

"He would be interested in the job, yes. But I fear his real motive is for me to marry him."

"Marry him, eh? You still going through with that?"

"Oh, Captain, I am not at all sure about marrying anyone just now." And then I choked up and had to struggle to keep back my tears. This seemed to embarrass him as it did me. He looked at the floor then back at me.

"To tell you the truth, that sets my mind at ease. I wondered if you were settling for less of a man that you are entitled to. Young ladies like you, with your spirit, deserve better. No offense, little lady, but that husband of yours . . . "

"Elmer."

"Yes, him. Don't take this wrong, but I always wondered what you ever saw in him."

"It is a long story, Captain. No point in going into it now."

"Still you'll need a man. What do you call that Chinaman?"

"Kwong Chung."

"Tell me more about him."

I related what I knew about Kwong Chung, ending it with, "Besides being one of the wisest and kindliest men I have ever known, he is as loyal as a dog to me and my little boy. And he is a regular wizard when it comes to figures."

"Maybe he is all the man you need to help you run the hotel, in case you decide against the Cousin Jack fellow for a husband."

"That is a possibility. But I hope that whether I am married to Will Tremelling or someone else or to no one, it will make no difference in our business arrangements."

"None whatsoever. Excuse me if I asked anything you found too personal."

"Not at all."

What more he might have said at that time, I will never know, for just then Chester came down the hotel stairs carrying a charmed Duncan on his shoulders.

"See there, young fellow. You wanted your mama and here she is."

Suddenly all business again, Captain McGee gathered up his papers and stuffed them back in his satchel.

"I'll let you know when the bids are ready. I like your ideas about the veranda. Now we got other business to see to in Nevada City. Come along, Chester."

Chester handed Duncan over to me with a grin and a wink, and followed the Captain out the hotel door. They left a very confused Annie Mundy Hixon in their wake.

3

In the space of a half hour, my head had been set to spinning, yes, and my heart as well. Unable to sit still and unwilling to talk to Opal lest she pry into the cause of my nervousness, I took Duncan's hand and led him down to the bridge that crossed Wolf Creek. There I stared at the water and tried to make sense of the morning's events.

The interview with Chester left me with much to consider. His letter had made it appear only that he was contemplating breaking his engagement. But now he had gone and told his Amy they were through, not that I blamed him for that. But to end their engagement so abruptly. What must the poor girl feel when she got his letter and her locket? And, unless he was lying, I was the cause of his reckless action.

Then there was that business about "laying siege to my heart." At first I had experienced a feeling of dread but, then, confound him, he had set me to laughing. And in truth I rather liked the idea of being openly courted by an intelligent, imaginative chap like him.

As long as his attentions did not interfere with plans for The Gold Mountain Hotel, what was the harm of friendship with him? Besides, I liked the idea of getting flowers and candy and such, as long as we stayed off politics.

The plans Captain McGee had shown me would have been excitement enough for one morning. What a grand opportunity he was offering me: to become part owner of a hotel that would put the Pacific—and with proper management maybe even the Wisconsin Hotel—to shame. And all that with no conditions except to do a competent job of managing the establishment. No one had ever shown such confidence in me.

All I really wanted in life now was to see that hotel built and to make of it a great success. Yet here I was with two men interested in marrying me. No, only Will Tremelling had made an out-and-out proposal. Chester Peebles, on the other hand, while making his interest in me more than plain, had not come right out and asked me to become his wife. He had merely implied that he would do so in time. Meanwhile, he had given me fair warning that he would be working away to win my affection.

My reveries were broken by Duncan trying to show me something. It was a silver dime.

"Where did you get that?"

"Uncle Chester give it to me."

"Did you say 'Uncle Chester'?"

"He give me this to call him Uncle Chester."

* * *

Although I was ashamed of my discourtesy to Kwong Chung on my last visit with him, there really was no one else in whom I could confide.

Holding Duncan on his lap, he listened closely without either smiling or frowning as I told him of the events of the morning. In my emotional state, I fear that I rattled on too long, but he did not interrupt. At last I ran down and asked, "So what do you think I should do?"

"Nothing. Do nothing. Confucius said that a wise and good man is composed and happy; a fool is always worried and full of distress. The same is true of a wise and good woman. You are a wise and good woman. You are kind and generous. You are determined. You have friends. You have nice son. Count your blessings. Enjoy building your hotel. Don't waste time with worry. There is no reason for distress. All will turn out for the best."

* * *

Kwong Chung gave me good advice, and I accepted it. Pushing aside all thoughts of marriage, I gave myself over completely to overseeing the construction of The Gold Mountain, too completely for the tastes of the contractor, his carpenters and brick masons. Twice I made them reject wagon loads of lumber so green the planks were curled. Once I refused to accept a load of improperly dried bricks that were full of cracks. And I made them reframe a doorway. I paid no attention to the way they looked sideways at each other when I took them to task. And I accepted no excuses.

Since the Captain had put me on salary from the start of the construction, I could afford to continue living at the Pacific Hotel but I spent most of my waking hours at the building site.

Although his job kept him in Sacramento most of the time, true to his word, Chester, without mention of marriage, began his campaign to win my heart. He wrote me charming letters at least twice a week and sent me boxes of candy almost as often. About every other week end, he appeared in Grass Valley, armed with bouquets and invitations to attend theatrical productions at Grass Valley's new Hamilton Hall or at Nevada City's Metropolitan Theater.

He amused me with imitations of his freighting customers. He brought little gifts for Duncan and Opal. And never once in all that period did he make any amorous advances.

As a result of his constant attention, I had no time for Will Tremelling. Gradually Opal stopped talking about him. And despite herself, she sometimes laughed at Chester's jokes.

Duncan, also, was seduced by the attentions of his "Uncle Chester." He abandoned the lap of Kwong Chung whenever Chester appeared.

Meanwhile, the hotel was taking form with surprising speed. I had vowed to the Captain that we would have the structure under roof before the first snow fell. Once that goal had been accomplished, I made a second vow that we would have the establishment open at least for dinner guests by Christmas.

Captain McGee dropped by occasionally to check on our progress. Our talks were always of business, and I wasn't about to discuss Chester's proposition with him.

Older and wiser now, I realize that we human beings are happiest when we have a grand project to take our minds off ourselves. Writing this account of my life serves that purpose today just as building The Gold Mountain Hotel did during the closing months of 1859. Never had I felt so alive and in control of my own fate. I enjoyed cracking the whip over the men working on the building. I enjoyed the amusing attentions of Chester Peebles without my happiness being in the least dependent upon them. Yes, always keep a new project going: that is my recipe for happiness in this uncertain world.

And I was happy. The problems of troublesome guests, of the tedious rendering and collection of accounts, the recruitment and supervision of chambermaids and kitchen staff, all such details of operating a hotel lay in the future.

*   *   *

We did in truth open the dining room of our hotel two days before Christmas and a grand opening it turned out to be. We decided to make of the occasion a memorable one for ourselves and the town. All the local big wigs were invited to a Friday night dinner and, since it was on the house, nearly all accepted.

Captain McGee was there, of course, and so was Chester. Will Tremelling and several of his friends were on hand as well.

Although the Captain and I stood at the entrance to our dining room to greet the guests, once they were inside it was Chester who jollied them up, introducing himself to them and telling jokes to all who would listen, and making sure glasses were filled with imported champagne.

"Hell of a fellow, that Peebles," I overheard Alonzo Delano say to Captain McGee.

"He is feeling his oats tonight," the Captain replied.

"He is a side kick of yours, isn't he?"

"He is my assistant."

"Doing a good job for you?"

"Too early to say," the Captain said, then in an abrupt change of subject, "Looks like our investment is going to pay off, don't it?"

Before I could hear more, Opal interrupted to say that dinner was ready to be served.

The local Episcopal rector asked God's blessings upon "this noble establishment" and prayed that it would always be "a house of honor." He gave thanks for "the meal of which we are about to partake" and well he might have given thanks for such a repast.

I wouldn't be surprised if the people back in Grass Valley are still talking about the dinner that Opal prepared in the new hotel kitchen, with the help of Kwong Chung and Mildred. Surely it was one the best I had ever eaten.

First came bowls of steaming oyster stew. This was followed by beef brisket simmered so long that it fell apart at the touch of a fork, roast turkey with sausage stuffing, Irish potatoes, well-mashed, laced with onion and drizzled with a rich gravy, plate after plate of celery, fruit and cheese, a delicious corn pudding, and, of course, platters of Opal's famous cornbread muffins.

Later, after her desserts of apple-raisin pies and sponge cakes with strawberry preserves and whipped cream, Captain McGee arose and made a few remarks to the effect that a booming town like Grass Valley "deserves a first-rate hotel, and, by God, I hope you all agree that is what we are offering you here."

He concluded by matter-of-factly praising me for my part in bringing the project to fruition, and then he sat down.

Instantly, Chester was on his feet. Raising his wine glass, he noted that he and "my cousin Zeb" had gone through many adventures in the Mexican War and afterwards. "And let me tell you, my friends. Whatever Zebulon McGee sets out to do, he does. He wanted to give this town an outstanding hotel and he has done it, but he has not done it alone. No, he showed the good judgment to enlist the aid of a young woman well-known to most of you. This is a young woman of great courage and dignity. She has survived the loss of a promising young husband on the trail out here three years ago. She has survived the loss of her restaurant in a ruinous fire. But like the mythical phoenix, she and her establishment have risen triumphantly from the ashes. Now as manageress and part owner of The Gold Mountain Hotel, she has launched a new career, one in which I am sure we all wish her even greater success. Ladies and gentlemen, please join me in toasting the good health of Annie Mundy Hixon, a young lady of rare spunk and vision."

In a moment whose memory I still cherish, everyone in that crowded dining room arose, drained their glasses and applauded until I grew embarrassed and motioned for them to sit.

Even in a raw sort of town like Grass Valley, it was unthought of for a respectable woman to make a formal speech. So all I did was curtsy, and quickly thank Chester for his kind words and Captain McGee for having the faith to support me, and Alonzo Delano for his financial backing, and my staff for their loyalty.

I sat down but Chester remained standing.

"Annie mentioned her staff. I want to ask them to come out of the kitchen so you all can see who produced the culinary delights of which we have partaken."

Out came Opal, Kwong Chung and Mildred along with our new employees.

Carried away by his own eloquence, Chester laid the praise on thick. And he concluded by insisting that everyone take a tour of the hotel to inspect the rooms.

After our guests had finally left, Chester remained to help clear the tables and wash the dishes.

Afterwards, when time came for us to retire. he took my hand and looking into my eyes said, "Annie, Zeb is right. You are the beatingest girl I ever saw."

Then, before I was aware of what was happening, he kissed me on the cheek. Surprised, I stood on tiptoe and returned his kiss. He beamed at me, clapped his hat on his head, and left for his lodgings at the Wisconsin Hotel.

Opal, who had witnessed this, rolled her eyes and said, "I don't know that I like what I just saw."

"You have to admit that he made the evening go well."

"I reckon you are right. That captain of yours acted like a stuffed owl. And there ain't many men that would have stayed behind to clean up."

When I finally went to bed, I was so excited that, despite my weariness, it was impossible to fall asleep quickly. I lay there reflecting on how just three years before, I had been living with my newborn child in a brothel, penniless and, except for Opal, friendless. Now I and the hotel of which I was part owner had become the toast of the town. Life was, after all, worth living.

*　　*　　*

The next day was Christmas eve, a Saturday. Caught up in completing work on the hotel and on preparing for our grand opening of the dining room, I forgot about Christmas until after breakfast.

So out I charged to shop for gifts for Opal, Kwong Chung, Mildred, and, of course, Duncan.

When I got back to our apartment at The Gold Mountain, I was surprised to find Chester there helping Opal decorate our rooms with holly and cedar branches he had brought. This struck me as a bit cheeky of him, but I overlooked it when he asked if he might return the following day "to deliver some gifts."

"That is sweet of you, Chester, but it really isn't necessary."

"Yours is the only family I have out here in California. Surely you wouldn't deny a lonely man the pleasure of being in your company." Then he paused and ducked his head in a pose of mock humility and added, "I promise not to be a nuisance."

It hit me then that I had not thought of either him or Captain McGee when I was buying gifts.

I laughed and said, "Of course you are more than welcome. And please invite Captain McGee as well."

"You bet. Zeb and I are going over to Nevada City this afternoon. Never mind that it's Christmas Eve. Business comes first for Zeb. So, Merry Christmas. What time tomorrow?"

"Ten o'clock."

As soon as he had gone, I put on my coat again and started for the door.

"Where you going now?" Opal asked.

"I forgot something."

What I had forgot was to buy gifts for Chester and the Captain. I had never bought a Christmas present for a man. What would they like? Clothing would be inappropriate. Besides I did not know their sizes. Yet I owed much to both: to the Captain for backing the hotel project; to Chester for making the opening night such a success and for his kindness to me and my family. Each man in his own way had made me feel better about myself, had given me self-confidence.

At last I settled on a shaving mug and brush for each.

The next morning, after we had opened our gifts for each other, and Duncan was whining because there were no more packages for him, I thought back to my childhood Christmas mornings back in North Carolina.

There we had been required to remain in our beds until Papa and Mama had gone downstairs and had built up the fire. Then Papa would roar, "Come see what St. Nicholas has left for you." The glass of buttermilk we had left on the hearth would be half empty and only a fragment of the tea cake remained on its plate. Each of our stockings now was filled with nuts and raisins, horehound candy canes, and oranges.

My reverie was broken when Chester burst into the room crying "Merry Christmas" and thrust a parcel into Opal's hands.

"Now that Annie has taught you to read so well, see how you like this book," he said, then watched while Opal unwrapped a leather-bound copy of UNCLE TOM'S CABIN.

Now Duncan was tugging at his sleeve and demanding to know "What you bring me, Uncle Chester?"

"Ah, you must close your eyes while I step outside."

In a moment he returned, carrying a grand rocking horse, complete with saddle and bridle.

My heart warmed to see the look of delight that came over my little son's face. He mounted his wooden steed and refused to get off for the rest of the day.

Thinking that surely Chester had bought me at least a small gift, I waited and waited while he played with Duncan and chatted with Opal. Finally, I gave up and said, "By the way, I have something for you and the Captain. Is he coming?"

"Zeb can't make it."

"That is a pity. Well, anyway, here is your present," I said, handing him his shaving mug and brush.

"Thank you, Annie. Just what I need."

"I will give the Captain his later."

He frowned at that remark, then grinned and said, "By the way, I almost forgot. Here is a little something for you, too, Annie."

At that he drew from his pocket a small, velvet-coated box.

"Sit down before you open it."

I sat in my rocker and raised the lid of the box. In it was a ring set with a diamond bigger than any I had ever seen.

"What on earth?"

"It is an engagement ring. Now, now, you don't have to wear it until you are ready."

"I can't accept this . . . "

"At least try it on to see if it fits. You can always give it back if it doesn't. There, Opal, what do you think? Don't it look like it belongs there?"

Opal shook her head and laughed with an air of resignation.

"I reckon it does, after all."

4

No sooner had Chester persuaded me to keep his ring before he began pushing for us to be married right away, but I resisted. There was too much to be done in running the hotel for me to jump into marriage so quickly. I preferred to wait until after summer, by which time The Gold Mountain would be operating smoothly enough on its own so that we could take a proper honeymoon trip to San Francisco where I had never been. We compromised by setting the date and place for Easter at the National Exchange Hotel in Nevada City. Chester promised to take me to San Francisco later.

We also agreed to keep our engagement a secret for the time being. Only Opal would know of our intentions. And I would not start wearing the ring until the engagement was announced.

What brought me around to say yes at all? Mainly it was the realization that Duncan needed a father and the fact that he was entranced by Chester. As for Opal, she said, "Like always, you going to do what you going to do anyway. Just don't come crying on my shoulder if it don't work out." To which I replied, "Why in heaven's name wouldn't it work out?"

Did I not love Chester then? It depends on what you mean by love. Part of his attraction for me, aside from our mutual interest in the theater and literature, was that I felt I could help him shape his destiny. No, I didn't want to boss him around. His dreams, aside from his rabid abolitionist sentiments, seemed to coincide with mine. He just needed a woman's stable influence. Besides all that, he was good company. He made me laugh. And then, I must admit, there was a growing physical attraction.

The clincher came when he announced that he was willing to give up his job with Captain McGee to devote himself to helping me manage the hotel. I protested that while admittedly The Gold Mountain could benefit from his hail-fellow-well-met presence in the saloon and reception areas, we could hardly afford another salary.

"I will work for my room and board and for the privilege of being in your company," he said. "Besides, I draw a quarterly stipend from the estate of my late grandparents, not a fortune, but enough to keep me in decent clothes and a bit besides."

"You never told me of your family. Were they so rich?"

He explained that he had been born late in his parents' lives, when his father was nearly 50 and his mother past 40. His father, the son of a Tory school master who died in the Battle of Kings Mountain during the Revolution, grew up in Philadelphia where his widowed mother married a shipping magnate named Jeremiah Martin.

As he explained it, "There was some problem with my father's younger half brother during the War of 1812. I never knew just what it was, but my father and mother—she was a Bostonian—moved to New York City. They died when I was only five. My maternal grandparents took me to live with them in Boston, where my grandfather was a Unitarian minister. My grandparents died soon after I came west. Maybe that explains why I haven't settled down. But dear Annie, in you I have found someone who can bring stability and purpose into my life."

Who could have resisted such sweet talk? So, yes, I agreed to marry him at Easter time. I thought that we could live happily ever after, but, alas, that happens only in fairy tales.

Those first few weeks after I said yes to Chester were busy and happy. Despite feeling bone weary from my hotel labors, I was full of hope and high expectations. Chester would show up on a Saturday with gifts and booming good cheer. Everyone, even Opal, was glad to see him. We spent hours talking to each other. We decided to say nothing to Captain McGee either of our engagement or of Chester's desire, after our wedding, to quit his freighting job to help me run the hotel. He was full of great plans not only to pitch in at the hotel but also to enter the newspaper business there in Nevada County and even to try his hand again at politics.

Meanwhile, Opal had finished reading her Christmas gift of UNCLE

TOM'S CABIN, with help from me with some of the more difficult passages. At her insistence, I read the book myself. The picture Mrs. Stowe painted of cruel overseers and harsh treatment of slaves did not accord with my limited experience of slavery, but I held my tongue. To tell the truth, Opal's loyalty and kindness to me, as well as her outspokenness and culinary skills, were far more convincing arguments for emancipation of slaves than the imagination of a woman writer from New England.

Chester was delighted at Opal's enjoyment of the book. And during his weekend visits to Grass Valley, he became the darling of the local Republicans, often holding court in the saloon of The Gold Mountain. Of course, with my Southern upbringing, I did not share his Republican views but at the time I could see no problems with that. Nor did it any longer bother me that he was a Yankee and a Unitarian. We enjoyed each other's company so much, I had every reason to look forward to a long and satisfying marriage.

So it was with shock and disbelief that I greeted his showing up unexpectedly a few weeks before our marriage date to announce that we would have to postpone the event well beyond Easter.

"Why? You are the one who was so eager to tie the knot."

"The Republicans are having their convention this year in Chicago, on May 16."

"What has the Republican convention to do with us?"

"They want me to go to Chicago as an alternate delegate from California. It is a great honor."

"But that is only ten weeks away. How can you possibly get there in time?"

"Our delegation has booked passage on a steamer from San Francisco down to Nicaragua. We will cross the isthmus and take another ship that will get us to Massachusetts. Then we'll take the trains to Chicago. Oh, don't look so downcast, Annie, my darling. This is the chance of a lifetime for me. Look, I can get out there and back by fall. In fact I will have to if I am to take part in the campaign. We can get married as soon as I return."

Dumbfounded, I said, "But what about your job?"

"I have given it up. Zeb didn't like it one whit. Called me a damned fool, as you might expect."

"When would you leave?"

"That is just it. There is a party of us from Nevada County due to depart tomorrow morning."

"And you are determined to go?"

"I must, Annie. This next presidential election will be the most important in our history. The slavery issue is coming to a head at last. There can be no peace until the issue is settled. And in my view there is only one man who can do this."

"And who might that be?"

"Some like Frémont, others, Seward. My choice is Abraham Lincoln, the rail splitter from Illinois."

I was too proud to beg him to stay even though I was hurt and baffled by his putting politics ahead of me and our wedding. Yet, at the same time, I was just a bit relieved by the thought that, in Chester's absence, I could give my full attention to running the hotel. I would miss him, certainly, but since it meant so much to him to go, who was I to stand in his way? After all, it had been I who originally had suggested waiting until later that year.

Often have I wondered what he might have done had I forced him to choose between going to that convention or marrying me, and how differently our lives would have turned out if I had persuaded him to remain with me . . . Or if he had left immediately that night instead of lingering until past bedtime.

Chester was on his knees, holding my hand and begging me not to be angry with him and promising to write as soon as he reached Chicago.

"You will wait for me, won't you, Annie?"

"Of course. But there will be conditions."

"Name them."

"Upon your return, you must settle down and stick to whatever it is you really want to do. I won't put up with any more flitting about from one profession to another."

"Agreed. And I further promise that I will consult you in my choice of occupation."

"In that case, I will not give you back your ring. I will wait for you."

To my amazement, his face crumpled and his eyes brimmed with tears.

Alarmed, I asked, "What is the matter?"

"I was so afraid you would say no."

"And if I had?"

"I don't know what I would have done. Oh, Annie, I am the luckiest fellow in the world to have you."

Opal and Duncan were asleep in an adjoining room. Had they been awake, again my story would be different. With Billy Joe Duncan, it had been I who had taken the initiative in my father's barn loft, and the experience had been unforgettably pleasant. In that single time with Elmer, I had given in to sympathy. Here with Chester Peebles, whom once I had scorned as a cock-sure Yankee, again it was sympathy but something more. For weeks, my sleep had been troubled by dreams of almost exactly what happened there in the living room of my third-floor apartment in The Gold Mountain.

Before I knew what was happening, Chester had his arms about me and was kissing, first my lips and then my neck, all the while moaning of his love for me.

At first, I held myself stiffly, trying to ward off his caresses until, unable to contain myself any longer, I began returning his kisses.

My experiences with Billy Joe had been furtive. Both he and I had been virgins. With Elmer, only he had been gratified by our brief coupling shortly before his death when I was already pregnant with Billy Joe's child. Neither Chester nor I were virgins, although it soon became evident that he was far more experienced than I.

Before I was fully aware of what was happening, he had led me into my bedroom and was helping me remove my clothing. Then, after I had slipped beneath the covers, he stripped off his own clothes and stood there briefly, smiling at me.

Except for that episode with Bart Corbett I had never gazed upon the naked form of a well-developed grown man.

"This isn't right, you know, Chester," I said as he joined me in bed.

"You are as good as my wife already, Annie."

"I suppose I am at that."

Afterwards, I put my arms around his neck and we fell into a deep sleep, from which I was awakened by his lips pressed afresh to mine. I quickly responded to his kisses. And what followed was even more deeply satisfying than the first time.

When we had finished, the first light of dawn was appearing through the window. Chester jumped from my bed, looked at his watch and said, "My God, Annie. I must go or I will miss the stage."

I had to bite my tongue to keep from urging him not to go, for him to stay and for us to be married right away. But pride held me back.

So I lay there watching him scramble into his clothes, thinking how pleasant it would be to be a married couple who could lie abed until after sunup without causing a scandal.

Once dressed, Chester came and sat on the edge of my bed and smiled at me.

"With or without being formally married, from this day forward I regard you as my wife."

He bent down and kissed me long and hard, then arose and tiptoed from my room. I would have called out to him or, at least, followed him to the door if Duncan had not stumbled into my room rubbing his eyes and asking, "Where is Uncle Chester?"

So, off went Chester Peebles III to take ship from San Francisco. For the first time in my life, I had experienced what true magic there could be between a fully grown man and woman. The memory of that too brief a night, untinged by guilt or regret, would comfort me for a long time thereafter.

True to his promise, Chester did write, and beautiful letters they were, too, full of assurances of his love and his determination to return, marry me, and devote the rest of his life to making me a happy woman.

His first letter came from Sacramento where he was to take the boat down the Sacramento River to San Francisco; the second from the Bay City just before embarking; and the third from San Juan del Sur on the west coast of Nicaragua. His letters made veiled references to our last night together and to his yearning for many more such nights following our marriage.

As expected, there was a hiatus in his correspondence for some weeks after that. During that period, I plunged into running the hotel by day while at night I reread Chester's letters and indulged myself in reliving my last night with him.

By then, the Pony Express was in operation between St. Joseph and Sacramento so that news from the East was coming through on a regular basis, and disturbing news it was, telling of the deadlock and splintering of the Democratic party on the issue of slavery and increasing talk of secession by the Southern states if an abolitionist Republican should win the presidency that fall of 1860.

In June, came the news that Abraham Lincoln, after three ballots, had been chosen by the Republican delegates over Seward. And also I received my first letter in several weeks from Chester. Written in tiny script on onion skin paper, it described his trip by mule train and boat across Nicaragua and his subsequent passage by ship to Boston, then by train to Chicago. I laid it to the $5-per-ounce cost of Pony Express mail that his letter did not contain so many professions of love as had his earlier ones. But he did cram in statements of his pleasure at Lincoln's nomination and of his determination to work hard to win California's votes for "the only man who can both save the Union and end the curse of slavery."

That same letter mentioned that his return to California would be delayed while he attended to the settlement of his late grandparents' estate in Boston. Although I regretted having to wait a few extra weeks for his return, I attached no importance to the delay.

* * *

As I have said, only Opal knew of my engagement to Chester, although it could hardly be kept a secret that he had been paying court to me. But Opal said little to me about my plans to marry Chester after his return from the East, partly because he had charmed her, as he had Duncan, and partly because of her growing involvement in the local African Methodist Episcopal Church.

There was a settlement of Negroes nearby, most of them free men and women from the border and northern states with a few runaway slaves such as Opal. Although members of her race were not allowed to vote even in a nominally free state like California, both she and her fellow church members took an increasingly strong interest in the presidential campaign.

For my part, I was too busy running the hotel to pay much attention to politics. All I wanted was for Chester to return, for us to marry, and for The Gold Mountain to continue to prosper.

During this period, Captain McGee continued to drop by occasionally, always for business reasons, or so I thought. He was not one for gossip or small talk, but I did enjoy his company and appreciated his continuing encouragement. So, while he could hardly have been ignorant of Chester's intentions toward me, he never referred to our relationship, even on the hot day in August when he stopped by to give me a letter that had been delivered to his Sacramento freight office.

It was addressed in very poor handwriting to "Anny Monday, care of Chester Peoples" and bore an Oregon return address.

I set the letter aside while Captain McGee went over our accounts with Kwong Chung and me. Then, after he had left, I opened and attempted to read the letter.

It was from Mrs. Mueller. I will not attempt to transcribe verbatim her highly original spelling or all of her unpunctuated and nearly illegible writing, nor will I try to describe the emotions I felt after, on my third reading, the significance of her message sank in.

Briefly, she explained that she and her family were prospering in Oregon and that she wished I could see the beautiful baby they had named Annie, after me. Then she chided me for not writing to her, noting that she had made Chester promise he would give me her address. She said that she hoped since I had achieved such reported success with my restaurant business that I had not forgotten faithful friends such as herself.

Then came the bombshell.

"After Chester's girl he was to marry back east throwed him over and I herd you was still single, I tole him he better haul hisself down to Californy and see would you marry him. I tole him he needs a woman like you to make a man out of him. I did not tell him nothing about you getting with child like you did. Far as he knows, Elmer was the daddy of yore baby. We been waiting and hoping for a letter from you. Sence you aint wrote I thought I would ask how things is working out for you and him. He was awful cut up when he got word his girl won't marry him after all them years. So do rite and tell us what is going on. Even if you have forgot us, we cant never forget you and our trip across the west. Your friend always, Hannah Mueller."

* * *

"What's the matter with you?" Opal asked when she saw me sitting with Mrs. Mueller's letter in my hand. "You look like you seen a ghost."

"Nothing is the matter. I am just tired. I think I will lie down for a while."

In the privacy of my bedroom, I pondered on the contrast between what Chester had told me of the ending of his engagement to Amy and Mrs. Mueller's version. Could she possibly have misunderstood? I dug Chester's old letter from my carpet bag. There it was in plain English: " . . . when I learned that you remained unmarried, I relayed this intelligence to Mrs. Mueller. and spoke of my discouragement at ever winning Amy's hand."

Then, not long after writing those words to me, he had said he had sent back her locket and written that he no longer wished to marry her. Yet, Mrs. Mueller's letter plainly read "Chester's girl he was to marry back east throwed him over."

I recalled that when he first appeared in Grass Valley, after he had told me about the Muellers and their baby girl, I had asked for and he had promised to give me their address. Had his failure to do this been deliberate?

Unless Mrs. Mueller was imagining things, Chester had been less than truthful in making it seem that it had been he, rather than Amy, who had broken their engagement and he had done so out of love for me.

Was the deception serious enough for me to confront him when he returned? But then what would he say if he were to learn of my out-of-wedlock pregnancy? Or that I had entered into a marriage with Elmer Hixon which I intended to annul? Or if he knew that I, and not Indians, had slain Bart Corbett?

So I had caught him on the rebound. Unless he was the biggest liar west of the Rocky Mountains, he had had strong feelings for me almost from our first meeting. What difference did it make who had ditched whom? Surely he would be mine once he returned from the East. He was not perfect. What man or woman was? And, as Mrs. Mueller said, he really did need "a woman like you to make a man out of him."

One thing was sure, here on the very bed where I lay, Chester had demonstrated that there was nothing I could teach him in one very important aspect of manhood.

So, I decided not only to overlook his deception but never to mention it to him. The important thing was that he was to be my lawful wedded husband. I missed him so I ached.

5

My next letter from Chester came in the form of a telegram sent from Boston to St. Joseph and thence to California via the Pony Express. It was a terse message informing me that the estate of his grandparents was both larger and more complicated than he had expected and, therefore, it would be the first of August before he could embark from Boston.

I would have preferred a proper letter full of sweet sentiments such as those in his earlier ones, but figured that telegraph messages were not meant to contain extravagant expressions of love.

Well, I had wanted to delay our wedding until after summer, hadn't I? It looked like I was getting my wish.

Caught up in my infatuation for Chester and my confidence that we would be married, I had given little thought to Will Tremelling. So I was surprised one evening when he showed up in the hotel lobby, smelling of whisky and acting nervous.

"I got to talk to you, Annie."

"Talk away, Will."

"Not here. Somewhere private."

I took him up to my apartment. There he removed his hat and fidgeted with the brim while I asked how he was doing with his job as assistant mine manager.

"That is one reason I have come. The owners are offering me the job of manager. I will be making more money than I ever dreamed of when I left Cornwall."

"Congratulations, Will."

"But that is not what I have come to talk about."

"And what might that be?"

"I told you a long time ago how I felt about you and how I wanted you to be my wife."

"And I told you how flattered I was."

"I still feel that way. Only since that Peebles fellow came here, you have had no time for me."

"It is nothing personal, Will. The hotel keeps me awfully busy."

"Not too busy to be seeing Peebles."

"I haven't seen him since early April, not since he went off to the Republican convention."

"Is he coming back?"

"I certainly hope so. What is your point, Will?"

"You turned me down when I offered to quit the mine and help you run this hotel. Now that my circumstances are about to improve, I will be making more than enough money to support a wife and children."

"I am pleased for you, but I don't understand . . ."

"There is an Irish girl that works for a rich family over in Nevada City. She is a Catholic but a good girl, all the same. I met her at a dance. I feel pretty certain she would marry me if I was to ask her. But I don't want to do that if there is any chance you might accept my offer. I still have that ring. So I must ask you straight out. Are things between you and Peebles serious, or is there still a chance for me?"

The poor fellow looked so distraught and vulnerable that I was tempted to put my arms around him. Of course, I didn't. I simply said in a low, gentle voice, "I am sorry, Will. Chester and I have an understanding, you might say. Nothing formal but an understanding all the same."

He looked down at his hat, then into my face.

"I was afraid of that."

"We have been friends for a long while, Will, and should remain so. I'd appreciate it if you'd keep this to yourself."

"So be it. I still think I would have made you a better husband than him."

He walked to the door and turned to face me.

"And I would appreciate it if you would never say anything of this to Noreen. In case she says yes, that is."

"We will keep all this a secret. And I am betting that your Noreen will say yes."

After he had left, I lay face down on my bed and wept, partly out of pity for Will but also out of frustration at Chester's failure to return promptly from the East.

Two days later Will appeared back at the hotel, accompanied by a shy, pretty little red-haired dumpling who seemed to adore him. She was wearing the ring Will had first offered me. I am not sure exactly why he brought her around; whether it was to rub it in for my having turned him down or because he wanted my approval.

At any rate they accepted my invitation to stay and have dinner on the house and I accepted theirs to attend their wedding the next month at the Catholic Church of St. Peter and Paul in Nevada City. Also I complimented Noreen on her little diamond ring.

* * *

My last letter-telegraph message from Chester arrived in mid-August.

Dated two weeks earlier, it was even more cryptic than the previous one. In it Chester reported "My circumstances much improved due to inheritance. Will depart tomorrow. Expect to arrive Frisco September 1. Will bring you up to date then."

Again I laid the tone of the message to the requirements of the telegraph, but that did not prevent my impatience to see the man I expected to marry, and to learn more about his mysterious news.

Although Opal knew of my unofficial engagement to Chester, she was unaware of the intimacy that had occurred between us the night before he departed. She did, however, note my increasing edginess, saying, "Wish that man would get himself back here so you will stop acting so anxious."

Chester's Republican friends in the area did not help my nerves by continually asking when I expected him to return to help rally voters to Lincoln. Although judging from the newspapers, the Breckenridge branch of the Democrats was dominating Southern politics, in California members of the party were becoming more unified around Stephen Douglas. The local Republicans were worried that Lincoln would not carry the state.

This annoyed me, for I knew that the minute Chester set foot back in Grass Valley he would become swept up in the increasingly heated campaign. Confound it, four months had passed since our night together. I had to do more than wait passively for him to show up.

*   *   *

Opal thought I was crazy when I told her my plan.

"You don't even know which ship he is going to be on."

"It generally takes a month to get here from the East Coast by ship. Surely I wouldn't have to wait very long."

"Who is going to run this place while you are gone?"

"Business is slow right now anyway. Captain McGee can find someone to fill in for me."

"What you going to do for money?"

"Mister Delano will give me an advance."

And so he did, and with it the name and address of a respectable boarding house where I would be safe while waiting for Chester's ship to arrive.

Captain McGee disapproved of my taking off two weeks. Not wanting to tell him the real reason for my request, I said, "Captain, I have been shut up in this town for four years now. It is time for me to see San Francisco. If not now, when?"

"You shouldn't be taking such a trip alone. San Francisco is full of some pretty rough characters."

"I will be perfectly safe. Mr. Delano has seen to that."

After some grumbling, he finally said, "I know you have had a hard life here, and expect you do need a break. I reckon it is all right, as long as you have a respectable place to stay. There is a hotel man over in Nevada City that owes me a favor. He will find us somebody to oversee things. But no longer than two weeks, now, you understand that don't you, little lady?"

* * *

I realized that it was a bold thing I was doing, but nonetheless I caught the morning stage to Sacramento where after a bumpy ride of some sixty miles I arrived in the evening and went directly to a hotel recommended by Mister DeLano. The next morning, I went aboard a crowded little steamer that was to carry me down the Sacramento River to San Francisco.

As I stood at the rail and watched the fertile fields and orchards of the rich Sacramento Valley glide past, my mood was joyous. I was headed to a meeting with the man I already considered my husband. In my imagination he would be surprised and delighted by my unexpected presence at the wharf. Surely there would be no reason why he would object to our getting married right there in San Francisco. Mr. Delano had advanced me more than enough money to pay for a honeymoon. Then after a few days to ourselves, we would return to Grass Valley to take up our lives together there.

I had brought along the lovely ring Chester had given me at Christmas. To give substance to my dream, I began wearing it on the boat.

Four years before, aboard The Polar Star on our trip up the Missouri from St. Louis to St. Joseph, there had been much political dissension over "the Kansas question." Now, on this day-long voyage I heard even more wrangling about the presidential campaign. A hard core of men with Southern drawls argued for the election of Vice President John C. Breckinridge of Kentucky. Their opinions were vociferously countered by other Democrats who favored the "Little Giant," Stephen Douglas. And then, speaking mostly in the accents of New England and New York, supporters of Abraham Lincoln extolled the virtues of their champion.

I was relieved when, in the late afternoon, the docks and jumbled buildings of San Francisco and beyond them the Golden Gate entrance to the great harbor came into view. Immediately I was caught up in the magic of that city. By comparison, Grass Valley was a raw frontier town. Every race of man and stripe of woman thronged the streets of that cosmopolitan city.

A hack delivered me and my bags to the boarding house where, I was gratified to learn from the landlady, Mr. Delano had telegraphed her a request that she accept me with courtesy, which she did. Not only had she reserved a lovely little private room at the rear of the second floor, she also sent me up a large bowl and pitcher of hot water with towels, a light supper, and a copy of a local newspaper.

Dog tired from my two days of travel, after taking a sponge bath, I donned my night gown and ate my supper. Then I thumbed through the paper, looking for notices of ship arrivals. Seeing none relating to arrivals from Nicaragua, I blew out my lamp, knelt by my bed and said an ardent prayer for the safe and early arrival of Chester, and fell quickly into a dreamless sleep.

The next morning, after partaking of an excellent breakfast downstairs, I put on my best bonnet and set forth on foot for the office of the harbor master. A kindly fellow, he listened with sympathy to my story of wanting to greet my fiance's ship.

"Tell you what, miss. To save you the trouble of hanging about these docks, why don't you give me your name and the address of your lodgings? When we get the signal from up on Telegraph Hill that a steamer is approaching the harbor, I'll send a messenger to your place so you can be ready and waiting to greet him."

I thanked the gentleman for his consideration and left thinking what a wonderful city San Francisco really was and how happy I was to be there.

Desiring more exercise, I took a roundabout route back to my boardinghouse, else I wouldn't have passed the theater outside which was posted a notice that "The Celebrated Courtenay Family" would start a new minstrel show the very next night. On impulse, I rapped on the glass window of the box office to attract the man who was sitting with his feet on his desk and smoking a cigar.

"Homer Courtenay? What do you want with him?"

"I am an old friend," I began. Then, when he raised his eyebrows, I quickly added, "and of his wife and two children. We crossed the West together on a wagon train back in fifty six."

"Did you now? I have heard enough about his adventures to write the book he keeps talking about, myself. Said he took part in the hanging of a horse thief. Is that true?"

"Very true," I said. "I witnessed it myself."

"In that case, let's see if he isn't about."

He opened the door that led into the lobby and yelled, "Hey, Courtenay. You in there? There's a lady out here to see you."

My apprehension that Mr. Courtenay, out of shame for never repaying my $50 loan, might not want to see me was baseless. He seized both my hands in his, looked into my eyes with a grin, and then gave me an enthusiastic hug.

My fear of loneliness at being in a strange city while waiting for Chester's ship, also vanished in an instant. Nothing would do but that I should accompany him to the family's lodgings several blocks away. There, in the shabby three-rooms the family occupied over a saloon, I was greeted with somewhat less enthusiasm by Mrs. Courtenay and the two children. Mrs. Courtenay had put on so much weight I could only assume that she could no longer play Cordelia in King Lear. But she gradually warmed up to me, after I told the reason why I had come to San Francisco.

They listened eagerly to my second-hand reports of the Oregon contingent of our expedition across the West. They were delighted by the story of the confrontation with Dr. Dormsby. And they seemed impressed by the news that I had graduated from operating a restaurant to being part-owner of a new hotel.

The longer I remained with them, the more at home I felt. There is nothing like coming up in the world to make you feel secure even with folk who once held you in lower esteem.

"But how did you capture the heart of that charming scamp, Peebles?" Mrs. Courtenay inquired.

I told them most of the story.

"And so you are to be married?"

"Yes, and soon, too," I said with confidence.

Then after a moment of reflection I added, "In fact if Chester is agreeable to the idea, we just might want to be wed right away, here in San Francisco."

Mr. Courtenay smote his hands together and exclaimed, "Wonderful. Perhaps you would do us the honor of letting us see the deed done."

To which I replied, "I'll go you one better. My father is a continent away. Would you stand in for him, Mr. Courtenay? And you, Mrs. Courtenay, perhaps you would be my matron of honor. You two are the closest thing to a family I have in this city. I am sure Chester would agree."

"Consider it done," Mr. Courtenay said. "Now then I have some time on my hands. What say you allow me to show you the sights of this grand city?"

It was an excellent tour that Mr. Courtenay treated me to, although you might say it was my treat since I ended up paying the hire of the carriage. Anyway I was enthralled by the sprawling Chinatown and by the grand view of the bay from Nob Hill and by the general vitality of that city of fifty-odd thousand widely assorted souls.

When we returned to my boarding house, as Mr. Courtenay and I were saying our good-bys, my landlady came out onto her porch.

"A fellow came a while ago from the harbor master's office. Said to tell you your ship was coming in."

Mr. Courtenay insisted on escorting me in our same hired carriage down to the wharves. Not knowing how to refuse him, after a brief attendance to my toilette in my room, I ran back downstairs and off we headed for the harbor area.

By the time we got there, a good-sized crowd had gathered to watch a trim, side-wheeler approach the wharf. The rails of the vessel were lined with passengers but because of the press of people in front of us, I could not distinguish Chester's face. Frustrated by this, I climbed down from our carriage, leaving behind a protesting Mr. Courtenay, and elbowed a path through the crowd in a most unladylike way, to where I could get a better view.

It was not until the ship had got close enough for a line to be cast to the wharf that I picked him out. How handsome and self assured he appeared. He was dressed in a fashionably cut suit, one I had never seen before, and was wearing a fine felt hat.

Good, I thought. It would not be necessary for him to buy a new suit for our wedding.

I waved, trying to catch his attention, but his face was averted now, as he looked back over his shoulder. What an agreeable profile he presented, I was thinking, when he turned his face back toward the shore and was joined at the rail by a slender, dark-haired young woman.

Then, to my horror, he put his arm around her shoulders and pointed toward the city.

Now the crewmen were attaching their lines to windlasses and were drawing the ship broadside up to the wharf.

Shielding my eyes from the late afternoon sun, I peered closer at Chester's companion. And then it struck me why that face looked so familiar. Surely it was the same countenance whose image had been contained in the locket he used to wear about his neck.

It was all I could do not to faint. I forced myself to gaze at the pair again. Now he was bending down and kissing her cheek.

In a stupor, fighting to keep back my tears, I thrust myself back through the crowd to where Mr. Courtenay waited with the carriage.

"Whatever is the matter, my dear? Is he not aboard?"

"He is aboard, all right."

"I don't understand. Are you ill?"

"Get me away from here, please . . . " were the last words I remember saying before I got back into the carriage and fell into a faint.

Only vaguely do I remember coming to myself as we drew away from the wharves area, then passing out again as the image of Chester and that girl, who could only be Amy, flashed into my brain again.

Although I implored him to carry me to my boardinghouse, the alarmed Mr. Courtenay insisted on delivering me to his wife at their own apartment. There I gave way to tears, sobbing out my story to a now sympathetic Mrs. Courtenay.

"You must get control of yourself. You may be mistaken," she said.

"There is no mistake. It was the girl he was to marry."

Again I broke into sobs as she bathed my face with cold water.

"There is only one thing to be done," she said.

"What is that?"

"Homer, you must hasten back to the wharf and ascertain who the woman or girl is. For all we know it might be his sister. He may have brought her along as a surprise."

"He doesn't have a sister. He is an only child."

"Whoever it is, let's get at the truth. Begone with you, Homer. You like to play the detective. Don't come back without the facts. Before you go, tell me where you now hide your brandy. I must help this poor girl revive herself."

"I don't want to be revived. I want to die."

Yet the shot of brandy did pick me up. And as the first shock of what

I had observed passed, I reflected on the strange tone of Chester's two messages from Boston. Why had he not told me, if he was married to his Amy?

I accepted yet another draught of brandy and then lay upon a couch with a wet cloth over my swollen eyes, thinking black thoughts about men in general.

My plight must have seemed a terrible one even for the normally unsympathetic Mrs. Courtenay, for, to my surprise, she took my hand and said, "You must relax and not think the worst. There may be some logical and innocent explanation."

"That is not possible."

"If your fears should be realized, whatever you do, you must not give in to despair. Your life is just beginning. You may have been saved from a dreadful and irretrievable mistake. I would trade places with you in a minute."

"You are just saying that."

"I am serious. You think I don't know what you feel? I could have married several men before I was your age and any one of them would have made a better husband than Homer Courtenay. Does that shock you? Look at me, living in miserable rented rooms above a saloon and forced to perform in black-face minstrel shows. My marriage was a mistake of which I am daily reminded."

"But you have never gone through what I just experienced. The sight of him with his arm around . . . "

"You don't know what you are saying. That is nothing compared to what Homer has done. Why do you think we left England? Or, for that matter, Richmond? Twice I have caught him flagrante delicto. If it had not been for the children or my own pride I would have left him years ago."

"You mean you don't love your husband?"

"I never said that. Once I loved him too much and now I am stuck with him. Hold, that is enough. I hear him on the stairs. Never breathe a word of what I have said. And whatever his report, bear it with dignity."

She went to intercept her husband in the hall, from which there came sounds of a low, muffled conversation. Then she opened the door and said, "Go ahead, Homer. The girl is made of strong stuff. She might as well hear the truth now. But for God's sake get to the point quickly. Don't embellish."

I removed the cloth from my eyes and sat up.

"My dear Annie," he said. "I went aboard the ship and saw the captain himself. It appears that the girl eloped with your Chester and left Boston by steamer. The captain of that ship performed a wedding ceremony as soon as they were clear of land. They came aboard this captain's ship in San Juan del sur and became the toast of the passengers, except for those who were Democrats who took offense at Peeble's political views."

"And is her name Amy?" I asked.

"According to the passenger list, yes."

At that I wailed in pain and jealousy. Mrs. Courtenay seized my shoulders and shook me until I shut up.

"You will gain nothing by giving in to your emotions. Now, Homer, is that all?"

"Not quite. The captain also told me where they asked their trunks to be sent. It is a hotel. So I had the carriage stop by there and, sure enough, they are registered as man and wife. They have reserved a room for a full week. By the way, Annie, the carriage driver is waiting downstairs to be paid and, confound it, I am a bit short of funds."

I arose and pushed away Mrs. Courtenay's restraining arms.

"I will pay the fellow when he delivers me back to my own boarding house."

"You are in no condition to be alone."

"You both have been most kind. I am sorry to have caused you so much trouble. No, no, I must leave you. Of course, I will not do anything foolish. I have already been far too foolish."

"Is there nothing more we can do for you?"

"Perhaps tomorrow I will ask one small favor before I return to Grass Valley."

"Anything, my dear."

I looked into the eyes of Mrs. Courtenay and saw there for the first time the sadness that lay behind her seeming pride.

"You have helped me more than you will ever know."

Then, before they could detain me further, I gathered up my bonnet, went downstairs and ordered the carriage man to transport me to my boarding house.

6

Early the next morning, on my way to the wharf from which the steamer to Sacramento would leave, I had the hack driver wait while I climbed the stairs to the Courtenay's apartment above the saloon.

Mrs. Courtenay and the children still slept, but Mr. Courtenay was awake and enjoying a cup of tea. I explained that my time was short and begged him to listen carefully to what I wished him to do.

"You want me to deliver this packet and letter to Chester Peebles today? Should I say that you . . . "

"Say only that you received these items and instructions from me, ten days ago, by mail from Grass Valley. Under no circumstances is he to know that I have been in San Francisco."

His face began to brighten at the prospect of pulling off yet another adventure.

"I see."

"The important thing is that he be made to think that I, without knowledge of his marriage, took the initiative to break off our relationship and return his ring. You understand?"

"Yes, but do you not wish to inflict upon him some punishment for deceiving you?"

"Trust me, Mr. Courtenay. My letter will punish him sufficiently, especially if you take care to deliver it and the ring in the presence of his bride. Now, why do you look perplexed?"

"Naturally I am delighted to perform this service. I only hope there will be no expenses involved."

"I can't think what they might be, but just in case, here is twenty dollars. Is that sufficient?"

"I should think so, although it does go against my grain to accept your money."

"Think nothing of it. However, I do insist that you require him to sign this receipt for the ring. Here is my address to which the receipt must be posted."

In his shirt sleeves and carpet slippers, he followed me down stairs and helped me into the hack.

"As I was saying to my lady wife last night, you are a brave and resourceful young woman."

"Thank you, Mr. Courtenay. Please remember to do exactly what I have asked. And please don't forget to send me my receipt."

* * *

On the cruise up the river to Sacramento, although inwardly I felt desolate, I maintained a stoical exterior. Whereas on the down-river trip, my mind had been occupied with dreams of a joyful reunion with Chester, now I took a grim pleasure in imagining the reaction that would greet the receipt of my letter and his ring.ABwouldn't it be an interesting scene if Amy should be present and Chester would have to explain the ring to her?

I doubted that he would share with her my sealed letter, however. I had sat up until midnight in my boarding house room, crafting that spiteful epistle. Not a word did I write of how I had pined for him when he had left for the East, nor of the happy future I had imagined our enjoying following his return. I made it seem that I had never relinquished my doubts about his steadfastness and that very soon after his departure I had begun to have second thoughts about marrying such an ineffective man.

Then I fired my broadside. I told him of that letter from Mrs. Mueller and how it revealed to me that he had lied about having been the instigator in breaking his engagement with Amy. I hated nothing more than a liar, I wrote, also that had I known his address in Boston, I would have sent him a letter by Pony Express saying I never wanted to see him again and asking for instructions on where to return his ring. Lacking such an address, I decided to kill two birds with one stone and enlist Mr. Courtenay to deliver both my letter and his ring to him upon his arrival in San Francisco.

Nothing in my missive gave any sign of my anguish, my sense of desolation. I expressed only a feeling of relief in having realized his true moral character in time to break our engagement.

They say hell hath no fury like a scorned woman. I could only hope that I had been able to cast Chester Peebles, that smooth-talking charmer, in the role of a scorned man. I figured that he who scorns first scorns best.

Later, on the stage back to Grass Valley, it occurred to me that what I might have done, rather than wounding Chester's feelings, had been to relieve him of any feelings of guilt. I wished now that I had asked Mr. Courtenay not only to send me that receipt but also to write an account of Chester's reaction.

Back in the sanctuary of The Gold Mountain, Opal was alarmed by my appearance.

"You wasn't to return for ten more days. And you look like death warmed over. Here, let me feel your forehead. Why you are burning up with a fever. We got to put you to bed." Then in a whisper, "Where is that Chester? Didn't he show up?"

Refusing to offer any explanation, I took myself off to bed and stayed there, too drained to cry any more, allowing only Duncan to spend very much time in my room.

I was sick both in body and soul. At Opal's insistance, Dr. Jacoby was sent for. He questioned me as to what I had eaten or drunk on my trip to San Francisco, a city he termed "a hotbed of disease." The potions he left did little enough for my bodily ailment, which he diagnosed as "river fever," and nothing at all for my crisis of spirit.

Earlier in this narrative I wrote of the pain and utter despair I experienced at having been dumped off like an unwanted pregnant cat at a wayside barn to bear my baby. Now I underwent a similar Gethsemene of the soul. As I lay in my darkened room, I flagellated myself by reliving all the mistakes I had made during the past five years, beginning when I first had laid eyes on Billy Joe Duncan at our Methodist camp meeting. It was my advances, not his, that had led to my becoming pregnant.

But then I thought had I been as shy as he, I would not be blessed with my handsome little boy who was one of the few bright spots in my life.

Then I reflected ruefully on my naive assumption that if Elmer Hixon and I did not consummate our marriage, it would be a simple matter to annul the union once we arrived in Oregon and his usefullness to me had ended. Wrongly as that turned out, had I not married Elmer, for whatever motive, the money he had won in his poker game with Bart Corbett would not have become my grubstake in California.

And I relived my shooting Corbett. Dreadful as that experience had been, it had resulted in a bond between me and Captain McGee. I doubted that he would have taken much notice of me had that awful thing not occurred, certainly not enough to inspire him with the confidence in my spunk to back my hotel project.

And that ridiculous episode in which Dr. Dormsby had sought to make me his number two wife had worked to my advantage. Had that silly little man not interfered in my life, I would have been forced to proceed to Oregon as an indentured servant.

My being left off to bear my child at a brothel had worked out to my advantage, too. Otherwise Opal would not have remained behind to become my devoted ally.

My mother used to say that it was an ill wind that blows no good. None of my previous experiences, not even being exiled by my father, had devastated me as thoroughly, however, as had the betrayal of Chester Peebles. No, that was more than merely an ill wind. It was a hurricane and I could not imagine how I would survive it.

* * *

My state of mind was not improved when Opal delivered to me an invitation to the wedding of Noreen Ryan to William Tremelling on the next Saturday.

The invitation plunged me into a deeper despondency. Will could so easily have been mine. As recently as three weeks before, all I would have had to do was say yes and it would be me about to wed that good, steady Cornishman, a man who would never have let me down as had Chester Peebles.

It was with a heavy heart and feeble hand that I wrote a note to Noreen saying that due to illness I could not attend their wedding but that I wished her and Will much happiness together.

With my normally sturdy constitution, I might have thrown off Dr. Jacoby's so-called river fever in a few days but in my distressed emotional state I lacked the will to fight the disease. My fever worsened. My bones began to ache as well as my head. Whether it was my doses of laudanum or my mounting fever, I cannot say, but I began to lapse into and out of periods of delirium. I was only faintly aware of Opal sitting by my bed or tenderly wiping the perspiration from my face.

Then came that awful moment when, briefly regaining consciousness, I heard Opal asking Dr. Jacoby, "She is going to pull through, isn't she?"

"I wouldn't bet on it."

"Wouldn't bet on it? If that is all you got to say, what you doing here?" She began to moan, "Oh, sweet Jesus, what will happen to us if we lose her? Who is going to raise her little boy? What can we do?"

"Are you a praying woman?" the doctor asked.

"If I wasn't, I couldn't have got this far in life."

"Then you better start praying. There is nothing more I can do for her."

They tell me that later that night I stopped breathing, and they could not detect a heart beat. I believe them. In fact, I remember feeling something, call it my soul if you will, rising right out of my poor wasted body and of my looking down on what had been myself, lying on the bed, yes, and of seeing Opal and Kwong Chung weeping, yes, even the normally inscrutable Kwong Chung. And I was conscious of a tall figure also standing in the shadows of the room, someone I did not recognize. In my delirium, I imagined him to be the Grim Reaper come to collect me. Then I felt myself rushing from my sick room toward a brilliant light and seeing my old Grandmother Shelton, smiling and holding out her arms.

My feeling of ecstasy was broken by the sound of Duncan's voice saying, "Mama" followed by Opal's demanding "What you bring that child in here for?" then by Mildred's replying, "I thought he ought to see his mama one more time. Is it too late?"

"Get him out of here. I think she is gone."

"No," I muttered. "Let him stay. I can't go. Not yet."

Instantly I felt myself surging back down into my wasted body. I opened my eyes and looked at Opal, tears glistening on her cheeks, and Mildred holding Duncan and Kwong Chung with the happiest look I had ever seen on his face.

And from the foot of my bed came the deep voice of Captain McGee saying, "By God, I believe she has come back to us after all."

After that Opal shooed everyone from my room. The last thing I recall before slipping into a deep, restful sleep was her kneeling by my bed and thanking "my sweet Jesus" for my return from the dead.

Later, as I was recovering, I tried to thank Opal for her devoted nursing.

"Don't thank me. Thank the Good Lord and the folks in my church."

"What do you mean the folks in your church?"

"They prayed you through. I laid the matter on our congregation and they took turns praying for you. I did my share of praying but I am just one woman."

After that my recovery was swift. The fellow Captain McGee had got to stand in for me while I was to have been in San Francisco agreed to stay on until I was strong enough to resume my duties. And the Captain himself dropped by almost every day, staying just long enough to inquire about my progress, until one day, when I was feeling well enough to sit in my rocking chair, I urged him to stay and talk.

"Opal has told me of the concern you expressed when I was so very ill."

"I was worried we might lose you."

"I am sorry to cause so much worry. It was my fault that I got sick. I had no business going down to San Francisco like that, by myself."

"It bothered me for you to go, only I didn't think it was my place to stop you. Did you have a good time there?"

"No. It was the worst time in my life."

"Anything you want to tell me about?"

"No. It is something I want to forget."

"Well, I'll not pry into your personal affairs."

"Nor I in yours, Captain."

A long, awkward silence followed which he broke by saying, "You remember that time we had dinner in Nevada City?"

"Of course."

"I am sorry I was so abrupt with you. I would have apologized and explained sooner but couldn't with Chester hanging about all the time."

"No need to apologize, Captain. I had no business asking about your past."

"I just didn't like to think I had hurt your feelings."

He cleared his throat as I assured him my feelings had not been injured. Then he spoke again, slowly, his eyes averted from my face.

"Chester told you the truth back there on the trail. I was married to a Sioux girl. Her name was Yellow Moon, too. I was only nineteen. She was about fifteen. I loved her and I enjoyed living among her people. They took me in their tribe natural as could be. Even gave me the name, 'Eyes of a Wolf' . . . "

He choked up at that point. I sat in silence until he recovered his voice.

"She died. Died in childbirth. It was a boy and he died, too. Life hasn't been the same for me since."

"I am sorry."

"They offered me other girls, including Yellow Moon's younger sister, but I turned them down. There is a lot of good in most all Indians, except maybe for the Utes and the Diggers. The Sioux are fine, brave people, but I didn't like their cruelty to other tribes. They kept trying to get me to go on raids against the Pawnee, to bring back horses and scalps, but I wanted no parts of that. So I divided all my worldly goods among Yellow Moon's relatives and moved up into the Rockies to trade furs with the Shoshones until the bottom dropped out of that business. Then went to California and got into the war with Mexico. Well, I didn't mean to bore you with my life story, but figured since you asked me, I had better satisfy your curiosity."

This time I had the good sense not to ask any questions that might plunge him back into silence. So all I said was, "Thank you for telling me your story, Captain. Believe me, I was not at all bored."

"Never thought I could care for another girl like I did Yellow Moon," he continued, paused to clear his throat again, and looked directly at me.

Then he said something that nearly caused me to fall off my chair.

"That was before I met you."

7

Perhaps if I had not been recovering from such a serious illness, I would have had the presence of mind to do more than blurt, "What?" followed by "Captain, I don't know what to say."

I was not used to being put off by a man like that. It galled me to feel so caught off guard and out of control.

With a hint of amusement in his eyes, he studied my face so long that I looked down in embarrassment at my hands in my lap.

He started to speak again, but I broke in with, "You are most kind, Captain, and please don't think me ungrateful for all you have done. It's just that . . . ."

"Hey, I didn't mean to upset you. What is the matter?"

"Could we talk some other time?" I said. "My head feels like it is splitting."

A look of alarm replaced that of amusement on his rugged face.

"Sure. Let's talk again. Maybe tomorrow. Now you take care of yourself, little lady."

As he closed the door, I forced myself to sit quietly with my eyes closed, trying to fight my way back from the verge of hysteria.

Surely he couldn't be serious about me, a girl of no more than half his age. How could he imagine that I might be interested in him? And yet as I thought back over my experiences with him, what other man had proved as steadfast and strong?

I recalled that day we assembled in St. Joseph and I saw him astride his big horse, the epitome of discipline and authority. Despite his seeming lack of warmth, it would be hard to imagine a better shepherd of such a flock of mismatched sheep, leading us west, helping us with our livestock, getting us safely across rivers and deserts.

Then I thought of his personal kindnesses to me, of his breaking up that duel with Bart Corbett, of his digging Elmer's grave with his own hands and then offering to see that I was returned safely to the East; of rescuing me from what could have been a humiliating experience following my encounter with Corbett, and his allowing me to join his contingent to California.

He had seen me waddling west in the last stages of pregnancy and had taken pains to leave me in a safe place to deliver my baby, had even heard my birthing screams.

Then I thought of the way he had helped set me up in the hotel business. The idea that he might have done that out of love, scared and thrilled me. I spent the rest of that day in a daze, eager for nightfall.

Despite my fatigue, sleep did not come easily. Images of that long trek across the West kept flashing through my mind, the hordes of insects, the choking clouds of dust, our encounters with Indians, yes, and the many interesting characters in our group.

When I finally fell asleep, I dreamed of the Captain grieving over the death of his great dog, Boris.

* * *

The first thing I did after breakfast the next morning was to send for Kwong Chung.

I got right to the point.

"Once you told me what Confucius might have said about Chester Peebles, that possibly he might be too glib for his own good, that he might lack moral character. And you were right. Now I want to know what he would have thought about Captain McGee."

Kwong Chung smiled and said, "The great teacher once said of a certain public character, 'He is a good man. He is independent.' Your captain is independent."

"That is true. He's more independent than anyone I ever met."

"You, too, are independent, don't you think?"

"I would like to be. But the captain, what else would your Confucius say of such a man?"

"Your captain makes me think of what the great warrior, Wu Chi, said about the qualities that make an excellent general. Wu Chi said, 'When he issues an order none dares disobey and wherever he is no rebels dare oppose.' Your captain is such a man."

"Why do you keep saying 'your captain'? We agree that he is a very independent man. He is hardly my captain."

"I think he might be."

"What makes you say such a silly thing?"

"I have observed how he stares at you when you are not aware. From the first I see longing in his eyes for you. Why you think I say send him telegram when your house burn?"

"Oh, Kwong Chung, you may be imagining things. But, still, I am confused. What shall I do if what you say is true?"

"Do nothing. Let nature take its course."

* * *

Later that day, Zeb was back, acting so embarrassed that I took pains to put him at his ease until he asked, "Well, little lady, have you thought about what I said yesterday?"

"About your feelings toward me?"

"Yes."

"I am flattered beyond all measure but I can hardly ignore the disparity between our ages. How old are you anyway, Captain?"

"I will be 41 my next birthday. For that matter, how old are you?"

"I will be 21 on my next birthday."

"Which means that when I am 80 you will be an old woman of 60. I reckon I could handle that," he said with one of his rare flashes of humor.

I laughed and replied, "My father was 30 and my mother only 14 when they were wed."

With that behind us, I decided to plow right into the matter that had been most on my mind, the matter of my own past.

"Before we go further in this conversation, there is something you should know about me."

As delicately but honestly as I could manage, I told him about Billy Joe Duncan and myself, and, of course, little Duncan. At the end of my revelation, I said, "You don't seem surprised. Don't you care?"

"I figured it was something like that. Didn't think that Hixon fellow could have been your first choice."

"True. I married him out of convenience. And then I should tell you about Chester."

"I know as much as I need to. After all the attention he paid you earlier this year, I'd have to be stupid not to understand why you wanted to go off to Frisco alone and then why you came back so soon and in such a sad condition. He is married, you know, to that girl he kept going on about. Brought her back from Boston. He has come into enough money so they can take up residence in Sacramento and he can spend his time beating the drums for Lincoln."

"I didn't know they had moved to Sacramento, only that they were married. Some day I may tell you how I found that out."

"No need to go into that. I just hope you are over him and that boy back in North Carolina."

"They both left their scars but nothing that time won't heal."

"Good. Is there anything you want to ask me?"

Remembering how he had bristled at my question about Yellow Moon, I hesitated but then decided that it was now or never and so plunged right in. The things that formerly reticent man told me about himself and what he had done since leaving his Indiana home for the West twenty five years before would make an adventure book.

There had been a string of other women since Yellow Moon, but none that he had loved enough to marry. His mysterious business in Salt Lake

City had been to spy out the Mormon defenses of the city and send a report back to the army at Fort Laramie. His limp was the result of being hit in the leg by a Mexican musket ball at the battle of San Pasqual. He had been knocked unconcious in falling from his horse. Chester had saved his life by stopping the flow of blood with a tourniquet and remaining with him until a doctor could reach him.

"You can understand why I try to look out for him," he said. "Chester gets under my skin sometimes but he has become more like a little brother than a cousin. He gets into trouble without me."

Not wanting to say anything more about Chester and thinking I might never have another such opportunity, I asked finally about Bart Corbett. "Was he still alive when you found him?"

"Just barely. He couldn't have lived through the night. I saw no reason to let him hang onto his miserable life long enough to involve you."

I shuddered as I looked at those big hands.

"So you . . . "

"Hurried him on his way to hell, which is where he belonged."

"And you did that for my sake?"

"Mainly. Saved us all a lot of trouble. Same as when I hanged that one-eyed friend of Corbett's. Same as I would do to anybody that would put you or your reputation in danger."

Now he was staring into my face as though his deep-set, gray-eyed gaze could penetrate my brain.

"So, little lady, now that you know all about me, what shall I do? Stay around or leave you alone so you can find yourself a younger fellow?"

"The first thing I want you to do is take a vow that never again will you refer to me as little lady. Just plain Annie will do very well, Captain."

He threw back his head to laugh, revealing a set of lovely white teeth. "And just plain Zeb will do fine for me. No more of that captain stuff. In the Mexican War I was only a sergeant. It was Chester that started folks calling me captain."

*   *   *

We waited until Christmas, after all the furor of the political campaign died down before getting married. Chester visited the area several times to make speeches for Lincoln and talk up the Republican cause but never came around to see me, which suited me fine.

Remembering what Kwong Chung's Confucius said about the importance of moral character, that a man who lacked it "cannot long put up with adversity, nor can he long enjoy prosperity," I wondered how long Chester would enjoy the prosperity gained by the settlement of his grandparents' estate.

At least one enterprise in which Chester took part did succeed. Lincoln won a narrow victory in California as he did in the rest of the nation, thereby hastening the slide into our great Civil War.

Although Zeb favored Stephen Douglas as the candidate best qualified to hold the nation together, he patched things up between himself and Chester to the point where he, Zeb, asked me if Chester might not make a good best man at our wedding.

Remembering the night Chester and I spent together before his departure for Chicago, I vetoed the idea. Instead I chose Kwong Chung for that duty. And to serve as my matron of honor, I, the daughter of a slave owner, chose Opal, a runaway slave.

Zeb accepted those decisions as well as my suggestion that we be married and spend our wedding night at the National Exchange Hotel in Nevada City.

* * *

It was a brief ceremony conducted by the Reverend Dryden, the same Methodist Episcopal minister Will Tremelling had once lined up to perform our aborted wedding. And Will and Noreen attended our ceremony along with Mildred and several of her former co-workers and some of Zeb's cronies.

Zeb insisted that we be given the finest room in the hotel, complete with a huge four-poster bed and an enormous down mattress.

I approached my wedding night with some apprehension, for I still held Zeb McGee in awe although no longer in fear.

My heart was quickly melted by his gentle tenderness. What a man was Zeb McGee.

The next morning, while he still slept, I drew back the covers and gazed at the lean, powerful body of the man who was now my husband. There was the scar marking the spot where the Mexican bullet had pierced his thigh and nearly ended his life. Across the smooth, pale skin of his chest a long gash ran, the result, I was to learn, of a sailor's knife in San Francisco. And in one shoulder a smaller scar had been left by a Ute's arrow.

He awoke to catch me scrutinizing his naked body and said, "Didn't you ever see a man before?"

"Not one like you," I replied as I drew the covers over us again.

EPILOGUE

Only in fairy tales does everyone live happily ever after. That does not mean, however, that, after certain crucial points in our lives, we can't enjoy a large measure of contentment and satisfaction.

Certainly that has been my own experience since that day back in September of 1860 when Zeb McGee first revealed how he felt toward me.

My big concern about marrying Zeb had been that with the difference in our ages and life experiences, he would try to dominate me, something I had sworn no man would do.

My fear was groundless. From the moment I agreed to be his wife, Zeb McGee consulted me in nearly every aspect of our life together. I was careful not to take advantage of his considerate attitude, however. I recognized that trying to tie such a man to my apron strings would be like trying to bridle an unbroken stallion. So I quickly learned how to couch my wishes in a conciliatory manner. And yet when he did ask my opinion about anything, I gave him straight answers. His appreciation of my judgment was most flattering.

We had only one big blow up and that came early in our marriage, in the first part of 1862 just as the Civil War was turning into an even bloodier conflict in the East than expected. And Chester Peebles was the cause.

I knew that Zeb often ran into Chester in Sacramento. Zeb returned from one of those encounters to report that Chester was talking about helping recruit several companies of Californian horsemen to go east and join a Massachusetts cavalry regiment.

"What's more," Zeb said, "he wants to put my name forward to serve as captain of one of the companies. Says if I make the grade, he'd like to go along as my lieutenant."

Neither Zeb nor I were prepared for my reaction. Oh, it embarrasses me to relate the tantrum I threw. I cried and threatened to divorce him. The more he talked, the louder grew my cries. Aside from my dismay at being left once more on my own, I was angered by Chester Peeble's interfering in my life, and just as my marriage was settling into a loving, comfortable routine.

Even more serious was my dread for Zeb's life. By then the telegraph line had been completed across the West, ending the Pony Express, and giving California's newspapers quick access to the news from the East. And very serious news it was, too.

When I caught my breath, the astonished Zeb said, "It don't sound like you want me to go."

I wiped my eyes on my apron and blew my nose.

"You idiot. I will die if you do."

"But, Annie, this country is being torn apart and I can't sit around doing nothing."

"What about the militia?" I asked. "Some of the newspapers make it sound like the rebels may try to hook California up with the Confederacy. Would you settle for serving in the militia?"

"I will consider it. Now, you just calm down. I didn't mean to upset you like that. It was just an idea."

Notice that by this time I was saying "rebels" rather than Confederates or Southerners. My attitude had undergone a big change after my nearly dying. I had been profoundly affected by the thoughts of Opal's fellow Negro Christians "praying me through" my illness. Then there was Opal's direct influence, her lack of servility and her examples of intelligence and loyalty. Almost against my will, my reading of UNCLE TOM'S CABIN helped change my perception of slavery. I was appalled, too, by the attack on Fort Sumter. Whatever the causes, by the winter of 1861–62 I had become an opponent of slavery and a staunch supporter of Abraham Lincoln. Yet, daughter of the South that I was, I was sickened by the thoughts of fellow Americans slaughtering each other on the battlefields. All I wanted was an early and peaceful end of the war with freedom for the slaves and a preserved Union. Meanwhile, I prayed that California in general and my husband in particular would remain out of the conflict.

The governor of California was delighted to have the services of a veteran of the Mexican War and of the western trail like Zebulon McGee for his militia. He became one of the some 16,000 Californians who did state service keeping the small, but intense segment of Confederate supporters in check. They even made Zeb a real captain. Having smugly and prematurely congratulated myself that he would remain safely at, or anyway, near home, I saw no reason to object when he was summoned to San Francisco to consult with the general in charge of the Department of the Pacific.

Imagine my dismay when I got a letter from Zeb explaining that he had been practically dragooned into joining up as a scout for an expedition, commanded by a Colonel Carleton, to kick a gang of Texas Confederates out of New Mexico. He wrote that he could not refuse and enclosed a power of attorney and instructions to close out his freighting business and salt the money down for him while he was gone.

At first I was furious at being frustrated in my efforts to keep my husband at home. But then, remembering Jesus's parable of the talents, I decided to show Zeb McGee for once and all the stuff I was made of. With the help of Mr. Delano, I sold off the freight-hauling business, and got a good price for it, too. But I did not hide our talents under a rock. No sir, I took that money and bought shares, first, in the Empire Gold Mine there in Grass Valley, and then in the Central Pacific Railroad, and finally in the newly formed Bank of California, three investments that paid off many times over.

The service of Zeb and his fellow members of what became known as The California Column paid off for the Union cause, too. That band of some 2,000 men not only kept Arizona and New Mexico out of the Confederacy but also subdued the Apache Indians who tried to harrass them along the way. His experiences would make a book in itself. Maybe someday I can get Zeb to write down what he did and saw, or anyway dictate it to me.

As for Chester Peebles, several months after Zeb's departure, he sailed with other Federal recruits from San Francisco for Boston, taking with him Amy to be reconciled with her parents and stay with them while he served with the Massachusetts cavalry. By that time he had wasted his legacy on several foolish business ventures. Although he probably saw himself as engaging in a noble effort to save the Union, in my opinion, he simply switched to yet another new enterprise, and one, like the others, that turned out badly for him.

Later, in 1864, Zeb received a letter from Amy herself. In it she related that in a fight with Mosby's Confederate partisans at Dranesville, Virginia, Chester and quite a few others of his company were captured. It was only after the end of the war that we learned that he and his comrades had been hauled off to that dreadful rebel prison camp at Andersonville in Georgia, where he died. Often have I wondered what would have been Zeb's fate had I not thrown my tantrum and prevented his signing up with Chester.

By the time he returned from his service with Carleton, our investments were doing so well that we decided to sell The Gold Mountain and quit Nevada County for the rich soil and more salubrious climate of the Napa Valley region of California. Zeb found us a ranch there and promised to build me the house of my dreams.

Opal had never forgiven Zeb for Lester's death. After my marriage, although we remained on good terms, she spent more and more of her time with her friends in the black community. At the close of the war, that community was joined by an unusual former slave from Oklahoma. Part Indian himself, he had run away from his half-Cherokee master to join the Union Army. Although several years younger than Opal, he and she seemed to suit each other, so I was not surprised when she announced that they would be wed.

I invited her and her husband to accompany us to Sonoma County, but she refused, saying, "You and me have done as much for each other as we can. Mr. Lincoln freed the slaves back home. It is time for me to be emancipated, too. But Lord, honey, I am going to miss you and Duncan."

With that, we both sobbed and hugged each other.

With Zeb's approval, I gave Opal and her husband a gift of more than enough money to buy themselves a building so she could realize her dream of once more operating a restaurant.

Kwong Chung decided that he now had saved enough money from his fortune telling and wages to return to his family in China. It wrung my heart to see him say good-by to Duncan. I had seen Kwong Chung cry only once before, at my near death in 1860.

"It is time for me to go," he said. "Duncan getting too big. Soon he outgrow this old Chinaman."

The ever generous Zeb paid for his passage on a steamer bound for Canton from San Franciso.

Although I got over my love for Chester Peebles, Duncan never quite did. Zeb went off with Carleton's column just as Duncan was beginning to warm up toward him. They had to start all over again after Zeb returned home. Once we got established in Sonoma County, however, Zeb bought the boy, now 10, a real pony—not a wooden one—and taught him to ride. They got along better after that.

Zeb liked to blame it on the water in Sonoma County that hardly had we got settled there when our daughters started arriving, first Sarah, then Rebecca, and after a few more years, little red-haired Laura. While a distance remained between Zeb and Duncan, this was not so with our daughters. Not in the least in awe of him, these three little girls turned him into a doting father.

So our investments prospered. Our ranch did well. Counted as a hero of the Civil War by California standards, Zeb was courted by local politicians who persuaded him to stand for the State Senate. He won by a landslide and has served several terms in Sacramento. Thus the man I once called captain became Senator McGee.

Still unreconciled with me, my father died in 1885. It was only after Uncle John had written me of his death and of the failing health of my mother that I decided to visit my family back in North Carolina.

By then, Duncan had taken a job in San Francisco and married a lovely girl there. Thinking it too much for me to take our entire brood of girls, Zeb agreed to stay at home and keep Sarah and Rebecca while only little Laura accompanied me.

Laura and I enjoyed a glorious trip on the train from Sacramento across the country. It took us only a few days and nights to cover the same distance it had taken five months to plod across back in 1856, and we traveled in far greater comfort. Finally, at the same little station where my father had put me aboard that wood-burning train with the Hixons thirty years earlier, we were met by my brother, Charles, now a middle-aged school teacher.

The home which I had remembered as a regular mansion, I now saw as a weather-beaten, unpainted old farm house. My poor mother, too, had shrunk in size. Her hair had turned snowy white. Uncle John and Aunt Mamie likewise had grown old and stooped.

They kept me up until midnight, looking at my photographs of Zeb and our family and of our ranch house, oh, yes, and talking of the war and its hardships and reciting the names of young men who had died and been maimed, or who just never returned home.

If Zeb had been with me, I would not have asked as I did of Uncle John, "And what about Billy Joe Duncan?"

"Didn't anyone tell you? He left the university to become a surgeon's assistant at Richmond. Came home from the war and set up in practice. In fact he took over my patients when I retired. Married of course but childless. Would you like to see him?"

"It would have to be his idea," I said.

The following Sunday afternoon, Dr. Billy Joe Duncan, accompanied by his wife, came to Uncle John's house for tea. I was there, too, with Laura and me dressed in our finest.

That strapping youth about whom I had dreamed for so many years had turned into a pot-bellied, red-faced fellow with only a fringe of hair around his ears, and that gone gray. Conversation between us might have been less awkward if his wife, a great, raw-boned Amazon, had not proved to be a regular Myrtle Mae Hixon when it came to interrupting her husband's talk and finishing his sentences for him.

It was not until she had got in their buggy and he had returned to the porch to shake my hand once more that he got the chance to say, "I'm sorry about what happened back in fifty seven, Annie."

"Actually it was in fifty-six," I replied. "And there is no need for apologies. All's well that ends well."

"William!" his wife called.

"In a minute, dear," he said. Then in a lower voice, "I understand you had a son."

"I have a son and two daughters, besides little Laura."

"What did you name the boy?"

"William! Stop dawdling. We must get home."

"Better go now, Billy Joe, or you may be in trouble."

Before he could say more, I stepped back into the house.

After a week with my family, I was more than ready to leave. I gave Mama a handsome gift of money, kissed my brothers, their wives and children and made them all promise to come out to California for a visit.

On the way back to the station, I had Charles detour by way of our Methodist church yard. Charles remained in the buggy with Laura while I stood by the big gravestone announcing to future generations that here lay the remains of Francis A. Monday, one time state legislator and justice of the peace.

"Well, Papa," I murmured. "Here I am again. Uncle John said years ago that sooner or later I had to forgive you. I am sorry I have taken so long doing that. You probably did what you thought best. So I reckon I do forgive you."

Back in the buggy, I would not let myself cry.

Uncle John had told me that my favorite cousin, Jim Mundy, had settled in Baltimore after Appomattox and there had established a prosperous printing business. Since Baltimore was the city where I would take the train for Chicago on our homeward journey, I sent Jim a wire. He met us at the station and took us home to spend a delightful two days with him and his wife, Jane.

Jim had lost an eye at Gettysburg where he was taken prisoner. He managed to escape by way of Canada and get back to Richmond for the last few months of the war. He then eloped with Jane, the daughter of a big plantation owner, to Baltimore. I hope someday he will write an account of his experiences, for they would make a better story than many of the adventure novels I have read.

    Jim and I agreed that the best thing we could have done was to escape from our native environments. He promised to come west some day. I thought he and Zeb would get along just fine, even though they fought on different sides. I am still waiting for Jim's visit.

    Speaking of Zeb, I never saw a man, or anyway that man, act so glad to see anyone as he did when he met our train in Sacramento. I thought he would crack my ribs with his hugs.

    We spent that night in a hotel in Sacramento, in two rooms, one for little Laura, and one for us. I didn't think that after 25 years, you could relive your wedding night, but we did.

    The next morning, we had breakfast brought to our rooms. As we drank our coffee and Zeb dandled an adoring Laura on his knee, he said, "So how did you find things back home?"

    "I'll tell you tomorrow when we get back there."

AFTERWORD

Once upon a time there was a real Annie Mundy. She was the oldest sister of my maternal grandfather who died before I was born. Her full name was Anne Eliza Monday (later Mundy). Born in North Carolina in 1838, she, like my fictional Annie, was packed off with a family going west when her pious Methodist parents learned she was pregnant. Both she and her boyfriend were too young to marry. She ended up in California where she married a successful man shortly before the Civil War.

I had never heard of this great-aunt until my mother told me about her shortly before she, my mother, died, in 1980 at 95.

I was fascinated by the story and asked why my mother had never told me of Annie Mundy.

"Oh, we were so ashamed," she said.

"But that was 125 years ago."

"I know. But we never spoke of it outside the family."

My mother remembered that when she was a little girl, her Aunt Annie, by then a respectable matron, had returned from California with her own daughter for a visit with her relatives.

"We were so impressed. She was such a stylish lady."

A mysterious thing occurred after my mother's death. My wife, Beverly, had intimated that she had a very special gift for my Christmas present. A few weeks before Christmas, I climbed the ladder to our attic and saw lying on a foot locker a photograph of a young woman in Victorian style dress. On the back of the carte de viste was printed the name of a San Francisco photographer. The name Annie Mundy was written on the back as well.

Not wanting to spoil Beverly's surprise, I put the photo back and said nothing. On Christmas morning, she explained that one of my gifts was not yet ready. I assumed that she had sent the photo off to be framed and the work had not been completed.

I forgot about the picture until the following summer when I asked Beverly, "Whatever happened to that picture of Annie Mundy that was in the attic last December?"

"What picture?" she said.

At first I thought she was teasing, but upon realizing that she knew nothing of the photograph, I climbed back into the attic and furiously turned the place upsidedown, all in vain.

The mystery of that missing photograph has haunted me ever since. I still have no logical explanation for the incident.

In April 1987 my wife was invited to attend a writers' workshop in San Francisco. I went along and while there visited the California Historical Society library. A librarian pulled out sheets of early accounts of marriages that had been copied from old newspapers in the 1930's as a WPA project. The WPA typist had recorded a newspaper notice that on April 29, 1859 an Anne Eliza Monday of Waloupa in Nevada County had been married to a Robert Wise in Nevada City on April 25 at the National Exchange Hotel. I was thrilled by this finding but then mystified a few pages later by a notation that an Annie E. Mundy had been married to William E. Parker in Sacramento October 4, 1860.

Surely there could not have been two women with practically the same name living in adjacent counties. Had Annie's first husband died, or was she a bigamist? Not having time for further research, I hired a geneologist in San Francisco to carry on the search.

The geneologist could find no Robert Wise with a wife named Anne in the 1860 or subsequent censuses. She could trace an Anne E. Parker through censuses up to 1910 but the woman claimed to have been born in Illinois, and her age didn't square with that of my great aunt. I despaired of ever learning more about her.

Then ten years ago, we built a new house not far from our old one and moved most of our possessions. We left boxes of our children's old school papers and other such things in the garage of our old house to be discarded.

I had put most of the stuff out on the curb for the garbage collector. There remained a box of my older daughter's texts and note books from her courses at Bryn Mawr College. Curious to see what she had written in one of her note books I opened it and out fell that mysterious photograph of Annie Mundy.

I don't believe in ghosts, or I didn't before that. Anyway, I locked that little portrait in my car, took it home and made photo copies. I still occasionally check to make sure the picture remains in my files.

Beverly felt that Annie Mundy was calling from beyond the beyond, as the Irish say, for me, as the writer in the family, to tell her story. Whatever the explanation, ever since I have been obsessed with the incident, determined to solve the mystery of Anne Eliza Monday.

In 1995, we visited the Family History Center maintained by the Church of Latter Day Saints. We did find Annie listed in the 1850 census as a 12-year-old student but nothing further.

Frustrated in my search for the real Annie Mundy, I decided to suspend my efforts and create a character of the same name and background, and have her crossing the West with a wagon train.

Before leaving Salt Lake City, I contracted with Carol Post, a professional geneologist, for her to continue the search for the real Annie while I turned my attention to learning about the great Western migration and life in the Gold Fields of California, to developing a plot and to creating characters for my novel.

If for nothing else, I am grateful to Carol for referring me to David Comstock's books about life in Nevada County, California between 1845 and 1869. Upon my return to Pennsylvania I called David and he offered to send me copies of his books on trust. This was the beginning of a rewarding friendship.

While I was beginning my crash course in the history of the American West, Carol Post was running into the same frustrations as had the San Francisco geneologist back in 1987. During a phone conversation with David Comstock, I mentioned our problem.

"What was your great aunt's maiden name?" he inquired.

He had me wait while he consulted his records, then said, "On April 29, 1859, the Nevada City Journal published this item: 'Married at the National Exchange Hotel on the 25th by Rev. D.A. Dryden, Mr. Robert West and Miss Anna E. Monday, all of Waloupa.'"

"West? She married a West, not a Wise?"

Suddenly, the scales fell from my eyes. That WPA typist back in the 1930's had miscopied the surname of Annie's groom, leading to many wasted hours and dollars.

I phoned Carol Post with this news and she soon called back to report that she had found an Annie E. West in the 1880 Census. She was listed as a native of North Carolina living in Healdsburg, in Sonoma County, with a son and five daughters. Carol could find nothing beyond that, so I asked her to call off her search.

By then I had become so engrossed in concocting a story about my fictional Annie, that I did not want to be further distracted by bits and pieces about the real one.

Not sure exactly when and how the real Annie got to California, I arbitrarily chose 1856 as the year of my heroine's passage and St. Joseph, Missouri as the jumping off spot for the trip.

In August of 1996, Beverly and I flew to Kansas City, rented a car and, starting out from St. Joseph, spent seventeen of the most interesting days of our lives following the wagon route Annie Mundy might have taken to Grass Valley, California, making notes and interviewing local historians along the way, among them David Comstock and his wife Ardis.

The National Exchange Hotel in nearby Nevada City, where Annie and Robert West were married, not only is still in business, it remains a popular place for weddings and receptions. Beverly and I enjoyed an excellent dinner there.

We ended our trip in Healdsburg. In the local museum we purchased a copy of a birdseye view of the town published in 1884. This showed the houses on the street listed as Annie's address in the 1880 census. We hurried to the very block where she would have lived. The houses were gone. On their old sites now stands the town library.

In Sonoma County, I hired another local geneologist, Eugenia Ohman, to learn more about Anne E. West and her family. She found that a Robert West had purchased a ranch in partnership with another man in 1872 for $5,000 and was part of a group that invested in a quicksilver mine in 1874. An 1877 atlas indicates that West had come to California in 1853 and to Sonoma County in 1871. But the trail grew cold after that 1880 Census listing.

Since then, through further probing by David Comstock, I have learned that in 1870, before moving to Sonoma County, Robert West had bought a half share in a meat market at You Bet in Little York Township. With that bit of knowledge, I asked Carol Post to take a closer look at the 1870 Census and, sure enough, she found the West family living in Little York Township in 1870 with the appropriate children..

Despite a few encouraging leads like these, one dead end after another has kept occurring in my search for the real Annie Mundy. Although determined sooner or later to find where she died and is buried, I set aside my search to concentrate on finishing my novel about the fictional Annie.

Incidentally, threads from all of my previous novels have come together in ANNIE MUNDY. I have made Annie herself a cousin of Jim Mundy, the hero of my first novel which was set in the Civil War. And the two guides who lead Annie's wagon train across the West, Zeb McGee and Chester Peebles III, turn out to be distant cousins who are descended from Jason McGee the hero of my second novel.

So now that I have finished with the fictional Annie, I plan to get back on the trail of the real Anne Eliza Monday, the great aunt who was exiled to the West to avoid a family scandal.

On the last Sunday of each July, my Mundy cousins congregate for a reunion at Rock Springs Methodist Camp Grounds near Denver, North Carolina on land that was donated by an ancestor in the early Nineteenth Century. I would like some day to locate descendants of the real Annie Mundy, to hear what they know of her life and to invite them to come and meet their kinfolk back in North Carolina.

Just in case one of the descendants of Anne E. Monday West and Robert West may read this novel, here is what the enumerator in the 1880 Census noted about the family: On June 5 of that year, they were living at 151 Piper Street, Healdsburg, in the California county of Sonoma. Annie is listed as a 49-year-old white female born in North Carolina. Her children are listed as Charles W., 20; Gertrude I., 18; Caroline B. 12; Annie E., 6; and Mary B., 1. Charles is listed as "apprentice miller." Whether he was fathered by the boy back in North Carolina or by Robert West, I cannot say.

I would be delighted to hear from anyone who thinks he or she is a descendant of him or one of his four sisters. My address is 1728 Cushing Greene, Camp Hill, PA 17011.

—Robert H. Fowler

PRINTED SOURCES

Asbury, Herbert. THE BARBARY COAST, Alfred A. Knopf, New York, 1933.

Browne, Juanita Kennedy. NUGGETS OF NEVADA COUNTY HISTORY, Nevada County Historical Society, Nevada City CA, 1983.

Clark, Malcolm Jr. EDEN SEEKERS, THE SETTLEMENT OF OREGON 1818–1862, Houghton Mifflin Co., Boston.

Comstock, David Allan. Three volumes: GOLD DIGGERS AND CAMP FOLLOWERS, 1845–1851, BRIDES OF THE GOLD RUSH, 1851–1859, and GREENBACKS AND COPPERHEADS, 1859–1869. Comstock Bonanza Press, Grass Valley CA. 1982, 1987 & 1995, respectively.

Confucius. DISCOURSES AND SAYINGS. Overseas Chinese Affairs Commission, Taipei, Taiwan.

Davis, H.P. GOLD RUSH DAYS IN NEVADA CITY. Nevada City: Berliner and McGinnis, 1948.

DeLafosse, Peter H. (editor). TRAILING THE PIONEERS, A GUIDE TO UTAH'S EMIGRANT TRAILS, 1829–1869, Utah State University Press, Logan, 1994.

De Voto, Bernard. ACROSS THE WIDE MISSOURI, Boston: Houghton Mifflin, 1947.

Dodd, Charles H. CALIFORNIA TRAIL, VOYAGE OF DISCOVERY, KC Publications, Inc., Las Vegas NV, 1996

Ellison, R.S. FORT BRIDGER, A BRIEF HISTORY, Wyoming State Archives, Museum and Historical Department. 1981.

Erickson, Paul. DAILY LIFE IN A COVERED WAGON, The Preservation Press, National Trust for Historic Preservation, Washington DC, 1994.

Faragher, John Mack. WOMEN AND MEN ON THE OVERLAND TRAIL, Yale University Press, New Haven and London, 1979.

Fischer, Christiane, ed. LET THEM SPEAK FOR THEMSELVES: WOMEN IN THE AMERICAN WEST, 1849–1900. Hamden, CT: The Shoe String Press, 1977.

Flanigan, Mike. THE OLD WEST DAY BY DAY, Facts on File, 1995.

Ford, George D. THESE WERE ACTORS. Library Publishers, New York, 1955.

Franzwa, Gregory M. THE OREGON TRAIL REVISITED, Patrice Press, Inc. 1972.

Gibson, J.W. RECOLLECTIONS OF A PIONEER, Privately printed, St. Joseph MO, 1912.

Gowans, Fred R. and Campbell, Eugene E. FORT BRIDGER, Brigham Young University Press, Provo UT, 1975.

Gudde, Erwin G. CALIFORNIA GOLD CAMPS, Berkeley: University of California Press, 1975.

Holliday, J.S. THE WORLD RUSHED IN, New York: Simon and Schuster, 1981.

Jackson, Russel. VICTORIAN THEATRE, A & C Black, London.

Lapp, Rudolph M. BLACKS IN GOLD RUSH CALIFORNIA, New Haven: Yale University Press, 1977.

Lavender, David. FORT LARAMIE AND THE CHANGING FRONTIER, National Park Service, 1983.

Laxalt, Robert. "The California Trail: To the Rainbow's End," TRAILS WEST, Washington: National Geographic Society, 1979. pp. 108–143.

Lescohier, Roger. GOLD GIANTS OF GRASS VALLEY, HISTORY OF THE EMPIRE AND NORTH STAR MINES, 1850–1956, Empire Mine Park Association, 1995.

Lewin, Jacqueline A. & Taylor, Marilyn S. THE ST. JOE ROAD, St. Joseph Museum Publication, 1992.

Mann, Ralph. AFTER THE GOLD RUSH: SOCIETY IN GRASS VALLEY AND NEVADA CITY, CALIFORNIA 1849–1870, Stanford: Stanford University Press, 1982.

Marcy, Capt. Randolph B. THE PRAIRIE TRAVELER, Applewood Books, 1859.

Mattes, Merrill J. THE GREAT PLATTE RIVER ROAD, University of Nebraska Press, Lincoln NB, 1969.

Morley, Jim, and Doris Foley. GOLD CITIES: GRASS VALLEY AND NEVADA CITY, Berkeley: Howell-North, 1965.

Myres, Sandra L. Myres. WESTERING WOMEN AND THE FRONTIER EXPERIENCE, 1800–1915, University of New Mexico Press, Albuquerque,1982.

Newell, Olive. TAIL OF THE ELEPHANT, THE EMIGRANT EXPERIENCE ON THE TRUCKEE ROUTE OF THE CALIFORNIA TRAIL 1844–1852, The Nevada County Historical Society, Cedar Ridge CA 1997.

Paden, Irene D. THE WAKE OF THE PRAIRIE SCHOONER, New York: The MacMillan Co., 1945.

Robinson, Fayetter. CALIFORNIA AND ITS GOLD REGIONS, New York: Stringer and Townsend, 1849 (reprinted New York: Promontory Press, 1974).

Royce, Sarah. A FRONTIER LADY: RECOLLECTIONS OF THE GOLD RUSH AND EARLY CALIFORNIA, New Haven: Yale University Press, 1932.

Schlissel, Lillian. WOMEN'S DIARIES OF THE WESTWARD JOURNEY. Schocken Books, New York, 1982.

Stewart, George R. THE CALIFORNIA TRAIL: AN EPIC WITH MANY HEROES, New York: McGraw-Hill, 1962.

Unruh, John D. Jr. THE PLAINS ACROSS, THE OVERLAND EMIGRANTS AND THE TRANS-MISSISSIPPI WEST, 1840–60, University of Illinois Press, Urbana and Chicago, 1979.

Vestal, Stanley. JIM BRIDGER, MOUNTAIN MAN, University of Nebraska Press, Lincoln/London, 1946.

Watkins, T.H. & Olmsted, R.R. MIRROR OF THE DREAM, AN ILLUSTRATED HISTORY OF SAN FRANCISCO, The Scrimshaw Press, Oakland CA, 1976.

Wilson, D. Ray. FORT KEARNY ON THE PLATTE, Crossroads Communications, Dundee IL, 1980.

MANUSCRIPTS

There remain in existence an estimated 800 diaries or memoirs written by persons who crossed the West during the mid-19th Century. One of the chief depositories of these can be found at The National Frontier Trails Center, Independence MO. In my reading of primary sources, I concentrated on those accounts written by persons who made the trip, as did my fictional Annie Mundy, in 1856, a year that saw relatively light traffic (only about 8,000 persons according to George R. Stewart) and no major Indian troubles along the trails.

A year-by-year collection of trail accounts compiled by the late Merrill J. Mattes includes summaries of 47 for 1856. By far the most interesting and useful of these is J. Robert Brown's 118-page "Journal of a trip across the plains of the U.S. from Missouri to California in the year 1856, giving a correct view of the country, anecdotes, Indian stories, mountaineers' tales, etc."

The Beinecke Library, Yale University, New Haven CT has one of the two known copies of this fascinating Brown journal which the author had privately printed in 1860. I am grateful to The Beinecke Library for making a copy available to me on microfilm through the West Shore Library of Camp Hill, Pennsylvania.

—Robert H. Fowler

We hope you enjoy this hardcover edition from Stealth Press.

Stealth was conceived and created with a simple premise in mind: that good books matter, and that good books deserve to be in print in the finest form possible, for as long as possible, for the betterment of all.

Privately owned and independently funded, Stealth specializes in high quality, hardcover editions from proven and talented writers, printed on acid-free paper and finely bound, and made directly available to our readers via the Internet.

Stealth believes that every book is a one-on-one experience for author and audience alike. We are dedicated to fostering the most direct and positive connection possible between writers and readers, and all who love books.

Our web site is constantly updated with information on our authors and our latest editions of their work. You can contact the author of this book directly -- and us, too at **www.stealthpress.com**

The Future Is Obvious.